MICHAEL MARSHALL SMITH
WHAT YOU MAKE IT

A book of short stories

 HarperCollins*Publishers*

HarperCollins*Publishers*
77–85 Fulham Palace Road,
Hammersmith, London W6 8JB

Published by HarperCollins*Publishers* 1999
1 3 5 7 9 8 6 4 2

ISBN 0-00-225602-9

Typeset in Minion by
Palimpsest Book Production Limited,
Polmont, Stirlingshire

Printed and bound in Great Britain by
Caledonian International Book Manufacturing Ltd, Glasgow

Dedication

This collection is dedicated to the three people without whom . . .
to Nicholas Royle, Stephen Jones and Howard Ely.

Acknowledgements

I would like to thank the people who've published and help shape my stories – Stephen Jones, Nicholas Royle, David Sutton, Ellen Datlow and Peter Crowther; the three authors who most made me want to write – KA, RB and SK; my parents for always being there, and my wife Paula for not being there then but being here now; and finally my editors, Jim Rickards and Jane Johnson, for their support, patience and friendship.

Contents

Introduction

I like short stories. I hope you do too, because this isn't a novel. If an honest-to-goodness *novel* is what you're looking for, then put this volume back on the pile. Propped up, so other people can see it. Or better still, take it with you anyway. You can snuggle down into novels, draw them over your head like a warm duvet and go away for a while. It's like taking a road trip in another country – while the land's got you in its clutches, you can't go home again. Short stories are different. They're evenings out, or day trips, an hour spent gazing out to sea. You don't have to do lots of packing beforehand or set timer switches or arrange for someone to feed the cat, but they leave their mark on your life all the same. Sometimes more so: short stories don't have the luxury of time to draw you in – so they have to come in low, under the radar, and hit you with the very first shot. They're doorways to other worlds, perpetually left ajar, dreams that you experience while you are still half awake.

Novels are time out of time: short stories are part of real life, and sometimes the shortest song can contain the longest single note.

What follows is a selection of the stories I have written in the last decade. Some of them are about fairly normal things, others less so. A few come at similar ideas from different angles, others stand alone; some have a life of their own now, having previously appeared in a variety of formats, while others are shiny new. They include both the first story I ever wrote, and the most recent. Everything else is bracketed between them. Through one of those coincidences which seem too telling to be merely random, while I was putting this collection together I was in Edinburgh for the Book Festival. In the evening I took my wife – who was but a dot on an unseen horizon when the first of these stories were written – to the place where I was sitting when I got the idea for that first short story, just over ten years previously. It was a strange feeling. Two days later, back in London, I attended a book launch for the writer who did more than any other to inspire me to write in the first place – and whose fiction I'd been avidly reading on that day in Edinburgh a decade before. This was the writer's first official visit to this country in seventeen years, and it seems odd that it should fall in the same week that I had stood on The Mound in Edinburgh and remembered how it had been.

But that's the way life is, a sea of coincidences and strange-nesses and dark heartbeats – and what follows is an attempt to capture something of it. Then it was 1987. Now it's 1998. These stories chart the journey from there to here, and I hope that amongst them you'll find a couple of evenings to remember.

Michael Marshall Smith
London, October 1998

MORE TOMORROW

I got a new job a couple of weeks ago. It's pretty much the same as my old job, but at a nicer company. What I do is trouble-shoot computers and their software – and yes, I know that sounds dull. People tell me so all the time. Not in words, exactly, but in their glassy smiles and their awkward 'let's be nice to the geek' demeanour.

It's a strange phenomenon, the whole 'computer people are losers' mentality. All round the world, at desks in every office and every building, people are using computers. Day in, day out. Every now and then, these machines go wrong. They're bound to: they're complex systems, like a human body, or society. When someone gets hurt, you call in a doctor. When a riot breaks out, it's the police that – for once – you want to see on your doorstep. It's their job to sort it out. Similarly, if your word processor starts dumping files or your hard disk goes non-linear, it's someone like me you need. Someone who actually *understands* the magic box which sits on your desk, and can make it all lovely again.

But do we get any thanks, any kudos for being the emergency services of the late twentieth century?

Do we fuck.

I can understand this to a degree. There are enough hard-line nerds and social zero geeks around to make it seem like a losing way of life. But there are plenty of pretty basic earthlings doing all the other jobs too, and no one expects them to turn up for work in a pin-wheel hat and a T-shirt saying: 'Programmers do it recursively'. For the record, I play reasonable blues guitar, I've been out with a girl and have worked undercover for the CIA. The last bit isn't true, of course, but you get the general idea.

Up until recently I worked for a computer company, which I'll admit *was* full of very perfunctory human beings. When people started passing around jokes which were written in C++, I decided it was time to move on. One of the advantages of knowing about computers is that unemployment isn't going to be a problem until the damn things start fixing themselves, and so I called a few contacts, posted a new CV up on my web site and within 24 hours had four opportunities to chose from. Most of them were other computer businesses, which I was kind of keen to avoid, and in the end I decided to have a crack at a company called the VCA. I put on my pin-wheel hat, rubbed pizza on my shirt, and strolled along for an interview.

The VCA, it transpired, was a non-profit organization dedicated to promoting effective business communication. The suave but shifty chief executive who interviewed me seemed a little vague as to what this actually entailed, and in the end I let it go. The company was situated in tidy new offices right in the centre of town, and seemed to be doing good trade at whatever it was they did. The reason they needed someone like me was they wanted to upgrade their system – computers, software and all. It was a month's contract work, at a very decent rate, and I said yes without a second thought.

Appleton, the guy in charge, took me for a gloating tour round the office. It looked the same as they always do, only emptier, because everyone was out at lunch. Then I settled down with their spreadsheet-basher to go find out what kind of system they could afford. His name was Cremmer, and he wasn't out at lunch because he was clearly one of those people who see working nine-hour days as worthy of some form of admiration. Personally I view it as worthy of pity, at most. He seemed amiable enough, in a curly-haired, irritating sort of way, and within half an hour we'd thrashed out the necessary. I made some calls, arranged to come back in a few days, and spent the rest of the afternoon helping build a hospital in Rwanda. Well actually I spent it listening to loud music and catching up on my Internet newsgroups, but I could have done the other had I been so inclined.

The Internet is one of those things that more and more people have heard of without having any real idea of what it means. It's actually very simple. A while back a group of universities and government organizations experimented with a way of linking up all their computers so they could share resources, send little messages and play *Star Trek* games with each other. There was also a military connection, and the servers linked in such a way that the system could take a hit somewhere and reroute information accordingly. After a time this network started to take on a momentum of its own, with everyone from Pentagon heavies to pin-wheeling wireheads taking it upon themselves to find new ways of connecting things up and making more information available. Just about every major computer on the planet is now connected, and if you've got a modem and a phone line, you can get on there too. I can tell you can hardly wait.

What you find when you're there almost qualifies as a parallel universe. There are thousands of pieces of software, probably billions of text files by now. You can check the records of the New York Public Library, send a message to someone in Japan which will arrive within minutes, download a picture of the far side of Jupiter, and monitor how many cans of Dr Pepper there are in soda machines in the computer science labs of American universities. A lot of this stuff is fairly chaotically organized, but there are a few systems which span the net as a whole. One of these is the World Wide Web, a hypertext-based graphic system. Another is the newsgroups.

There are about 40,000 of these groups now, covering anything from computers to fine art, science fiction to tastelessness, the books of Stephen King to quirky sexual preferences. If it's not outright illegal, out there on the Infobahn people will be yakking about it 24 hours a day, every day of the year. Either that or posting images of it: there are paintings and animals, NASA archives and abstract art, and in the alt.binaries.pictures.tasteless group you can find anything from close-up shots of roadkills to people with acid burns on their face. Not very nice, but trust me, it's a minority interest. Now that I think of it, there is some illegal stuff (drugs, mainly) – there's a system by which you can send untraceable and anonymous messages, though I've never bothered to check it out.

Basically, the newsgroups are the Internet for traditionalists – or people who want the news as it breaks. They're little discussion centres that stick to their own specific topic, rather than wasting time with graphics and java applets which play weird tunes at you until you go insane. People read each other's messages and reply, or forward their own pronouncements or questions. Some groups are repositories of computer files, like software or pictures, others just have text messages. No one, however sad, could hope to keep abreast of all of them, and nor would you want to. I personally don't give a toss about recent developments in Multilevel Marketing Businesses or the Nature of Chinchilla Farming in America Today, and have no interest in reading megabytes of losing burblings about them. So I, like most people, stick to a subset of the groups that carry stuff I'm interested in – Mac computers, guitar music, cats and the like.

So now you know.

The following Tuesday I got up bright and early and made my way to the VCA for my first morning's work. England was doing its best to be summery, which as always meant that it was humid without being hot, bright without being sunny, and every third commuter on the hellish tube journey was intermittently pebble-dashing nearby passengers with hayfever sneezes. I emerged moist and irritable from the station, more determined than ever to find a way of working that meant never having to leave my apartment. The walk from the station to VCA was better, passing through an attractive square and a selection of interesting sidestreets with restaurants featuring unusual cuisines, and I was feeling chipper again by the time I got there.

My suppliers had done their work, and the main area of VCA's open-plan office was piled high with exciting boxes. When I walked in just about all the staff were standing around the pile, coffee mugs in hand, regarding it with the wary enthusiasm of simple country folk confronted with a recently landed UFO. There was a slightly toe-curling five minutes of introductions, embarrassing merely because I don't enjoy that kind of thing. Only one person, Clive, seemed to view me with the sniffy disdain of someone greeting an underling whose services are, unfortunately, in the ascendant. Everybody else seemed nice, some very much so.

Appleton eventually oiled out of his office and dispensed a few weak jokes which had the – possibly intentional – effect of scattering everyone back to their desks to get on with their work. I took off my jacket, rolled up my sleeves and got on with it.

I spent the morning cabling like a wild thing, placing the hardware of the network itself. As this involved a certain amount of disrupting everyone in turn by drilling, pulling up carpet and moving their desks, I was soon on apologetic grinning terms with most of them. I guess I could have done the wire-up over the weekend when nobody was there, but I like my weekends as they are. Clive gave me the invisibility routine that people once used on servants, but everyone else was fairly cool about it. One of the girls, Jeanette, actually engaged me in conversation while I worked nearby, and seemed genuinely interested in understanding what I was doing. When I broke it to her that it was actually pretty dull, she smiled.

The wiring took a little longer than I was expecting, and I stayed on after everybody else had gone. Everyone but Cremmer, that was, who stayed, probably to make sure that I didn't run off with their plants, or database, or spoons. Either that or to get some brownie points with whoever it was he thought cared about people putting in long hours. The invoicing supremo was in expansive mood, and chuntered endlessly about his adventures in computing, which were, to be honest, of slender interest to me. In the end he got bored of my monosyllabic grunts from beneath desks, and left me with some keys instead.

The next day was pretty much the same, except I was setting

up the computers themselves. This involved taking things out of boxes and installing interminable pieces of software on the server. This isn't quite such a sociable activity as disturbing people, and I spent most of the day in the affable but distant company of Sarah, their PR person. At the end of the day everyone gathered in the main room and then left together, apparently for a meal to celebrate someone's birthday. I thought I caught Jeanette casting a glance in my direction at one point, maybe embarrassed at the division between me and them. It didn't bother me much, so I just got my head down and got on with swapping floppy disks in and out of the machines.

Well, it did bother me a little, to be honest. It wasn't their fault – there was no reason why they should make the effort to include someone they didn't know, who wasn't really a part of their group. People seldom do. You have to be a little thick-skinned about that kind of thing if you work freelance. There are tribes, you know, everywhere you go. They owe their allegiance to shared time (if they're friends), or to an organization (if they're colleagues): but they're still tribes, just as much as if they'd tilled the same patch of desert for centuries. As a freelancer, especially in the cyber-areas, you tend to spend a lot of time wandering between them; occasionally being granted access to their watering hole, but never being one of the real people. Sometimes it can get on your nerves. That's all.

I finished up, locked the building carefully – I'm a complete anal-retentive about such things – and went home. I used my mobile to call for a pizza while I was en route, and it arrived two minutes after I got out of the shower. A perfect piece of timing, which sadly no one was on hand to appreciate. My last experiment with living with someone did not end well, mainly because she was a touchy and irritable woman who needed her own space 23½ hours a day. Well it was more complicated than that, of course, but that was the main impression I took away with me. I mulled over those times as I sat and munched my 'Everything on it, and then a few more things as well' pizza, vague-eyed in front of white noise television, and ended up feeling rather grim.

Food event over, I made a jug of coffee and settled down in front of the Mac. I tweaked my invoicing database for a while, exciting young man that I am, and then wrote a letter to my sister in Australia. She doesn't have access to email, unfortunately, otherwise she'd hear from me a lot more often. Write letter, print letter, put it in envelope, get stamps, get it to a post office. A chain of admin of that magnitude usually takes me about two weeks to get through, and it's a bit primitive, really, compared to write letter, press button, there in five minutes.

I called my friend Greg, who's a freelance sub-editor on a trendy magazine, but he was chasing a deadline and not disposed to chat. I tried the television, but it was still outputting someone else's idea of entertainment. By nine o'clock I was very bored, and so I logged on to the net.

Probably because I was bored, and feeling a bit isolated, after I'd done my usual groups I found myself checking out alt.binaries.pictures.erotica. 'alt' means the group is an unofficial one; 'binaries' means it holds computer files rather than just messages; 'pictures' means those files are images. As for the last word, I'm prepared to be educational about this but you're going to have to work that one out for yourself.

The media has the impression that the minute you're in cyberspace countless pictures of this type come flooding at you down the phone, pouring like ravening hordes onto your hard disk and leaping out of the screen to take over your mind. This is not the case, and all of you worried about your little Timmy's soul can afford to relax a bit. Even if you're only talking about the web, you need a computer, a modem, access to a phone line, and a credit card to pay for your internet feed. With Usenet you need to find the right newsgroup, and download about three segments for each picture. You require several bits of software to piece them together, convert the result, and display it.

The naughty pictures don't come and get you, and if you see one, it ain't an accident. If your little Timmy has the kit, finance and inclination to go looking, then maybe it's you who needs the talking to. In fact, maybe you should be grounded.

The flipside of that, of course, is the implication that *I* have the inclination to go looking, which I guess I occasionally do. Not very often – honest – but I do. I don't know how defensive to feel about that fact. Men of all shapes and sizes, ages and creeds, and states of marital or relationship bliss enjoy, every now and then, the sight of a woman with no clothes on. It's just as well we do, you know, otherwise there'd be no new little earthlings, would there? If you want to call that oppression or sexism or the commodification of the female body then go right ahead, but don't expect me to talk to you at dinner parties. I prefer to call it sexual attraction, but then I'm a sad fuck who spends half his life in front of computer, so what the hell do I know?

Still, it's not something that people feel great about, and I'm not going to defend it too hard. Especially not to women, because that would be a waste of everyone's time. Women have a little bit of their brain missing which means they cannot understand the attraction of pornography. I'm not saying that's a *bad* thing, just that it's true. On the other hand they understand the attraction of babies, shoe shops and the detail of other people's lives, so I guess it's swings and roundabouts.

I've talked about it for too long now, and you're going to think I'm some Neanderthal with his tongue hanging to the ground who goes round looking up people's skirts. I'm not. Yes, there are rude pictures to be found on the net, and yes I sometimes find them. What can I say? I'm a bloke.

Anyway, I scouted round for a while, but in the end didn't even download anything. From the descriptions of the files they seemed to be the same endless permutations of badly lit mad people, which is ultimately a bit tedious. Also, bullish talk notwithstanding, I don't feel great about looking at that kind of thing. I don't think it reflects very well upon one, and you only have to read a few other people's slaverings to make you decide it is too sad to be a part of.

So in the end I played the guitar for a while and went to bed.

*   *   *

The next few days at VCA passed pretty easily. I installed and configured, configured and installed. The birthday meal went pretty well, I gathered, and featured amongst other highlights the secretary Tanya literally sliding under the table through drunkenness. That was her story, at least. By the Monday of the following week everyone was calling me by name, and I was being included in the coffee-making rounds. England had called off its doomed attempt at summer, or at least imposed a time out, and had settled for a much more bearable cross between spring and autumn instead. All in all, things were going fairly well.

And as the week progressed, slightly better even than that. The reason for this was a person. Jeanette, to be precise.

I began, without even noticing at first, to find myself veering towards the computer nearest her when I needed to do some testing. I also found that I was slightly more likely to offer to go and make a round of coffees in the kitchen when she was already standing there, smoking one of her hourly cigarettes. Initially, it was just because she was the politest and most approachable of the staff, and it was a couple of days before I realized that I was looking out for her return from lunch, trying to be less dull when she was around, and noticing what she wore.

It was almost as if I was beginning to fancy her, for heaven's sake.

By the beginning of the next week I passed a kind of watershed, and went from undirected, subconscious behaviour to actually facing the fact that I was attracted to her. I did this with a faint feeling of dread, coupled with occasional, mournful tinges of melancholy. It was like being back at school. It's awful, when you're grown-up, to be reminded of what it was like when a word from someone, a glance, even just their presence, can be like the sun coming out from behind cloud. While it's nice, in a lyric, romantic novel sort of way, it also complicates things. Suddenly it matters if other people come into the kitchen when you're talking to her, and the way they interact with other people becomes more important. You start trying to engineer things, try to be near them, and it all just gets a bit weird.

Especially if the other person hasn't a clue what's going on in your head – and you've no intention of telling them. I'm no good at that, the telling part. Ten years ago I carried a letter round with me for two weeks, trying to pluck up the courage to give it to someone. It was a girl who was part of the same crowd at college, who I knew well as a friend, and who had just split up from someone else. The letter was a very carefully worded and tentative description of how I felt about her, ending with an invitation for a drink. Several times I was on the brink, I swear, but somehow I didn't give it to her. I just didn't have what it took.

The computer stuff was going okay, if you're interested. By the middle of the week the system was pretty much in place, and people were happily sending pop-up messages to each other. Cremmer, in particular, thought it was just fab that he could boss people around from the comfort of his own den. Even Clive was bucked up by seeing how the new system was going to ease the progress of whatever dull task it was he performed, and all in all my stock at the VCA was rising high.

It was time, finally, to get down to the nitty-gritty of developing their new databases. I tend to enjoy that part more than the wireheading, because it's more of a challenge, gives scope for design and creativity, and I don't have to keep getting up from my chair. When I settled down to it on Thursday morning, I realized that it was going to have an additional benefit. Jeanette was the VCA's events organizer, and most of the databases they needed concerned various aspects of her job. In other words, it was her I genuinely had to talk to about them, and at some length.

We sat side by side at her desk, me keeping a respectful distance, and I asked her the kind of questions I had to ask. She answered them concisely and quickly, didn't pipe up with a lot of damn fool questions, and came up with some reasonable requests. It was rather a nice day outside, and sunlight that was for once not hazy and obstructive angled through the window to pick out the lighter hues in her chestnut hair, which was long, and wavy, and as far as I could see entirely beautiful. Her hands played carelessly with a biro as we talked, the fingers slender and purposeful, the forearms a pleasing shade of skin colour. I hate people who go sprinting out into parks at the first sign of summer, to spend their lunchtimes staked out with insectile brainlessness in the desperate quest for a tan. As far as I was concerned the fact that Jeanette clearly hadn't done so – in contrast to Tanya, for example, who already looked like a hazelnut (and probably thought with the same fluency as one) – was just another thing to like her for.

It was a nice morning. Relaxed, and pleasant. Over the last week we'd started to speak more and more, and were ready for a period of actually having to converse with each other at length. I enjoyed it, but didn't get overexcited. Despite my losing status as a technodrone, I am wise in the ways of relationships. Just being able to get on with her, and have her look as if she didn't mind being with me – that was more than enough for the time being. I wasn't going to try for anything more.

Then, at 12.30, I did something entirely unexpected. We were in the middle of an in-depth and speculative wrangle on the projected nature of their hotel-booking database, when I realized that we were approaching the time at which Jeanette generally took her lunch. Smoothly, and with a nonchalance which I found frankly impressive, I lofted the idea that we go grab a sandwich somewhere and continue the discussion outside. As the sentences slipped from my mouth I experienced an out-of-body sensation, as if I was watching myself from about three feet away, cowering behind a chair. 'Not bad,' I found myself thinking, incredulously. 'Clearly, she'll say no, but that was a good, businesslike way of putting it.'

Bizarrely, instead of poking my eye out with a ruler, she said yes. We rose together, I grabbed my jacket, and we left the office, me trying not to smirk like a businessman recently ennobled for doing a lot of work for charity. We took the lift down to the lobby and stepped outside, and I chattered inanely to avoid coming to terms with the fact that I was now standing with her *outside* work.

She knew a snack bar round the corner, and within ten minutes we found ourselves at a table outside, ploughing through sandwiches. She even ate attractively, holding the food fluently and wolfing it down, as if she was a genuine human taking on sustenance rather than someone appearing in amateur dramatics. I audibly mulled over the database for a while, to give myself time to settle down, and before long we'd pretty much done the subject.

Luckily, as we each smoked a cigarette she pointed out with distaste a couple of blokes walking down the street, both of whom had taken their shirts off, and whose paunches were hanging over their jeans.

'Summer,' she said, with a sigh, and I was away. There are few people with a larger internal stock of complaints to make about Summer than me, and I let myself rip.

Why, I asked her, did everyone think it was so nice? What were supposed to be the benefits? One of the worst things about summer, I maintained hotly, as she smiled and ordered a coffee, was the constant pressure to enjoy oneself in ways which are considerably less fun than death.

Barbecues, for example. Now I don't mind barbies, especially, except that *my* friends never have them. It's just not their kind of thing. If I end up at a barbecue it's because I've been dragged there by my partner, to stand round in someone else's scraggy back garden as the sky threatens rain, watching drunken blokes teasing a nasty barking dog and girls I don't know standing in hunched clumps gossiping about people I've never heard of, while I try to eat badly cooked food that I could have bought for £2.50 in McDonald's *and* had somewhere to sit as well. That terrible weariness, a feeling of being washed out, exhausted and depressed, that comes from getting not quite drunk enough in the afternoon sun while standing up and either trying to make conversation with people I'll never see again, or putting up with them doing the same to me.

And going and sitting in parks. I hate it, as you may have gathered. Why? Because it's fucking *horrible*, that's why. Sitting on grass which is both papery and damp, surrounded by middle-class men with beards teaching their kids to unicycle, the air rent by the sound of some arsehole torturing a guitar to the delight of his fourteen-year-old hippy girlfriend. Drinking lukewarm soft drinks out of overpriced cans, and all the time being repetitively told how nice it all is, as if by some process of brainwashing you'll actually start to enjoy it.

Worst of all, the constant pressure to *go outside*. 'What are you doing inside on a day like this? You want to go outside, you do, get some fresh air. You want to go outside.' No. Wrong. I don't want to go outside. For a start, I like it inside. It's nice there. There are sofas, drinks, cigarettes, books. There is shade. Outside, there's nothing but the sun, the mindless drudgery of suntan cultivation, and the perpetual sound of droning voices, yapping dogs and convention shouting at you to enjoy yourself. And always the constant refrain from everyone you meet, drumming on your mind like torrential rain on a tin roof: 'Isn't it a beautiful day?', 'Isn't it a beautiful day?', 'Isn't it a beautiful day?', 'Isn't it a beautiful day?'

No, say I. No, it fucking *isn't*.

There was all that, and some more, but I'm sure you get the drift. By halfway through Jeanette was laughing, partly at what I was saying, and partly – I'm sure – at the fact that I was getting quite so worked up about it. But she was fundamentally on my side, and chipped in some valuable observations about the horrors of sitting outside dull country pubs surrounded by red-faced career girls and loud-mouthed estate agents in shorts, deafened by the sound of open-topped cars being revved by people who clearly had no right to live. We banged on happily for quite a while, had another cup of coffee, and then were both surprised to realize that we'd gone into overtime on lunch. I paid, telling her she could get the next one, and although that sounds like a terrible line, it came out pretty much perfect and she didn't stab me or anything. We strode quickly back to the office, still chatting, and the rest of the afternoon passed in a hazy blur of contentment.

I could have chosen to leave the office at the same time as her, and walked to whichever station she used, but I elected not to. I judged that enough had happened for one day, and I didn't want to push my luck. Instead I went home alone, hung out by myself, and went to sleep with, I suspect, a small smile upon my face.

Next day I sprang out of bed with an enthusiasm which is utterly unlike me, and as I struggled to balance the recalcitrant taps of my shower I was already plotting my next moves. Part of my mind was sitting back with folded arms and watching me with indulgent amusement, but in general I just felt really quite happy and excited.

For most of the morning I quizzed Jeanette further on her database needs. She was lunching with a friend, I knew, so I wasn't expecting anything there. Instead, I ambled vaguely round a couple of bookshops, wondering if there was any book I could legitimately buy for Jeanette. It would have to be something very specific, relevant to a conversation we'd had – and sufficiently inexpensive that it looked like a throwaway gift. In the end I came back empty-handed, which was probably just as well. Buying her a present was a ridiculous idea, out of proportion to the current situation. As I walked back to the office I told myself to be careful. I was in danger of getting carried away and disturbing the careful equilibrium of my life and mind.

Then, in the afternoon, something happened. I was off the databases for a while, trying to work out why one of the servers was behaving like an arse. Tanya wandered up to ask Jeanette about something, and before she went reminded her that there'd been talk of everyone going out for a drink that evening. Jeanette hummed and ha-ed for a moment, and I bent further over the keyboard, giving them a chance to ignore me. Then, as from nowhere, Tanya said the magic words.

Why, she suggested, didn't I come too?

Careful to be nonchalant and cavalier, pausing as if sorting through my myriad of other options, I said yes, why the hell not. Jeanette then said yes, she could probably make it, and for a moment I saw all the locks and chains around my life fall away, as if a cage had collapsed around me leaving only the open road.

For a moment it was like that, and then suddenly it wasn't. 'I'll have to check with Chris, though,' Jeanette added, and I realized she had a boyfriend.

I spent the rest of the afternoon alternating between trying to calm myself down and violently but silently cursing. I should have known that someone like her would already be taken – after all, they always are. Of course, it didn't mean it was a no-go area. People sometimes leave their partners. I know, I've done it myself. And people have left me. But suddenly it had changed, morphed from something that might – in my dreams, at least – have developed smoothly into a Nice Thing. Instead it become a miasma of potential grief which was unlikely to even start.

For about half an hour I was furious, with what I don't know. With myself, for letting my feelings grow and complicate. With her, for having a boyfriend. With life, for always being that bit more disappointing than it absolutely has to be.

Then, because I'm an old hand at dealing with my inner conditions, I talked myself round. It didn't matter. Jeanette could simply become a pleasant aspect of a month-long contract, someone I could chat to. Then the job would end, I'd move on, and none of it would matter. I had to nail that conclusion down on myself pretty hard, but thought I could make it stick.

I decided that I might as well go out for the drink anyway. There was another party I could go to but it would involve trekking halfway across town. Greg was busy. I might as well be sociable, now that they'd made the offer.

So I went, and I wish I hadn't.

The evening was okay, in the way that they always are when

people from the same office get together to drink and complain about their boss. Appleton wasn't there, thankfully, and Cremmer quickly got sufficiently drunk that he didn't qualify as a Appleton substitute. The evening was fine, for everyone else. It was just me who didn't have a good time.

Jeanette disappeared just before we left the office, and I found myself walking to the pub with everyone else. I sat drinking Budweisers and making conversation with Clive and Sarah, wondering where she was. She'd said she'd meet everyone there. So where was she?

At about half past eight the question was answered. She walked into the pub and I started to get up, a smile of greeting on my face. Then I realized she looked different somehow, and I noticed the man standing behind her.

The man was Chris Ayer. He was her boyfriend. He was also the nastiest man I've met in quite some time. That's going to sound like sour grapes, but it's not. He was perfectly presentable, in that he was good-looking and could talk to people, but everything else about him was wrong. There was something odd about the way he looked at people, something both arrogant and closed off. There was an air of restrained violence about him that I found unsettling, and his sense of his possession of Jeanette was complete. She sat at his side, hands in her lap, and said very little throughout the evening. I couldn't get over how different she looked to the funny and confident woman I'd had lunch with the day before, but nobody else seemed to notice it. After all, she joined in the office banter as usual, and smiled with her lips quite often. Nobody apart from me was looking for any more than that.

As the evening wore on I found myself feeling more and more uncomfortable. I exchanged a few tight words with Ayer, mainly concerning a new computer he'd bought, but wasn't bothered when he turned to talk to someone else. The group from the office seemed to be closing in on itself, leaning over the table to shout jokes which they understood and I didn't. Ayer's harsh laugh cut across the smoke to me, and I felt impotently angry that someone like him should be able to sit with his arm around someone like Jeanette.

I drank another couple of beers and then abruptly decided that I simply wasn't having a good enough time. I stood up and took my leave, and was mildly touched when Tanya and Sarah tried to get me to stay. Jeanette didn't say anything, and when Ayer's eyes swept vaguely over me I saw that for him I didn't exist. I backed out of the pub smiling, and then turned and stalked miserably down the road.

By Sunday evening I was fine. I met my ex-girlfriend-before-last for lunch on the Saturday, and we had a riotous time bitching and gossiping about people we knew. In the evening I went to a restaurant that served food only from a particular four-square-mile region of Nepal, or so Greg claimed, such venues being his speciality. It tasted just like Indian to me, and I didn't see any sherpas, but the food was good. I spent Sunday doing my kind of thing, wandering round town and sitting in cafés to read. I called my folks in the evening, and they were on good form, and then I watched a horror film before going to bed when I felt like it. The kind of weekend that only happily single people can have, in other words, and it suited me just fine.

Monday was okay too. I was regaled with various tales of drunkenness from Friday night, as if for the first time I had a right to know. I had all the information I needed from Jeanette for the time being, so I did most of my work at a different machine. We had a quick chat in the kitchen while I made some coffee, and it was more or less the same as it had been the week before – because she'd always *known* she had a boyfriend, of course. I caught myself sagging a couple of times in the afternoon, but bullied my mood into holding up. In a way it was kind of a relief, not to have to care.

The evening was warm and sunny, and I took my time walking home. Then I rustled myself up a chef's salad, which is my only claim to culinary skill. It has iceberg lettuce, black olives, grated cheese, julienned ham (that's 'sliced', to you and me), diced tomato and two types of home-made dressing: which is more than enough ingredients to count as cooking in my book. When I was sufficiently gorged on roughage I sat in front of the computer and tooled around, and by the time it was dark outside found myself cruising round the net.

And, after a while, I found myself accessing alt.binaries.pictures.erotica. I was in a funny sort of mood, I guess. I scrolled through the list of files, not knowing what I was after. What I found was the usual stuff, like '-TH2xx.jpg-{m/f}-hot sex!'. Hot sex wasn't really what I was looking for, especially if it had an exclamation mark after it. Of all the people who access the group, I suspect it's less than about 5% who actually put pictures up there in the first place. It seems to be a matter of intense pride with them, and they compete with each other on the volume and 'quality' of their postings. Their tragically sad bickering is often more entertaining than the pictures themselves.

It's complete pot luck what is available at any given time, and no file stays on there for more than about two days. The servers which hold the information have only limited space, and files get rolled off the end pretty quickly in the high-volume groups. I was about to give up when something suddenly caught my attention.

j1.gif-{f}-"Young_woman, fully_clothed (part 1/3).

Fuck *me*, I thought, that's a bit weird. The group caters for a wide spectrum of human sexuality, and I'd seen titles which promised fat couples, skinny girls, interracial bonding and light S&M. What I'd never come across was something as perverted as a woman with all her clothes on. Intrigued, I did the necessary to download the picture's three segments onto my hard disk.

By the time I'd made a cup of coffee they were there, and I severed the net connection and stitched the three files together. Until they were converted they were just text files, which is one of the weird things about the newsgroups. Absolutely anything, from programs to articles to pictures, is up there as plain text. Without the appropriate decoders it just looks like nonsense, which I guess is as good a metaphor as any for the net as a whole. Or indeed for life. Feel free to use that insight in your own conversations.

When the file was ready, I loaded up a graphics package and opened it. I was doing so with only half an eye, not really expecting anything very interesting. But when, after a few seconds of whirring, the image popped onto the screen, I dropped my cup of coffee and it teetered on the desk before falling to shatter on the floor.

It was Jeanette.

The image quality was not especially high, and looked as if it had been taken with some small automatic camera. But the girl in the picture was Jeanette, without a shadow of a doubt. She was perched on the arm of an anonymous armchair, and with a lurch I realized it was probably taken in her flat. She was, as advertised, fully clothed, wearing a shortish skirt and a short-sleeved top which buttoned up at the front. She was looking in the general direction of the camera, and her expression was unreadable. She looked beautiful, as always, and somehow much, much more appealing than any of the buck-naked women who cavorted through the usual pictures to be found on the net.

After I'd got over my jaw-dropped surprise, I found I was feeling something else. Annoyance, possibly. I know I'm biased, but I didn't think it right that a picture of her was plastered up in cyberspace for everyone to gawk at, even if she was fully clothed. I realize that's hypocritical in the face of all the other women up there, but I can't help it. It was different.

Because I knew her.

I was also angry because I could only think of one way it could have got there. I'd mentioned a few net-related things in Jeanette's presence at work, and she'd showed no sign of recognition. It was a hell of a coincidence that I'd seen the picture at all, and I wasn't prepared to speculate about stray photos of her falling into unknown people's hands. There was only one person who was likely to have uploaded it. Her boyfriend.

The usual women (and men) in the pictures are getting paid

for it. It's their job. Jeanette wasn't, and might not even know the picture was there.

I quickly logged back onto the net and found the original text files. I extricated the uploader information and pulled it onto the screen, and then swore.

Remember a while back I said it was possible to hide yourself when posting up to the net? Well, that's what he'd done. The email address of the person who'd uploaded the picture was listed as 'anon99989@penet.fi'. That meant that rather than posting it up in his real name, he'd routed the mail through an anonymity server in Finland called PENET. This server strips the journey information out of the posting and assigns a random address which is held on an encrypted database. I couldn't tell anything from it at all. Feeling my lip curl with distaste, I quit out.

By the time I got to work the next day I knew there wasn't anything I could say about it. I could hardly pipe up with 'Hey! Saw your pic on the Internet porn board last night!' And after all, it was only a picture, the kind that people have plastic folders stuffed full of. The question was whether Jeanette knew Ayer had posted it up. If she did then, well, it just went to show that you didn't know much about people just because you worked with them. If she didn't, then I think she had a right both to know, and to be annoyed.

I dropped a few net references into the conversations we had, but nothing came of them. I even mentioned the newsgroups, but got mild interest and nothing more. It was fairly clear she hadn't heard of them. In the end I sort of mentally shrugged. So her unpleasant boyfriend had posted up a picture. There was nothing I could do about it, except bury still further any feelings I might have entertained for her. She already had a life with someone else, and I had no business interfering.

In the evening I met up with Greg again, and we went and got quietly hammered in a small drinking club we frequented. I successfully fought off his ideas on going and getting some food, doubtless the cuisine of one particular village on the top of Kilimanjaro, and so by the end of the evening we were pretty far gone. I stumbled out of a cab, flolloped up the stairs and mainlined coffee for a while, in the hope of avoiding a hangover the next day. And it was as I sat, weaving slightly, on the sofa, that I conceived the idea of checking a certain newsgroup.

Once the notion had taken hold I couldn't seem to dislodge it. Most of my body and soul was engaged in remedial work, trying to save what brain cells they could from the onslaught of alcohol, and the idea was free to romp and run as it pleased. So I found myself slumped at my desk, listening to my hard disk doing its thing, and muttering quietly to myself. I don't know what I was saying. I think it was probably a verbal equivalent of that letter I never gave to someone, an explanation of how much better off Jeanette would be with me. I can get very maudlin when I'm drunk.

When the newsgroup appeared in front of me I blearily ran my eye over the list. The group had seen serious action in the last 24 hours, and there were over 300 titles to contend with. I was beginning to lose heart and interest when I saw something about two thirds of the way down the list.

'j2.gif-{f}-"Young_woman"', one line said, and it was followed by 'j3.gif-{f}-"Young_woman"'.

These two titles started immediately to do what half a pint of coffee hadn't: sober me up. At a glance I could tell that there were two differences from the description of the first picture of Jeanette I'd seen. The numerals after the 'j' were different, implying they were not the same picture. Also, there were two words missing at the end of the title: 'fully clothed'.

I called the first few lines of the first file onto the screen, and saw that it too had come from anon99989@penet.fi. Then, reaching shakily for a cigarette, I downloaded the rest. When my connection was over I slowly stitched the text files together and then booted up the viewer.

It was Jeanette, again. Wincing slightly, hating myself for having access to photos of her under these circumstances when

I had no right to know what they might show, I looked briefly at first one and then the other.

j2.gif looked as if it had been taken immediately after the first I'd seen. It showed Jeanette, still sitting on the arm of the chair. She was undoing the front of her top, and had got as far as the third button. Her head was down, and I couldn't see her face. Trembling slightly from a combination of emotions, I looked at j3.gif. Her top was now off, showing a flat stomach and a dark blue lacy bra. She was steadying herself on the chair with one arm, and her position looked uncomfortable. She was looking off to one side, away from the camera, and when I saw her face I thought I had the answer to at least one question. She didn't look very happy. She didn't look as if she was having fun.

She didn't look as if she wanted to be doing this at all.

I stood up suddenly and paced around the room, unsure of what to do. If she hadn't been especially enthralled about having the photos taken in the first place, I couldn't believe that Jeanette condoned or even knew about their presence on the net. Quite apart from anything else, she wasn't that type of girl, if that type of girl indeed existed at all.

This constituted some very clear kind of invasion by her boyfriend, something that negated any rights he may have felt he had upon her. But what could I do about it?

I copied the two files onto a floppy, along with j1.gif, and threw them off my hard disk. It may seem like a small distinction to you, but I didn't want them on my main machine. It would have seemed like collusion.

I got up the next morning with no more than a mild headache, and before I left for work decided to quickly log onto the net. There were no more pictures, but there was something that made me very angry indeed. Someone had posted up a message whose total text was the following.

'Re: j-pictures {f}: EXCELLENT! More pleeze!'.

The pictures had struck a chord with some nameless net-pervert, and they wanted to see some more.

I spent the whole morning trying to work out what to do. The only way I could think of broaching the subject would involve mentioning the alt.binaries.pictures.erotica group itself, which would be a bit of a nasty moment – I wasn't keen on revealing the fact that I was a nameless net-pervert myself. I hardly got a chance to talk to her all morning anyway, because she was busy on the phone. She also seemed a little tired, and little disposed to chat on the two occasions we found ourselves in the kitchen together.

It felt as if parts of my mind were straining against each other, pulling in different directions. If she didn't know about it, it was wrong, and she should be put in the picture. If I told her, however, she'd never think the same of me again. There was a chance, of course, that the problem might go away: despite the net-loser's request, the expression on Jeanette's face in j3.gif made it seem unlikely there were any more pictures. And ultimately the whole situation probably wasn't any of my business, however much it felt like it was.

In the event, I missed the boat. About 4.30, I emerged from a long and vicious argument with the server software to discover that Jeanette had left for the day. 'A doctor's appointment'. In most of the places I've worked that phrase translates directly to: 'A couple of hours off from work, *obviously* not spent at the doctor's', but that didn't seem to be the general impression at the VCA. She'd probably just gone to the doctor's. Either way she was no longer in the office, and I was slightly ashamed to find myself relaxing now that I could no longer talk to her.

At 8.30 that evening, after my second salad of the week, I logged on and checked the group again. There was nothing there. I fretted and fidgeted around the apartment for a few hours, and then tried again at 11.00. This time I found two more: j4.gif, and j5.gif, both from the anonymous address.

In the first, Jeanette was standing. She was no longer wearing her skirt, and her long legs led up to underwear that matched the bra I'd already seen. She wasn't posing for the picture. Her hands were on her hips, and she looked angry. In j5 she was leaning back against the arm of the chair, and no longer wearing her bra. Her face was blank.

I stared at the second picture for a long time, mind completely split in two. If you ignored the expression on her face, she looked gorgeous. Her breasts were small but perfectly shaped, exactly in proportion to her long, slender body. It was, undeniably, an erotic picture. Except for her face, and the fact that she obviously didn't want to be photographed, and the fact that someone was doing it anyway. Not only that, but broadcasting it to the planet.

I decided that enough was enough. After a while I came up with the best that I could. I loaded up my email package, and sent a message to anon99989@penet.fi. The double-blind principle the server operated on meant that the recipient wouldn't know where it had come from, and that was fine by me. The message was this . . .

'I know who you are.'

It wasn't much, but it was something. The idea that someone out there could know his identity *might* be enough to stop him. It was only a stop-gap measure, anyway. I now knew I had to do something about the situation. It simply wasn't on.

And I had to do it soon. When I checked the next morning there were no more pictures, but two messages from people who'd downloaded them. 'Keep 'em cumming!' one wit from Japan had written. Some slob from Texas had posted in similar vein, but added a small request: 'Great, but pick up the pace a little. I want to see more FLESH!'

All the way to work I geared myself up to talking to Jeanette, and I nearly punched the wall when I heard she was out at a venue meeting for the whole morning and half the afternoon. I got rid of the morning by concentrating hard on one of her databases, wanting to bring at least something positive into her life. I know it wasn't much, but all I know is computers, and that's the best that I could do.

At last three o'clock rolled round and Jeanette reappeared in the office. She seemed tired and a little preoccupied, and sat straight down at her desk to work. I loitered in the main office area, willing people to fuck off out of it so hard my head started to ache. I couldn't get anywhere near the topic if there were other people around. It would be hard enough if we were alone.

Finally, bloody *finally*, she got up from her desk and went into the kitchen. I got up and followed her in. She smiled faintly and vaguely on seeing me, and, noticing that she had a bandage on her right forearm, I used that to start a conversation. A small mole, apparently, hence the visit to the doctor. I let her finish that topic, keeping half an eye out to make sure that no one was approaching the kitchen.

'I bought a camera today,' I blurted, as cheerily as I could. It wasn't great, but I wanted to start slowly. She didn't respond for a moment, and then looked up, her face expressionless.

'Oh yes?' she said, eventually. 'What are you going to photograph?'

'Oh, you know, buildings, landscape. Black and white, that kind of thing.' She nodded distantly, and I ran out of things to say.

I ran out because in retrospect the topic didn't lead anywhere, but I stopped for another reason too. I stopped because as she turned to pick up the kettle, the look on her face knocked the wind out of me. The combination of unhappiness and loneliness, the sense of helplessness. It struck me again that despite the anger in her face in j4, in j5 she had not only taken her bra off but looked resigned and defeated. Suddenly I didn't care how it looked, didn't care what she thought of me.

'Jeanette,' I said, firmly, and she turned to look at me again. 'I saw a pict-'

'Hello boys and girls. Having a little tea party, are we?'

At the sound of Appleton's voice I wanted to turn round and smash his face in. Jeanette laughed prettily at her employer's sally, and moved out of the way to allow him access to the kettle. Appleton asked me some balls-achingly dull questions about the computer system, obviously keen to sound as if he had the faintest conception of what it all meant. By the time I'd finished answering him Jeanette was back at her desk.

The next hour was one of the longest of my life. I'd gone over, crossed the line. I knew I was going to talk to her about what I'd seen. More than that, I'd realized that it didn't have to be as difficult as I'd assumed.

The first picture, j1.gif, simply showed a pretty girl sitting on a chair. It wasn't pornographic, and could have been posted up in any number of places on the net. All I had to do was say I'd seen that picture. It wouldn't implicate me, and she would know what her boyfriend was up to.

I hovered round the main office, ready to be after her the minute she looked like leaving, having decided that I'd walk with her to the tube and tell her then. So long as she didn't leave with anyone else, it would be perfect. While I hovered I watched her work, her eyes blank and isolated. About quarter to five she got a phone call. She listened for a moment, said, 'Yes, alright' in a dull tone of voice, and then put the phone down. There was nothing else to distract me from the constant recycling of draft gambits in my head.

At five, she started tidying her desk, and I slipped out and got my jacket. I waited in the hallway until I could hear her coming, and then went downstairs in the lift. I walked through the lobby as slowly as I could, and then went and stood outside the building. My hands were sweating and I felt wired and frightened, but I knew I was going to go through with it. A moment later she came out.

'Hi,' I said, and she smiled warily, surprised to see me, I suppose. 'Look Jeanette, I need to talk to you about something.'

She stared at me, looked around, and then asked what.

'I've seen pictures of you.' In my nervousness I blew it, and used the plural rather than singular.

'Where?' she said, immediately. She knew what I was talking about. From the speed with which she latched on I realized that whatever fun and games were going on between her and Ayer were at the forefront of her mind.

'The newsgroups. It's . . .'

'I know what they are,' she said. 'What have you seen?'

'Five so far,' I said. 'Look, if there's anything I can do . . .'

'Like what?' she said, and laughed harshly, her eyes beginning to blur. 'Like what?'

'Well, anything. Look, let's go talk about it. I could . . .'

'There's no use,' she said hurriedly, and started to pull away. I followed her, bewildered. How could she not want to do anything about it? I mean, alright, I may not have been much of a prospect, but surely some help was better than none.

'Jeanette . . .'

'Let's talk tomorrow,' she hissed, and suddenly I realized what was happening. Her boyfriend had come to pick her up. She walked towards the kerb where a white car was coming to a halt, and I rapidly about-faced and started striding the other way. It wasn't fear, not purely. I also didn't want to get her in trouble.

As I walked up the road I felt as if the back of my neck was burning, and at the last moment I glanced to the side. The white car was just passing, and I could see Jeanette sitting bolt upright in the passenger seat. Her boyfriend was looking out of the side window. At me. Then he accelerated and the car sped away.

That night brought another two photographs. j6 had Jeanette naked, sitting in the chair with her legs slightly apart. Her face was stony. In j7 she was on all fours, photographed from behind. As I sat in my chair, filled with impotent fury, I noticed something in both pictures, and blew them up with the magnifier tool. In j6 one side of her face looked a little red, and when I looked carefully at j7 I could see that there was a trickle of blood running from a small cut on her right forearm.

There had never been a mole on her arm. She hadn't got the bandage because of the doctor. She had it because of him.

I hardly slept that night. I stayed up till three, keeping an eye on the newsgroup. Its denizens were certainly becoming fans of the 'j' pictures, and I saw five requests for some more. As far as they knew all this involved was a bit more scanning originals from some magazine. They didn't realize that someone I knew was having them taken against her will. I considered trying to do something within the group, like posting a message telling what I knew. While its frequenters are a bit sad, they tend to have a strong moral stance about such things. It's not like the alt.binaries.pictures.tasteless group – where anything goes, the sicker the better. If the a.b.p.erotica crowd were convinced the pictures were being taken under coercion, there was a strong chance they might mailbomb Ayer off the net. It would be a big war to start, however, and one with potentially damaging consequences. The mailbombing would have to go through the anonymity server, and would probably crash it. While I couldn't give a fuck about that, it would draw the attention of all manner of people. In any event, because of the anonymity, nothing would happen directly to Ayer apart from some inconvenience.

I decided to put the idea on hold, in case talking to Jeanette tomorrow made it unnecessary. Eventually I went to bed, where I thrashed and turned for hours. Some time just before dawn I drifted off, and dreamed about a cat being caught in a lawnmower.

I was up at seven, there being no point in me staying in bed. I checked the group, but there were no new files. On an afterthought I checked my email, realizing that I'd been so out of it that I hadn't done so for days. There were about thirty messages for me, some from friends, the rest from a variety of virtual acquaintances around the world. I scanned through them quickly, seeing if any needed urgent attention, and then slap in the middle I noticed one from a particular address.

anon99989@penet.fi.

Heart thumping, I opened the email. In the convention of such things, he'd quoted my message back at me, with a comment. The entire text of the mail read:

> I know who you are.
>

Maybe. But I know where you live.

*   *   *

30

When I got to work, at the dot of nine, I discovered Jeanette wasn't there. She'd left a message at eight-thirty announcing she was taking the day off. Sarah was a bit sniffy about this, though she claimed to be great pals with Jeanette. I left her debating the morality of such cavalier leave-taking with Tanya in the kitchen, as I walked slowly out to sit at Jeanette's desk to work. After five minutes' thought I went back to the kitchen and asked Sarah for Jeanette's number, claiming I had to ask her about the database. Sarah seemed only too pleased to provide the means of contacting a friend having a day off. I grabbed my jacket, muttered something about buying cigarettes, and left the office.

Round the corner I found a public phone box and called her number. As I listened to the phone ring I glanced at the prostitute cards which liberally covered the walls, but soon looked away. I didn't find their representation of the female form amusing any more. After six rings, an answering machine cut in. A man's voice, Ayer's, announced that they were out. I rang again, with the same result, and then left the phone box and stood aimlessly on the pavement.

There was nothing I could do.

I went back to work. I worked. I ran home.

At six-thirty I logged on for the first time, and the next two pictures were already there. I could tell immediately that something had changed. The wall behind her was a different colour, for a start. The focus of the action seemed to have moved, to the bedroom, presumably, and the pictures were getting worse. j8 showed Jeanette spread-eagled on her back. Her legs were very wide open, and both her hands and feet were out of shot. j9 was much the same, except you could see that her hands were tied. You could also see her face, with its hopeless defiance and fear. As I erased the picture from my disk I felt my neck spasming.

Too late I realized that what I should have done was get Jeanette's address while I was at work. It would have been difficult, and viewed with suspicion, but I might have been able to do it. Now I couldn't. I didn't know the home numbers of anyone else from the VCA, and couldn't trace her address from her number. The operator wouldn't give it to me. If I'd had the address I could have gone round. Maybe I would have found myself in the worst situation of my life, but it would have been something to try. The idea of her being in trouble somewhere in London, and me not knowing where, was almost too much to bear. Suddenly, I decided that I had to do the one small thing I could. I logged back on to the erotica group and prepared to start a flame war.

The classic knee-jerk reaction that people on the net use to express their displeasure is known as 'flaming'. Basically, it involves bombarding the offender with massive mail messages until their virtual mail box collapses under the load. This draws the attention of the site administrator, and they get chucked off the net. What I had to do was post a message providing sufficient reason for the good citizens of pornville to dump on anon99989@penet.fi.

So it might cause some trouble. I didn't fucking care.

I had a mail slip open and my hands poised over the keyboard before I noticed something which stopped me in my tracks.

There were two more files. Already. The slob from Texas was getting his wish: the pace was being picked up.

In j10 Jeanette was on her knees on a dirty mattress. Her hands appeared to be tied behind her, and her head was bowed. j11 showed her lying awkwardly on her side, as if she'd been pushed over. She was glaring at the camera, and when I magnified the left side of the image I could see a thin trickle of blood from her right nostril.

I leapt up from the keyboard, shouting. I don't know what I was saying. It wasn't coherent. Jeanette's face stared up at me from the computer and I leant wildly across and hit the switch to turn the screen off. Just quitting out didn't seem enough. Then I realized that the image was still there, even though I couldn't see it. The computer was still sending the information to the screen, and the minute I turned it back on, it would be there. So I hard-stopped the computer by just turning it off at the mains. Suddenly, what had always been my domain felt like the outpost of someone very twisted and evil, and I didn't want anything to do with it.

Then, like a stone through glass, two ideas crashed into each other in my head.

Gospel Oak.

Police.

From nowhere came a faint half-memory, so tenuous that it might be illusory, of Jeanette mentioning Gospel Oak station. I knew where that was.

An operator wouldn't give me an address from a phone number. But the police would be able to get it. They had reverse directories.

I couldn't think of anything else.

I rang the police. I told them I had reason to believe that someone was in danger, and that she lived at the house with this phone number. They wanted to know who I was and all manner of other shit, but I rang off quickly, grabbed my coat and hit the street.

Gospel Oak is a small area, filling up the gap between Highgate, Chalk Farm and Hampstead. I knew it well because Greg and I used to go play pool at a pub on Mansfield Road, which runs straight through it. I knew the entrance and exit points of the area, and I got the cab to drop me off as near to the centre as possible. Then I stood on the pavement, hopping from foot to foot and smoking, hoping against hope that this would work.

Ten minutes later a police car turned into Mansfield Road. I was very pleased to see them, and enormously relieved. I hadn't been particularly sure about the Gospel Oak part. I shrank back against the nearest building until it had gone past, and then ran after it as inconspicuously as I could. It took a left into Estelle Road and I slowed at the corner to watch it pull up outside number 6. I slipped into the doorway of the corner shop and watched as two policemen took their own good time about untangling themselves from their car.

They walked up to the front of the house. One leant hard against the doorbell, while the other peered around the front of the house as if taking part in an officiousness competition. The door wasn't answered, which didn't surprise me. Ayer was hardly going to break off from torturing his girlfriend to take social calls. One of the policemen nodded to the other, who visibly sighed, and made his way round the back of the house.

'Oh come on, come on,' I hissed in the shadows. 'Break the fucking door down.'

About five minutes passed, and then the policeman reappeared. He shrugged flamboyantly at his colleague, and pressed the doorbell again.

A light suddenly appeared above the door, coming from the hallway behind it. My breath caught in my throat and I edged a little closer. I'm not sure what I was preparing to do. Dash over there and force my way in, past the policemen, to grab Ayer and smash his head against the wall? I really don't know.

The door opened, and I saw it wasn't Ayer or Jeanette. It was an elderly man with a crutch and grey hair that looked like it had seen action in a hurricane. He conversed irritably with the policemen for a moment and then shut the door in their faces. The two cops stared at each other for a moment, clearly considering busting the old tosser, but then turned and made their way back to the car. Still looking up at the house, the first policeman made a report into his radio, and I heard enough to understand why they then got into the car and drove away.

The old guy had told them that the young couple had gone away for the weekend. He'd seen them go on Thursday evening. I was over 24 hours too late.

When the police car had turned the corner I found myself panting, not knowing what to do. The last two photographs, the one with the dirty mattress, hadn't been taken here at all. Jeanette was somewhere in the country, but I didn't know where, and there was no way of finding out. The pictures could have been posted from anywhere.

Making a decision, I walked quickly across the road towards the house. The policemen may not have felt they had just cause, but I did, and I carefully made my way around the back of the house. This involved climbing over a gate and wending through the old guy's crowded little garden, and I came perilously close to knocking over a pile of flower pots. As luck would have it there was a kind of low wall which led to a complex exterior plumbing fixture, and I quickly clambered on top of it. A slightly precarious upward step took me next to one of the second-floor windows. It was dark, like all the others, but I kept my head bent just in case.

When I was closer to the window I saw that it wasn't fastened at the bottom. They might have gone, and then come back. Ayer could have staged it so the old man saw them go, and then slipped back when he was out.

It was possible, but not likely. On the other hand, the window was ajar. Maybe they were just careless about such things. I slipped my fingers under the pane and pulled it open. Then I leant with my ear close to the open space and listened. There was no sound, and so I boosted myself up and quickly in.

I found myself in a bedroom. I didn't turn the light on, but there was enough coming from the moon and streetlights to pick out a couple of pieces of Jeanette's clothing, garments that I recognized, strewn over the floor. She wouldn't have left them like that, not if she'd had any choice in the matter. I walked carefully into the corridor, poking my head into the bathroom and kitchen, which were dead. Then I found myself in the living room.

The big chair stood in front of a wall I recognized, and at the far end a computer sat on a desk next to a picture scanner. Moving as quickly but quietly as possible, I frantically searched over the desk for anything that might tell me where Ayer had taken her. There was nothing there, and nothing in the rest of the room. I'd broken – well, opened – and entered for no purpose.

There were no clues. No sign of where they'd gone. An empty box under the table confirmed what I'd already guessed: Ayer had a laptop computer as well. He could be posting the pictures onto the net from anywhere that had a phone socket. Jeanette would be with him, and I needed to find her. I needed to find her soon.

I paced around the room, trying to pick up speed, trying to work out what I could possibly do. No one at VCA knew where they'd gone – they hadn't even known Jeanette wasn't going to be in. The old turd downstairs hadn't known. There was nothing in the flat that resembled a phone book or personal organizer, something that would have a friend or family member's number. I was prepared to do anything, call anyone, in the hope of finding where they'd gone. But there was nothing, unless . . .

I sat down at the desk, reached behind the computer and turned it on. Ayer had a fairly flash deck, together with a scanner and laserprinter. He knew the net. Chances were he was wirehead enough to keep his phone numbers somewhere on his computer.

As soon as the machine was booted up I went rifling through it, grimly enjoying the intrusion, the computer-rape. His files and programs were spread all over the disk, with no apparent system. Each time I finished looking through a folder, I erased it. It seemed the least I could do.

Then after about five minutes I found something, but not what I was looking for. I found a folder named 'j'.

There were files called j12 to j16 in the folder, in addition to all the others that I'd seen. Wherever Jeanette was, Ayer had come back here to scan the pictures. Presumably that meant they were still in London, for all the good that did me.

I'm not telling you what they were like, except that they showed Jeanette, and in some she was crying, and in j15 and j16 there was a lot of blood running from the corner of her mouth. She was twisted and tied, face livid with bruises, and in j16 she was staring straight at the camera, face slack with terror.

Unthinkingly, I slammed my fist down on the desk. There was a noise downstairs and I went absolutely motionless until I was sure the old man had lost interest. Then I turned the computer off, opened up the case and removed the hard disk. I climbed out the way I'd come and ran out down the street, flagged a taxi by jumping in front of it and headed for home.

I was going to the police, but I needed a computer, something to shove the hard disk into. I was going to show them what I'd found, and fuck the fact it was stolen. If they nicked me, so be it. But they had to do something about it. They had to try and find her. If he'd come back to do his scanning he had to be keeping her somewhere in London. They'd know where to look, or where to start. They'd know what to do.

They had to. They were the police. It was their job.

I ran up the stairs and into the flat, and then dug in my spares cupboard for enough pieces to hack together a compatible computer. When I'd got them I went over to my desk to call the local police station, and then stopped and turned my computer on. I logged onto the net and kicked up my mail package, and sent a short, useless message.

'I'm coming after you,' I said.

It wasn't bravado. I didn't feel brave at all. I just felt furious, and wanted to do anything which might unsettle him, or make him stop. Anything to make him stop.

I logged quickly onto the newsgroups, to see when anon99989@-penet.fi had most recently posted. A half hour ago, when I'd been in his apartment, j12-16 had been posted up. Two people had already responded: one hoping the blood was fake and asking if the group really wanted that kind of picture – the other asking for more. I viciously wished a violent death upon the second person, and was about to log off, having decided not to bother phoning but to just go straight to the cops, when I saw another text-only posting at the end of the list.

'Re: j-series' it said. It was from anon99989@penet.fi.

I opened it. 'End of series,' the message said. 'Hope you all enjoyed it. Next time, something tasteless.'

'And I hope,' I shouted at the screen, 'that you enjoy it when I ram your hard disk down your fucking throat.'

Then suddenly my blood ran cold.

Next time, something tasteless.

I hurriedly closed the group, and opened up alt.binaries.pictures.tasteless. As I scrolled past the titles for roadkills and people crapping I felt the first heavy, cold tear roll out onto my cheek. My hand was shaking uncontrollably, my head full of some dark mist, and when I saw the last entry I knew suddenly and exactly what Jeanette had been looking at when j16 was taken.

'j17.gif,' it read. '{f} Pretty amputee'.

EVERYBODY GOES

I saw a man yesterday. I was coming back from the wasteground with Matt and Joey and we were calling Joey dumb because he'd seen this huge spider and he thought it was a Black Widow or something when it was just, like, a *spider*, and I saw the man.

We were walking down the road towards the block and laughing and I just happened to look up and there was this guy down the end of the street, tall, walking up towards us. We turned off the road before he got to us, and I forgot about him.

Anyway, Matt had to go home then because his family eats early and his mom raises hell if he isn't back in time to wash up and so I just hung out for a while with Joey and then he went home too. Nothing much happened in the evening.

This morning I got up early because we were going down to the creek for the day and it's a long walk. I made some sandwiches and put them in a bag, and I grabbed an apple and put that in too. Then I went down to knock on Matt's door.

His mom answered and let me in. She's okay really, and quite nice-looking for a mom, but she's kind of strict. She's the only person in the world who calls me Peter instead of Pete. Matt's room always looks like it's just been tidied, which is quite cool actually though it must be a real pain to keep up. At least you know where everything is.

We went down and got Joey. Matt seemed kind of quiet on the way down as if there was something he wanted to tell me, but he didn't. I figured that if he wanted to, sooner or later he would. That's how it is with best friends. You don't have to be always talking. The point will come round soon enough.

Joey wasn't ready so we had to hang round while he finished his breakfast. His dad's kind of weird. He sits and reads the paper at the table and just grunts at it every now and then. I don't think I could eat breakfast with someone who did that. I think I would find it disturbing. Must be something you get into when you grow up, I guess.

Anyway, *finally* Joey was ready and we left the block. The sun was pretty hot already though it was only nine in the morning and I was glad I was only wearing a T-shirt. Matt's mom made him wear a sweatshirt in case there was a sudden blizzard or something and I knew he was going to be pretty baked by the end of the day but you can't tell moms anything.

As we were walking away from the block towards the wasteground I looked back and I saw the man again, standing on the opposite side of the street, looking at the block. He was staring up at the top floor and then I thought he turned and looked at us, but it was difficult to tell because the sun was shining right in my eyes.

We walked and ran through the wasteground, not hanging around much because we'd been there yesterday. We checked on the fort but it was still there. Sometimes other kids come and mess it up but it was okay today.

Matt got Joey a good one with a scrunched-up leaf. He put it on the back of his hand when Joey was looking the other way and then he started staring at it and saying 'Pete . . .' in this really scared voice; and I saw what he was doing and pretended to be scared too and Joey bought it.

'I told you,' he says – and he's backing away – 'I *told* you there was Black Widows,' and we could have kept it going but I started laughing. Joey looked confused for a second and then he just grunted as if he was reading his dad's paper and so we jumped on him and called him Dad all afternoon.

We didn't get to the creek till nearly lunchtime, and Matt took his sweatshirt off and tied it round his waist. It's a couple miles from the block, way past the wasteground and out into the bush. It's a good creek though. It's so good we don't go there too often, like we don't want to wear it out.

You just walk along the bush, not seeing anything, and then

suddenly there you are, and there's this baby canyon cut into the earth. It gets a little deeper every year, I think, except when there's no rain. Maybe it gets deeper then too, I don't know. The sides are about ten feet deep and this year there was rain so there's plenty of water at the bottom and you have to be careful climbing down because otherwise you can slip and end up in the mud. Matt went down first. He's best at climbing, and really quick. He went down first so that if Joey slipped he might not fall all the way in. For me, if Joey slips, he slips, but Matt's good like that. Probably comes from having such a tidy room.

Joey made it down okay this time, hold the front page, and I went last. The best way to get down is to put your back to the creek, slide your feet down, and then let them go until you're hanging onto the edge of the canyon with your hands. Then you just have to scuttle. As I was lowering myself down I noticed how far you could see across the plain, looking right along about a foot up from the ground. You can't see anything for miles like that, nothing but bushes and dust. I think the man was there too, off in the distance, but it was difficult to be sure and then I slipped and nearly ended up in the creek myself, which would have been a real pain and Joey would have gone on about it for ever.

We walked along the creek for a while and then came to the ocean. It's not really the ocean, it's just a bit where the canyon widens out into almost a circle that's about fifteen feet across. It's deeper than the rest of the creek, and the water isn't so clear, but it's really cool. When you're down there you can't see anything but this circle of sky, and you know there's nothing else for miles around. There's this old door there which we call our ship and we pull it to one side of the ocean and we all try to get on and float it to the middle. Usually it's kind of messy and I know Matt and Joey are thinking there's going to be trouble when their moms see their clothes, but today we somehow got it right and we floated right to the middle with only a little bit of water coming up.

We played our game for a while and then we just sat there for a long time and talked and stuff. I was thinking how good it was to be there and there was a pause and then Joey tried to say something of his own like that. It didn't come out very well, but we knew what he meant so we told him to shut up and made as if we were going to push him in. Matt pretended he had a spider on his leg just by suddenly looking scared and staring and Joey laughed, and I realized that that's where jokes come from. It was our own joke, that no one else would ever understand and that we would never forget however old we got.

Matt looked at me one time, as if he was about to say what was on his mind, but then Joey said something dumb and he didn't. We just sat there and kept talking about things and moving around so we didn't get burned too bad. Once when I looked up at the rim of the canyon I thought maybe there was a head peeking over the side but there probably wasn't.

Joey has a watch and so we knew when it was four o'clock. Four o'clock is the latest we can leave so that Matt gets back for dinner in time. We walked back towards the wasteground, not running. The sun had tired us out and we weren't in any hurry to get back because it had been a good afternoon, and they always finish when you split up. You can't get back to them the next day, especially if you try to do the same thing again.

When we got back to the street we were late and so Matt and Joey ran on ahead. I would have run with them but I saw that the man was standing down the other side of the block, and I wanted to watch him to see what he was going to do. Matt waited back a second after Joey had run and said he'd see me after dinner. Then he ran, and I just hung around for a while.

The man was looking back up at the block again, like he was looking for something. He knew I was hanging around, but he didn't come over right away, as if he was nervous. I went and sat on the wall and messed about with some stones. I wasn't in any hurry.

'Excuse me,' says this voice, and I looked up to see the man standing over me. The slanting sun was in his eyes and he was shading them with his hand. He had a nice suit on and he was younger than people's parents are, but not much. 'You live here, don't you?'

I nodded, and looked up at his face. He looked familiar.

'I used to live here,' he said, 'when I was a kid. On the top floor.' Then he laughed, and I recognized him from the sound. 'A long time ago now. Came back after all these years to see if it had changed.'

I didn't say anything.

'Hasn't much, still looks the same.' He turned and looked again at the block, then back past me towards the wasteground. 'Guys still playing out there on the 'ground?'

'Yeah,' I said, 'it's cool. We have a fort there.'

'And the creek?'

He knew I still played there: he'd been watching. I knew what he really wanted to ask, so I just nodded. The man nodded too, as if he didn't know what to say next. Or more like he knew what he wanted to say, but didn't know how to go about it.

'My name's Tom Spivey,' he said, and then stopped. I nodded again. The man laughed, embarrassed. 'This is going to sound very weird, but . . . I've seen you around today, and yesterday.' He laughed again, running his hand through his hair, and then finally asked what was on his mind. 'Your name isn't Pete, by any chance?'

I looked up into his eyes, then turned away.

'No,' I said. 'It's Jim.'

The man looked confused for a moment, then relieved. He said a couple more things about the block, and then he went away. Back to the city, or wherever.

After dinner I saw Matt out in the back parking lot, behind the block. We talked about the afternoon some, so he could get warmed up, and then he told me what was on his mind.

His family was moving on. His dad had got a better job somewhere else. They'd be going in a week.

We talked a little more, and then he went back inside, looking different somehow, as if he'd already gone.

I stayed out, sitting on the wall, thinking about missing people. I wasn't feeling sad, just tired. Sure, I was going to miss Matt. He was my best friend. I'd missed Tom for a while, but then someone else came along. And then someone else, and someone else. There's always new people. They come, and then they go. Maybe Matt would return some day, like Tom. Sometimes they do come back. But everybody goes.

HELL HATH ENLARGED HERSELF

WHAT YOU MAKE IT

I always assumed I was going to get old. That there would come a time when just getting dressed left me breathless, and I would count a day without a nap as a victory; when I would go into a barber's and some young girl would lift up the remaining grey stragglers on my pate and look dubious if I asked her for anything more than a trim. I would have tried to be charming, and she would have thought to herself how game the old bird was, while cutting off rather less than I'd asked her to. I thought all that was going to come, some day, and in a perverse sort of way I had even looked forward to it. A diminuendo, an ellipsis to some other place.

But now I know it will not happen, that I will remain unresolved, like some fugue which didn't work out. Or perhaps more like a voice in an unfinished symphony, because I won't be the only one.

I regret that. I'm going to miss having been old.

I left the facility at 6.30 yesterday evening, on the dot, as had been my practice. I took care to do everything as I always had, carefully collating my notes, tidying my desk, and leaving upon it a list of things to do the next day. I hung my white coat on the back of my office door as always, and said goodbye to Johnny on the gate with a wink. For six months we have been engaged in a game which involves making some joint statement on the weather every time I enter or leave the facility, without either of us recoursing to speech. Yesterday, Johnny raised his eyebrows at the dark and heavy clouds overhead, and rolled his eyes – a standard gambit. I turned one corner of my mouth down and shrugged with the other shoulder, a more adventurous riposte, in recognition of the fact that this was the last time the game would ever be played. For a moment I wanted to do more, to say something, reach out and shake his hand; but that would have been too obvious a goodbye. Perhaps no one would have stopped me anyway, as it has become abundantly clear that I am as powerless as everyone else – but I didn't want to take the risk.

Then I found my car among the diminishing number which still park there, and left the compound for good.

The worst part, for me, is that I knew Philip Ely, and understand how it all started. I was sent to work at the facility because I am partly to blame for what has happened. The original work was done together, but I was the one who had always given credence to the paranormal. Philip had never paid much heed to such things, not until they became an obsession. There may have been some chance remark of mine which made him open to the idea. Just having known me for so long may have been enough. If it was, then I'm sorry. There's not a great deal more I can say.

Philip and I met at the age of six, our fathers having taken up new positions at the same college – the University of Florida, in Gainesville. My father was in the Geography Faculty, his in Sociology, but at that time – the late '80s – the departments were drawing closer together and the two men became friends. Our families mingled closely, in shared holidays on the coast and countless back-yard barbecues, and Philip and I grew up more like brothers than friends. We read the same clever books and hacked the same stupid computers, and even ended up losing our virginity on the same evening. One spring when we were both sixteen I borrowed my mother's car and the two of us loaded it up with books and a laptop and headed off to Sarasota in search of sun and beer. We found both, in quantity, and also two young English girls on holiday. We spent a week in courting spirals of increasing tightness, playing pool and talking fizzy nonsense over cheap and exotic pizzas, and on the last night two couples walked up the beach in different directions.

Her name was Karen, and for a while I thought I was in love. I wrote a letter to her twice a week, and to this day she's probably received more mail from me than everyone else put together. Each morning I went running down to the mailbox, and ten years later the sight of an English postage stamp could still bring a faint rush of blood to my ears. But we were too far apart, and too young. Maybe she had to wait a day too long for a letter once, or perhaps it was me who without realizing it came back empty-handed from the mailbox one too many times. Either way the letters started to slacken in frequency after six months and then, without either of us ever saying anything, they simply stopped altogether.

A little while later I was with Philip in a bar and, in between shots, he looked up at me.

'You ever hear from Karen any more?' he asked.

I shook my head, only at that moment realizing that it had finally died. 'Not in a while.'

He nodded, and then took his shot, and missed, and as I lined up for the black I thought that he'd probably been through a similar thing. For the first time in our lives we'd lost something. It didn't break our hearts. It had only lasted a week, after all, and we were old enough to know that the world was full of girls, and that if we didn't hurry we'd hardly have got through any of them before it was time to get married.

But does anyone ever replace that first person? That first kiss, first fierce hug hidden in dunes and darkness? Sometimes, I guess. I kept the letters from Karen for twenty years. Never read them, just kept them. Last week I threw them all away.

What I'm saying is this. I knew Philip for a long, long time, and I understood what we were trying to do. He was just trying to salve his own pain, and I was trying to help him.

What happened wasn't our fault.

I spent the evening driving slowly down 75, letting the freeway take me down towards the Gulf coast of the panhandle. There were a few patches of rain, but for the most part the clouds just scudded overhead, running to some other place. I didn't see many other cars. Either people have given up fleeing, or all those capable of it have already fled. I got off just after Jocca, and headed down minor roads, trying to cut round Tampa and St Petersburg. I managed it, but it wasn't easy, and I ended up getting lost more than a few times. I would have brought a map but I thought I could remember the way. I couldn't. It had been too long.

We'd heard on the radio in the afternoon that things weren't going so hot around Tampa. It was the last thing we heard, just before the signal cut out. The six of us remaining in the facility just sat around for a while, as if we believed the radio would come back on again real soon now. When it didn't, we got up one by one and drifted back to work.

As I passed the city I could see it burning in the distance, and I was glad I had gone the back way, no matter how long it took. If you've seen what it's like when a large number of people go together, you'll understand what I mean.

Eventually I found 301 and headed down towards 41, and the old Coast Road.

Summer of 2005. For Philip and I it was time to make a decision. There was no question but that we would go to college – both our families were book-bashers from way back. The money was already in place, some from our parents but most from holiday jobs we'd played at. The question was what we were going to study.

I thought long and hard, but in the end still couldn't come to a decision. I postponed for a year, and decided to take off round the world. My parents shrugged, said 'Okay, keep in touch, try not to get killed, and stop by your Aunt Kate's in Sydney.' They were that kind of people. I remember my sister bringing a friend of hers back to the house one time; the girl called herself Yax and her hair had been carefully dyed and sculpted to resemble an orange explosion. My mother just asked her where she had it done, and kept looking at it in a thoughtful way. I guess my dad must have talked her out of it.

Philip went for computers. Systems design. He got a place at Jacksonville's new centre for Advanced Computing, which was a coup but no real surprise. Philip was always a hell of a bright guy. That was part of his problem.

It was strange saying goodbye to each other after so many years in each other's pockets, but I suppose we knew it was going to happen sooner or later. The plan was that he'd come out and hook up with me for a couple of months during the year. It didn't happen, for the reason that pacts between old friends usually get forgotten.

Someone else entered the picture.

I did my grand tour. I saw Europe, started to head through the Middle East and then thought better of it and flew down to Australia instead. I stopped by and saw Aunt Kate, which earned me big brownie points back home and wasn't in any way arduous. She and her family were a lot of fun, and there was a long drunken evening when she seemed to be taking messages from beyond, which was kind of interesting. My mother's side of the family was always reputed to have a touch of the medium about them, and Aunt Kate certainly did. There was an even more entertaining evening when my cousin Jenny and I probably overstepped the bounds of conventional morality in the back seat of her jeep. After Australia I hacked up through the Far East for a while until time and money ran out, and then I went home.

I came back with a major tan, an empty wallet, and no real idea of what I was going to do with my life. With a couple months to go before I had to make a decision, I went to go visit Philip. I hopped on a bus and made my way up to Jacksonville on a day which was warm and full of promise. Anything could happen, I believed, and everything was there for the taking. Adolescent naïveté perhaps, but I was an adolescent. How was I supposed to know otherwise? I'd led a pretty charmed life up until then, and I didn't see any real reason why it shouldn't continue. I sat in the bus and gazed out the window, watching the world and wishing it the very best. It was a good day, and I'm glad it was. Because though I didn't know it then, the new history of the world probably started at the end of it.

I got there late afternoon, and asked around for Philip. Someone pointed me in the right direction, to a house just off campus. I found the building and tramped up the stairs, wondering whether I shouldn't maybe have called ahead.

Eventually I found his door. I knocked, and after a few moments some man I didn't recognize opened it. It took me a couple of long seconds to work out it was Philip. He'd grown a beard. I decided not to hold it against him just yet, and we hugged like, well, like what we were. Two best friends, seeing each other after what suddenly seemed like far too long.

'*Major* bonding,' drawled a female voice. A head slipped into view from round the door, with wild brown hair and big green eyes. That was the first time I saw Rebecca.

Four hours later we were in a bar somewhere. I'd met Rebecca properly, and realized she was special. In fact, it's probably a good thing that they'd met six months before, and that she was so evidently in love with Philip. Had we met her at the same time, she could have been the first thing we'd ever fallen out over. She was beautiful, in a strange and quirky way that always made me think of forests; and she was clever, in that particularly appealing fashion which meant she wasn't always trying to prove it and was happy for other people to be right some of the time. She moved like a cat on a sleepy afternoon, but her eyes were always alive – even when they couldn't co-operate with each other enough to allow her to accurately judge the distance to her glass. She was my best friend's girl, she was a good one, and I was very happy for him.

Rebecca was at the School of Medical Science. Nanotech was just coming off big around then, and it looked like she was going to catch the wave and go with it. In fact, when the two of them talked about their work, it made me wish I hadn't taken the year off. Things were happening for them. They had a direction. All I had was goodwill towards the world, and the belief that it loved me too. For the first time I had that terrible sensation that life is leaving you behind and you'll never catch up again; that if you don't match your speed to the train and jump on you'll be forever left standing in the station.

At 1 a.m. we were still going strong. Philip lurched in the general direction of the bar to get us some more beer, navigating the treacherously level floor like a man using stilts for the first time.

'Why don't you come here?' Rebecca said suddenly. I turned to her, and she shrugged. 'Philip misses you, I don't think you're too much of an asshole, and what else are you going to do?'

I looked down at the table for a moment, thinking it over. Immediately it sounded like a good idea. But on the other hand, what would I do? And could I handle being a third wheel, instead of half a bicycle? I asked the first question first.

'We've got plans,' Rebecca replied. 'Stuff we want to do. You could come in with us. I know Philip would want you to. He always says you're the cleverest guy he's ever met.'

I glanced across at Philip, who was conversing affably with the barman. We'd decided that to save energy we should start buying drinks two at a time, and Philip appeared to be explaining this plan. As I watched, the barman laughed. Philip was like that. He could get on with absolutely anyone.

'And you're sure I'm not too much of an asshole?'

Deadpan: 'Nothing that I won't be able to kick out of you.'

And that's how I ended up applying for, and getting, a place on Jacksonville's nanotech program. When Philip got back to the table I wondered aloud whether I should come up to college, and his reaction was big enough to seal the decision there and then. It was him who suggested I go nanotech, and him who explained their plan.

For years people had been trying to crack the nanotech nut. Building tiny biological 'machines', some of them little bigger than large molecules, designed to be introduced into the human body to perform some function or other: promoting the secretion of certain hormones; eroding calcium build-ups in arteries; destroying cells which looked like they were going cancerous. In the way that these things have, it had taken a long time before the first proper results started coming through – but in the last three years it had really been gathering pace. When Philip had met Rebecca, a couple of weeks into the first semester, they'd talked about their two subjects, and Philip had immediately realized that sooner or later there would be a second wave, and that they could be the first to ride it.

Lots of independent little machines was one thing. How about lots of little machines which worked together? All designed for particular functions, but co-ordinated by a neural relationship with each other, possessed of a power and intelligence that was greater than the sum of its parts. Imagine what *that* could do.

When I heard the idea I whistled. I tried to, anyway. My lips had gone all rubbery from too much beer and instead the sound came out as a sort of parping noise. But they understood what I meant.

'And no one else is working on this?'

'Oh, probably,' Philip smirked, and I had to smile. We'd always both nurtured plans for world domination. 'But with the three of us together, no one else stands a chance.'

And so it was decided, and ratified, and discussed, over just about all the beer the bar had left. At the end of the evening we crawled back to Philip and Rebecca's room on our hands and knees, and I passed out on the sofa. The next day, trembling under the weight of a hangover which passed all understanding, I found a place to stay in town and went to talk to someone in the faculty of Medical Science. By the end of the week it was confirmed.

On the day I was officially enrolled in the next year's intake the three of us went out to dinner. We went to a nice restaurant, and we ate and drank, and then at the end of the meal we placed our hands on top of each other's in the centre of the table. Philip's went down first, then Rebecca's, and then mine on top. With our other hands we raised our glasses.

'To us,' I said. It wasn't very original, I know, but it's what I meant. It felt like there should have been a photographer present to immortalize the moment. We drank, and then the three of us clasped each other's hands until our knuckles were white.

Ten years later Rebecca was dead.

The Coast Road was deserted, as I had expected. The one thing nobody is doing these days is heading off down to the beach to hang out and play volleyball. I passed a few vehicles abandoned on the verge, but took care not to drive too close. Often people will hide inside or behind and then leap out at anyone who passes, regardless of whether that person is in a moving vehicle or not.

I kept my eyes on the sea for the most part, concentrating on what was the same, rather than what was different. The ocean looked exactly as it always had, though I suppose usually there would have been ships to see, out on the horizon. There probably still are a few, floating aimlessly wherever the tide takes them, their decks echoing and empty. But I didn't see any.

When I reached Sarasota I slowed still further, driving out onto Lido Key until I pulled to a halt in the centre of St Armand's Circle. It's not an especially big place, but it has a certain class. Though the stores around the circle were more than full enough of the usual kind of junk, the restaurants were good and some of the old, small hotels were attractive in a dated kind of way. Not as flashy as the deco strips on Old Miami Beach, but pleasant enough.

Last night the circle was littered with burnt-out cars, and the up-scale pizzeria where we used to eat was still smoldering, the embers glowing in the fading light.

We worked through our degrees and out into post-graduate years. At first I had a lot to catch up on. Sometimes Rebecca snuck me into classes, but mostly I just pored over their notes and books, and we talked long into the night. Catching up wasn't so hard, but keeping up with both of them was a struggle. I never understood the nanotech side as well as Rebecca, or the computing as deeply as Philip, but that was probably an advantage. I stood between the two of them, and it was in my mind where the two disciplines most equally met. Without me there, it's probable none of it would ever have come to fruition. So maybe if you get right down to it, and it's anyone's fault, it's mine.

Philip's goal was designing a system which would take the input and imperatives of a number of small component parts, and synthesize them into a greater whole – catering for the fact that the concerns of biological organisms are seldom clear cut. The fuzzy logic wasn't difficult – God knows we were familiar enough with it, most noticeably in our ability to reason that we needed another beer when we couldn't even remember where the fridge was. More difficult was designing and implementing the means by which the different machines, or 'beckies', as we elected to call them, interfaced with each other.

Rebecca concentrated on the physical side of the problem, synthesizing beckies with intelligence coded into artificial DNA in a manner which enabled the 'brain' of each type to link up with and transfer information to the others. And remember, when I say 'machines' I'm not talking about large metal objects which sit in the corner of the room making unattractive noises and drinking a lot of oil. I'm talking about strings of molecules hardwired together, invisible to the naked eye.

I helped them both with their specific areas, and did most of the development work in the middle, designing the overall system. It was me who came up with the first product to aim for, 'ImmunityWorks'.

The problem of diagnosing malfunction in the human body has always been the number of variables, many of which are difficult to monitor effectively from the outside. If someone sneezes, they could just have a cold. On the other hand, they could have flu, or the bubonic plague – or some dust up their nose. Unless you can test all the relevant parameters, you're not going to know what the real problem is – or the best way of treating it. We were aiming for an integrated set of beckies which could examine all of the pertinent conditions, share their findings, and determine the best way of tackling the problem – all at the molecular level, without human intervention of any kind. The system had to be robust – to withstand interaction with the body's own immune system – and intelligent. We weren't intending to just tackle things which made you sneeze, either: we were never knowingly underambitious. Even for ImmunityWorks 1.0 we were aiming for a system which could cope with a wide range of viruses, bacteria and general senescence: a first-aid kit which lived in the body, anticipating problems and solving them before they got started. A kind of guardian angel, which would coexist with the human system and protect it from harm.

We were right on the edge of knowledge, and we knew it. The roots of disease in the human body still weren't properly understood, never mind the best ways to deal with them. An individual trying to do what we were doing would have needed about 300 years and a research grant bigger than God's. But we weren't just one person. We weren't even just three. Like the system we were trying to design, we were a perfect symbiosis, three minds whose joint product was incomparably greater than the sum of its parts. Also, we worked like maniacs. After we'd received our Doctorates we rented an old house together away from the campus, and turned the top floor into a private lab. Obviously, there were arguments for putting it in the basement, historical 'mad scientist' precedents for example, but the top floor had a better view and as that's where we spent most of our time, that kind of thing was an issue. We got up in the mornings, did enough to maintain our tenure at the University, and worked on our own project in secret.

Philip and Rebecca had each other. I had an intermittent string of short liaisons with fellow lecturers, students or waitresses, each of which felt I was being unfaithful to something, or to someone. It wasn't Rebecca I was thinking of. God knows she was beautiful enough, and lovely enough, to pine after, but I didn't. Lusting after Rebecca would have felt like one of our beckies deciding only to work with some, not all, of the others in its system. The whole system would have imploded.

Unfaithful to us, I suppose is what I felt. To the three of us.

It took us four years to fully appreciate what we were getting into, and to establish just how much work was involved. The years after that were a process of slow, grinding progress. Philip and I modelled an artificial body on the computer, creating an environment in which we could test virtual versions of the beckies Rebecca and I were busy trying to synthesize. Occasionally we'd enlist the assistance of someone from the medical faculty, when we needed more of an insight into a particular disease; but this was always done covertly, and without letting on what we were doing. This was our project, and we weren't going to share it with anyone.

By July of 2016, the software side of ImmunityWorks was in beta, and holding up well. We'd created code equivalents of all of the major viruses and bacteria, and built creeping failures into the code of the virtual body itself – to represent the random processes of physical malfunction. An initial set of 137 different virtual beckies was doing a sterling job of keeping an eye out for problems, then charging in and sorting them out whenever they occurred.

The physical side was proceeding a little more slowly. Creating miniature biomachines is a difficult process, and when they didn't do what they were supposed to you couldn't exactly lift up the hood and poke around inside. The key problem, and the one which took the most time to solve, was that of imparting a sufficient degree of 'consciousness' to the system as a whole – the aptitude for the component parts to work together, exchanging information and determining the most profitable course of action in any given circumstance. We probably built in a lot more intelligence than was necessary, in fact I know we did; but it was simpler than trying to hone down the necessary conditions right away. We could always streamline in ImmunityWorks 1.1, we felt, when the system had proved itself and we had patents nobody could crack. We also gave the beckies the ability to perform simple manipulations of the matter around them. It was an essential part of their role that they be able to take action on affected tissue once they'd determined what the problem was. Otherwise it would only have been a diagnostic tool, and we were aiming higher than that.

By October we were closing in, and were ready to run a test on a monkey which we'd infected with a copy of the Marburg strain of the Ebola virus. We'd pumped a whole lot of other shit into it as well, but it was the filovirus we were most interested in. If ImmunityWorks would handle that, we reckoned, we were really getting somewhere.

Yes *of course* it was a stupid thing to do. We had a monkey jacked full of one of the most communicable viruses known to mankind *in our house*. The lab was heavily secured by then, but it was still an insane risk. In retrospect I realize that we were so caught up in what we were doing, in our own joint mind, that normal considerations had ceased to really register. We didn't even need to do the Ebola test. That's the really tragic thing. It was unnecessary. It was pure arrogance, and also wildly illegal. We could have just tested ImmunityWorks on plain vanilla viruses, or artificially-induced cancers. If it had worked we could have contacted the media and owned our own Caribbean islands within two years.

But no. We had to go the whole way.

The monkey sat in its cage, looking really very ill, with any number of sensors and electrodes taped and wired on and into its skull and body. Drips connected to bioanalysers gave a second-by-second readout of the muck that was floating around in the poor animal's bloodstream. About two hours before the animal was due to start throwing clots, Philip threw the switch which would inject a solution of ImmunityWorks 0.9b7 into its body.

The time was 16:23, October 14th, 2016, and for the next 24 hours we watched.

At first the monkey continued to get worse. Arteries started clotting, and the heartbeat grew ragged and fitful. The artificial cancer which we'd induced in the animal's pancreas also appeared to be holding strong. We sat, and smoked, and drank coffee, our hearts sinking. Maybe, we began to think, we weren't so damned clever after all.

Then . . . that moment.

Even now, as I sit here in an abandoned hotel and listen for sounds of movement outside, I can remember the moment when the read-outs started to turn around.

The clots started to break up. The cancerous cells started to lose vitality. The breed of simian flu which we'd acquired illicitly from the University's labs went into remission.

The monkey started getting better.

And we felt like gods, and stayed that way even when the monkey suddenly died of shock a day later. We knew by then that there was more work to do in buffering the stress effects the beckies had on the body. That wasn't important. It was just a detail. We had screeds of data from the experiment, and Philip's AI systems were already integrating it into the next version of the ImmunityWorks software. Becky and I made the tweaks to the beckies, stamping the revised software into the biomachines and refining the way they interfaced with the body's own immune system.

We only really came down to earth the next day, when we realized that Rebecca had contracted Marburg.

Eventually the sight of the St Armand's dying heart palled, and I started the car up again. I drove a little further along the coast to the Lido Beach Inn, which stands just where the strip starts to diffuse into a line of beach motels. I turned into the driveway and cruised slowly up to the entrance arch, peering into the lobby. There was nobody there, or if there was, they were crouching in darkness. I let the car roll down the slope until I was inside the hotel court proper, and then pulled into a space.

I climbed out, pulled my bag from the passenger seat, and locked the car up. Then I went to the trunk and took out the bag of groceries which I'd carefully culled from the stock back at the facility. I stood by the car for a moment, hearing nothing but the sound of waves over the wall at the end, and looked around. I saw no one, and no signs of violence, and so I headed for the stairs to go up to the second floor, and towards room 211. I had an old copy of the key, 'accidentally' not returned many years ago, which was just as well. The hotel lobby was a pool of utter blackness in an evening which was already dark, and I had no intention of going anywhere near it.

For a moment, as I stood outside the door to the room, I thought I heard a girl's laughter, quiet and far away. I stood still for a moment, mouth slightly open to aid hearing, but heard nothing else.

Probably it was nothing more than a memory.

Rebecca died two days later in an isolation chamber. She bled and crashed out in the small hours of the morning, as Philip and I watched through glass. My head hurt so much from crying that I thought it was going to split, and Philip's throat was so hoarse he could barely speak. Philip wanted to be in there with her, but I dissuaded him. To be frank, I punched him out until he was too groggy to fight any more. There was nothing he could do, and Rebecca didn't want him to die. She told me so through the intercom, and as that was her last comprehensible wish, I decided it would be so.

We knew enough about Marburg that we could almost feel her body cavities filling up with blood, smell the blackness as it coagulated in her. When she started bleeding from her eyes I turned away, but Philip watched every moment. We talked to her until there was nothing left to speak to, and then watched powerless as she drifted away, retreating into some upper and hidden hall while her body collapsed around her.

Of course we tried ImmunityWorks. Again, it nearly worked. Nearly, but not quite. When Rebecca's vital signs finally stopped, her body was as clean as a whistle. But it was still dead.

Philip and I stayed in the lab for three days, waiting. Neither of us contracted the disease.

Lucky old us.

We dressed in biohazard suits and sprayed the entire house with a solution of ImmunityWorks, top to bottom. Then we put the remains of Rebecca's body into a sealed casket, drove upstate, and buried it in a forest. She would have liked that. Her parents were dead, and she had no family to miss her, except us.

Philip left the day after the burial. We had barely spoken in the intervening period. I was sitting numbly in the kitchen on that morning and he walked in with an overnight bag. He looked at me, nodded, and left. I didn't see him again for two years.

I stayed in the house, and once I'd determined that the lab was clean, I carried on. What else was there to do?

Working on the project by myself was like trying to play chess with two thirds of my mind burned out: the intuitive leaps which had been commonplace when the three of us were together simply didn't come, and were replaced by hours of painstaking, agonizingly slow experiment. On the other hand, I didn't kill anyone.

I worked. I ate. I drove most weekends to the forest where Rebecca lay, and became familiar with the paths and light beneath the trees which sheltered her.

I refined the beckies, eventually understanding the precise nature of the shock reaction which had killed our two subjects. I pumped more and more intelligence into the system, amping the ability of the component parts to interact with each other and make their own decisions. In a year I had the system to a point where it was faultless on common viruses like flu. Little did the world know it, but while they were out there sniffing and coughing I had stuff sitting in ampoules which could have sorted them out for ever. But that wasn't the point. ImmunityWorks had to work on everything. That had always been our goal, and if I was going to carry on, I was going to do it our way. I was doing it for us, or for the memory of how we'd been. The two best friends I'd ever had were gone, and if the only way I could hang onto some remnant of them was through working on the project, that was what I would do.

Then one day one of them reappeared.

I was in the lab, tinkering with the subset of the beckies whose job it was to synthesize new materials out of damaged body cells. The newest strain of biomachines were capable of far, far more than the originals had been. Not only could they fight the organisms and processes which caused disease in the first place, but they could then directly repair essential cells and organs within the body to ensure that it made a healthy recovery.

'Can you do anything about colds yet?' asked a voice, and I turned to see Philip, standing in the doorway to the lab. He'd lost about two stone in weight, and looked exhausted beyond words. There were lines around his eyes that had nothing to do with laughter. As I stared at him he coughed raggedly.

'Yes,' I said, struggling to keep my voice calm. Philip held his arm out and pulled his sleeve up. I found an ampoule of my most recent brew and spiked it with a hypo. 'Where did you pick it up?'

'England.'

'Is that where you've been?' I asked, as I slipped the needle into his arm and sent the beckies scurrying into his system.

'Some of the time.'

'Why?'

'Why not?' He shrugged, and rolled his sleeve back up.

I waited in the kitchen while he showered and changed, sipping a beer and feeling obscurely nervous. Eventually he reappeared, looking better but still very tired. I suggested going out to a bar, and we did, carefully but unspokenly avoiding those we used to go to as a threesome. Neither of us had mentioned Rebecca yet, but she was there between us in everything we said and didn't say. We walked down winter streets to a place I knew had opened recently, and it was almost as if for the first time I felt I was grieving for her properly. While Philip had been away, it had been as if they'd just gone away somewhere together. Now he was here, I could no longer deny that she was dead.

We didn't say much for a while, and all I learnt was that Philip had spent much of the last two years in Eastern Europe. I didn't push him, but simply let the conversation take its own course. It had always been Philip's way that he would get round to things in his own good time.

'I want to come back,' he said eventually.

'Philip, as far as I'm concerned you never left.'

'That's not what I mean. I want to start the project up again, but different.'

'Different in what way?'

He told me. It took me a while to understand what he was talking about, and when I did I began to feel tired, and cold, and sad. Philip didn't want to refine ImmunityWorks. He had lost all interest in the body, except in the ways in which it supported the mind. He had spent his time in Europe visiting people of a certain kind, trying to establish what it was about them that made them different. Had I known, I could have recommended my Aunt Kate to him – not, I felt, that it would have made any difference. I watched him covertly as he talked, as he became more and more animated, and all I could feel was a sense of dread, a realization that for the rest of his life my friend would be lost to me.

He had come to believe that mediums, people who can communicate with the spirits of the dead, do not possess some special spiritual power, but instead a difference in the physical make-up of their brain. He believed that it was some fundamental but minor difference in the wiring of their senses which enabled them to bridge a gap between this world and the next, to hear voices which had stopped speaking, see faces which had faded away. He wanted to pin-point where this difference lay, and learn to replicate it. He wanted to develop a species of becky which anyone could take, which would rewire their soul and enable them to become a medium.

More specifically, he wanted to take it himself, and I understood why, and when I realized what he was hoping for I felt like crying for the first time in two years.

He wanted to be able to talk with Rebecca again, and I knew both that he was not insane and that there was nothing I could do, except help him.

*   *   *

211 was as I remembered it. Nondescript. A decent-sized room in a low-range motel. I put my bags on one of the twin beds and checked out the bathroom. It was clean and the shower still gave a thin trickle of lukewarm water. I washed and changed into one of the two sets of casual clothes I had brought with me, and then I made a sandwich out of cold cuts and processed cheese, storing the remainder in the small fridge in the corner by the television. I turned the latter on briefly and got snow across the board, though I heard the occasional half-word which suggested that someone was still trying somewhere.

I propped the door to the room open with a bible and dragged a chair out onto the walkway, and then I sat and ate my food and drank a beer looking down across the court. The pool was half full, and a deck chair floated in one end of it.

Our approach was very simple. Using some savings of mine we flew to Australia, where I talked Aunt Kate into letting us take minute samples of tissue from different areas of her brain, using a battery of lymph-based beckies. We didn't tell her what the samples were for, simply that we were researching genetic traits. Jenny was now married to an accountant, it transpired, and they, Aunt Kate and Philip and I sat out that night on the porch and watched the sun turn red.

The next day we flew home and went straight on to Gainesville, where I had a much harder time persuading my mother to let us do the same thing. In the end she relented, and despite claiming that the beckies had 'tickled', had to admit it hadn't hurt. She seemed fit, and well, as did my father when he returned from work. I saw them once again, briefly, about two months ago. I've tried calling them since, but the line is dead.

Back at Jacksonville, Philip and I did the same thing with our own brains, and then the real work began. If, we reasoned, there really was some kind of physiological basis to the phenomena we were searching for, then it ought to show up to varying degrees in my family line, and less so – or not at all – in Philip. We had no idea whether it would be down to some chemical balance, a difference in synaptic function, or a virtual 'sixth sense' which some sub-section of the brain was sensitive to – and so in the beginning we just used part of the samples to find out exactly what we'd got to work with. Of course we didn't have a wide enough sample to make any findings stand up to scrutiny: but then we weren't ever going to tell anyone what we were doing, so that hardly mattered.

We drew the blinds and stayed inside, and worked eighteen hours a day. Philip said little, and for much of the time seemed only half the person he used to be. I realized that until we succeeded in letting him talk with his love again, I would not see the friend I knew.

We both had our reasons for doing what we did.

It took a little longer than we'd hoped, but we threw a lot of computing power at it and in the end began to see results. They were complex, and far from conclusive, but appeared to suggest that all three possibilities were partly true. My aunt showed a minute difference in synaptic function in certain areas of her brain, which I shared, but not the fractional chemical imbalances which were present in both my mother and me. On the other hand, there was evidence of a loose meta-structure of apparently unrelated areas of her brain which was only present in trace degrees in my mother, and not at all in me. We took these results and correlated them against the findings from the samples of Philip's brain, and finally came to a tentative conclusion.

The ability, if it truly was related to physiological morphol-ogy, seemed most directly related to an apparently insignifi-cant variation in general synaptic function which created an almost intangible additional structure within certain areas of the brain.

Not, perhaps, one of the most memorable slogans of scientific discovery, but that night Philip and I went out and got more drunk than we had in five years. We clasped hands on the table once more, and this time we believed that the hand that should have been between ours was nearly within reach. The next day we split into two overlapping teams, dividing our time and minds as always between the software and the beckies. The beckies needed redesigning to cope with the new environment, and the software required yet another quantum leap to deal with the complexity of the tasks of synaptic manipulation. As we worked we joked that if the beckies got much more intelligent we'd have to give them the vote. It seemed funny back then.

September 12th, 2019 ought to have a significant place in the history of science, despite everything that happened afterwards. It was the day on which we tested MindWorks 1.0, a combination of computer and corporeal which was probably more subtle than anything man has ever produced. Philip insisted on being the first subject, despite the fact that he had another cold, and in the early afternoon of that day I injected him with a tiny dose of the beckies. Then, in a flash of solidarity, I injected myself. Together till the end, we said.

We sat there for five minutes, and then got on with some work. We knew that the effects, if there were any, wouldn't be immediate. To be absolutely honest, we weren't expecting much at all from the first batch. As everyone knows, anything with the version number '1' will have teething problems, and if it has a '.0' after it then it's going to crash and burn. We sat and tinkered with the plans for a 1.1 version, which was only different in that some of the algorithms were more elegant, but we couldn't seem to concentrate. Excitement, we assumed.

Then late afternoon Philip staggered and dropped a flask of the solution he was working on. It was full of MindWorks, but that didn't matter – we had a whole vat of it in storage. I made Philip sit down and ran a series of tests on him. Physically he was okay, and protested that he felt fine. We shrugged and went back to work. I printed out ten copies of the code and becky specifications, and posted them to ten different places around the world. Of course, the computers already laid automated and encrypted email backups all over the place, but there's no substitute for a physical object with a date stamped on it. If this worked it was going to be ours, and no one else was taking credit for it. Such considerations were actually less important to us by then, because there was only one thing we wanted from the experiment – but old habits die hard. Ten minutes later I had a dizzy spell myself, but apart from that nothing seemed to be happening at all.

We only realized that we might have succeeded when I woke to hear Philip screaming in the night.

I ran into his room and found him crouched up against the wall, eyes wide, teeth chattering uncontrollably. He was staring at the opposite corner of the room. He didn't seem to be able to hear anything I said to him. As I stood there numbly, wondering what to do, I heard a voice from behind me – a voice I half-thought I recognized. I turned, but there was no one there. Suddenly Philip looked at me, his eyes wide and terrified.

'Fuck,' he said. 'I think it's working.'

We spent the rest of the night in the kitchen, sitting round the table and drinking coffee in harsh light. Philip didn't seem to be able to remember exactly what it was he'd seen, and I couldn't recapture the sound of the voice I'd heard, or what it might have said. Clearly we'd achieved something, but it wasn't clear what it might be. When nothing further happened by daybreak, we decided to get out of the house for a while. We were both too keyed up to sit around any longer or try to work, but felt we should stay together. Something was happening, we knew: we could both feel it. We walked around campus for the morning, had lunch in the cafeteria, then spent the afternoon downtown. The streets seemed a little crowded, but nothing else weird happened.

In the evening we went out. We had been invited to a dinner party at the house of a couple on the medical staff, and thought we might as well attend. Philip and I were rather distracted at first, but once everyone had enough wine inside them we started to have a good time. The hosts got out their stock of dope, doubtless supplied by an accommodating member of the student body, and by midnight we were all a little high, comfortably sprawled around the living room.

And of course, eventually, Philip started talking about the work we'd been doing. At first people just laughed, and that made me realize belatedly just how far outside the scope of normal scientific endeavour we had moved. It also made me determined that we should be taken seriously, and so I started to back Philip up. It was stupid, and we should never have mentioned it. It was one of the people at that party who eventually gave our names to the police.

'So prove it,' this man said at one stage. 'Hey, is there a ouija board in the house?'

The general laughter which greeted this sally was enough to tip the balance. Philip rose unsteadily to his feet, and stood in the centre of the room. He sneezed twice, to general amusement, but then his head seemed to clear. Though he was swaying gently, the seriousness of his face was enough to quieten most people, although there was a certain amount of giggling. He looked gaunt, and tired, and everybody stopped talking, and the room went very quiet as they watched him.

'Hello?' he said quietly. He didn't use a name, for obvious reasons, but I knew who he was asking for. 'Are you there?'

'And if so, did you bring any grass?' the hostess added, getting a big laugh. I shook my head, partly at how foolish we were seeming, partly because there seemed to be a faint glow in one corner of the room, as if some of the receptors in my eyes were firing strangely. I made a note to check the beckies when we got back, to make sure none of them could have had an effect on the optic nerve.

I was about to say something to help Philip out of an embarrassing position when he suddenly turned to the hostess.

'Jackie, how many people did you invite tonight?'

'Eight,' she said. 'We always have eight. We've only got eight complete sets of tableware.'

Philip looked at me. 'How many people do you see?' he asked.

I looked round the room, counting.

'Eleven,' I said.

One of the guests laughed nervously. I counted them again. There were eleven people in the room. In addition to the eight of us who were slouched over the settees and floor, three people stood round the walls.

A tall man, with long and not especially clean brown hair. A woman in her forties, with blank eyes. A young girl, maybe eight years old.

Mouth hanging open, I stood up to join Philip. We looked from each of the extra figures to the other. They looked entirely real, as if they'd been there all along.

They stared back at us, silently.

'Come on guys,' the host said, nervously. 'Okay, great gag – you had us fooled for a moment there. Now let's have another smoke.'

Philip ignored him, turning to the man with the long hair.

'What's your name?' he asked him. There was a long pause, as if the man was having difficulty remembering. When he spoke, his voice sounded dry and cold.

'Nat,' he said. 'Nat Simon.'

'Philip,' I said. 'Be careful.'

Philip ignored me, and turned back to face the real guests. 'Does the name "Nat Simon" mean anything to anyone here?' he asked.

For a moment I thought it hadn't, and then we noticed the hostess. The smile had slipped from her face and her skin had gone white, and she was staring at Philip. With a sudden, ragged beat of my heart I knew we had succeeded.

'Who was he?' I asked quickly. I wish I hadn't. In a room that was now utterly silent she told us.

Nat Simon had been a friend of one of her uncles. One summer, when she was nine years old, he had raped her just about every day of the two weeks she'd spent on vacation with her relatives. He was killed in a car accident when she was fourteen, and since then she'd thought she'd been free.

'Tell Jackie I've come back to see her,' Nat said proudly. 'And I'm all fired up and ready to go.' He had taken his penis out of his trousers and was stroking it towards erection.

'Go away,' I said. 'Fuck off back where you came from.'

Nat just smiled. 'Ain't ever been anywhere else,' he said. 'Like to stay as close to little Jackie as I can.'

Philip quickly asked the other two figures who they were. I tried to stop him, but the other guests encouraged him, at least until they heard the answers. Then the party ended abruptly. Voyeurism becomes a lot less amusing when it's you that people are staring at.

The blank-eyed woman was the first wife of the man who had joked about ouija boards. After discovering his affair with one of his students she had committed suicide in their living room. He'd told everyone she'd suffered from depression, and that she drank in secret.

The little girl was the host's sister. She died in childhood, hit by a car while running across the road as part of a dare devised by her brother.

By the time Philip and I ran out of the house, two of the other guests had already started being able to see for themselves, and the number of people at the party had risen to fifteen.

After four beers my mind was a little fuzzy, and for a while I was almost able to forget. Then I heard a soft splashing sound from below, and looked to see a young boy climbing out of the stagnant water in the pool. He didn't look up, but just walked over the flagstones to the gate, and then padded out through the entrance to the motel. I could still hear the soft sound of his wet feet long after he'd disappeared into the darkness. The brother who'd held his head under a moment too long; the father who'd been too busy watching someone else's wife putting lotion on her thighs; or the mother who'd fallen asleep. Someone would be having a visitor tonight.

When we got back to the house after the party, and tried to get into the lab, we found that we couldn't open the door.

The lock had fused. Something had attacked the metal of the tumblers, turning the mechanism into a solid lump. We stared at each other, by now feeling very sober, and then turned to look through the glass upper portion of the door. Everything inside looked the way it always had, but I now believe that even earlier, before we knew what was happening, everything had already been set in motion. The beckies work in strange and invisible ways.

Philip got the axe from the garage, and we broke through the door to the laboratory. We found the vat of MindWorks empty. A small hole had appeared in the bottom of the glass, and there was a faint trail where the contents had crawled across the floor, cutting right through the wooden boards at several points. It had doubled back on itself, and in a couple of places it had also flowed against gravity. It ended in a larger hole which, it transpired, dripped through into a pipe which went out back into the municipal water system.

The first reports were on CNN at seven o'clock the next morning. Eight murders in downtown Jacksonville, and three on the university campus. All committed by people who must have been within sneezing distance of David on our walk the day before. Reports of people suddenly going crazy, screaming at people who weren't there, running in terror from voices in their head and acting on impulses that they claimed weren't theirs. By lunchtime the problem wasn't just confined to people we might have come into contact with: it had started to spread on its own.

I don't know why it happened like this. Maybe we just made a mistake somewhere. Perhaps it was something as small and simple as a chiral isomer, some chemical which the beckies created in a mirror image of the way it should be. That's what happened with Thalidomide, and that's what we created. A Thalidomide of the soul.

Or maybe there was no mistake. Perhaps that's just the way it is. Maybe the only spirits who stick around are the ones you don't want to see. The ones who can turn people into psychotics who riot, murder, or end their lives, through the hatred or guilt they bring with them. These people have always been here, all the time, staying close to the people who remember them. Only now they are no longer invisible, or silent.

A day later there were reports in European cities, at first just the ones where I'd sent my letters, then spreading rapidly across the entire land mass. By the time my letters reached their recipients, the beckies I'd breathed over them had multiplied a thousandfold, breaking the paper down and reconstituting the molecules to create more of themselves. They were so clever, our children, and they shared the ambitions of their creators. If they'd needed to, they could probably have formed themselves into new letters, and lay around until someone posted them all over the world. But they didn't, because coughing, or sneezing, or just breathing is enough to spread the infection. By the following week a state of emergency was in force in every country in the world.

A mob killed Philip before the police got to him. He never got to see Rebecca. I don't know why. She just didn't come. I was placed under house arrest, and then taken to the facility to help with the feverish attempts to come up with a cure. There is none, and there never will be. The beckies are too smart, too aggressive, and too powerful. They just take any antidote, break it down, and use it to make more of themselves.

They don't need the vote. They're already in control.

The moon is out over the ocean, casting glints over the tides as they rustle back and forth with a sound like someone slowly running their finger across a piece of paper. A little while ago I heard a siren in the far distance. Apart from that all is quiet.

I think it's unlikely I shall riot, or go on a killing spree. In the end, I will simply go.

The times when Karen comes to see me are bad. She didn't stop writing to me because she lost interest, it turns out. She stopped writing because she had been pregnant by me, and didn't want me involved, and died through some nightmare of childbirth without ever telling her mother my name. I hadn't brought any contraception. I think we both figured life would let you get away with things like that. When Philip and I talked about Karen over that game of pool she was already dead. She will come again tonight, as she always does, and maybe tonight will be the night when I decide I cannot bear it any longer. Perhaps seeing her here, at the motel where Philip and I stayed that summer, will be enough to make me do what I have to do.

If it isn't her who gives me the strength, then someone else will, because I've started seeing other people now too. It's surprising quite how many – or maybe it isn't, when you consider that all of this is partly my fault. So many people have died, and will die, all of them with something to say to me. Every night there are more, as the world slowly winds down. There are two of them here now, standing in the court and looking up at me. Perhaps in the end I shall be the last one alive, surrounded by silent figures in ranks that reach out to the horizon.

Or maybe, as I hope, some night Philip and Rebecca will come for me, and I will go with them.

A PLACE TO STAY

'John, do you believe in vampires?'

I took a moment to light a cigarette. This wasn't to avoid the issue, but rather to prepare myself for the length and vitriol of the answer I intended to give – and to tone it down a little. I hardly knew the woman who'd asked the question, and had no idea of her tolerance for short, blunt words. I wanted to be gentle with her, but if there's one star in the pantheon of possible nightmares which I certainly *don't* believe in, then it has to be bloody vampires. I mean, really.

I was in New Orleans, and it was nearly Halloween. Children of the Night have a tendency to crop up in such circumstances, like talk of rain in London. Now that I was here, I could see why. The French Quarter, with its narrow streets and looming balconies frozen in time, almost made the idea of vampires credible, especially in the lingering moist heat of the fall. It felt like a playground for suave monsters, a perpetual reinventing past, and if vampires lived anywhere, I supposed, then these dark streets and alleyways with their fetid, flamboyant cemeteries would be as good a place as any.

But they *didn't* live anywhere, and after another punishing swallow of my salty margarita, I started to put Rita-May right on this fact. She shifted herself comfortably against my chest, and listened to me rant.

We were in Jimmy Buffett's bar on Decatur, and the evening was developing nicely. At nine o'clock I'd been there by myself, sitting at the bar and trying to work out how many margaritas I'd drunk. The fact that I was counting shows what a sad individual I am. The further fact that I couldn't seem to count properly demonstrates that on that particular evening I was an extremely *drunk* sad individual too. And I mean, yes, Margaritaville is kind of a tourist trap, and I could have been sitting somewhere altogether heavier and more authentic across the street. But I'd done that the previous two nights, and besides, I liked Buffett's bar. I was, after all, a tourist. You didn't feel in any danger of being killed in his place, which I regard as a plus. They only played Jimmy Buffett on the juke box, not surprisingly, so I didn't have to worry that my evening was suddenly going to be shattered by something horrible from the post-melodic school of popular music. Say what you like about Jimmy Buffett, he's seldom hard to listen to. Finally, the barman had this gloopy eye thing, which felt pleasingly disgusting and stuck to the wall when you threw it, so that was kind of neat.

I was having a perfectly good time, in other words. A group of people from the software convention I was attending were due to be meeting somewhere on Bourbon at ten, but I was beginning to think I might skip it. After only two days my tolerance for jokes about Bill Gates was hovering around the zero mark. As an Apple Macintosh developer, they weren't actually that funny anyway.

So. There I was, fairly confident that I'd had around eight margaritas and beginning to get heartburn from all the salt, when a woman walked in. She was in her mid-thirties, I guessed, the age where things are just beginning to fade around the edges but don't look too bad for all that. I hope they don't, anyway: I'm approaching that age myself and my things are already fading fast. She sat on a stool at the corner of the bar, and signalled to the barman with a regular's upward nod of the head. A minute later a margarita was set down in front of her, and I judged from the colour that it was the same variety I was drinking. It was called a Golden something or other, and had the effect of gradually replacing your brain with a sour-tasting sand which shifted sluggishly when you moved your head.

No big deal. I noticed her, then got back to desultory conversation with the other barman. He'd visited London at some point, or wanted to – I never really understood which. He was either asking me what London was like, or telling me; I was either listening, or telling him. I can't remember, and probably didn't know at the time. At that stage in the evening my responses would have been about the same either way. I eventually noticed that the band had stopped playing, apparently for the night. That meant I could leave the bar and go sit at one of the tables. The band had been okay, but very loud, and without wishing them any personal enmity I was glad they had gone. Now that I'd noticed, I realized they must have been gone for a while. An entire Jimmy Buffett CD had played in the interval.

I lurched sedately over to a table, humming 'The Great Filling Station Holdup' quietly and inaccurately, and reminding myself that it was only about twenty after nine. If I wanted to meet up with the others without being the evening's comedy drunk, I needed to slow down. I needed to have not had about the last four drinks, in fact, but that would have involved tangling with the space-time continuum to a degree I felt unequal to. Slowing down would have to suffice.

It was as I was just starting the next drink that the evening took an interesting turn. Someone said something to me at fairly close range, and when I looked up to have another stab at comprehending it, I saw it was the woman from the bar.

'Wuh?' I said, in the debonair way that I have. She was standing behind the table's other chair, and looked diffident but not very. The main thing she looked was good-natured, in a wary and toughened way. Her hair was fairly blonde and she was dressed in a pale blue dress and a dark blue denim jacket.

'I said – is that chair free?'

I considered my standard response, when I'm trying to be amusing, of asking in a soulful voice if *any* of us are truly free. I didn't feel up to it. I wasn't quite drunk enough, and I knew in my heart of hearts that it simply wasn't funny. Also, I was nervous. Women don't come up to me in bars and request the pleasure of sitting at my table. It's not something I'd had much practice with. In the end I settled for straightforwardness.

'Yes,' I said. 'And you may feel absolutely free to use it.'

The woman smiled, sat down, and started talking. Her name, I discovered rapidly, was Rita-May. She'd lived in New Orleans for fifteen years, after moving there from some god-forsaken hole called Houma, out in the Louisiana sticks. She worked in one of the stores further down Decatur near the square, selling Cajun spice sets and cookbooks to tourists, which was a reasonable job and paid okay but wasn't very exciting. She had been married once and it had ended four years ago, amid general apathy. She had no children, and considered it no great loss.

This information was laid out with remarkable economy and a satisfying lack of topic drift or extraneous detail. I then sat affably drinking my drink while she efficiently elicited a smaller quantity of similar information from me. I was 32, she discovered, and unmarried. I owned a very small software company in London, England, and lived with a dozy cat named Spike. I was enjoying New Orleans' fine cuisine but had as yet no strong views on particular venues – with the exception of the muffelettas in the French Bar, which I liked inordinately, and the po-boys at Mama Sam's, which I thought were overrated.

After an hour and three more margaritas our knees were resting companionably against each other, and by eleven-thirty my arm was laid across the back of her chair and she was settled comfortably against it. Maybe the fact that all the dull crap had been got out of the way so quickly was what made her easy to spend time with. Either way, I was having fun.

Rita-May seemed unperturbed by the vehemence of my feelings about vampires, and pleasingly willing to consider the possibility that it was all a load of toss. I was about to raise my hand to get more drinks when I noticed that the bar staff had all gone home, leaving a hand-written sign on the bar which said: LOOK, WILL YOU TWO JUST *FUCK OFF*.

They hadn't really, but the well had obviously run dry. For a few moments I bent my not inconsiderable intelligence towards solving this problem, but all that came back was a row of question marks. Then suddenly I found myself out on the street, with no recollection of having even stood up. Rita-May's arm was wrapped around my back, and she was dragging me down Decatur towards the square.

'It's this way,' she said, giggling, and I asked her what the hell I had agreed to. It transpired that we were going to precisely the bar on Bourbon where I'd been due to meet people an hour-and-a-half ago. I mused excitedly on this coincidence, until Rita-May got me to understand that we were going there because I'd suggested it.

'Want to buy some drugs?' Rita-May asked, and I turned to peer at her.

'I don't know,' she said. 'What have you got?' This confused me until I realized that a third party had asked the original question, and was indeed still standing in front of us. A thin black guy with elsewhere eyes.

'Dope, grass, coke, horse . . .' the man reeled off, in a bored monotone. As Rita-May negotiated for a bag of spliffs I tried to see where he was hiding the horse, until I realized I was being a moron. I turned away and opened my mouth and eyes wide to stretch my face. I sensed I was in a bit of a state, and that the night was as yet young.

It was only as we were lighting one of the joints five minutes later that it occurred to me to be nervous about meeting a gentleman who was a heroin dealer. Luckily, he'd gone by then, and my attention span was insufficient to let me worry about it for long. Rita-May seemed very relaxed about the whole deal, and as she was a local, presumably it was okay.

We hung a right at Jackson Square and walked across towards Bourbon, sucking on the joint and slowly caroming from one side of the sidewalk to the other. Rita-May's arm was still around my back, and one of mine was over her shoulders. It occurred to me that sooner or later I was going to have to ask myself what the hell I thought I was doing, but I didn't feel up to it just yet.

I wasn't really prepared for the idea that people from the convention would still be at the bar when we eventually arrived. By then it felt as if we had been walking for at least ten days, though not in any bad way. The joint had hit us both pretty hard, and my head felt as if it had been lovingly crafted out of warm brown smoke. Bourbon Street was still at full pitch, and we slowly made our way down it, weaving between half-dressed male couples, lean local blacks and pastel-clad, pear-shaped tourists from Des Moines. A stringy blonde popped up from nowhere at one point, waggling a rose in my face and asking, 'Is she ready?' in a keening, nobody's-home kind of voice. I was still juggling responses to this when I noticed that Rita-May had bought the rose herself. She broke off all but the first four inches of stem in a business-like way, and stuck the flower behind her ear.

Fair enough, I thought, admiring this behaviour in a way I found difficult to define.

I couldn't actually remember, now we were in the area, whether it was the Absinthe Bar we were looking for, the *Old* Absinthe Bar, or the *Original Old* Absinthe Bar. I hope you can understand my confusion. In the end we made the decision on the basis of the bar from which the most acceptable music was pounding, and lurched into the sweaty gloom. Most of the crowd inside applauded immediately, but I suspect this was for the blues band rather than us. I was very thirsty by then, partly because someone appeared to have put enough blotting paper in my mouth to leech all the moisture out of it, and I felt incapable of doing or saying anything until I was less arid. Luckily Rita-May sensed this, and immediately cut through the crowd to the bar.

I stood and waited patiently for her return, inclining slightly and variably from the vertical plane like some advanced form of children's top. 'Ah ha,' I was saying to myself. 'Ah ha.' I have no idea why.

When someone shouted my name, I experienced little more than a vague feeling of well-being. 'They know me here,' I muttered, nodding proudly to myself. Then I saw that Dave Trindle was standing on the other side of the room and waving his arm at me, a grin of outstanding stupidity on his face. My first thought was that he should sit down before someone in the band shot him. My second was a hope that he would continue standing, for the same reason. He was part, I saw, of a motley collection of second-rate shareware authors ranged around a table in the corner, a veritable rogues' gallery of dweebs and losers. My heart sank, with all hands, two cats and a mint copy of the Gutenberg Bible on deck.

'Are they the people?'

On hearing Rita-May's voice I turned thankfully, immediately feeling much better. She was standing close behind, a large drink in each hand and an affectionate half-smile on her face. I realized suddenly that I found her very attractive, and that she was nice, too. I looked at her for a moment longer, and then leant forward to kiss her softly on the cheek, just to the side of the mouth.

She smiled, pleased, and we came together for another kiss, again not quite on the mouth. I experienced a moment of peace, and then suddenly I was very drunk again.

'Yes and no,' I said. 'They're from the convention. But they're not the people I wanted to see.'

'They're still waving at you.'

'Christ.'

'Come on. It'll be fun.'

I found it hard to share her optimism, but followed Rita-May through the throng.

It turned out that the people I'd arranged to meet up with *had* been there, but I was told that they'd left in the face of my continued failure to arrive. I judged it more likely that they'd gone because of the extraordinary collection of berks they had accidentally acquired on the way to the bar, but refrained from saying so.

The conventioneers were drunk, in a we've-had-two-beers-and-hey-aren't-we-bohemian sort of way, which I personally find offensive. Quite early on I realized that the only way of escaping the encounter with my sanity intact was pretending that they weren't there and talking to Rita-May instead. This wasn't allowed, apparently. I kept being asked my opinion on things so toe-curlingly dull that I can't bring myself to even remember them, and endured fifteen minutes of Davey wank-face telling me about some GUI junk he was developing. Luckily Rita-May entered the spirit of the event, and we managed to keep passing each other messages on how dreadful a time we were having. With that and a regular supply of drinks, we coped.

After about an hour we hit upon a new form of diversion, and while apparently listening avidly to the row of life-ectomy survivors in front of us, started – tentatively at first, then more deliciously – to stroke each other's hands under the table. The conventioneers were now all well over the limit, some of them having had as many as four beers, and were chattering nineteen to the dozen. So engrossed were they that after a while I felt able to turn my head towards Rita-May, look in her eyes, and say something.

'I like you.'

I hadn't planned it that way. I'd intended something much more grown-up and crass. But as it came out I realized that it was true and that it communicated what I wanted to say with remarkable economy.

She smiled, skin dimpling at the corners of her mouth, wisps of her hair backlit into golden. 'I like you too,' she said, and squeezed my hand.

Wow, I thought foggily. How weird. You think you've got the measure of life, and then it throws you what I believe is known as a 'curve-ball'. It just went to show. 'It just goes to show,' I said, aloud. She probably didn't understand, but smiled again anyway.

The next thing that I noticed was that I was standing with my back against a wall, and that there wasn't any ground beneath my feet. Then that it was cold. Then that it was quiet.

'Yo, he's alive,' someone said, and the world started to organize itself. I was lying on the floor of the bar, and my face was wet.

I tried to sit upright, but couldn't. The owner of the voice, a cheery black man who had served me earlier, grabbed my shoulder and helped. It was him, I discovered, who'd thrown water over me. About a gallon. It hadn't worked, so he'd checked my pulse to make sure I wasn't dead, and then just cleared up around me. Apart from him and a depressed-looking guy with a mop, the bar was completely empty.

'Where's Rita?' I asked, eventually. I had to repeat the question in order to make it audible.

The man grinned down at me. 'Now I wouldn't know *that*, would I?' he said. 'Most particularly 'cos I don't know who Rita *is*.'

'What about the others?' I managed. The barman gestured eloquently around the empty bar. As my eyes followed his hand, I saw the clock. It was a little after five a.m.

I stood up, shakily thanked him for his good offices on my behalf, and walked very slowly out into the street.

I don't remember getting back to the hotel, but I guess I must have done. That, at any rate, is where I found myself at ten the next morning, after a few hours of molten sleep. As I stood pasty-faced and stricken under the harsh light of the bathroom, I waited in horror while wave after wave of The Fear washed over me. I'd passed out. Obviously. Though uncommon with me, it's not unknown. The conventioneers, rat-finks that they were, had pissed off and left me there, doubtless sniggering into their beards. Fair enough. I'd have done the same for them.

But what had happened to Rita-May?

While I endured an appalling ten minutes on the toilet, a soothing fifteen minutes under the shower, and a despairing, tearful battle with my trousers, I tried to work this out. On the one hand, I couldn't blame her for abandoning an unconscious tourist. But when I thought back to before the point where blackness and The Fear took over, I thought we'd been getting on very well. She didn't seem the type to abandon anyone.

When I was more or less dressed I hauled myself onto the bed and sat on the edge. I needed coffee, and needed it very urgently. I also had to smoke about seventy cigarettes, but seemed to have lost my packet. The way forward was clear. I had to leave the hotel room and sort these things out. But for that I needed shoes.

So where were they?

They weren't on the floor, or in the bathroom. They weren't out on the balcony, where the light hurt my eyes so badly I retreated back into the gloom with a yelp. I shuffled around the room again, even getting down onto my hands and knees to look under the bed. They weren't there. They weren't even in the bed.

They were entirely absent, which was a disaster. I hate shoes, because they're boring, and consequently I own very few pairs. Apart from some elderly flip-flops which were left in the suitcase from a previous trip, the ones I'd been wearing were the only pair I had with me. I made another exhausting search, conducting as much of it as possible without leaving the bed, with no success. Instead of just getting to a café and sorting out my immediate needs, I was going to have to put on the flip-flops and go find a fucking shoe store. Once there I would have to spend money which I'd rather commit to American-priced CDs and good food on a pair of fucking *shoes*. As a punishment from God for drunkenness this felt a bit harsh, and for a few minutes the walls of the hotel room rang with rasped profanities.

Eventually, I hauled myself over to the suitcase and bad-temperedly dug through the archaeological layers of socks and shirts until I found something shoe-shaped. The flip-flop was, of course, right at the bottom of the case. I tugged irritably at it, unmindful of the damage I was doing to my carefully stacked shorts and ties. Up came two pairs of trousers I hadn't worn yet – one of which I'd forgotten I'd brought – along with a shirt, and then finally I had the flip-flop in my hand.

Except it wasn't a flip-flop. It was one of my shoes.

Luckily I was standing near the end of the bed, because my legs gave way. I sat down suddenly, staring at the shoe in my hand. It wasn't hard to recognize. It was a black lace-up, in reasonably good condition but wearing on the outside of the heel. As I turned it slowly over in my hands like some holy relic, I realized it even smelled slightly of margaritas. Salt had dried on the toe, where I'd spilt a mouthful laughing at something Rita-May had said in Jimmy Buffett's.

Still holding it in one hand, I reached tentatively into the bowels of my suitcase, rootling through the lower layers until I found the other one. It was underneath the towel I'd packed right at the bottom, on the reasoning that I was unlikely to need it because all hotels had towels. I pulled the shoe out, and stared at it.

Without a doubt, it was the other shoe. There was something inside. I carefully pulled it out, aware of little more than a rushing sound in my ears.

It was a red rose, attached to about four inches of stem.

The first thing that strikes you about the Café du Monde is that it isn't quite what you're expecting. It isn't nestled right in the heart of the old town, on Royal or Dauphin, but squats on Decatur opposite the square. And it isn't some dinky little café, but a large awning-covered space where rows of tables are intermittently served by waiters of spectacular moroseness. On subsequent visits, however, you come to realize that the *café au lait* really is good and that the beignet are the best in New Orleans; that the café is about as bijou as it can be given that it's open 24 hours a day, every day of the year; and that anyone wandering through New Orleans is going to pass the Decatur corner of Jackson Square at some point, so it is actually pretty central.

Midday found me sitting at one of the tables at the edge, so I wasn't surrounded by other people and had a good view of the street. I was on my second coffee and third orange juice. My ashtray had been emptied twice already, and I had an order of beignet inside me. The only reason I hadn't had more was that I was saving myself for a muffeletta. I'd tell you what they are but this isn't a travel guide. Go and find out for yourself.

And, of course, I was wearing my shoes. I'd sat in the hotel for another ten minutes, until I'd completely stopped shaking. Then I'd shuffled straight to Café du Monde. I had a book with me, but I wasn't reading it. I was watching people as they passed, and trying to get my head in order. I couldn't remember what had happened, so the best I could do was try to find an explanation that worked, and stick with it. Unfortunately, that explanation was eluding me. I simply couldn't come up with a good reason for my shoes being in my suitcase, under stuff which I hadn't disturbed since leaving Roanoke.

About nine months before, at a convention in England, I rather overindulged an interest in recreational pharmaceuticals in the dissolute company of an old college friend. I woke the next morning to find myself in my hotel bed, but dressed in different clothes to those I'd been wearing the night before. Patient reconstruction led me to believe that I could *just about* recall getting up in the small hours, showering, getting dressed – and then climbing back into bed. Odd behaviour, to be sure, but there were enough hints and shadows of memory for me to convince myself that's what I had done.

Not this time. I couldn't remember a thing between leaving the Old Original Authentic Genuine Absinthe Bar and waking up. But strangely, I didn't have The Fear about it.

And then, of course, there was the rose.

The Fear, for those unacquainted with it, is something you may get after very excessive intake of drugs or alcohol. It is, amongst other things, the panicky conviction that you have done something embarrassing or ill-advised that you can't quite remember. It can also be more generic than that, a simple belief that at some point in the previous evening, something happened which was in some way not ideal. It usually passes off when your hangover does, or when an acquaintance reveals that yes, you did lightly stroke one of her breasts in public, without being requested to do so.

Then you can just get down to being hideously embarrassed, which is a much more containable emotion.

I had mild Fear about the period in Jimmy Buffett's, but

probably only born of nervousness about talking to a woman I didn't really know. I had a slightly greater Fear concerning the Absinthe Bar, where I suspected I might have referred to the new CEO of a company who was a client of mine as a 'talentless fuckwit'.

I felt fine about the journey back to the hotel, however, despite the fact I couldn't remember it. I'd been alone, after all. Everyone, including Rita-May, had disappeared. The only person I could have offended was myself. But how had my shoes got into the suitcase? Why would I have done that? And at what point had I acquired Rita-May's rose? The last time I could remember seeing it was when I'd told her that I liked her. Then it had still been behind her ear.

The coffee was beginning to turn on me, mingling with the hangover to make it feel as if points of light were slowly popping on and off in my head. A black guy with a trumpet was just settling down to play at one of the other sides of the café, and I knew this guy from previous experience. His key talent, which he demonstrated about every ten minutes, was that of playing a loud, high note for a very long time. Like most tourists, I'd applauded the first time I'd heard this. The second demonstration had been less appealing. By the third time I'd considered offering him my Visa card if he'd go away.

And if he did it now, I was likely to simply shatter and fall in shards upon the floor.

I needed to do something. I needed to move. I left the café and stood outside on Decatur.

After about two minutes I felt hot and under threat, buffeted by the passing throng. No one had yet filled the seat I'd vacated, and I was very tempted to just slink right back to it. I'd be quiet, no trouble to anyone: just sit there and drink a lot more fluids. I'd be a valuable addition, I felt, a show tourist provided by the town's management to demonstrate to everyone else how wonderful a time there was to be had. But then the guy with the trumpet started a rendition of 'Smells Like Teen Spirit' and I really had to go.

I walked slowly up Decatur towards the market, trying to decide if I was really going to do what I had in mind. Rita-May worked at one of the stores along that stretch. I couldn't remember the name, but knew it had something to do with cooking. It wouldn't be that difficult to find. But should I be trying to find it? Perhaps I should just turn around, leave the Quarter and go to the Clarion, where the convention was happening. I could find the people I liked and hang for a while, listen to jokes about Steve Jobs. Forget about Rita-May, take things carefully for the remaining few days, and then go back home to London.

I didn't want to. The previous evening had left me with emotional tattoos, snapshots of desire which weren't fading in the morning sun. The creases round her eyes when she smiled; the easy southern rhythm of her speech, the glissando changes in pitch; her tongue, as it lolled round the rim of her glass, licking off the salt. When I closed my eyes, in addition to a slightly alarming feeling of vertigo, I could feel the skin of her hand as if it was still there against my own. So what if I was an idiot tourist. I was an idiot tourist who was genuinely attracted to her. Maybe that would be enough.

The first couple of stores were easy to dismiss. One sold quilts made by American craftspeople; the next, wooden children's toys for parents who didn't realize how much their kids wanted video games. The third had a few spice collections in the window, but was mainly full of other souvenirs. It didn't look like the place Rita-May had described, but I plucked up my courage and asked. No one of that name worked there. The next store was a bakery, and then there was a fifty-yard open stretch which provided table space for the restaurant which followed it.

The store after the restaurant was called The N'awlins Pantry, and tag-lined 'The One Stop Shop For All Your Cajun Cooking Needs'. It looked, I had to admit, like it was the place.

I wanted to see Rita-May, but I was scared shitless at the thought of just walking in. I retreated to the other side of the street, hoping to see her through the window first. I'm not sure how that would have helped, but it seemed like a good idea at the time. I smoked a cigarette and watched for a while, but the constant procession of cars and pedestrians made it impossible to see anything. Then I spent a few minutes wondering why I wasn't just attending the convention, listening to dull, safe panels like everybody else. It didn't work. When I was down to the butt I stubbed my cigarette out and crossed back over the road. I couldn't see much through the window even from there, because of the size and extravagance of the window display. So I grabbed the handle, opened the door and walked in.

It was fantastically noisy inside, and crowded with sweating people. The blues band seemed to have turned a second bank of amplifiers on, and virtually everyone sitting at the tables in front of them was clapping hands and hooting. The air was smeared with red faces and meaty arms, and for a moment I considered just turning around and going back into the toilet. It had been quiet in there, and cool. I'd spent ten minutes splashing my face with cold water, trying to mitigate the effect of the joint we'd smoked. While I stood trying to remember where the table was, the idea of another few moments of water-splashing began to take on a nearly obsessive appeal.

But then I saw Rita-May, and realized I had to go on. Partly because she was marooned with the conventioneers, which wouldn't have been fair on anyone, but mainly because going back to her was even more appealing than the idea of water.

I carefully navigated my way through the crowd, pausing halfway to flag down a waitress and get some more drinks on the way. Because obviously we needed them. Obviously. No way were we drunk enough. Rita-May looked up gratefully when she saw me. I plonked myself down next to her, glared accidentally at Dave Trindle, and lit another cigarette. Then, in a clumsy but necessary attempt to rekindle the atmosphere which had been developing, I repeated the last thing I had said before setting off on my marathon journey to the gents. 'It just goes to show,' I said.

Rita-May smiled again, probably in recognition at the feat of memory I had pulled off. 'Show what?' she asked, leaning towards me and shutting out the rest of the group. I winked, and then pulled off the most ambitious monologue of my life.

I said that it went to show that life took odd turns, and that you could suddenly meet someone you felt very at home with, who seemed to change all the rules. Someone who made stale, damaged parts of you fade away in an instant, who let you feel strange magic once again: the magic of being in the presence of a person you didn't know, and realizing that you wanted them more than anything else you could think of.

I spoke for about five minutes, and then stopped. It went down very well, not least because I was patently telling the truth. I meant it. For once my tongue got the words right, didn't trip up, and I said what I meant to say. In spite of the drink, the drugs, the hour, I said it.

At the same time I was realizing that something was terribly wrong.

This wasn't, for example, a cookery store.

A quick glance towards the door showed it also wasn't early afternoon. The sky was dark and Bourbon Street was packed with night-time strollers. We were sitting with the conventioneers in the Absinthe Bar, I was wearing last night's clothes, and Rita-May's rose was still behind her ear.

It was last night, in other words.

As I continued to tell Rita-May that I was really very keen on her, she slipped her hand into mine. This time they weren't covered by the table, but I found I didn't care about that. I did, however, care about the fact that I could clearly remember standing outside the Café du Monde and wanting her to touch my hand again.

The waitress appeared with our drinks. Trindle and his cohorts decided that they might as well be hung for a lamb as for an embryo, and ordered another round themselves. While this transaction was being laboriously conducted I stole a glance at the bar. In a gap between carousing fun-lovers I saw what I was looking for. The barman who'd woken me up.

He was making four margaritas at once, his smooth face a

picture of concentration. He would have made a good photograph, and I recognized him instantly. But he hadn't served me yet. I'd been to the bar once, and been served by a woman. The other drinks I'd bought from passing waitresses. Yet when I'd woken up, I'd recognized the barman *because he'd served me.* That meant I must have bought another drink before passing out and waking up in the bar by myself.

But I couldn't have woken up at all. The reality of what was going on around me was unquestionable, from the smell of fresh sweat drifting from the middle-aged men at the table next to us to the way Rita-May's skin looked cool and smooth despite the heat. One of the conventioneers had engaged Rita-May in conversation, and it didn't look as if she was having too bad a time, so I took the chance to try to sort my head out. I wasn't panicking, exactly, but I was very concerned indeed.

Okay, I *was* panicking. Either I'd spent my time in the toilet hallucinating about tomorrow, or something *really* strange was happening. Did the fact that I hadn't been served by the barman yet prove which was right? I didn't know. I couldn't work it out.

'What do you think of Dale Georgio, John? Looks like he's really gonna turn WriteRight around.'

I didn't really internalize the question Trindle asked me until I'd answered it, and my reply had more to do with my state of mind than any desire to cause offence.

'He's a talentless fuckwit,' I said.

Back outside on the pavement I hesitated for a moment, not really knowing what to do. The N'awlins Pantry was indeed where Rita-May worked, but she was out at lunch. This I had discovered by talking to a very helpful woman, who I assume also worked there. Either that, or she was an unusually well-informed tourist.

I could either hang around and accost Rita-May on the street, or go and get some lunch. Talking to her outside the store would be preferable, but I couldn't stand hopping from foot to foot for what could be as long as an hour.

At that moment my stomach passed up an incomprehensible message of some kind, a strange liquid buzzing that I felt sure most people in the street could hear. It meant one of two things. Either I was hungry, or my mid-section was about to explode taking the surrounding two blocks along with it. I elected to assume I was hungry and turned to walk back towards the square, in search of a muffeletta.

At Café du Monde I noticed that the dreadful trumpet player was in residence, actually in the middle of one of his trademark long notes. As I passed him, willing my head not to implode, the penny dropped.

I shouldn't be noticing that he was there. I knew he was there. I'd just been at Café du Monde. He was one of the reasons I'd left.

I got far enough away that the trumpet wasn't hurting me any more, and then ground to a halt. For the first time I was actually scared. It should have been reassuring to be back in the right time again. Tomorrow I could understand. I could retrace my steps here. Most of them, anyway. But I couldn't remember a thing of what had happened in the cookery store. I'd come out believing I'd had a conversation with someone and established that Rita-May worked there. But as to what the interior of the store had been like, I didn't have a clue. I couldn't remember. What I could actually remember was being in the Absinthe Bar.

I looked anxiously around at tourists dappled by bright sunshine, and felt the early-afternoon heat seeping in through my clothes. A hippy face-painter looked hopefully in my direction, judged correctly that I wasn't the type, and went back to juggling with his paints.

On impulse, I lifted my right hand and sniffed my fingers. Cigarette smoke and icing sugar, from the beignets I'd eaten half an hour ago. This had to be real.

Maybe there had been something weird in the joint last night. That could explain the blackout on the trip back to the hotel, and the Technicolor flashback I'd just had. It couldn't have been acid, but some opium-based thing, possibly? But why would the man have sold us it? Presumably that kind of thing was more expensive. Dealers tended to want to rip you off, not give you little presents. Unless Rita-May had known, and had asked and paid for it – but that didn't seem very likely either.

More than that, I simply didn't believe it was a drug hangover. It didn't feel like one. I felt exactly as if I'd just had far too much to drink the night before, plus one strong joint – except for the fact that I couldn't work out where in time I actually was.

If you close one of your eyes you lose the ability to judge space. The view flattens out, like a painting. You know, or think you know, which objects are closer to you – but only because you've seen them before when both of your eyes have been open. Without that memory, you wouldn't have a clue. And that's how I felt now. I couldn't seem to tell what order things should be in. The question almost felt inappropriate.

Suddenly thirsty, and hearing rather than feeling another anguished appeal from my stomach, I crossed the road to a place that sold po-boys and orange juice from a hatch in the wall. It was too far to the French Bar. I needed food immediately. I'd been okay all the time I was at Café du Monde – maybe food helped tether me in some way.

The ordering process went off okay, and I stood and munched my way through French bread and sauce piquante on the street, watching the door to the N'awlins Pantry. As much as anything else, the tang of lemon juice on the fried oysters convinced me that what I was experiencing was real. When I'd finished, I took a sip of my drink, and winced. It was much sweeter than I'd been expecting. Then I realized that was because it was orange juice, rather than a margarita. The taste left me unfulfilled, like those times when you know you've only eaten half a biscuit, but can't find the other piece. I knew I'd bought orange juice, but also that less than a minute ago I had taken a mouthful of margarita.

Trembling, I slugged the rest of the juice back. Maybe this was something to do with blood sugar levels.

Or maybe I was rapidly going off my head.

As I drank I stared fixedly at the other side of the street, watching out for Rita-May. I was beginning to feel that until I saw her again, until something happened which conclusively locked me into today, I wasn't going to be able to stabilize. Once I'd seen her the day after the night before, it had to be that next day. It really had to, or how could it be tomorrow?

Unless, of course, I was back in the toilet of the Absinthe Bar, projecting in eerie detail what might happen the next day. About the only thing I was sure of was that I wanted to see Rita-May. She probably wouldn't be wearing what I'd seen her in last night, but I knew I'd recognize her in an instant. Even with my eyes open, I could almost see her face. Eyes slightly hooded with drink, mouth parted, wisps of clean hair curling over her ears. And on her lips, as always, that beautiful half-smile.

'We're going,' Trindle shouted, and I turned from Rita-May to look blearily at him. They hadn't abandoned me after all: they were leaving, and I was still conscious. My habitual irritation towards Trindle and his colleagues faded somewhat on seeing their faces. They'd clearly all had a lovely time. In a rare moment of maturity, I realized that they were rather sweet, really. I didn't want to piss on their fireworks.

I nodded and smiled and shook hands, and they trooped drunkenly off into the milling crowd. It had to be well after two o'clock by now, but the evening was still romping on. I turned back to Rita-May and realized that it hadn't been such a bad stroke of luck, running into the Trindle contingent. We'd been kept apart for a couple of hours, and passions had quietly simmered to a rolling boil. Rita-May was looking at me in a way I can only describe as frank, and I leant forward and kissed her liquidly on the mouth. My tongue felt like some glorious sea creature, lightly oiled, rolling for the first time with another of its species.

After a while we stopped, and disengaged far enough to look in each other's eyes. 'It just goes to show,' she whispered, and we rested our foreheads together and giggled. I remembered thinking much earlier in the evening that I needed to ask myself what I thought I was doing. I asked myself. The answer was 'having an exceptionally nice evening', which was good enough for me.

'Another drink?' It didn't feel time to leave yet. We needed some more of being there, and feeling the way we did.

'Yeah,' she said, grinning with her head on one side, looking up at me as I stood. 'And then come back and do that some more.'

I couldn't see a waitress so I went to the bar. I'd realized by now that the time switch had happened again, and I wasn't surprised to find myself being served by the smooth-faced barman. He didn't look too surprised to see me either.

'Still going?' he asked, as he fixed my drinks. I knew I hadn't talked to him before, so I guessed he was just being friendly.

'Yeah,' I said. 'Do I look like I'm going to make it?'

'You look fine,' he grinned. 'Got another hour or so in you yet.'

Only when I was walking unsteadily back to our table did this strike me as a strange thing to have said. Almost as if he knew that in a little while I was going to pass out. I stopped, turned, and looked back at the bar. The barman was still looking at me. He winked, and then turned away.

He knew.

I frowned. That didn't make sense. That didn't work. Unless this was all some flashback, and I was putting words into his mouth. Which meant that it was really tomorrow. Didn't it? Then why couldn't I remember what was going to happen?

I turned back towards Rita-May, and it finally occurred to me to ask her about what was going on. If she didn't know what I was talking about, I could pass it off as a joke. If the same thing was happening to her, then we might have had a spiked joint. Either way I would have learned something. Galvanized by this plan, I tried to hurry back through the crowd. Unfortunately I didn't see a large drunken guy in a check shirt lurching into my path.

'Hey! Watch it,' he said, but fairly good-humouredly. I grinned to show I was harmless and then stepped back away from the kerb. The woman I'd thought was Rita-May hadn't been. Just some tourist walking quickly in the sunshine. I looked at my watch and saw I'd been waiting opposite the store for only twenty minutes. It felt like I'd been there for ever. She had to come back soon. She had to.

Then:

Christ, back here again, I thought. The switches seemed to be coming on quicker as time wore on, assuming that's what it was doing. So, eating the food hadn't worked.

By the time I reached the hotel I'd started to forget, but I'd had enough sense left in me to take Rita-May's rose from my pocket and slip it into one of my shoes. Then I buried the shoes as deeply in the suitcase as I could. 'That'll fuck you up,' I muttered to myself. 'That'll make you remember.' I seemed to know what I meant. It was six in the morning by then, and I took a random selection of my clothes off and fell onto the bed. My head was a mess, and my neck hurt. Neither stopped me from falling asleep instantly, to find myself on Decatur, still waiting opposite the N'awlins Pantry.

That one took me by surprise, I have to admit. I was beginning to get the hang of the back and forth thing, even if it was making me increasingly terrified. I couldn't stop it, or understand it, but at least it was following a pattern. But to flick back to being at the hotel earlier that morning, and find that I'd hidden the shoes myself, was unexpected.

It was all getting jumbled up, as if the order didn't really matter, only the sense, of which there was none.

The people in the po-boy counter were beginning to look at me strangely, so I crossed back over to stand outside N'awlins Pantry itself. It felt like I had been going back and forth over the road for most of my life. There was a lamppost directly outside the store and I grabbed hold of it with both hands, as if I believed that holding something physical would keep me where I was. All I wanted in the whole wide world was for Rita-May to get back.

When she did, she walked right up to the table, straddled my knees and sat down on my lap facing me. She did this calmly, without flamboyance, and no one on the nearby tables seemed to feel it was in any way worthy of note. I did, though. As I reached out to pull her closer to me, I felt like I was experiencing sexual attraction for the very first time. Every cell in my body shifted nervously, as if aware that something rather unusual and profound was afoot. The band was still pumping out twelve-bar at stadium concert volume, which normally blasts all physical sensation out of me: I can't, to put it bluntly, usually do it to music. That didn't appear to be the case on this occasion. I nuzzled into Rita-May's face and kissed her ear. She wriggled a little closer to me, her hand around the back of my head, gently twisting in the roots of my hair. My entire skin felt as if it had been upgraded to some much more sensitive organ, and had I stood up too quickly, in those jeans, I suspect something in my trousers would have just snapped.

'Let's go,' she said suddenly.

I stood up, and we went.

It was about three a.m. by then, and Bourbon Street was much quieter. We went up it a little way, and then took a turn to head back down towards Jackson Square. We walked slowly, wrapped up in each other, watching with interest the things our hands seemed to want to do. I don't know what Rita-May was thinking, but I was hoping with all of my heart that we could stay this way for a while. I was also still girding myself up to asking her if she was having any problems keeping track of time.

We got to the corner of the square, and she stopped. It looked very welcoming in the darkness, empty of people and noise. I found myself thinking that leaving New Orleans was going to be more difficult than I'd expected. I'd spent a lot of my life leaving places, taking a quick look and then moving on. Wasn't going to be so easy this time.

Rita-May turned to me, and took my hands. Then she nodded down Decatur, at a row of stores. 'That's where I work,' she said.

I drew her closer. 'Pay attention.' She smiled. 'It's going to be important.'

I shook my head slightly, to clear it. It was going to be, I knew. I was going to need to know where she worked. I stared at the N'awlins Pantry for a moment, memorizing its location. I would always forget, as it turned out, but perhaps that is part of the deal.

Rita-May seemed satisfied that I'd done my best, and reached up with her hand to pull my face towards hers.

'It's not going to be easy,' she said, when we'd kissed. 'For you, I mean. But please stick with it. I want you to catch up with me some day.'

'I will,' I said, and I meant it. Slowly, I was beginning to understand. I let go of the lamppost with my left hand, and looked at my watch. Only another minute had passed. There was still no sign of Rita-May, just the swarming mass of tourists, their holiday clothes glaring like a merry-go-round in the sun. From a little way down the road I could hear the peal of one long trumpet note, and it didn't sound so bad to me. I glanced down Decatur towards the sound, wondering how far away she was, how many times I would have to wait. I decided to ask.

'As long as it takes,' she said. 'Are you sure this is what you want?'

In a minute, Rita-May would give me the rose, and I'd go back to the bar to pass out as I had so many times before. But for now I was still here, in the silent square, where the only sign of life was a couple of tired people sipping *café au lait* in darkness at the Café du Monde. The air was cool, and soft somehow, like the skin of the woman I held in my arms. I thought of my house, and London. I would remember them with affection, but not miss them very much. My sister would look after the cat. One day I would catch up with Rita-May, and when I did, I would hold on tight.

In the meantime the coffee was good, the beignets were excellent, and there would always be a muffeletta just around the corner. Sometimes it would be night, sometimes day, but I would be travelling in the right direction. I would be at home, one of the regulars, in the corner of all the photographs which showed what a fine place it was to stay. And always there would be Rita-May, and me inching ever closer every day.

'I'm sure,' I said. She looked very happy, and that sealed my decision for ever. She kissed me once on the forehead, once on the lips, and then angled her head.

'I'll be waiting,' she said, and then she bit me softly on the neck.

ATER

WHAT YOU MAKE IT

I remember standing in the bedroom before we went out, fiddling with my tie and fretting mildly about the time. As yet we had plenty, but that was nothing to be complacent about. The minutes had a way of disappearing when Rachel was getting ready, early starts culminating in a breathless search for a taxi. It was a party we were going to, so it didn't really matter what time we left, but I tend to be a little dull about time. I used to, anyway.

When I had the tie as close to a tidy knot as I was able I turned away from the mirror, and opened my mouth to call out to Rachel. But then I caught sight of what was on the bed, and closed it again. For a moment I just stood and looked, and then walked over to it.

It wasn't anything very spectacular, just a dress made of sheeny white material. A few years ago, when we started going out together, Rachel used to make a lot of her clothes. She didn't do it because she had to, but because she enjoyed it. She used to haul me endlessly round dress-making shops, browsing patterns and asking my opinion on a million different fabrics, while I half-heartedly protested and moaned.

On impulse I leant down and felt the material, and found I could remember touching it for the first time in the shop on Mill Road, could recall surfacing up through contented boredom to say that yes, I liked this one. On that recommendation she'd bought it, and made this dress, and as a reward for traipsing around after her she'd bought me dinner too. We were poorer then, so the meal was cheap, but there was lots and it was good.

The strange thing was, I didn't even really mind the dress

shops. You know how sometimes, when you're just walking around, living your life, you'll see someone on the street and fall hopelessly in love with them? How something in the way they look, the way they are, makes you stop dead in your tracks and stare? How for that instant you're convinced that if you could just meet them, you'd be able to love them for ever? Wild schemes and unlikely chance meetings pass through your head, and yet as they stand on the other side of the street or the room, talking to someone else, they haven't the faintest idea of what's going through your mind. Something has clicked, but only inside your head. You know you'll never speak to them, that they'll never know what you're feeling, and that they'll never want to. But something about them forces you to keep looking, until you wish they'd leave so you could be free.

The first time I saw Rachel was like that, and now she was in my bath. I didn't call out to hurry her along.

A few minutes later a protracted squawking noise announced the letting out of the bath water, and Rachel wafted into the bedroom swaddled in thick towels and glowing high spirits. Suddenly I lost all interest in going to the party, punctually or otherwise. She marched up to me, set her head at a silly angle to kiss me on the lips and jerked my tie vigorously in about three different directions. When I looked in the mirror I saw that somehow, as always, she'd turned it into a perfect knot.

Half an hour later we left the flat, still in plenty of time. If anything, I'd held her up.

'Later,' she said, smiling in the way that showed she meant it. 'Later, and for a long time, my man.'

I remember turning from locking the door to see her standing on the pavement outside the house, looking perfect in her white dress, looking happy and looking at me. As I walked smiling down the steps towards her she skipped backwards into the road, laughing for no reason, laughing because she was with me.

'Come on,' she said, holding out her hand like a dancer, and a yellow van came round the corner and smashed into her. She spun backwards as if tugged on a rope, rebounded off a parked car and toppled into the road. As I stood cold on the bottom step she half sat up and looked at me, an expression of wordless surprise on her face, and then she fell back again.

When I reached her, blood was already pulsing up into the white of her dress and welling out of her mouth. It ran out over her make-up and I saw she'd been right: she hadn't quite blended the colours above her eyes. I'd told her it didn't matter.

She tried to move her head again and there was a sticky sound as it almost left the tarmac and then slumped back. Her hair fell back from around her face, but not as it usually did. There was a faint flicker in her eyelids, and then she died.

I knelt there in the road beside her, holding her hand as the blood dried a little. I heard every word the small crowd said, but I don't know what they were muttering about. All I could think was that there wasn't going to be a later, not to kiss her some more, not for anything. It was as if everything had come to a halt, and hadn't started up again. Later was gone.

When I got back from the hospital I phoned her mother. I did it as soon as I got back, though I didn't want to. I didn't want to tell anyone, didn't want to make it official. It was a bad phone call, very, very bad. Then I sat in the flat, looking at the drawers she'd left open, at the towels on the floor, at the party invitation on the dressing table, feeling my stomach crawl. I was back at the flat, as if we'd come back home from the party. I should have been making coffee while Rachel had yet another bath, coffee we'd drink on the sofa in front of the fire. But the fire was off and the bath was empty. So what was I supposed to do?

I sat for an hour, feeling as if somehow I'd slipped too far forward in time and left Rachel behind, as if I could turn and see her desperately running to try to catch me up. I called my parents and they came and took me home. My mother gently made me change my clothes, but she didn't wash them. Not until I was asleep, anyway. When I came down and saw them clean I hated her, but I knew she was right and the hate went away. There wouldn't have been much point in just keeping them in a drawer.

The funeral was short. I guess they all are, really, but there's no point in them being any longer. Nothing more would be said. I was a little better by then, and not crying so much, though I did before we went to the church because I couldn't get my tie to sit right.

Rachel was buried near her grandparents, which she would have liked. Her parents gave me her dress afterwards, because I'd asked for it. It had been thoroughly cleaned and large patches had lost their sheen and died, looking as much unlike Rachel's dress as the cloth had on the roll. I'd almost have preferred the bloodstains still to have been there: at least that way I could have believed that the cloth still sparkled beneath them. But they were right in their way, as my mother was. Some people seem to have pragmatic, accepting souls, an ability with death. I don't, I'm afraid. I don't understand it at all.

Afterwards I stood at the graveside for a while, but not for long because I knew that my parents were waiting at the car. As I stood by the mound of earth that lay on top of her I tried to concentrate, to send some final thought to her, some final love, but the world kept pressing in on me through the sound of cars on the road and some bird that was cawing up in a tree. I couldn't shut it out. I couldn't believe that I was noticing how cold it was, or that somewhere lives were being led and televisions being watched, that the inside of my parents' car would smell the same as it always had. I wanted to feel something, wanted to sense her presence, but I couldn't. All I could feel was the world round me, the same old world. But it wasn't a world that had been there a week ago, and I couldn't understand how it could look so much the same.

It was the same because nothing had changed, and I turned and walked to the car. The wake was worse than the funeral, much worse, and I stood with a tuna sandwich feeling something very cold building up inside. Rachel's oldest friend Lisa held court with her old school friends, swiftly running the range of emotions from stoic resilience to trembling incoherence.

'I've just realized,' she sobbed to me, 'Rachel's not going to be at my wedding.'

'Yes, well she's not going to be at mine either,' I said numbly, and immediately hated myself for it. I went and stood by the window, out of harm's way. I couldn't react properly. I knew why everyone was standing here, that in some ways it was like a wedding. Instead of gathering together to bear witness to a bond, they were here to prove she was dead. In the weeks to come they'd know they'd stood together in a room, and would be able to accept she was gone. I couldn't.

I said goodbye to Rachel's parents before I left. We looked at each other oddly, and shook hands, as if we were just strangers again. Then I went back to the flat and changed into some old clothes. My 'Someday' clothes, Rachel used to call them, as in 'some day you must throw them away'. Then I made a cup of tea and stared out of the window for a while. I knew damn well what I was going to do, and it was a relief to give in to it.

That night I went back to the cemetery and I dug her up. What can I say? It was hard work, and it took a lot longer than I expected, but in another way it was surprisingly easy. I mean yes, it was creepy, and yes, I felt like a lunatic, but after the shovel had gone in once, the second time seemed less strange. It was like waking up in the mornings after the accident. The first time I clutched at myself and couldn't understand, but after that I knew what to expect. There were no cracks of thunder, there was no web of lightning and I actually felt very calm. There was just me and, beneath the earth, my friend. I simply wanted to find her.

When I did, I laid her down by the side of the grave and then filled it back up again, being careful to make it look undisturbed. Then I carried her to the car in my arms and brought her home.

The apartment seemed very quiet as I sat her on the sofa, and the cushion rustled and creaked as it took her weight again. When she was settled, I knelt and looked up at her face. It looked much the same as it always had, though the colour of the skin was different, didn't have the glow she always had. That's where life is, you know, not in the heart but in the little things, like the way hair falls around a face. Her nose looked the same and her forehead was smooth. It was the same face.

I knew the dress she was wearing was hiding a lot of things I would rather not see, but I took it off anyway. It was her going away dress, bought by her family specially for the occasion, and it didn't mean anything to me or to her. I knew what the damage would be and what it meant. As it turned out the patchers and menders had done a good job, not glossing because it wouldn't be seen. It wasn't so bad.

When she was sitting up again in her white dress I walked over and turned the light down, and I cried a little then, because she looked so much the same. She could have fallen asleep, warmed by the fire and dozy with wine, as if we'd just come back from the party.

I went and had a bath then. We both used to when we came back in from an evening, to feel clean and fresh for when we slipped between the sheets. It wouldn't be like that this evening, of course, but I had dirt all over me, and I wanted to feel normal. For one night at least I just wanted things to be as they had.

I sat in the bath for a while, knowing she was in the living room, and slowly washed myself clean. I really wasn't thinking much. It felt nice to know that I wouldn't be alone when I walked back in there. That was better than nothing, was part of what had made her alive. I dropped my Someday clothes in the bin and put on the ones from the evening of the accident. They didn't mean as much as her dress, but at least they were from before.

When I returned to the living room her head had lolled slightly, but it would have done if she'd been asleep. I made us both a cup of coffee. The only time she ever took sugar was in the last cup of the day, so I put one in. Then I sat down next to her on the sofa and I was glad that the cushions had her dent in them, that as always they drew me slightly towards her, didn't leave me perched there by myself.

The first time I saw Rachel was at a party. I saw her across the room and simply stared at her, but we didn't speak. We didn't meet properly for a month or two, and first kissed a few weeks after that. As I sat there on the sofa next to her body I reached out tentatively and took her hand, as I had done on that night. It was cooler than it should have been, but not too bad because of the fire, and I held it, feeling the lines on her palm, lines I knew better than my own.

I let myself feel calm and I held her hand in the half-light, not looking at her, as also on that first night, when I'd been too happy to push my luck. She's letting you hold her hand, I'd thought, don't expect to be able to look at her too. Holding her hand is more than enough: don't look, you'll break the spell. My face creased then, not knowing whether to smile or cry, but it felt all right. It really did.

I sat there for a long time, watching the flames, still not thinking, just holding her hand and letting the minutes run. The longer I sat the more normal it felt, and finally I turned slowly to look at her. She looked tired and asleep, so deeply asleep, but still there with me and still mine.

When her eyelid first moved I thought it was a flicker of light cast by the fire. But then it stirred again, and for the smallest of moments I thought I was going to die. The other eyelid moved and the feeling just disappeared, and that made the difference, I think.

She had a long way to come, and if I'd felt frightened, or rejected her, I think that would have finished it then. I didn't question it. A few minutes later both her eyes were open, and it wasn't long before she was able to slowly turn her head.

I still go to work, and put in the occasional appearance at social events, but my tie never looks quite as it did. She can't move her fingers precisely enough to help me with that any more. She can't come with me, and nobody can come here, but that doesn't matter. We always spent a lot of time by ourselves. We wanted to.

I have to do a lot of things for her, but I can live with that.

Lots of people have accidents, bad ones: if Rachel had survived she could have been disabled, or brain-damaged, so that her movements were as they are now, so slow and clumsy. I wish she could talk, but there's no air in her lungs, so I'm learning to read her lips. Her mouth moves slowly, but I know she's trying to speak, and I want to hear what she's saying.

But she gets round the apartment, and she holds my hand, and she smiles as best she can. If she'd just been injured I would have loved her still. It's not so very different.

HE MAN WHO DREW CATS

Tom was a very tall man. He was so tall he didn't even have a nickname for it. Ned Black, who was at least a head shorter, had been 'Tower Block' since the sixth grade, and Jack had a sign up over the door saying, 'Mind Your Head, Ned'. But Tom was just Tom. It was like he was so tall it didn't bear mentioning even for a joke: be a bit like ragging someone for breathing.

Course there were other reasons too for not ragging Tom about his height or anything else. The guys you'll find perched on stools round Jack's bar watching the ball game and buying beers, they've know each other for ever. Gone to Miss Stadler's school together, gotten under each other's mom's feet, double-dated together right up to giving each other's best man's speech. Kingstown is a small place, you understand, and the old boys who come regular to Jack's mostly spent their childhoods in the same tree-house. Course they'd gone their separate ways, up to a point: Pete was an accountant now, had a small office down Union Street just off the square and did pretty good, whereas Ned was still pumping gas and changing oil and after forty years he did that pretty good too. Comes a time when men have known each other so long they forget what they do for a living most the time because it just don't matter. When you talk there's a little bit of skimming stones down the quarry in second grade, a bit of dolling up to go to that first dance, and going to the housewarming when they moved ten years back. There's all that and so much more than you can say that none of it's important except for having happened.

So we'll stop by and have a couple of beers and talk about the town and rag each other and the pleasure's just in shooting the

117

breeze and it don't really matter what's said, just the fact that we're all still there to say it.

But Tom, he was different. We all remember the first time we saw him. It was a long hot summer like we haven't seen in the ten years since and we were lolling under the fans at Jack's and complaining about the tourists. And Kingstown gets its share in the summer, even though it's not near the sea and we don't have a McDonald's and I'll be damned if I can figure out why folk'll go out of their way to see what's just a quiet little town near some mountains. It was as hot as Hell that afternoon and as much as a man could do to sit in his shirtsleeves and drink the coolest beer he could find, and Jack's is the coolest for us, and always will be, I guess.

Then Tom walked in. His hair was already pretty white back then, and long, and his face was brown and tough with grey eyes like diamonds set in leather. He was dressed mainly in black with a long coat that made you hot just to look at it, but he looked comfortable like he carried his very own weather around with him and he was just fine. He got a beer and sat down at a table and read the town *Bugle* and that was that.

It was special because there wasn't anything special about it. Jack's Bar isn't exactly exclusive and we don't all turn round and stare at anyone new if they come in, but that place is like a monument to shared times and if a tourist couple comes in out of the heat and sits down nobody says anything – and maybe nobody even notices at the front of their mind – but it's like there's a little island of the alien in the water and the currents just don't ebb and flow the way they usually do, if you get what I mean. Tom just walked in and sat down and it was all right because it was like he was there just like we were, and could've been for thirty years. He sat and read his paper like part of the same river and everyone just carried on downstream the way they were.

Pretty soon he goes up for another beer and a few of us got talking to him. We got his name and what he did, painting, he said, and after that it was just shooting the breeze. That quick. He came in that summer afternoon and just fell into the conversation like he'd been there all his life, and sometimes it was hard to imagine he hadn't been. Nobody knew where he came from, or where he'd been, and there was something real quiet about him. A stillness, a man in a slightly different world. But he showed enough to get along real well with us, and a bunch of old friends don't often let someone in like that.

Anyway, he stayed that whole summer. Rented himself a place just round the corner from the square, or so he said: I never saw it. I guess no one did. He was a private man, private like a steel door with four bars and a couple of six-inch padlocks, and when he left the square at the end of the day he could have vanished as soon as he turned the corner for all we knew. But he always came from that direction in the morning, with his easel on his back and paintbox under his arm, and he always wore that black coat like it was a part of him. But he always looked cool, and the funny thing was when you stood near him you could swear you felt cooler yourself. I remember Pete saying over a beer that it wouldn't surprise him none if, assuming it ever rained again, Tom would walk round in his own column of dryness. He was just joking, of course, but Tom made you think things like that.

Jack's bar looks right out onto the square, the kind of square towns don't have much anymore: big and dusty with old roads out each corner, tall shops and houses on all the sides and some stone paving in the middle round a fountain that ain't worked in living memory. Well, in the summer that old square is just full of out-of-towners in pink towelling jumpsuits and nasty jackets standing round saying, 'Wow' and taking pictures of our quaint old hall and our quaint old stores and even our quaint old selves if we stand still too long. Tom would sit out near the fountain and paint and those people would stand and watch for hours – but he didn't paint the houses or the square or the old Picture House. He painted animals, and painted them like you've never seen. Birds with huge blue speckled wings and cats with cutting green eyes; and whatever he painted it looked like it was just coiled up on the canvas ready to fly away. He didn't do them in their normal colours, they were all reds and purples and deep blues and greens – and yet they fair sparkled with life. It was a wonder to watch: he'd put up a fresh paper, sit looking at nothing in particular, then dip his brush into his paint and draw a line, maybe red, maybe blue. Then he'd add another, maybe the same colour, maybe not. Stroke by stroke you could see the animal build up in front of your eyes and yet when it was finished you couldn't believe it hadn't always been there. After he was done he'd spray it with some stuff to fix the paints and put a price on it and you can believe me those paintings were sold before they hit the ground. Spreading businessmen from New Jersey or somesuch and their bored wives would come alive for maybe the first time in years, and walk away with one of those paintings and their arms round each other, looking like they'd found a bit of something they'd forgotten they'd lost.

Come about six o'clock Tom would finish up and walk across to Jack's, looking like a sailing ship among rowing boats and saying yes he'd be back again tomorrow and yes, he'd be happy to do a painting for them. He'd get a beer and sit with us and watch the game and there'd be no paint on his fingers or his clothes, not a spot. I figured he'd got so much control over that paint it went where it was told and nowhere else.

I asked him once how he could bear to let those paintings go. I know if I'd been able to make anything that right in my whole life I couldn't let it out of my life, I'd want to keep it to look at sometimes. He thought for a moment and then he said he believed it depends how much of yourself you've put into it. If you've gone deep down and pulled up what's inside and put it down, then you don't want to let it go: you want to keep it, so's you can check sometimes that it's still safely tied down. Comes a time when a painting's so right and so good that it's private, and no one'll understand it except the man who put it down. Only he is going to know what he's talking about. But the everyday paintings, well they were mainly just because he liked to paint animals, and liked for people to have them. He could only put a piece of himself into something he was going to sell, but they paid for the beers and I guess it's same as us fellows in Jack's Bar: if you like talking, you don't always have to be saying something important.

Why animals? Well if you'd seen him with them I guess you wouldn't have to ask. He loved them, is all, and they loved him right back. The cats were always his favourites. My old Pa used to say that cats weren't nothing but sleeping machines put on the earth to do some of the human's sleeping for them, and whenever Tom worked in the square there'd always be a couple curled up near his feet.

Whenever he did a chalk drawing he'd always do a cat.

Once in a while, you see, Tom seemed to get tired of painting on paper, and he'd get out some chalks and sit down on the baking flagstones and just do a drawing right there on the dusty rock. Now I've told you about his paintings, but these drawings were something else again. It was like because they couldn't be bought but would be washed away, he was putting more of himself into it, doing more than just shooting the breeze. They were just chalk on dusty stone and they were still in these weird colours but I tell you children wouldn't walk near them because they looked so real, and they weren't the only ones, either. People would stand a few feet back and stare and you could see the wonder in their eyes. If they could've been bought there were people who would have sold their houses. I'm telling you. And it's a funny thing but a couple of times when I walked over to open the store up in the mornings I saw a dead bird or two on top of those drawings, almost like they had landed on it and been so terrified to find themselves right on top of a cat they'd dropped dead of fright. But they must have been dumped there by some real cat, of course, because some of those birds looked like they'd been mauled a bit. I used to throw them in the bushes to tidy up and some of them were pretty broken up.

Old Tom was a godsend to a lot of mothers that summer, who found they could leave their little ones by him, do their shopping in peace and have a soda with their friends and come back to find the kids still sitting quietly watching Tom paint. He didn't mind them at all and would talk to them and make them laugh, and kids of that age laughing is one of the best sounds there is. It's the kind of sound that makes the trees grow. They're young and curious and the world spins round them and when they laugh the world seems a brighter place because it takes you back to the time when you knew no evil and everything was good, or if it wasn't, it would be over by tomorrow.

And here I guess I've finally come down to it, because there was one little boy who didn't laugh much, but just sat quiet and watchful, and I guess he probably understands more of what happened that summer than any of us, though maybe not in words he could tell.

His name was Billy McNeill, and he was Jim Valentine's kid. Jim used to be a mechanic, worked with Ned up at the gas station and raced beat-up cars after hours. Which is why his kid is called McNeill now: one Sunday Jim took a corner a mite too fast and the car rolled and the gas tank caught and they never did find all the wheels. A year later, his Mary married again. God alone knows why. Her folks warned her, her friends warned her, but I guess love must just been blind. Sam McNeill's work schedule was at best pretty empty, and mostly he just drank and hung out with friends who maybe weren't always this side of the law. I guess Mary had her own sad little miracle and got her sight back pretty soon, because it wasn't long before Sam got free with his fists when the evenings got too long and he'd had a lot too many. You didn't see Mary around much anymore. In these parts people tend to stare at black eyes on a woman, and a deaf man could hear the whisperings of 'We Told Her So'.

One morning, Tom was sitting painting as usual, and little Billy was sitting watching him. Usually he just wandered off after a while but this morning Mary was at the doctor's and she came over to collect him, walking quickly with her face lowered. But not low enough. I was watching from the store

– it was kind of a slow morning. Tom's face never showed much. He was a man for a quiet smile and a raised eyebrow, but he looked shocked that morning. Mary's eyes were puffed and purple and there was a cut on her cheek an inch long. I guess we'd sort of gotten used to seeing her like that and if the truth be known some of the wives thought she'd got remarried a bit on the soon side and I suppose we may all have been a bit cold towards her, Jim Valentine having been so well-liked and all.

Tom looked from the little boy who never laughed much to his mom with her tired unhappy eyes and her beat-up face and his own face went from shocked to stony and I can't describe it any other way but that I felt a cold chill cross my heart from right across the square.

But then he smiled and ruffled Billy's hair and Mary took Billy's hand and they went off. They turned back once and Tom was still looking after them and he gave Billy a little wave and he waved back and mother and child smiled together.

That night in Jack's, Tom put a quiet question about Mary and we told him the story. As he listened his face seemed to harden from within, his eyes growing flat and dead. We told him that old Lou Lachance who lived next door to the McNeills said that sometimes you could hear him shouting and her pleading till three in the morning and on still nights the sound of Billy crying for even longer than that. Told him it was a shame, but what could you do? Folks keep themselves out of other people's faces round here, and I guess Sam and his drinking buddies didn't have much to fear from nearly-retirders like us anyhow. Told him it was a terrible thing, and none of us liked it, but these things happened.

Tom listened and didn't say a word. Just sat there in his black coat and listened to us pass the buck. After a while the talk sort of petered out and we sat and watched the bubbles in our beers. I guess the bottom line was that none of us had really thought about it much except as another chapter of small-town gossip and Jesus Christ did I feel ashamed about that by the time we'd finished telling it. Sitting there with Tom was no laughs at all. He had a real edge to him, and seemed more unknown than known that night. He stared at his laced fingers for a long time, and then he began, real slow, to talk.

He'd been married once, he said, a long time ago, and he lived in a place called Stevensburg with his wife Megan. When he talked about her the air seemed to go softer and we all sat quiet and supped our beers and remembered how it had been way back when we first loved our own wives. He talked of her smile and the look in her eyes and when we went home that night I guess there were a few wives who were surprised at how tight they got hugged, and who went to sleep in their husband's arms feeling more loved and contented than they had in a long while.

He'd loved her and she him and for a few years they were the happiest people on earth. Then a third party had got involved. Tom didn't say his name, and he spoke real neutrally about him, but it was a gentleness like silk wrapped round a knife. Anyway his wife fell in love with him, or thought she had, or leastways she slept with him. In their bed, the bed they'd come to on their wedding night. As Tom spoke these words some of us looked up at him, startled, like we'd been slapped across the face.

Megan did what so many do and live to regret till their dying day. She was so mixed up and getting so much pressure from the other guy that she decided to plough on with the one mistake and make it the biggest in the world.

She left Tom. He talked with her, pleaded even. It was almost impossible to imagine Tom ever doing that, but I guess the man we knew was a different guy from the one he was remembering.

And so Tom had to carry on living in Stevensburg, walking the same tracks, seeing them around, wondering if she was as free and easy with him, if the light in her eyes was shining on him now. And each time the man saw Tom he'd look straight at him and crease a little twisted smile, a grin that said he knew about the pleading and he and his cronies had had a good laugh over the wedding bed and yes I'm going home with your wife tonight and I know just how she likes it, you want to compare notes?

And then he'd turn and kiss Megan on the mouth, his eyes on Tom, smiling. And she let him do it.

It had kept stupid old women in stories for weeks, the way Tom kept losing weight and his temper and the will to live. He took three months of it and then left without bothering to sell the house. Stevensburg was where he'd grown up and courted and loved and now wherever he turned the good times had rotted and hung like fly-blown corpses in all the cherished places. He'd never been back.

It took an hour to tell, and then he stopped talking a while and lit a hundredth cigarette and Pete got us all some more beers. We were sitting sad and thoughtful, tired like we'd lived it ourselves. And I guess most of us had, some little bit of it. But had we ever loved anyone the way he'd loved her? I doubt it, not all of us put together. Pete set the beers down and Ned asked Tom why he hadn't just beaten the living shit out of the guy. Now, no one else would have actually asked that, but Ned's a good guy, and I guess we were all with him in feeling a piece of that oldest and most crushing hatred in the world, the hate of a man who's lost the woman he loves to another, and we knew what Ned was saying. I'm not saying it's a good thing and I know you're not supposed to feel like that these days but show me a man who says he doesn't and I'll show you a liar. Love is the only feeling worth a tin shit but you've got to know that it comes from both sides of a man's character and the deeper it runs the darker the pools it draws from.

My guess is he just hated the man too much to hit him. Comes a time when that isn't enough, when nothing is ever going to be enough, and so you can't do anything at all. And as he talked the pain just flowed out like a river that wasn't ever going to be stopped, a river that had cut a channel through every corner of his soul. I learned something that night that you can go your whole life without realizing: that there are things that can be done that can mess someone up so badly for so long that they just cannot be allowed; that there are some kinds of pain that you cannot suffer to be brought into the world.

And then Tom was done telling and he raised a smile and said that in the end he hadn't done anything to the man except paint him a picture, which I didn't understand, but Tom looked like he'd talked all he was going to.

And so we got some more beers and shot some quiet pool before going home. But I guess we all knew what he'd been talking about. Billy McNeill was just a child. He should have been dancing through a world like a big funfair full of sunlight and sounds and instead he went home at night and saw his mom being beaten up by a man with shit for brains who struck out at a good woman because he was too stupid to deal with the world. Most kids go to sleep thinking about bikes and climbing apple trees and skimming stones and he was lying there hearing his mom get smashed in the stomach and then hit again as she threw up in the sink. Tom didn't say any of that, but he did. And we knew he was right.

The summer kept up bright and hot, and we all had our businesses to attend to. Jack sold a lot of beer and I sold a lot of ice cream (Sorry Ma'am, just the three flavours, and no, Bubblegum Pistachio ain't one of them) and Ned fixed a whole bunch of cracked radiators. Tom sat right out there in the square with a couple of cats by his feet and a crowd around him, magicking up animals in the sun.

And I think that after that night Mary maybe got a few more smiles as she did her shopping, and maybe a few more wives stopped to talk to her. She looked a lot better too: Sam had a job by the sound of it and her face healed up pretty soon. You could often see her standing holding Billy's hand as they watched Tom paint for a while before they went home. I think she realized they had a friend in him. Sometimes Billy was there all afternoon, and he was happy there in the sun by Tom's feet and oftentimes he'd pick up a piece of chalk and sit scrawling on the pavement. Sometimes I'd see Tom lean over and say something to him and he'd look up and smile a simple child's smile that beamed in the sunlight. The tourists kept coming and the sun kept shining and it was one of those summers that go on for ever and stick in a child's mind, and tell you what summer should be like for the rest of your life. And I'm damn sure it sticks in Billy's mind, just like it does in all of ours.

Because one morning Mary didn't come into the store, which had gotten to being a regular sort of thing, and Billy wasn't out there in the square. After the way things had been the last few weeks that could only be bad news and so I left the boy John in charge of the store and hurried over to have a word with Tom. I was kind of worried.

I was no more than halfway across to him when I saw Billy come running from the opposite corner of the square, going straight to Tom. He was crying fit to burst and just leapt up at Tom and clung to him, his arms wrapped tight round his neck. Then his mother came across from the same direction, running as best she could. She got to Tom and they just looked at each other. Mary's a real pretty girl but you wouldn't have believed it then. It looked like he'd actually broken her nose this time, and blood was streaming out of her lip. She started sobbing, saying Sam had lost his job because he was back on the drink and what could she do and then suddenly there was a roar and I was shoved aside and Sam was standing there, still wearing his slippers, weaving back and forth and radiating that aura of violence that keeps men like him safe. He started shouting at Mary to take the kid the fuck back home and she just flinched and cowered closer to Tom like she was huddling round a fire to keep out the cold. This just got Sam even wilder and he staggered forward and told Tom to get the fuck out of it if he knew what was good for him, and grabbed Mary's arm and tried to yank her towards him, his face terrible with rage.

Then Tom stood up. Now Tom was a tall man, but he wasn't a young man, and he was thin. Sam was thirty and built like the town hall. When he did work it usually involved moving heavy things from one place to another, and his strength was supercharged by a whole pile of drunken nastiness. But at that moment the crowd stepped back as one and I suddenly felt very afraid for Sam McNeill. Tom looked like you could take anything you cared to him and it would just break, like he was a huge spike of granite wrapped in skin with two holes in the face where the rock showed through. And he was mad, not hot and blowing like Sam, but mad and *cold*.

There was a long pause. Then Sam weaved back a step and shouted: 'You just come on home, you hear? Gonna be real trouble if you don't, Mary. Real trouble . . .' and then stormed off across the square the way he came, knocking his way through the tourist vultures soaking up some spicy local colour.

Mary turned to Tom, so afraid it hurt to see, and said she guessed she'd better be going. Tom looked at her for a moment and then spoke for the first time.

'Do you love him?'

Even if you wanted to, you ain't going to lie to eyes like that, for fear something inside you will break. Real quiet she said, 'No,' and began crying softly as she took Billy's hand and walked slowly back across the square.

Tom packed up his stuff and walked over to Jack's. I went with him and had a beer but I had to get back to the shop and Tom just sat there like a trigger waiting to be pulled. And somewhere down near the bottom of those still waters something was stirring. Something I thought I didn't want to see.

About an hour later it was lunchtime and I'd just left the shop to have a break and suddenly something whacked into the back of my legs and nearly knocked me down. It was Billy. It was Billy and he had a bruise round his eye that was already closing it up.

I took his hand and led him across to the bar, feeling a hard anger pushing against my throat. When he saw Tom, Billy ran to him again and Tom took him in his arms and looked over Billy's shoulder at me and I felt my own anger collapse utterly in the face of a fury I never could have generated. I tried to find a word to describe it but they all just seemed like they were in the wrong language. All I can say is I wanted to be somewhere else and it felt real cold standing there facing that stranger in a black coat.

Then the moment passed and Tom was holding the kid close, ruffling his hair and talking to him in a low voice, murmuring the words I thought only mothers knew. He dried Billy's tears and checked his eye and then he got off his stool, smiled down at him and said: 'I think it's time we did a bit of drawing, what d'you say?' and, taking the kid's hand, he picked up his chalkbox and walked out into the square.

I don't know how many times I looked up and watched them that afternoon. They were sitting side by side on the stone, Billy's little hand wrapped round one of Tom's fingers, and Tom doing one of his chalk drawings. Every now and then Billy would reach across and add a little bit and Tom would smile and say something and Billy's gurgling laugh would float across the square. The store was real busy that afternoon and I was chained to that counter but I could tell by the size of the crowd that a lot of Tom was going into that picture, and maybe a bit of Billy too.

It was about four o'clock before I could take a break. I walked across the crowded square in the mid-afternoon heat and shouldered my way through to where they sat with a couple of cold Cokes. And when I saw it my mouth just dropped open and took a five-minute vacation while I tried to take it in.

It was a cat alright, but not a normal cat. It was a life-size tiger. I'd never seen Tom do anything near that big before, and as I stood there in the beating sun trying to get my mind round it, it almost seemed to stand in three dimensions, a nearly living thing. Its stomach was very lean and thin, its tail seemed to twitch with colour, and as Tom worked on the eyes and jaws, his face set with a rigid concentration quite unlike his usual calm painting face, the snarling mask of the tiger came to life before my eyes. And I could see that he wasn't just putting a bit of himself in at all. This was a man at full stretch, giving all of himself and reaching down for more, pulling up bloody fistfuls and throwing them down. The tiger was all the rage I'd seen in his eyes, and more, and like his love for Megan that rage just seemed bigger than any other man could comprehend. He was pouring it out and sculpting it into the lean and ravenous creature coming to pulsating life in front of us on the pavement, and the weird purples and blues and reds just made it seem more vibrant and alive.

I watched him working furiously on it and thought I understood what he'd meant that evening a few weeks back. He said he'd done a painting for the man who'd given him so much pain. Then, as now, he must have found what I guess you'd call something fancy like catharsis through his skill with chalks, had wrenched the pain up from within him and nailed it down onto something solid that he could walk away from. And now he was helping that little boy do the same, and the boy did look better, his bruised eye hardly showing with the wide smile on his face as he watched the big cat conjured up from nowhere in front of him.

We all just stood and watched, like something out of an old story, the simple folk and the magical stranger. It always feels like you're giving a bit of yourself away when you praise someone else's creation, and it's often done grudgingly, but you could feel the awe that day like a warm wind. Comes a time when you realize something special is happening, something you're never going to see again, and there isn't anything you can do but watch.

I had to go back to the store after a while. I hated to go but, well, John is a good boy, married now of course, but in those days his head was full of girls and it didn't do to leave him alone in a busy shop for too long.

And so the day drew slowly to a close. I kept the store open till eight, when the light began to turn and the square emptied out with all the tourists going away to write postcards and see if we didn't have even just a *little* McDonald's hidden away someplace. I suppose Mary had troubles enough at home, realized where the boy would be and figured he was safer there than anywhere else, and I guess she was right.

Tom and Billy finished up drawing and then Tom sat and talked to him for some time. Then they got up and the kid walked slowly off to the corner of the square, looking back to wave at Tom a couple times. Tom stood and watched him go and when Billy had gone he stayed there a while, head down, like a huge black statue in the gathering dark. He looked kind of creepy out there and I don't mind telling you I was glad when he finally moved and started walking over towards Jack's. I ran out to catch up with him and drew level just as we passed the drawing. And then I had to stop. I just couldn't look at that and move at the same time.

Finished, the drawing was like nothing on earth, and I suppose that's exactly what it was. I can't hope to describe it to you, although I've seen it in my dreams many times in the last ten years. You had to be there, on that heavy summer night, had to know what was going on. Otherwise it's going to sound like it was just a drawing.

That tiger was out and out terrifying. It looked so mean and hungry, Christ I don't know what: it just looked like the darkest parts of mankind, the pain and the fury and the vengeful hate nailed down in front of you for you to see, and I just stood there and shivered in the humid evening air.

'We did him a picture,' Tom said quietly.

'Yeah,' I said, and nodded. Like I said, I know what 'catharsis' means and I thought I understood what he was saying. But I really didn't want to look at it much longer. 'Let's go have a beer, hey?'

The storm in Tom wasn't passed, I could tell, and he still seemed to thrum with crackling emotions looking for an earth, but I thought the clouds might be breaking and I was glad.

And so we walked slowly over to Jack's and had a few beers and watched some pool being played. Tom seemed pretty tired, but still alert, and I relaxed a little. Come eleven most of the guys started going on their way and I was surprised to see Tom get another beer. Pete, Ned and I stayed on, and Jack of course, though we knew our loving wives would have something to say about that. It just didn't seem time to go. Outside it had gotten pretty dark, though the moon was keeping the square in a kind of twilight and the lights in the bar threw a pool of warmth out of the front window.

Then, about twelve o'clock, it happened, and I don't suppose any of us will ever see the same world we grew up in again. I've told this whole thing like it was just me who was there, but we all were, and we remember it together.

Because suddenly there was a wailing sound outside, a thin cutting cry, getting closer. Tom immediately snapped to his feet and stared out the window like he'd been waiting for it. As we looked out across the square we saw little Billy come running and we could see the blood on his face from there. Some of us got to get up but Tom snarled at us to stay there and so I guess we just stayed there, sitting back down like we'd been pushed. He strode out the door and into the square and the boy saw him and ran to him and Tom folded him in his cloak and held him close and warm. But he didn't come back in. He just stood there, and he was waiting for something.

Now there's a lot of crap talked about silences. I read novels when I've the time and you read things like, 'Time stood still' and so on and you think bullshit it did. So I'll just say I don't think anyone in the world breathed in that next minute. There was no wind, no movement. The stillness and silence were there like you could touch them, but more than that: they were like that's all there was and all there ever had been.

We felt the slow red throb of violence from right across the square before we could even see the man. Then Sam came staggering into view waving a bottle like a flag and cursing his head off. At first he couldn't see Tom and the boy because they were the opposite side of the fountain, and he ground to a wavering halt, but then he started shouting, rough jags of sound that seemed to strike against the silence and die instead of breaking it, and he began charging across the square and if ever there was a man with murder in his thoughts then it was Sam McNeill. He was like a man who'd given his soul the evening off. I wanted to shout to Tom to get the hell out of the way, to come inside, but the words wouldn't come out of my throat and we all just stood there, knuckles whitening as we clutched the bar and stared, our mouths open like we'd made a pact never to use them again. And Tom just stood there too, watching Sam come towards him, getting closer, almost as far as the spot where Tom usually painted. It felt like we were looking out of the window at a picture of something that happened long ago in another place and time, and the closer Sam got the more I began to feel very afraid for him.

It was at that moment that Sam stopped dead in his tracks, skidding forward like in some kids' cartoon, his shout dying off in his ragged throat. He was staring at the ground in front of him, his eyes wide and his mouth a stupid circle. Then he began to scream.

It was a high shrill noise like a woman, and coming out of that bull of a man it sent fear racking down my spine. He started making thrashing movements like he was trying to move backwards, but he just stayed where he was.

His movements became unmistakable at about the same time his screams turned from terror to agony. He was trying to get his leg away from something.

Suddenly, he seemed to fall forward on one knee, his other leg stuck out behind him, and he raised his head and shrieked at the dark skies and we saw his face then and I'm not going to forget that face so long as I live. It was a face from before there were any words, the face behind our oldest fears and earliest nightmares, the face we're terrified of seeing on ourselves one night when we're alone in the dark and It finally comes out from under the bed to get us.

Then Sam fell on his face, his leg buckled up and still he thrashed and screamed and clawed at the ground with his hands, blood running from his broken fingernails as he twitched and struggled. Maybe the light was playing tricks, and my eyes were sparkling anyway on account of being too paralysed with fear to even blink, but as he thrashed less and less it became harder and harder to see him at all, and as the breeze whipped up stronger his screams began to sound a lot like the wind. But still he writhed and moaned and then suddenly there was the most godawful crunching sound and then there was no movement or sound anymore.

Like they were on a string, our heads all turned together and we saw Tom still standing there, his coat flapping in the wind. He had a hand on Billy's shoulder and as we looked we could see that Mary was there too now and he had one arm round her as she sobbed into his coat.

I don't know how long we just sat there staring but then we were ejected off our seats and out of the bar. Pete and Ned ran to Tom but Jack and I went to where Sam had fallen, and we stared down, and I tell you the rest of my life now seems like a build up to and a climb down from that moment.

We were standing in front of a chalk drawing of a tiger. Even now my scalp seems to tighten when I think of it, and my chest feels like someone punched a hole in it and tipped a gallon of ice water inside. I'll just tell you the facts: Jack was there and he knows what we saw and what we didn't see.

What we didn't see was Sam McNeill. He just wasn't there. We saw a drawing of a tiger in purples and greens, a little bit scuffed, and there was a lot more red round the mouth of that tiger than there had been that afternoon and I'm sure that if either of us could have dreamed of reaching out and touching it, it would have been warm too.

And the hardest part to tell is this. I'd seen that drawing in the afternoon, and Jack had too, and we knew that when it was done it was lean and thin.

I swear to God that tiger wasn't thin anymore. What Jack and I were looking at was one fat tiger.

After a while I looked up and across at Tom. He was still standing with Mary and Billy, but they weren't crying anymore. Mary was hugging Billy so tight he squawked and Tom's face looked calm and alive and creased with a smile. And as we stood there the skies opened for the first time in months and a cool rain hammered down. At my feet colours began to run and lines became less distinct. Jack and I stood and watched till there were just pools of meaningless colours and then we walked slowly over to the others not even looking at the bottle lying on the ground and we all stayed there a long time in the rain, facing each other, not saying a word.

Well that was ten years ago, near enough. After a while Mary took Billy home and they gave us a little wave before they turned the corner. The cuts on Billy's face healed real quick, and he's a good-looking boy now: he looks a lot like his dad and he's already fooling about in cars. Helps me in the store sometimes. His mom ain't aged a day and looks wonderful. She never married again, but she looks real happy the way she is.

The rest of us just said a simple goodnight. Goodnight was all we could muster and maybe that's all there was to say. Then we walked off home in the directions of our wives. Tom gave me a small smile before he turned and walked off alone. I almost followed him, I wanted to say something, but in the end I just stayed where I was and watched him go. And that's how I'll always remember him best, because for a moment there was a spark in his eyes and I knew that some pain had been lifted deep down inside there somewhere.

He walked and no one has seen him since, and like I said it's been about ten years now. He wasn't there in the square the next morning and he didn't come in for a beer. Like he'd never been, he just wasn't there. Except for the hole in our hearts: it's funny how much you can miss a quiet man.

We're all still here, of course, Jack, Ned, Pete and the boys, and all the same, if even older and greyer. Pete lost his wife and Ned retired but things go on the same. The tourists come in the summer and we sit on the stools and drink our cold beers and shoot the breeze about ballgames and families and how the world's going to shit and sometimes we'll draw close and talk about a night a long time ago, and about paintings and cats, and about the quietest man we ever knew, wondering where he is, and what he's doing. And we've had a sixpack in the back of the fridge for ten years now, and the minute he walks through that door and pulls up a stool, that's his.

HE FRACTURE

Signing with a vehemence that made his lips vibrate, Richard dropped his pen and waved his right hand about in the air. While he waited for the cramp to ease he sipped a mouthful of tepid coffee and gazed vaguely out at the street. The short crescent his house was in started to turn outside his window, and with the trees just beginning to come into leaf looked almost like a little square. A bedraggled old woman with nicotine-stained hair struggled past on the other side of the road, and he watched her as he dredged his mind for any event of the past week which could be pressed into service as a letter-lengthener.

He couldn't think of any, and found the effort both tiring and actively depressing. Instead he settled for a long concluding paragraph, stopping himself at the last moment from including an excuse for the shortness of the letter. He'd used pressing appointments, the lateness of the hour and a desire to catch the post all before, and a letter was a letter, after all. Susan's were only longer than his because she drew from a much wider net of material. Her last letter had included over half a page on a couple he was fairly confident he'd never even heard of, much less met, and he was far from sure how he was supposed to feel about the problems they were having. He'd wondered in the past if there was some subtle point being made in these obscure vignettes, but had never been able to discern one and had long since given up trying.

They did make for long newsy letters though, whereas at less than two sides this was his shortest yet. Still, as they were seeing each other at the weekend, surely it was the thought that counted.

Pushing the completed letter aside, he lit a cigarette and

turned his attention to the other lying on his desk. As he reread it he quickly saw that he was in no position to criticize Susan's letter-writing. The minutiae of his life were all here, interspersed with little reflections and jokes, described in happy detail over five pages. The difference, he realized, was not just due to the fact that he wouldn't be seeing Isobel for almost two weeks. Even the final paragraph was longer, and he hadn't needed to think of padding it out with an excuse.

The chore finally over, he sat back and stared at the two unequal piles of paper on his desk. He hated writing letters, especially by hand. On a word processor you could just let the words flow down, carried forward by the speed of the typing and the momentum of transcription. More importantly, you could go back and fix anything which didn't come out right. Slogging it out by hand was different. For a start it was much slower, and worse, it was uncorrectable. If he was halfway down the second side and a sentence didn't come out right, he couldn't face the idea of tearing up and starting again. Instead he'd try to fix it in the next sentence, taking back streets and B-roads in an effort to cut back towards the point he'd been trying to make. Usually the sense ended up having to stay the night at some motel within striking distance of the intended destination, hoping to make it there the next time. The alternative was coldly planning and drafting, orchestrating a progression of facts in a letter that had duty rather than love between the lines. Neither was ideal, and he wished at least one of them didn't mind getting typewritten letters.

Absently pulling a piece of jotting paper off the desk pad for the checklist, Richard ran his eyes over the letter to Susan a final time. It was okay. He sounded like him in it, at least. Or the him that Susan knew, anyway. He sounded like him in the one to Isobel too, of course, but it was a different him, and he shuddered at the idea of Susan ever finding out that he existed.

As he pulled two envelopes out of the drawer, one blue, the other lilac, the phone went. Richard winced at finding

Mr Baum on the other end, and immediately started feeling guilty. Mr Baum always had that effect on him. Having him as a client was like perpetually sitting in the corridor outside some headmaster's office.

Mr Baum expressed himself keen, even anxious, to know when he was likely to see the preliminary designs for his new stationery. Babbling slightly, Richard rootled through the papers on his desk until he found the work he was supposed to have done for the businessman. By pure chance he'd actually finished it, and his hand went back into the drawer for a manila envelope.

As Mr Baum chuntered on Richard glanced at the clock. To stand any chance of catching a post which would land the work on the man's mat tomorrow morning he would have to leave the house almost immediately, but he couldn't afford to irritate one of his most regular clients still further by chucking him off the phone. So while he made the assorted noises of agreement and contrition which seemed to be all that was required of him he folded the two letters and slipped them into the envelopes, writing Susan's address from memory and copying Isobel's current crashpad from his filofax.

The conversation ended in an amicable draw, with Richard managing to slip in a deft reference to an unpaid invoice. He gathered his various envelopes to him, grabbed his coat and made it as far as the door. Then he went back to the desk, checked all the cigarettes were out in the ashtray, and headed for the door again. Swearing at himself, he then returned to the desk, picked up the ashtray and carried it to the sink. Quickly filling it with water he walked away without looking back, and finally made it out of the flat.

He got to the mailbox at the bottom of the street with a couple of minutes to spare, and lobbed the envelopes through the slot with a feeling of relief. He was about to head back to the flat when he realized that he wasn't half as cold as he'd been expecting. In fact, he saw, the sun was in the sky and there was even a touch of spring in the air. On impulse he decided to take a walk down to the high street, maybe pick up something different for lunch. What the hell, he thought. Go wild. Buy a scotch egg.

When he reached the high street he slowed from his usual intent stride to a more desultory stroll. This was partly forced upon him by the unusually high numbers of young mothers and old people meandering blinking into the sunlight, and partly an attempt to relax. Susan always said he shouldn't work so hard, and on that she was probably right. He felt tired.

Within a few minutes he was back to walking quickly, barely glancing at the shops as he passed. Something about the street didn't feel right. Both Susan and Isobel had visited him here in the couple of months since he'd moved, and with them the high street had a purpose, a comfortable set of points to amble between. Susan liked to browse in the poster shop, and could never resist a pastry from the Jewish bakery on the other side. Isobel enjoyed poking around in the second-hand bookshop, and resolutely refused to pass the Italian café without going in for a coffee, issuing the laconic waitress with precise but forgivable instructions on how much cocoa powder she'd like on top.

Richard thought he liked the high street, but today it seemed different. Today there was no track for him to follow, no reason for being here. He felt oddly displaced and lost, adrift in a gap between paths. Though the sun was weak his coat was heavy, and before long he was hot and irritable, buffeted by squealing children and peevish tramps. In the end he shopped briefly at the supermarket and turned back for home, feeling bluntly rejected by everything around him, as if he had no place there by himself.

On the way back to the flat he tried to shake himself out of his mood, realizing it was the letters that had started it. Writing them always made him feel depressed, and lonely too.

He knew that some men would think of themselves as pretty flash for having two women to write to, two women who had shared his double bed and lounged swaddled in his worn-out bathrobe in the mornings. Richard didn't. He realized it made him a bit of a bastard, and he didn't like to think of himself in that way. It didn't seem to fit, somehow. Or he didn't want it to.

It didn't seem to fit because he hadn't courted the situation, and because he felt guilty about it about all the bloody time. He hated the constant undercurrent of potential disaster, hated having to find excuses to put the answering machine on when he was actually worried that the other might call, hated the idea of hurting either of them in any way. Feeling bad wasn't the same as doing something about it, of course, but surely it counted for something.

He really *hadn't* gone looking for the situation, either. Somehow it had just happened. Susan had been his girlfriend since college, on and off. Fair-skinned and blonde, she still lived in Nottingham, wielding a variety of power suits as an up-and-coming solicitor. One of them made the trip to the other about every third weekend, and in between it was letters, phone calls, and mixed memories. Every now and then they talked of changing the situation, but it remained the same, and as time went on neither seemed more inclined to do anything about it.

Isobel was dark with an unruly volley of thick brown hair, and a mouth that seemed always on the verge of a smirk. The first time Richard had seen her had been across the room at a friend's party, and the memory of her grin then could still make him shiver. They had been too drunk to stand by the end of the evening, but somehow they'd managed to swop numbers and meet up for dinner. For five minutes it was strange, and then it was warm, and dark, and very exciting. She was an actress, in the sense that she'd been to drama college and the thing she spent most of her time not doing was acting. At the moment she was in Bristol, rehearsing for a play that seemed increasingly unlikely to ever make it to the stage.

Both girls were slim, and tall, but there any resemblance ended. Susan was solid, dependable, and Richard knew when he could call and find her in. Isobel worked on Martian time, never being where she'd said she would, and calling him at random times in the small hours to tell him that she loved him. With Susan he went to plays and watched films with subtitles where nothing happened, but with Isobel he prowled drunkenly down alleyways and dark canal banks, trying to keep her in hand as she shouted up at windows and then ran gleefully away. Susan had a time and place for contact, and would never have suddenly clamped her mouth over his in public as Isobel sometimes did, but Susan always knew what he meant, and Isobel sometimes didn't. Susan held his hand and Isobel gripped it, Susan put her arms round his waist and Isobel draped them round his shoulders, Susan smiled at him and Isobel grinned that grin.

So many differences, but in the end there was only one. With Susan there was always a backdrop, a context. Sorting out their problems, forgetting the past, getting back together, putting the bad things behind them: those were the things their dreams were made of. With Isobel everything was new, and different, and nothing had ever gone wrong between them. It was Love, not love, and after two quiet years he didn't think he could give it up now he'd found it again. Just as he couldn't give up the slow, tidal reassurance of shared times and thoughts, the comfort that comes with years and old love.

As he unlocked the flat door Richard made a determined effort to put the whole thing out of his mind. He knew he didn't possess the willpower to deny himself either of them, and five months had passed without either finding out about the other. Okay, yes, he was a bit of a bastard. Maybe even a complete bastard. Fair enough. But let it go on a little longer, he asked quietly: it makes me happy.

After lunch he sat back at his desk and kicked his computer into life. As today was Thursday he had plenty of time to clear his desk before the weekend. An afternoon spent hard at work would leave him comfortably ahead of schedule on his various commitments, which meant that he could take the evening off to watch television or do something equally untaxing. Remembering ahead of time for once that he should go shopping on Friday to get in the kind of food Susan liked, he reached across to make a note on the deskpad. Then, hand hovering over it, he stopped.

Lying behind his keyboard there was already a piece of jotting paper. For a moment he wondered what it was doing there, and then he knew.

He picked it up and turned it over, and then looked back at the front. There were no marks on the paper. None at all. Quickly, he tilted the monitor of his computer back enough to check if a piece of paper could have slipped underneath it. There was nothing there. He lit a cigarette and picked up the piece of paper again, feeling hollow.

He hadn't done his checklist.

Clasping his hands tightly in front of his face, he tried to remember the ten minutes before he'd left the flat, tried to picture himself doing the list, and perhaps throwing it away. He couldn't, and didn't bother to check the bin. He knew he hadn't done it.

Suddenly it was as if for once there was only one thought in his head, and he went cold with the purest fear, the fear of being found out. Then parts of his mind leapt different ways to huddle up against the wall, taking terrified glances at the fear in the centre. Nothing to do with me, they squealed: someone else's problem. Wide-eyed, he got up and put the kettle on, trying not to pace around the kitchen area as he waited for it to boil.

The checklist had developed slowly, as had his cigarette rituals. It was only in the last couple of years that he'd become so paranoid about leaving a smouldering butt behind that he'd felt compelled to do what he could to ensure they were all out. At first just rigorously re-stubbing all of them had been enough. That was okay, normal, and had only taken a few seconds.

But once the worry had taken root it got worse and worse. After stubbing had come leaving the ashtray in the sink, and then filling the ashtray with water as well. Together with checking and rechecking that all of the windows were locked it took him about five minutes to ever leave the house. Unless he was in a real hurry, like today.

By the time the kettle pinged at him, Richard was not only pacing but rubbing his upper lip with his forefinger as well.

Somehow, and for some reason he didn't understand, he just didn't believe he did things. Setting the alarm clock every night took five minutes of checking and rechecking that the time was right, the alarm time was right, that the alarm time was a.m. not p.m., and that the alarm function was in fact on. He did this time and again, staring at the numerals as if this would somehow make the adjustment more real, more something that he had done.

Coffee in hand, he sat back down at the desk and fruitlessly turned the piece of paper over again. It still had no marks on it.

The checklist had arisen out of the fact that he always sat down to write to Susan and Isobel at the same time. It generally took him at least a day to build himself up to letter-writing mode, and he couldn't face doing that twice in one week. The problem being that he ended up an utter disaster waiting to happen, in the shape of two contradictory piles of paper. If they should ever reach the wrong people, all hell would break loose and nothing in the world he valued would be left at the end of it.

At first he'd tried writing one and then the other, making sure the first was safely sealed inside its addressed envelope before starting on the next. The problem was that he couldn't refer to the first letter as a reminder of events already tediously dredged up out of his memory, and it also meant that he couldn't reread the first letter, which he liked to do before adding the final paragraph.

In the end he'd developed the checklist, and had settled with that. He wrote the two letters simultaneously, and then put addresses on two different coloured envelopes. He noted the number of pages of each letter on a piece of paper, and rechecked it. He checked the name at the beginning of the letter, and the pet name used at the end of it, twice each before tucking the letter into the envelope with Susan's address on it. Then he wrote the name 'Susan' over her number on the checklist. After he'd gone through the same procedure with Isobel's letter, he took Susan's letter out, quickly scanned through it to make sure all of the pages were hers, bundled it into the envelope and immediately sealed it. Then he did the same with Isobel's.

He knew the system wasn't foolproof, but that wasn't the point. Checking and rechecking the door didn't increase the likelihood of it being shut when he knew he'd done it properly the first time. He did know, in some sense, that he wouldn't have dropped a cigarette to the floor without noticing, just as he knew that he set the alarm properly first time. But in some other sense, he didn't know. He didn't trust his memory of events, even when he had no reason to doubt it. If you thought too hard about things you believed you'd done it became harder and harder to remember doing them with any degree of certainty, almost as if it wasn't really you who'd done them. And what was true for trivial things was even more so with the most important things in his life. Isobel and Susan.

And today, thanks to Mr-fucking-Baum, he hadn't done his checklist. For once he'd behaved like a normal human being, which would have been fine if he hadn't found out he'd done it.

But he had.

When his hands were no longer actively trembling, he booted his illustration program and set about coming up with a logo for a local printers. At least, he set up a blank page. After that he moved the mouse around, watching the pointer flash over the screen. He typed in the name of the firm, and then erased it. He drew a series of shapes, and then deleted them too. He did all of this as if under time pressure, working quickly and accurately, foot tapping unconsciously on the floor.

It would all be over in the first line, he knew. Both were easily well-acquainted enough with his handwriting to know it was him who'd written this letter to a girl with another name. They'd know before they were an inch down the page.

He typed the firm's name again, and tried it in several typefaces. They all looked the same. He erased again.

After that, the rest would just be the shit on the cake. Susan would read slowly through a letter that was over twice as long as the ones she normally received, seeing all the detail in his life he told her didn't exist. Isobel would see references to old times and deep friendship which she and Richard didn't have. And just as the horrible, fascinating novelty of yet another unfaithful sentence was beginning to wear off, they'd both read the other's final paragraph, and find new reserves of hate for him.

No they fucking *wouldn't*. Furiously, Richard spun the mouse across the desk and stood up. He jammed his hands into his pockets and walked stiffly across the room to the other window. They wouldn't because he hadn't put the letters in the wrong envelopes. He hadn't done the checklist, but that didn't mean he'd done it wrong. It didn't mean anything.

He walked back to the desk and tried to sit down, but was up again immediately. He took another cigarette out but before realizing there was one still burning in the ashtray, the end of the filter turning brown. He'd forgotten all about it.

He stubbed it out viciously and lit the other. He had to do something. He couldn't tune this out. He knew he hadn't made a mistake. He knew that he was a normal, efficient human being, and that like anyone else, he'd have put the letters in the right envelope. But he couldn't remember doing so. He couldn't recall the moment clearly enough, and the harder he thought about it, the fuzzier it became.

He got up. He sat down again. He looked at the screen for a while but didn't even bother to retrieve the mouse from where it had fetched up. He stared out of the window at the street, taking manic interest in a passing child. He considered cleaning the bath.

It was no good. He had to do something about it.

Suddenly, something occurred to him. He looked at his watch. It was 3.20. He carried the ashtray to the sink, filled it with water and flicked the ash from the current one into the grey sludge. He closed the window and twisted the lock hard, and then, struggling into his coat, headed for the street.

As he walked quickly down Leighton Road, Richard rehearsed reasonable-sounding excuses in his head. By the time he got to the Kentish Town Sorting Office he knew that, if necessary, he'd tell the truth.

He rang the bell at the enquiry desk and stood fretfully reading very dull and badly designed posters until a man appeared. He didn't ask if he could help or even raise an eyebrow in signification of readiness for enquiry, but simply stood behind the desk in a resigned fashion, waiting for Richard to speak.

In the end, Richard didn't even get to use his first excuse for wanting to retrieve two pieces of mail. Once provoked into speech, the man proved surprisingly well-informed and helpful. Yes, he confirmed, it was possible to take back a piece of mail once it had been put into a mailbox. All that was required was a detailed description of the article in question, and comprehensive proof of identity.

Feeling relief wash over him, Richard reached for his wallet to produce credit cards, video library memberships, whatever it took. He was about to explain that there were actually two envelopes he wanted to take back when the man suddenly held up his hand.

'Hang on,' he said. 'When did you post it?'

'Twelve-thirty,' Richard replied quickly, trying to be helpful. 'Just before the lunchtime pick-up.'

The man shook his head regretfully.

'No use you showing me anything, then,' he said. 'We're only part-time here, see. Only the first collection gets sorted here.'

'What happens to the rest?' Richard moaned.

'Goes straight to King's Cross Sorting Office.'

'And then?'

The man looked at him carefully.

'It gets sorted,' he said.

'Yes, but what then?'

'It gets put on a train,' the man said slowly, obviously hoping that he wasn't going to have to explain the postal system from first principles.

'Yes. When? At what time?' Richard asked frantically, struggling to remain polite. The man looked at his watch.

'Lunchtime, you said. Well, quite soon then. Ten, fifteen minutes.'

Armed with the address and phone number of the King's Cross Sorting Office, Richard ran back out to the street and looked quickly up and down it. The man's regret at professing himself unable to let Richard use his phone had been genuine, but final. The main sorting office was at least 25 minutes away by tube and foot. He didn't have time to find the nearest working phone booth, which was probably in Germany. So he trotted back towards his flat.

The light was flashing on his answering machine, but he ignored it and grabbed the handset.

The number was engaged.

Swearing wildly, Richard stomped over to the kettle and switched it on. He tried the number but it was still engaged, or engaged again. He fished the waterlogged buts out of the ashtray in the sink and slopped them into the bin. When he'd washed and dried the ashtray he set it on his desk, lit a cigarette and tried again.

This time he got a ringing tone. He continued to have a ringing tone for quite some time. Eventually it was answered by a female voice that seemed to conjure up endless, monumental vistas of boredom, a tumbleweed-strewn desert of futility.

It took Richard a few moments to get the person on the other end to understand that he was enquiring about the current status of the lunchtime pick-up of mail from a particular mailbox in Kentish Town. Once that was finally clear, the precise information that Richard didn't want to hear was immediately forthcoming. The mail had been sorted, and was beyond reaching.

Richard put the phone down, and watched the light on the answering machine flash for a while. He made a cup of coffee, and sat back down at the desk.

In a way it was a relief, of a terrible kind. There was nothing else he could do. The letters were on their way.

For a brief moment he had a sudden flash of rationality. There really was, he realized, no reason for him to suspect they'd gone in the wrong envelopes. There was a very strong chance that everything was going to be all right.

The moment faded, but left him feeling calmer than he had since discovering the blank checklist. He took a sip of coffee, feeling his heartbeat return to something like normal, and pressed the play button on the answering machine.

The message was from Isobel. She wasn't going to be in that evening, so she was calling now instead. She sounded disappointed not to have reached him, but chipper enough to have filled three minutes of tape with cheerful banter. At the end, her tone changed abruptly. I love you, she said, I love you very much.

When the message ended Richard sat motionless for a long time, listening to the sound of the words in his head, and wondering if this was the last time he would ever hear her say them. Say them like that, anyway. Say them like Isobel, instead of like Susan, with unthinking vehemence rather than considered resignation.

He managed to get a little work done in the remainder of the afternoon, but not much. At six he stood up for the tenth time in two hours, and this time elected not to sit down again. He took a shower and fixed a minimal meal, chewing it blankly in front of the evening news. Interest rates were up. England had won the cricket.

And some moron in Kentish Town had completely fucked up his life.

After trying to watch the television for a couple of hours he walked down to the corner newsagents/grocery/video library and took out the most gripping-looking film he could find. On the way down the idea of calling Susan popped into his head. He spent the time in the newsagents and during the walk back telling himself that there was absolutely nothing he could achieve by doing so, and then picked the phone up as soon as he was back in the flat.

She was out, which was unusual. Thursday was generally her night for staying in and catching up on work. It was probably just as well: as soon as he'd put the phone back down Richard realized just how impossible it would have been to have done anything useful by phoning her. What could he have said? By the way, please don't open the letter which arrives tomorrow?

The film, despite the outlandish claims to the contrary plastered all over the cover, failed to grip him or even hold his attention. His mind kept going back to the phone call at lunchtime, trying to picture his hands putting paper into envelopes, trying to see what had happened. The film ended, and he rewound it.

Two hours later he was in bed, and still awake. The door was locked, the alarm definitely set. Lying flat on his back, eyes lightly shut, he listened to the sound of traffic on faraway roads, and in his mind heard it mingle with the sound of a train, a train which held a sack, a sack which held two letters. He knew that by now the letters would be on different trains, heading for different parts of the country, but in his mind they lay together, rustling against each other with the rhythm of the train as it rushed through dark fields under a clear black sky.

When the alarm went he slapped it off and sat bolt upright, filled with dread before he remembered why. It felt like the opposite of Christmas morning, a long-awaited bad thing that was finally here. He showered and shaved quickly, expecting the phone to ring at any moment.

Because they would ring immediately. He would. Or would he? He thought he probably would. Some people, in some relationships, might save it up for the evening, let their anger ferment and refine the murderously cool way in which they'd reveal what had happened. Neither Susan nor Isobel were like that. In their different ways, they were very similar.

When by ten o'clock the phone still hadn't rung, Richard cautiously began to reassess the situation. They hadn't rung, which meant one of three things. The letters hadn't arrived. Possible, but unlikely given that they'd been out of the central sorting office at four. They'd arrived, but the girls had left before the post. Possible in Susan's case, unthinkably unlikely in Isobel's case. With her it was easier to believe she hadn't got up yet, but ten was pushing it even for her on a weekday.

Three. The right letters had landed on the right doorsteps. Richard sagged where he sat. After all that, he hadn't screwed up after all.

The phone rang.

Richard stared at it for a moment, utterly paralysed, and then picked the handset up carefully. Mr Baum told him he'd received the designs, and was actually pleased with them. After noting down a few points, Richard put the phone down again, panting.

By the time he was beginning to think about lunch Richard felt fine, if a little foolish. The real moral of the last 24 hours was that he was becoming dangerously reliant on artificial reassurances. When he finished a cigarette, he put it out properly. When he shut a door, it was shut. When he put letters into envelopes, he put them in the right ones. It wasn't a matter of trusting his memory. It was simply a case of trusting himself.

The printers now had two alternatives for their logo, and concocting another to make up the numbers would only take half an hour or so. As he waited for the file to finish saving Richard gazed contentedly out of the window at the street, where a black cat was sitting in the intermittent sunlight. It was lying down, technically, but something in its demeanour seemed to undermine this, as if it was taking a rest prescribed by protocol rather than need, part of some corporate relaxation regime that even senior managers were encouraged to follow. I'm lying down now, its manner said, but that doesn't alter the fact that what's really important is maintaining an up-to-date stock breakdown, and that's what I'll be going back to just as soon as this is over.

Then suddenly the cat leapt to its feet and scurried under a nearby car. Richard smiled at this, as there was absolutely no apparent cause for it. The computer pinged at him to signify completion of its task, and he hit the buttons which would quit the program before glancing back out to see if the cat had re-emerged.

A man was standing on the opposite side of the street, looking up at the house. He was in his late fifties and tall, with a lean face and tidy greying hair. His clothes were nondescript but light in colour, and he was wearing a dark coat. As Richard frowned on realizing that the man was not just looking at the house in general, but actually at his window, the man smiled gravely and started to walk away up the crescent. As he turned, he reached into his pocket and pulled something out. Still looking at Richard, he held it up for a moment, the minimal good humour vanishing from his face.

He was holding up two envelopes. One was blue, the other lilac. The man put the letters back in his pocket and held Richard's eyes for a long moment before walking away.

For a second Richard remained absolutely still, too shocked to move. Then he scrambled out of his chair to look through the next window along. He caught a brief glimpse of the back of the man's coat, and then he was out of vision again.

The man had his letters.

Richard turned wildly and stared at his desk for no reason, and then back out of the window. Abruptly, his mind caught up with events and he ran towards the door and slung it open. Feeling angry, bewildered and ashamed he hurtled down the steps and out of the building, leaving the door hanging wide.

There was no sign of him. Richard ran up to the nearest corner and looked down it, but the street was empty and so he sprinted up to the next road. The way to the right led down to the main junction with the Camden Road. It was wide and empty. There was no sign of the man in the other direction either, but that had to be the way he'd gone. Richard jogged up the road, trying to hang on to his anger. It seemed important.

After fifty yards he looked round the next corner, and saw that the man could not have gone that way either. He backtracked quickly and ran down the only side road he'd passed. Though the road curved he could see to the bottom, and there was nobody there. Then he noticed an alleyway on the left-hand side, and headed towards that.

The alley ran between high buildings, and was surprisingly dark. As he approached a recessed doorway he discovered what the anger had been masking. Fear. He moved carefully over to the opposite side of the alley, hugging the wall so as to see anything that might be in the doorway as soon as possible. Aware that his eyelid was twitching slightly, he peered into the doorway. It was empty, and he was very glad.

Casting occasional glances behind, he walked quickly down the remainder of the alley until he emerged on the side road that led into Torriano Crescent. He paused for a moment outside the door of the house, his heart beating quickly, and then stepped in.

Back inside the flat he walked to the window immediately and looked out, as if he hoped that would give him another chance. The road was still empty, which made him feel both desperate and relieved. He wanted his letters back, but he'd realized something in the alley. He didn't want to see the man again. Ever. There was something very wrong about him.

He grabbed a nearby packet of cigarettes, found it empty and crumpled it into the bin. Fumbling open another packet he paced round the room, barely aware that he was doing so.

He knew that he ought to feel furious. Someone had intercepted his letters, taken them out of the post and then come round to show him they'd done it. That was an outrageous invasion of privacy, and almost certainly illegal too. He ought to feel angry. He had every right to. So why did his anger feel so thin and abstract? Why was he allowing himself to feel as if he'd been caught?

Why did he feel afraid?

Cigarette finally lit, his pacing reached escape velocity and he strode off towards the phone. Someone in the employ of the postal service was going to receive the bollocking of their lives.

The handset was under his ear before he realized the problem with this, and it stayed there while he stared unseeingly out of the window, following the thought to the end.

Who was he going to accuse?

He hadn't described the envelopes to the man at Kentish Town, hadn't even told him there were two of them. Likewise, the voice at King's Cross had told him there was no hope before he'd had time to say what he was after. Neither of them could have known what to look for, and it couldn't have been them even if they had. He knew what the man at Kentish Town looked like, and the voice at King's Cross had been female.

Richard put the phone back down. Suddenly unable to remain in the flat, he grabbed his coat and wallet and left.

As he passed the postbox on the way to the high street he paused and stared at it. It occurred to him that either of the two people he'd spoken to could have got somebody else to come round with the letters. But it still didn't make sense. According to the man at Kentish Town, the letters would never have been there, and by the time he'd spoken to the woman at King's Cross the letters had been beyond reaching. He supposed it was possible that the man could have waited until he'd left and then called straight through. But why would he have done that, and how would they have known what to look for? Nothing he'd said to the man would have made two envelopes to different people an obvious target.

Still worrying the problem in his mind Richard absent-mindedly culled what he needed for the weekend from the shelves of the Pricefighter supermarket. He picked up the low-fat yoghurts and cottage cheeses that Susan would want, together with salad materials and a bottle of wine. At the counter he got an armful of packets of cigarettes too, partly to allay the assistant's probable displeasure at him paying by cheque, and partly because he felt he needed them.

At the bottom of his road he stopped, and moved slowly round until he could see the street opposite his house. There was no one there, and he walked up the crescent. Outside his house he stood and looked up at the window. From street-level you could see the back of the computer, the edges of the curtains and a patch of ceiling. It wasn't at all clear what he'd demonstrated by establishing this, and he crossed the road and let himself in.

Taking the fact that he had the letters as a given, however inexplicable, the real question was what the man hoped to gain from them. Not blackmail, surely. Richard felt that he'd have to be famous and far richer before that became a serious possibility. So what?

All the man had done was stand outside, and show him he had them. That, and looking unforgiving and stern. So he must have known what was in the letters. What was he going to do about it? Withhold them for purposes of his own, or send them on? If the latter, why take them out in the first place?

Crouched in front of the fridge, tucking yoghurts away, Richard suddenly stood up. This was absolutely ridiculous. What fucking business was it of anyone else's? Richard knew well enough that the situation wasn't ideal, felt guilty enough about it as it was. Okay, he was running two girlfriends at once, but that was no one's business but his. Or his and theirs. Certainly not that of some old shag who went round fishing in mailboxes or sorting offices or wherever the hell he'd got the letters from.

Armed with a coffee he sat down at the desk to work out what to do, beginning at last to feel self-righteously angry. It had taken a while in coming, he thought; too long. Because he'd felt guilty and worried all night, his first reaction had been off-base.

So what now? There didn't seem a lot of point in calling the police. He could imagine both their polite suspicion and complete inability to help without going through the grief of observing it first hand. He thought briefly about trying to get hold of Susan or Isobel, and then realized again the pointlessness of doing so. There didn't seem to be anything he could do. Except wait. Wait and see if the man turned up again. And if he did?

Richard felt his anger falter for a moment. The man was

absolutely in the wrong, however he'd got hold of the letters. Richard had every right to have them back. And yet . . . the idea of confronting the man was more unappealing than most things he could think of. He reached for the ashtray, feeling unsure.

Then he stopped, staring at the table. On it, by the side of the ashtray, there was a small pile of ash and a warped brown filter. The remains of a cigarette were lying on an intensely black burn about an inch long and a centimetre wide. The position of the debris left no doubt as to what had happened. When he'd gone out he'd left a cigarette burning. It had fallen out and burned the table.

Whimpering quietly, he pointlessly dashed to get a wet cloth. A little of the black smear came off, but not much. The table was scarred for life. It wasn't his table, but worse, what if the butt had rolled onto the carpet, or against the curtain?

Hadn't he checked?

Richard flung the cloth back towards the sink and stood, hands on hips, glaring unhappily at the ashtray. Somehow, and in some way he couldn't closely define, this made things worse. Suddenly he knew with absolute certainty that he'd put the letters in the wrong envelopes. Not because he remembered doing so, but because he'd left a cigarette burning, and the two were the same thing. His mind had been elsewhere, and the robot in charge of envelope filling had made a mistake.

Richard spent the next two hours drinking coffee, sitting on the sofa, leaning forward on his knees and staring out of the window. If the man passed by again, he didn't want to miss him, wanted to be out of the door as soon as he was in sight. He didn't know what he could say to him. He just knew that he had to get the letters back.

He also knew something else. If he didn't get them back, he was going to have to tell Susan and Isobel. The emotional balls he'd been able to keep juggling for five months had fallen out of sequence and landed heavily in his hands. Now they were there he knew, with a terrified relief, that he was going to have to tell.

He tried to dislodge the thought, but it felt as if his centre of gravity had irrevocably shifted, as if the whole thing had shocked him out of his previous equilibrium. It was no longer a case of whether he was going to do it, but simply when, and how.

At six, he shook himself out of a kind of awful reverie in which he'd mulled over different ways of breaking the news to Susan. He had a shower and picked through a joyless meal, and then left the house. He couldn't work, and couldn't face spending the whole evening staring pointlessly out of the window. Instead, he grabbed a book and walked down the road to the Porcupine, the nearest pub where the clientele weren't actively frightening. Not all the time, anyway.

The pub was busy, but Richard was able to get his favoured seat, in the raised area next to the window which looked out onto the main road. He sat with his pint and tried to get into the book, but the increasingly strident levels of noise outside and inside his head made it difficult to concentrate.

He ought to tell them both, as soon as possible. He'd been a bastard to them for too long, and he owed them the truth.

Maybe if he just explained everything, and said he was sorry, he'd get away with it. He hadn't set out to hurt them, after all. It was an accident. It wasn't his fault. Maybe they would see that.

If he was lucky enough to be able to choose, which would he go with? With a changed, sourer Isobel, who rightfully wouldn't trust him an inch, or back to Susan as so many times before, with a new debit in the complex scoring system they tended?

He didn't deserve either of them, and should be left alone, hated by both of them, the bad man in both their pasts whose legacy future boyfriends would have to deal with.

Everything he thought seemed to vacillate, to lurch from one viewpoint to another. It wasn't as if he kept changing his mind, but rather as if he had three or four consistent sets of opinions in his head, and kept ricocheting between them.

At nine there was a new influx of locals into the pub, and the noise leaped in volume. It was crowded now, the ceiling almost invisible above a pall of cigarette smoke. It was hot too, and the dangerous-looking lads on the big table next to Richard's kept banging into him on the way to the bar. He shook his head to try to stop the constant cycle of thought, and attempted manfully to get into his book.

The noise kept coming, and the room got more and more sweltering until he found himself wiping his hand across his forehead to dry it. The lads next to him got increasingly raucous until they were shouting almost constantly. He felt a self-righteously liberal thread of distaste as their tales of sexual derring-do got more and more frank and degrading, and then realized he wasn't in a position to get self-righteous about anything at all.

'Whaa fuck s'matter with you?'

Startled, Richard looked up. One of the men on the next table, about his own age, had twisted round in his seat and was staring at him with deeply alarming aggression.

'I'm sorry?' Richard replied, before he had time to loosen his accent.

'I said, what the fuck is the matter with you, *wanker*?'

The pub was now delirious with noise, and the other lads on the table were still merrily shouting at each other. The man stared at him and Richard felt his head run clear with fear.

'I'm sorry,' he stammered, 'I don't understand . . .'

The man twisted further round, until the full force of his apparent hatred was directed firmly at Richard. Still the pub raged, and still the man's companions seemed oblivious to what was going on. Richard gripped his book with hands that were now slick, and tried not to look as terrified as he felt.

'I fucking hate you wankers,' the man continued, slowly and deliberately, 'bunch of fucking arseholes. Put you in charge, then one little problem and you lose it.'

'I'm sor-'

'Course you fucking are. That's your whole fucking problem.' Suddenly and viciously the man mimicked Richard's voice. '"Oh dear, I've fucked up, what shall I do." What a *wanker*.'

Richard felt the back of his scalp crawl and he stared at the man. It was probably the smoke in the pub, and probably fear, but it was almost as if he was looking at the man down a tunnel of clearness.

'Fuck 'em. They give you any lip, just tell them to fuck off. Better still, just lie your fucking head off. So you shagged them both. So fucking what – that's what they're fucking *there* for. Tell you what mate, you want to try and get the two of them together.'

The man broke off to guffaw. Richard felt around him for his cigarettes, swallowing compulsively. This was bad. He had to get out.

'My advice to you,' the man concluded, winking with a kind of horrific intimacy, 'is to stop being such a cunt.'

Richard stood up and walked quickly across the raised area. He slipped going down the couple of steps and almost fell, but survived to shoulder his way through the crowds to the door. Just before he stepped out he glanced hurriedly back at the table. The man was still staring at him, a crooked grin on his face. He winked, and then turned his back on Richard, melting back into his group as if he'd never turned round. Richard fell out of the door into the cooler air outside.

He walked home as quickly as he could, pausing only to rest with his hands on his knees, sucking in great lungfuls of air. Occasionally, his mind was able to come up with a concrete thought, but most of the time it just whirled and flinched, balking against what had just happened.

The man had known what was going on. He had known.

As he fumbled with his keys outside the house Richard thought he heard a sound behind him and spun round, but there was no one there. He hurried up the stairs to his flat and let himself in.

The flat was hot, stifling. Richard wrenched open the fridge and grabbed the bottle of Diet Coke. Most of what he poured went into a glass. Then the phone rang in the silence and he dropped the glass.

The phone rang again. He should answer it. Carefully, Richard stepped over the broken glass. It rang again.

Then there was a clicking sound, and Richard remembered the answering machine was on. He listened to his voice saying he wasn't there, and waited with his hand over the handset for it to finish. He wouldn't be able to hear himself speak with it on.

'Well,' said a voice from the speaker when the answering message was finished. Richard pulled his hand back. 'What a lot of bother over nothing.'

Eyes wide, Richard straightened. He didn't recognize the voice. It was suave but oily, the voice of a plump, self-satisfied man.

'We're all adults here, we know these things happen.' There was a chortle, and Richard felt his flesh crawl as he stared. 'It's not ideal, I'll grant you. But what's done is done.'

Teeth clenched, Richard reached his hand out towards the phone.

'After all, you were what they both wanted, and what they didn't know didn't hurt them. So why should it now?'

Richard lightly put his hand on the handset.

'Really, they've been lucky to both be able to have you. I'm sure that if you point that out, calmly but firml-' Richard yanked the phone up to his ear.

'Who the hell . . .' he shouted, but too late. All he could hear was a dial tone. Blinking, he shook the phone, but the tone remained. Then Richard noticed that the answer button was flashing on the machine. Of course: the machine would have been running. He hit the play button to hear the man's voice again.

After assorted beeping sounds a voice came over the speaker, but it wasn't the one he was expecting. It was Susan. She'd finished work early and was coming down this evening instead of tomorrow lunchtime. She expected to be at Kentish Town tube at 10.30 p.m. Would he meet her?

Shocked, Richard glanced at his watch. It was ten o'clock. What on earth was she playing at? He could have been out with

Isobel this evening. Worse still, they could have been spending the evening in. What was she doing, suddenly coming early? His heart stopped as he thought of one possible reason for the change in plan, but then he discounted it: she couldn't have received the wrong letter, because some bastard was running round London with them. So why? What was going on?

The machine beeped again, and noise poured suddenly out of it, the sound of lots of people talking and shouting at once. Richard stared at it as a low, guttural voice spoke.

'She's my favourite. The one with the tits. Good mouth on the other one, but give me the tits any time.'

There was a laugh that distorted the speaker, and the message ended. Richard found he was breathing very heavily, heart juddering. That was him. That was the man from the pub. The machine beeped again, and after a pause, rewound. Richard jabbed the button again, bewildered. Where was the message from the oily man? Why wasn't it there?

He listened carefully to Susan's message again, trying to hear some expression in her voice. It was casual, conversational. There was no way of telling what she might be thinking. Maybe it was all right. Maybe she was just coming early because she wanted to see him. Maybe not.

The machine beeped and Richard clapped his hands over his ears when he heard the noise of the pub again. He sang loudly for ten seconds, eyes tightly shut. He didn't want to hear the man's voice again. There was still no other message.

Richard walked to the sofa on legs that felt very shaky and sat down. His chest was still hitching unevenly, his forehead beaded with sweat and his eyes were taking in next to nothing. While part of his mind ran calmly over the change in plan, trying to see if it would cause any problems, the rest of him tried to flee. The oily man, he was sure, was not the man who'd stood outside his window. His voice would have been dry and quiet with firm authority. He wouldn't have delivered that smug homily with its fatuous arrogance. He would have calmly told him he was a shit.

163

Was that fair? Was he simply a bastard? He hadn't meant to do it, had only wanted to be with both of them. Surely he hadn't acted as badly as all that? These things happened, after all.

Suddenly Richard realized that he *was* a shit, that he was simply unlucky to have been caught, and that he did want to sleep with both of them, and keep doing so. Whoever the fuck they were, and however they'd found out about him, the three men were each right. They didn't understand the whole story, but they had bits of it. The oily man could have been a friend of the stern man, or an accomplice, together with the yob in the pub. The first man could have shown them the letters. In fact, he must have done. Why? Why were they doing this? He wished he could talk to them, tell them that it wasn't the way it looked, that he did care about both of them. But what business was it of theirs?

Shaking his head violently, he stood up, and then realized he had nowhere to go. Not yet, anyway; in a little while he had to walk down to the station and face the music. Face the fucking *Ring Cycle*, in fact.

Then, puzzled, he came to a mental halt. He'd got it wrong again. He wasn't going to have to face anything. Susan couldn't have received a letter, unless the stern man had hopped on a train and delivered it personally. Why did he keep forgetting that?

He turned and looked round for his cigarettes. He had to do something to fill up the minutes, and smoking seemed as good a bet as anything. He also grabbed the copy of *Time Out* that he'd dropped by the armchair, to see if anything worth seeing was on. Without noticing he was hunched over slightly, as if flinching against the phone ringing again, he searched through the cinema listing. Lots of foreign shite: Susan wouldn't fancy that. No point looking in the theatre listings either: after rehearsing all week the last thing she'd want to do was watch other people standing on a stage. Drawing heavily on his cigarette Richard switched to the clubs section to see what was happening at the Dome. Then he stopped.

What the hell was he thinking of?

Aghast at his own stupidity, Richard threw his cigarette butt out of the window, moving slowly as if under water. What on *earth* was he doing? Foreign films were *exactly* Susan's thing, and he knew there were at least two plays she wanted to see. She wouldn't, of course, have been anywhere near a bloody stage, and wild horses couldn't have dragged her into the Dome. He'd been thinking of the wrong one. He'd been thinking of Isobel.

But he hadn't, not really. All he'd been doing was reacting, behaving normally. The only problem was that it had been Isobel's Richard who'd been doing the thinking, not Susan's.

Then, very late, he snapped his head up and stared at the window. It was open. He hadn't opened it since he got back. When he came in he went straight to the fridge, then the phone. He hadn't opened the window. So it had been open all the time. He had left the window open when he went out. Part of him had known that, and had unthinkingly aimed the butt out of the window.

Suddenly feeling sick, Richard hurled the magazine at the bookcase, and leapt up and slammed the window shut. He also left the window open and put the magazine back near the armchair, and then looked at his watch. It was time to go.

He marched quickly along the crescent towards Leighton Road. He didn't look up at the window. It didn't matter whether he'd shut it or not. He wasn't going to be gone long.

Leighton Road was deserted, eerily wide beneath sallow street-lights. Head down, he walked as quickly as he could. Halfway down, as he passed a side road, he heard a sound and turned to look. He couldn't see anything, and took a couple of steps into the dark turning. The sound got louder until he recognized it. It was someone crying.

About five yards up the road stood a little boy. He was dressed in shorts and a T-shirt, and his hands were pressed into his eyes. Richard took a careful step towards him. The boy's chest was heaving spasmodically, and he was oblivious to the world around him, trapped in some private grief alone by himself in a side road in Kentish Town.

'Are you all right?' Richard asked. He knew it was a stupid question, but it seemed to be the only one available. The boy didn't answer. Richard tried again, hating himself for being conscious of the fact that he ought to be hurrying to the station. 'Are you hurt?'

The boy didn't even look up, and Richard realized with a chill how alone he looked, as if he'd been wandering the earth for ever, with no home to go to and no one to care for him. His chest hitched again and Richard took another step towards him.

Suddenly the boy looked up, a flash of tears and cheeks that were swollen red. He stared directly at Richard for a second, and then screamed at him.

'I hate you,' he shouted, and then turned and ran into the darkness. Stunned, Richard stared after him.

'What?' he shouted, 'Why? Who are you?' But the boy was gone.

Richard turned slowly and went back the way he had come, continually casting glances behind him. There was no sign of the boy, and no sound of footsteps. Head down, feeling like crying, Richard walked onto the main road.

'Richard?'

Startled, he looked up. Susan was standing in front of him, overnight bag in hand.

'Suz?' He stared at her stupidly.

'Was that you shouting?'

'Er, yes. What are you doing here?'

'I rang . . .'

'I know, I mean, here?' His heart beating more slowly, Richard began to feel slightly more normal.

'Train was early.' She smiled. 'I got bored with hanging about. Thought I'd brave the streets alone for once.'

Richard nodded, and smiled tentatively back. Then he consciously broadened his smile. Susan was very good at noticing when something was wrong.

'Why were you shouting?' Susan asked as they turned and headed for Torriano Crescent.

'Oh, just some kid. He seemed upset.' At me, Richard could have added, but didn't. Susan took his arm.

'You are good,' she said. 'Most people wouldn't have given a toss.' Richard smiled painfully at the compliment. With a lurch he remembered his earlier vow to talk to her this evening, to tell her what was going on. Then suddenly he heard footsteps, and turned to look behind them. There was nobody there.

'What?'

'Nothing,' he said. 'Thought I heard someone.' Susan turned to look. 'There's nobody there,' he added quickly.

'Is there any food in the house? I didn't have time to eat.'

'Oh yes,' Richard said heartily, listening carefully for any sound behind them. 'Tons of rabbit food and some of that white grunge in pots.'

'Oh, super,' she said, squeezing his arm and laughing. Richard found that it hurt badly for her to do that, for her to love him. He didn't want her to love him. Not tonight, not with what he'd done, with what he had to tell her. There was the sound of a loud guffaw from the window of an estate they were passing, and he looked up quickly.

'You're as bad as me.' Susan grinned. 'Don't worry. I'll protect you.'

Richard glanced behind again, and had to fight against jumping with fright. There was a man about thirty yards away, on the other side of the street, walking the same way as them. It was too far to see clearly, but Richard thought he knew who he was. There was something in the way he stood, the unforgiving uprightness and the long stride. Richard started walking more quickly, babbling at Susan to prevent her from turning round and seeing the man, or sensing the waves of disapproval.

As he let them into the flat he sent up a brief prayer that there wouldn't be any messages on the machine. Susan would see the light flashing and he'd have to play them. As she lay her coat over the chair, fished cigarettes out of her bag and generally made herself at home he covertly glanced at the machine, but it was all right. No messages.

'Now what I want,' Susan announced, 'before anything else, before even the cup of coffee you're going to make me, is a kiss.' She stepped towards him and put her arms round his shoulders. Heart tightening, Richard put his round her waist. This wasn't the way they normally kissed. Susan slowly moved her face towards his, eyes soft and warm, and he shut his so he couldn't see them.

The kiss went okay, as far as he could tell, and he pulled her towards him, hoping his arms could make up for anything his lips weren't giving. He couldn't remember how he kissed her.

Then he heard a sound, and his eyes flew open. He looked past Susan's, which were closed, and at the dark hallway. There seemed to be a shadow back in there, and he knew he'd heard something. Either a sob or a chuckle. He couldn't tell which.

Susan pulled back, a quizzical expression on her face.

'Are you all right?'

'Yes, why?' he said carefully.

She shrugged.

'Don't know. That just seemed a little . . . quiet.'

'I'm fine,' Richard lied, glancing at the corridor, 'It's just . . . I need to go to the toilet.'

'Do you?' Susan asked, pretending to be a schoolteacher, and Richard realized thankfully he'd been given a way out of a potentially awkward moment.

'Yus,' he said, sounding like a child, and Susan laughed.

'Off you go then. I'll put the kettle on. Would you dump my bag in the bedroom?'

Richard walked carefully into the corridor. He wanted to put the light on, but knew that was stupid. It was only five yards long, and enough light seeped from the living room to see that there was no one there. He walked into the bedroom and turned the light on. Leaving Susan's bag on the bed he stepped into the bathroom. He really did need to go, he discovered. In fact, he couldn't remember when he'd last been. After getting a result with the erratic flush he took a deep breath and opened the door. Then he covered his mouth with his hands just in time to stifle a yelp.

The stern man was standing in the doorway to the corridor, leaning against the wall. The man from the pub was stretched out on the bed, smoking, and the little boy was standing by the window, not crying now, but just staring at him. A chubby, well-dressed man whose fat face seemed to shine like plastic paced in the centre of the room, and turned to smile at Richard.

'Hello there, Number One,' he said, and the yob on the bed snorted. Richard stared at them, hands trembling. He didn't think he could handle this. This, he thought, might just be that little bit too much.

'Who the hell are you?' he managed, quietly. The oily man chortled, and then tutted.

'You know very well,' he said, keeping his voice low. 'Now. Situation is this. We're not happy.' The man on the bed snorted again, more angrily this time. The man in the doorway just looked balefully at Richard, and the little boy turned to look out of the window, nodding his head. This isn't happening, thought Richard. This is not happening.

'Not happy at all,' the man continued. 'There was talk of doing away with you altogether, after the fracture.' Richard just stared at him. 'But,' the man said, smiling brightly, 'I'm happy to say I won the various parties over, and that's not going to happen. Instead, we're just going to revoke your status. As you can see, things are going to be run a little differently from now on. We're all on a par now. There is no Number One any more. Understood?'

Richard didn't answer, and the man nodded his head curtly in a businesslike way.

'Good. No hard feelings then. Oh, and one more thing: the alarm *is* set properly. I do it myself.'

'And I look after the fag butts,' smirked the man on the bed. 'Don't you worry. Trust me.' He grinned, showing his nicotine-stained teeth, and sat up. Richard decided he really couldn't cope with this any more, stepped back into the bathroom and shut the door.

When he no longer looked as if he'd been crying he opened it again. The bedroom was empty. There was no depression on the bed.

He breathed deeply for a while, composing himself before going back in to Susan. Then he noticed a flash of colour in the gap in her bag, and leant forward. He reached silently in and pulled out the envelope. He slipped the letter out and read the first line. It said 'Dear Suz'.

He walked into the corridor. Everything felt different now. Some balance had shifted, some scale tipped. He stepped into the living room.

The stern man was sitting in the armchair, gazing with distaste at the furnishings. Richard thought it was probably him who needed the checklist, but also him who made sure the letters went in the right envelopes. It was definitely him who disapproved of the infidelity. The little boy was sitting on the floor. He looked a little more cheerful, almost hopeful. He didn't mind who or how many he had, so long as he had someone. The oily man stood, arms folded, and smiled beneficently at Susan, who was sitting on the sofa. The man from the pub was kissing her hard, his hand squeezing her breast through her blouse. He bit her lip for a moment in the way she liked, and Susan slipped her hand onto his thigh.

Richard stood aimlessly in the doorway for a moment, and then moved to lean against the bookcase, to wait his turn in the limelight, to get used to no longer being Number One, but just one of many.

SAVE AS...

WHAT YOU MAKE IT

As soon as I walked out of the hospital I knew what I was going to do. It was one a.m. by then, for what little difference that made. I was on hospital time, crash time, blood time: surprised by how late it was, as if I'd believed that what happened must have taken place in some small pocket of horror outside the real world, where the normal rules of progression and chronology didn't apply. Of course it must have taken time, for the men and women in white coats to run the stretcher trolleys down the corridors, shouting for crash teams and saline; to cut through my wife's matted clothes and expose wet ruins where only an hour ago all had been smooth and dry; to gently move my son's head so that its position in relation to his body was the same as it had always been. All of this took time, as did the eventual slow looks up at me, the quiet shakes of the doctors' heads, the forms I had to sign and the words I had to listen to.

Then the walk from the emergency room to the outside world, my shoes tapping softly on the linoleum as I passed rows of people with bandaged fingers. That took the most time of all.

The air in the car park was cool and moist, freshened by the rain. I could smell the grass which grew in the darkness beyond the pools of yellow lamplight, and hear in the distance the sound of wet tyres on the freeway.

I suddenly realized that I had no means of getting home. The remains of the Lexus were presumably lying by the side of the road where the accident had taken place, or had been carted off to a wrecker's yard. For a moment the problem took up the whole of my mind, unnaturally luminescent: and then I realized both that I could presumably call a cab from reception, and that I didn't really care.

Two orderlies walked across the far side of the lot, a faint laugh carrying to me. The smell of smoke in their wake reminded me I was a smoker, and I fumbled a cigarette from the packet in my jacket pocket. The carton was perfectly in shape, the cigarette unbent. One of the very few things Helena and I had ever argued about was my continued inability to resist toying with death in the form of tubes of rolled tobacco. Her arguments were never those of the zealot, just measured and reasonable. She loved me, and Jack loved me, and she didn't want the two of them to be left alone. The fact that the crash which had crushed her skull had left my cancer sticks entirely unmolested was a joke which she would have liked and laughed at hard.

For a moment I hesitated. I couldn't decide whether Helena's death meant I should smoke the cigarette or not.

Then I lit it and walked back to reception. If I was going to go through with it, I didn't have much time.

The cab dropped me at the corner of Montaigne and 31st. I overtipped the driver – who'd had to put up with a sudden crying jag which left me feeling cold and embarrassed – and watched the car swish away down the deserted street. The crossroads was bleak and exposed; an empty used car lot and burnt-out gas station taking two corners, run-down buildings of untellable purpose squatting kitty corner on the others. It couldn't have been more different from the place where I'd originally gone to visit the Same Again Corporation, an altogether more gleaming street in the heart of the business district. I guessed space was cheaper out here, and maybe they needed a lot of it: though I couldn't really understand why. Data storage is pretty compact these days.

Whatever. The card I'd kept in my wallet was adamant that I should go to the address on Montaigne in case of emergency, and so I walked quickly down towards 1176. I saw from across the street that a light was on behind the frosted glass of the door, and picked up the pace with relief. It was open, just as the card said it would be.

As I crossed the street a man came out of Same Again's front door, holding a very wet towel. He twisted the towel round on itself, squeezing as much of the water out of it as he could. It joined the rain already on the sidewalk and disappeared.

When he saw where I was heading he suddenly looked up.

'Help you?' he asked, warily. I showed him the card. An unreadable expression crossed his face. 'Go inside,' he said. 'Be right with you.'

The reception area was small but smart. And very quiet. I waited at the desk for a few moments while the man finished whatever the hell he was doing. Then I noticed a soft dripping sound. A patch of carpet near one of the walls was damp, and there was a similar spot on the ceiling.

I turned to find the man reaching out a hand to me.

'Sorry about that,' he said, but didn't offer any more explanation. 'Okay, can I have that card?'

He took it and went behind the desk, tapped my customer number into the terminal there.

'My name's . . .' I said, but he held up his hand.

'Don't tell me,' he said quickly. 'Not a thing. I assume something pretty major has happened.' He looked at my face for a moment, and decided he didn't have to wait for an answer. 'So it's very important that I know as little as possible. How many people have already been involved?'

'Involved?'

'Are aware of whatever event it is that has brought you here.'

'I don't know.' I didn't know who counted. The doctors and nurses, presumably, and the people who'd loaded up the ambulance. They'd seen the faces. Others knew something had happened, in that they'd driven past the mess on the freeway, or walked past me as I stood in the parking lot of the hospital. But maybe they didn't count, because they had no knowledge of who had been involved in what. 'Maybe ten, twelve?'

The man nodded briskly. 'That's fine. Okay, I've processed the order. Go through that door and a technician will take you from there. May I just remind you of the terms of the contract you entered into with Same Again, most specifically that you are legally bound not to reveal to anyone either that you are a subscriber to our service or that you have made use of it on this or any other occasion?'

'Fine,' I said. It was illegal. We both knew that, and I was the last person who wanted any trouble.

The door led me into a cavernous dark area where a young woman in a green lab coat waited for me. Without looking directly at my face she indicated that I should follow her. At the end of the room was a chair, and I sat in it and sat quietly while she applied conductant gel to my temples and attached the wires.

When she was finished she asked if I was comfortable. I turned my head towards her, clamping my lips tightly together. My teeth were chattering inside my head, the muscles of my jaw and neck spasming. I could barely see her through a haze of grief I knew I could not bear. In the end I nodded.

She loaded up a hypo and injected something into the vein on the back of my hand. I started counting backwards from twenty but made it no further than nine.

I got home about four o'clock that afternoon. After I'd locked the Lexus I stood in the driveway for a moment, savouring a breeze which softened the heat like a ceiling fan in a noisy bar. The weather men kept saying summer was going to burst soon, but they were evidently as full of shit as their genus had always been. Chaos theory may have grooved a lot of people's lives but the guys who stood in front of maps for a living were obviously still at the stage of consulting entrails. It hadn't rained for weeks and didn't look like it was going to start anytime soon – and that was good, because in the evening we had a bunch of friends coming round for a cook-out in the back yard.

I let myself into the house and went straight through into the kitchen. Helena was standing at the table, basting chicken legs, half an eye on an old Tom Hanks film playing on the set in the corner. I noticed with approval that it was an old print, one which hadn't been parallaxed.

'Good movie,' I said.

'Would be,' she replied, 'if you could see what the hell was going on.'

I'm against the 'enhancing' of classics: Helena takes the opposite view, as is her wont. We'd had the discussion about a hundred times and as neither of us really cared, we only put ourselves through it for fun. I kissed her on the nose and dunked a stick of celery in the barbecue sauce.

'Dad!' yelped a voice, and I turned in time to catch Jack as he leapt up at me. He looked like he'd been dragged through a hedge sideways by someone who was an internationally acknowledged expert in the art of interfacing humans and hedges to maximum untidying effect. I raised an eyebrow at Helena, who shrugged.

'How many pairs of hands do you see?' she said.

I set Jack down, endured him boxing my kneecaps for a while, and then sent him upstairs for a bath – promising I'd come up and talk to him. I knew what he really wanted was to rehearse yet again the names of the kids who'd be coming tonight. He's a sociable kid, much more than I was at his age – but I think I was looking forward to the evening as much as him. The secret of good social events is to only invite the people you like having in your life, not the ones you merely tolerate. Tonight we had my boss – who was actually my best friend – and his wife; a couple of Helena's old girlfriends who were as good a time as anyone could handle; and another old colleague of mine over from England with his family.

I hung with Helena in the kitchen for a while, until she tired of me nibbling samples of everything she'd painstakingly arranged on serving plates. She was too tall to box my kneecaps and so bit me on the neck instead, a bite which turned into a kiss and became in danger of throwing her cooking schedule out of whack. She shooed me out and I left her to it and went through into the study.

There were screeds of email to be sent before I could consign the day to history and settle down into the evening and weekend, but most of it was already written and the rest didn't take long. As my software punted them out I rested my chin on my hands and gazed out onto the yard. A trestle table was already set up, stacks of paper plates at the ready. The old cable spool we used as a table when it was just family had been rolled to over by the tree, and bottles of red wine were open and breathing in the air. Beer would be frosting in the fridge and the fixings for Becky and Janny's drink of choice – Mint Juleps, for chrissake – ready and waiting in the kitchen. I could hear Helena viciously chopping some errant vegetable in the kitchen, and Jack hollering in the bath upstairs.

For a moment I felt perfectly at peace. I was 36, had a wife I'd die for and a happy, intelligent kid; a job I actually enjoyed and more money than we needed; and a house that looked and felt like an advert for The American Way. So what if it was schmaltzy: it was what I wanted. After my twenties, a frenetic nightmare of bad relationships and shitty jobs – and my early thirties, when no one around me seemed to be able to talk about anything other than houses, marriage or children – my life had finally found its mark. The good things were in place, but with enough perspective to let me exist in the outside world too.

I was a lucky guy, and not too stupid to realize it.

The machine told me it had accomplished its task, and that I had new mail. I scanned the sender addresses: one from my sister in Europe, and a spam about 'Outstanding business opportunities ($$$$$$)!'. I was mildly surprised to see that there was also one from my own email address – entitled 'Read This!' – but not very. As part of my constant battle to design a killfile which would weed out email invitations to business opportunities of any kind – regardless of the number of suffixed dollar signs – I was often sending test messages to myself. Evidently the new version of the killfile wasn't cutting it. I could tool around with it a little more on Sunday afternoon, maybe aided by a glass of JD. Right now it hardly seemed important.

I told the computer to have a nap and went upstairs to confront the dripping chaos that our bathroom would be.

Doug and Julia arrived first, as usual: they were always invited on a 'turn up when you feel like it' basis. Helena was only just out of the shower so Julia went up to chat with her; meanwhile Doug and I stood in the kitchen with bottles of beer and chewed a variety of rags, him nibbling on Helena's cooking, me trying to rearrange things so she wouldn't notice.

We moved out into the yard when Becky and Janny arrived, and I started the Weber up, supervising the coals with foreman-ship from Helena at the table. I'd strung a couple of extension speakers out the door from the stereo in the living room, and one of Helena's compilation minidiscs played quietly in the background: something old, something new, something funky and something blue. Jack sat neatly on a chair at the end of the trestle in his new pants and checked shirt, sipping at a diet coke and waiting for the real fun to begin. Becky chatted with him in the meantime, while Janny reran horror stories of her last relationship: she's working on being the Fran Liebowitz of her generation, and getting there real fast. When everyone round the table erupted as she got to the end of yet another example of why her ex-boyfriend had not been fit to walk the earth, Helena caught my eye, and smiled.

I knew what she meant. There but for the grace of God, she was thinking, could have gone you or I.

Being funny is cool; being happy is better. I left the coals to themselves for a bit, and went and stood behind Helena with my hand on her shoulder.

But then the doorbell went and she jumped up to let Adam and Carol in. Jack stood uncertainly, waiting for them to come through into the garden. Their two kids, whose names I could never remember, walked out behind them. There was a moment of quiet mutual appraisal, and then all three ran off towards the tree to play some game or other. They'd only ever met once before, on a trip we took to England, but obviously whatever they'd got up to then was still good for another day. As the evening began to darken, and the adults sat round the table and drank and ate, I could hear always in the background one of my favourite sounds of all, the sound of Jack laughing.

And smell Helena's barbecue sauce, wafting over from the grill; and feel Helena's leg, her thigh warm against my leg, her ankle hooked behind mine.

At ten I came out of the house, clutching more beers, and realized two things. The first was that I was kind of drunk. Negotiating the step down from the kitchen was a little more difficult than it should have been, and the raucous figures around the trestle table looked less than clear. I shook my head, trying to get it back together: I didn't want to appear inebriated in front of my son. Not that he was on hand to watch – the kids were still tirelessly cavorting off in the darkness of the far end of the yard.

The second thing I noticed was less tangible. Something to do with atmosphere. While I'd been in the kitchen, it had changed. People were still laughing, and laughing hard, but they'd moved round, were sitting in different positions at the table. I guess I'd been in the kitchen longer than I thought. Becky and Jan were huddled at one end of the table, and I perched myself on a chair nearby. But they were talking seriously about something, and didn't seem to want to involve me.

There was another burst of laughter from the other end, and I looked blearily towards it. There was something harsh in the sound. Helena and Carol were leaned in tight together, their faces red and shiny. Adam was chortling with Doug and Julia. It was good to see them getting on together, but I hadn't realized they were all so chummy. Adam had only been with the firm for a year before upping stakes and going with Carol back to her own country. Doug and I had been friends for twenty years. Still, I guess it showed the evening was going well.

Then I saw something I couldn't understand. Helena's hand, reaching out and taking a cigarette from the packet lying on the table. I frowned vaguely, knowing something wasn't right, but she stuck the cigarette in her mouth and lit it with her lighter.

Then I remembered that she'd started a few months before, finally dragged into my habit. I felt guilty again, wishing I'd been able to stop before she started. Too late now, I suppose.

I reached for the bottle of beer I'd perched on the end of the table, and missed. Well, not quite missed: I made enough contact to knock it off the table. Janny rolled her eyes and started to lean down for it, but I beat her to it.

'It's okay, I'm not that drunk,' I said, slightly stiffly. This wasn't true, of course, because it took me rather longer than it should to find the bottle. In the end I had to completely lean over and look for where it had gone. This gave me a view of all the legs under the table, which was kind of neat, and I remained like that for a moment. Lots of shins, all standing together.

Some more together than others, I saw. Helena's foot was resting against Doug's.

I straightened up abruptly, cracking my head on the end of the table. Conversation around the table stopped, and I found myself with seven pairs of eyes looking at me.

'Sorry,' I said, and went back into the kitchen to get another beer.

A couple later, really pretty drunk by then. Didn't want to sit back down at the table, felt like walking around a bit. Besides, Janny and Becky were still in conference, Janny looking odd; Adam and Carol and Julia talking about something else. I didn't feel like butting in.

Headed off towards the tree, thinking I'd see what the kids were up to. Maybe they'd play with me for a while. Better make an effort to talk properly – didn't want Jack to see Daddy zonked. Usually it's okay, as my voice stays pretty straight unless I'm completely loaded, and as I couldn't score any coke that afternoon, that wasn't the case.

Coke? What the fuck was I talking about?

I ground to a halt then, suddenly confused. I didn't take coke, never had. Well, once, a few years back: it had been fun, but not worth the money – and an obvious slippery slope. Too easy to take until it was all gone, and then just buy some more. Plus Helena would have gone ballistic – she didn't even like me *smoking*, for God's sake.

Then I remembered her taking a cigarette earlier, and felt cold. She hadn't started smoking. That was nonsense.

So why did I think she had?

I started moving again, not because I felt I'd solved anything, but because I heard a sound. It wasn't laughing. It was more like quiet tears.

At the far end of the yard I found Jack's camp, a little clearing huddled up against wisteria that clung to the fence. I pushed through the bushes, swearing quietly.

Jack was sitting in the middle, tears rolling down his moon-like face. His check shirt was covered in dirt, the leg of his pants torn. Adam's kids were standing around him, giggling and pointing. As I lumbered towards them the little girl hurled another clump of earth at Jack. It struck him in the face, just above the eye.

For a moment I was totally unable to move, and then I lunged forward and grabbed her arm.

'Piss off, you little bastards,' I hissed, yanking them away from my son. They stared up at me, faces full of some thought I couldn't read. Then the little boy pulled his arm free, and his sister did the same. They ran off laughing towards the house.

I turned again to Jack, who was staring at the fence.

'Come on, big guy,' I said, bending down to take him in my arms. 'What was that all about?'

His face slowly turned to mine, and my heart sank at what was always there to see. The slight glaze in the eyes, the slackness at one corner of his mouth.

'Dada,' he said. 'They dirt me.'

I fell down onto my knees beside him, wrapping my arms around his thin shoulders. I held him tight, but as always sensed his eyes looking over my shoulder, gazing off into the middle distance at something no one else could see.

Eventually I let go of him and rocked to my feet again, hand held down towards him. He took it and struggled to his feet. I led him out of the bushes and into the yard.

As we came close to the tree I saw Helena and Doug approaching out the darkness. I sensed some kind of rearrangement taking place as they saw us, but couldn't work out what it might have been.

'Oh shit, what's happened now?' Helena said, reading Jack's state instantly and stepping towards us. Doug hung back, in the deep shadows.

I couldn't answer her. Partly just because I was drunk; I'd obviously over-compensated for my dealer's coke famine by drinking way more than usual. But mainly because there was something wrong with her face. Not her face, which was as beautiful as ever. Her lipstick. It was smudged all over.

'Christ, you're useless,' she snapped, and grabbed Jack's hand. I didn't watch as she hauled him back towards the house. Instead I stared into the darkness under the tree, where a faint glow showed Doug was lighting a cigarette.

'Having a good evening?' I asked.

'Oh yeah,' he said, laughing quietly. 'You guys always throw such great parties.'

We walked back to the trestle table, neither of us saying anything.

I sat down next to the girls, glanced across at Becky. She looked a lot worse than the last time we'd seen her. The chemo obviously wasn't working.

'How are you feeling?' I asked.

She looked up at me, smiled tightly. 'Fine, just fine,' she said. She didn't want my sympathy, and never had since the afternoon I'd called round at her place, looking for some company.

Behind me I heard Doug getting up and going through into the kitchen. I'd never liked Julia, nor she me, and so it would be no comfort to look round and see her eyes following her husband into the house, where Helena would already have dispatched Jack up to bed with a slap on the behind, and would maybe be standing at the sink, washing something that didn't need washing.

Instead, I watched Adam and Carol talking together. They at least looked happy.

I stood at the front door as the last set of tail-lights turned into the road and faded away. Helena stood behind me. When I turned to take her hand she smiled meaninglessly, her face hard and distant, and walked away. I lumbered into my study to turn the computer off.

Instead I found myself waking it from sleep, and clicked into my mail program. I read the letter from my sister, who seemed to be doing fine. She was redecorating her new house with her new boyfriend. I nodded to myself; it was good that things were finally going her way.

I turned at a sound behind me to find Helena standing there. She plonked a cup of coffee down on the desk beside me.

'There you go, Mister Man,' she said, and I smiled up at her. I didn't need the coffee, because I hadn't drunk very much. Sitting close to Helena all evening was still all the intoxication I needed. But it would be nice anyway.

'Good evening?' she asked, running her fingers across the back of my neck.

'Good evening,' I said, looping my arm around her waist.

'Well don't stay down here too long,' she winked, 'because we could make it even better.'

After she'd gone I applied myself to the screen, but before I could starting writing a reply to my little sis I heard Helena's voice again. This time it was hard, and came as usual from outside the study.

'Put your fucking son to bed,' she said. 'I can't deal with him tonight.'

I turned, but she was already gone. I sat with my head in

my hands for a little while, then reached out for the coffee. It wasn't there.

Then something on the screen caught my eye. Something I'd dismissed earlier. 'Read This!' it said.

As much to avoid going upstairs as anything, I double-clicked on the mail icon. A long text message burped up onto the screen, and I frowned. My killfile tests usually only ran a couple of lines. Blinking against the drunkenness slopping through my head I tried to focus on the first sentence.

I managed to read it, in the end. And then the next, and as I read all the way through I felt as if my chair was sinking, dropping lower and lower into the ground.

The message was from me. It was about Same Again, and finally I remembered.

Before I'd come home that afternoon, I'd gone to their offices in the business district. It was the second time I'd been, the first when I signed up for the service and had a preliminary backup done a year before. When I'd got up that morning, woken by Jack's cheerful chatter and feeling the warmth of Helena's buttocks against mine under the sheets, I'd suddenly realized that if there were any day on which to make a backup of my life, today was surely that day.

I'd driven over to their offices, sat in the chair and they'd done their thing, archiving the current state of affairs into a data file. A file which, as their blurb promised, I could access at any time life had gone wrong and I needed to return to the saved version.

I heard a noise out in the hallway, the sound of a small person bumping into a piece of furniture. Jack. In a minute I should go out and help him, put him to bed. Maybe read to him a little, see if I could get a few more words into his head. If not, just hold him a while, as he slipped off into a sleep furnished with a vagueness I could never understand.

All it takes is one little sequence of DNA out of place, one infinitesimal chemical reaction going wrong. That's all the difference there is between the child he was, and could have been. Becky would understand that. One of her cells had misbehaved too, like a 1 or 0 the wrong way round in some computer program.

Wet towels. Heavy rain. A leaking ceiling.

Suddenly I remembered going to a dark office on Montaigne in the wet small hours of some future morning. The strange way the man with the towel had reacted when I said I needed to do a restore from a backup they held there. And I knew what had happened. There'd been an accident.

The same rain which had totalled the car which for the moment still sat out in the drive, had corrupted the data I'd spent so much money to save.

At the bottom of the mail message was a number. I called it. Same Again's 24-hour switchboard was unobtainable. I listened to a recorded voice for a while, and then replaced the handset.

Maybe they'd gone out of business. Backing up was, after all, illegal. Too easy for criminals to leap backwards before their mistakes, for politicians to run experiments. Wide scale, it would have caused chaos. So long as not many people knew, you could get away with it. The disturbance was undetectable.

But now I knew, and this disturbance was far too great.

I could feel, like a heavy weight, the aura of the woman lying in the bed above my head. Could predict the firmness with which her back would be turned towards me, the way Doug and I would dance around each other at work the next day, and the endless drudgery of the phone calls required to score enough coke to make it all go away for a while.

'Hi Dad – you still up?'

Jack stood in the doorway. He'd taken three apples from the kitchen, and was attempting to juggle them. He couldn't quite do it yet, but I thought it wouldn't be too long now. Perhaps I would learn then, and we could do that stuff where you swap balls with one another. That might be kind of cool.

'Yep,' I said, 'but not for much longer. How about you go up, get your teeth brushed, and then I'll read you a story?'

But he'd corrupted again by then, and the apples fell one by one, to bruise on the hardwood floor. His eyes stared, slightly out of kilter, at my dusty bookcase, his fingers struggling at a button on his shirt. I reached forward and wiped away the thin dribble of saliva that ran from the bad corner of his mouth.

'Come on, little guy,' I said, and hoisted him up.

As I carried him upstairs into the darkness, his head lolling against my shoulder, I wondered how much had changed, whether in nine months the crash would still come as we drove back from a happy evening in Gainesville.

And I wondered, if it did, whether I would do anything to avoid it.

Or if I would steer the car harder this time.

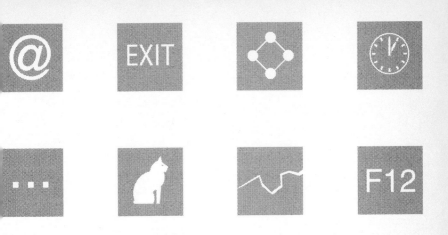

MORE BITTER THAN DEATH

'That was *bollocks*,' said Nick amiably, leaning on his cue. 'You've produced some terrible shots this evening, but that really has to take it. Go to the library, get out a book on basic physics. Start again from the ground up.'

I stepped back from the table and replied with a cheerful obscenity before taking a sip of my beer. I wasn't playing that badly on the whole, but the last couple of games had been very erratic. When I play a pool shot, it's either very good or abysmal. There doesn't seem to be a middle ground in my game, any 'fairly good' or 'not bad' shots. How I'm playing depends solely on the ratio of the sublime to the ridiculous.

'If this comes off . . .' Nick muttered, lining up an ambitious double cannon. 'You'll have confirmed your standing as the luckiest player in the cosmos,' I finished for him.

Not only did the shot not come off, it sent the cue ball clear off the table to bounce loudly on the wooden floor and rocket off towards the other side of the hall. Because I was nearest, I went after it. Players at the other tables watched impassively as I tried not to look as if I was scurrying.

The pool hall in the Archway Tavern is on the first floor, a large bare rectangular room with high ceilings that covers the area of the two bars on the floor below. There are two snooker tables and five for pool, an area of seats and tables around the nuclear-powered juke box, and a bar set into the wall near the door. Not an especially prepossessing room, in a fairly rough Irish pub (painted entirely green on the outside, just in case anyone should be in any doubt), but I'd been going there to play pool regularly for over a year, and there'd never been any trouble. While the locals are generally too taciturn to be called friendly they always seem fairly affable, and with discs full of the Fureys and the Dubliners in the juke box the atmosphere on a good night is pretty good.

The cue ball made it all the way to the far corner of the room, banging to rest under the pool table there.

'Sorry,' I said, trying not to sound too English, and crouched down to retrieve it. The two youths at the table continued playing. Reaching under, I scrabbled with my fingertips and eventually dislodged the ball. I stood up rather quickly and felt my head dizzy for a moment as I turned to head back to the other side of the room.

Then suddenly the evening, which was already fine, took a turn for the better.

They had arrived.

I walked back to our table, trying to look nonchalant, willing myself not to look back at the bar.

'Two shots,' Nick conceded.

'No, really? I had to catch a fucking bus.'

I took my time putting the cue ball in position, ostensibly lining up the next break, but in fact covertly glancing up the room. The only free table was the next but one to ours. If they were going to play pool rather than just hang around and chat with their mates near the juke box, then they would be less than five yards away.

I sent the cue ball rocketing towards a stray red near the end of the table, not really expecting it to go in. The hidden agenda of the shot was to get Nick back on the table so that I could carry on looking up the room. Unfortunately, I'd judged it too well and the ball smacked into the pocket. Nick tapped his cue sagely on the floor in approval. Choosing a shot which would allow me to glance up to the bar, I leaned over the table to see that, drinks in hand, they were indeed heading towards the free table, a gaggle of their mates in tow. I tightened up and missed an easy shot into the centre pocket.

Nick shook his head. 'Sometimes I wonder if there are two

completely different people inside you,' he said. 'A twenty-six-year-old veteran and a five-year-old paraplegic, taking alternate shots. Oh.' Noticing the new arrivals, he gave me a knowing smile. 'I see. Distraction.'

I grinned sheepishly, feeling like a fourteen-year-old accused of fancying a girl in the sixth form. This time the relationship was completely the opposite, but it still evoked the same mixed feelings of pride and utter stupidity.

The source of these emotions was the girl at the next table but one. She and her virtually identical twin sister were regulars at the Tavern, sometimes playing pool, sometimes just hanging out with a group of other locals. The twins were both tall, extremely slim and unnecessarily pretty. The difference between them was that my one had slightly more prominent cheekbones, and her long wavy brown hair was cut slightly shorter than her sister's. Her skin was pale, and her lips were red. She and her sister were, I guessed, about seventeen.

'Any day now. When you're ready.' Nick sighed theatrically.

'What?'

'It's your shot.'

Down at the other table they were racking up the balls, the second twin talking to another of the regular girl players. My one was standing slightly apart, taking her jacket off, causing a simultaneous feeling of joy and despair in me. The loose jeans she was wearing I could cope with, but her top appeared to be the upper half of a grey leotard, and clung to her like a swimming costume. It wasn't worn smugly, which made it even worse. She was just wearing it because she could, and I knew that faced with that length of slim perfection I was going to find it impossible not to keep looking at her.

'Jesus wept,' I whispered to myself, and tried to concentrate on the shot. The centre pocket pot was easy, but I had to do some work to get position on the next shot. Aiming at the bottom of the cue ball I dug in hard for maximum backspin. The white leapt neatly over the red and left the table, nearly hitting Nick in the stomach.

'Shame,' he said, when his hysterics had subsided, 'they were watching.'

I smiled at him, hoping he was joking. He didn't look as if he was, and my smile turned rather tight-lipped as I sat down to wait. Given two shots and the position of the yellows, he'd almost certainly finish up with this break. As he moved methodically round the table, potting away, I sipped my warm Budweiser and looked up the room.

Intent on her shot, she was bending over the table, her back to me. I let my eyes wander over the slim strength of her lovely long back, and felt a crushing weight of unhappiness settle into me. I felt like I was watching her through glass, staring in from the outside, as she chatted with a friend, waiting for her next shot while her sister made a creditable attempt at a long pot. Her voice, which I heard for the first time, was pure London, though the accent was pleasantly mild for the area. As she leant over to take her next shot, this time in profile, the misery I was feeling deepened. There are some things I find unbearably attractive in a woman: cheekbones, a definite nose, long and thick brown hair, slim upper arms and shoulders, a long back and willowy stomach, a small chest and graceful hands. She had every single one of these. And she was seventeen, and I was pathetic.

A resounding *thwak* signalled the end of the game as Nick drilled the black into one of the end pockets. He was having a very good evening.

'Your set-up,' I said, climbing to my feet. 'You ready for another?'

As I was waiting for attention at the bar I wandered over to the juke box and put on my two favourite songs of the time, Heart's 'Secret' and Bruce Springsteen's 'I'm on Fire'. I was obviously in a queue, however, because the next to come on was a delightful piece entitled 'Yeah Baby, Do It Again', by some American heavy metal band. Returning to the table I shook my head at Nick to signal that this wasn't my choice.

'Thought not,' he said, accepting his cider. 'Can I guess what you've put on?'

'Probably,' I grunted, and broke the pack. Nick always gives me a hard time for the songs I select, claiming that they are without exception morbid and about failed relationships. Nick is in a position to laugh about things like that, because he's happily married. He has someone who cares about him, someone to love, and he's not so fucked up that he can get obsessed with slim girls he'll never speak to who are ten years younger than he is.

As the game wore on my play improved. Reds are usually a good colour for me. The girl sat out the next game as her sister played the blonde-haired regular. She sat staring into space, semi-expertly dragging on a cigarette. I wondered what she was thinking about. I forced myself to be more cheerful, not wanting to spoil Nick's evening.

Basically, in most areas, I'm fairly together. I have a reasonable job as editor of a video trade magazine, and pick up good money on the side as a freelance journalist. I don't have that many friends, but the ones I have are good, and I'm not lonely much more often than anyone else, I don't think. Emotionally, things aren't quite so good, but I don't really want to talk about that. I've been over my last relationship in my head so many times that it's boring even to me, and I've given up hope of ever making sense of it or exorcizing it from my mind. It's no big deal, just another relationship that started off well and then took a very long time going off the rails. I was hurt, and now it's over. So what.

Nick missed an easy black and set me up nicely to take the game.

'Once more the god of pool craps on my head,' he said mildly, reaching for the chalk.

I like playing Nick because he doesn't care who wins, and for a non-competitor like me, that's essential. As I bent to take the shot the song on the juke box finished, and after a pause I heard the piano introduction and then the crashing opening chords of 'Secret'. Nick groaned from behind me.

'Not *again.*'

I smiled, feeling buoyed up by the music, and slotted the

penultimate red down. Songs about the trials of love and how much grief it is to be alive always cheer me up, and as I lined up the last red I felt my heart loosen. Mooning after a perfectly ordinary, if unusually beautiful, seventeen-year-old was beneath even my currently sterile life. I was just lonely, and being silly. Fuck it, I told myself, relax. Forget about it. As the song slammed into the first chorus I glanced up at the girl, a wry smile at myself unthinkingly on my lips.

She was looking at me.

For a long moment time stopped as our eyes met. The moment went well beyond a casual coincidence, and far into extra time. Around us the chorus raged, telling of a love that must remain a secret, ooh yeah, and still we looked down a long tunnel at each other, unblinkingly staring into each other's eyes. Her eyes were blue, and beautiful, and there were no scars round them.

'You better come quickly, Doctor. The patient's blown a fuse again.'

When I looked back after registering Nick's crack, she had turned the other way, talking to the blonde-haired girl. For a moment I doubted that it had happened, but from the tightness in my chest and the perspiration on my forehead, I knew it had. I cracked the cue ball down the table and the red zipped into the pocket as if pulled on a piece of taut elastic. The white reversed with perfect backspin and edged the black off the cushion and over a pocket.

'My friend's body has been taken over by an alien force,' Nick said, tapping his cue on the floor again, 'one that is considerably better at pool than he is.' Grinning, I ignored the open pocket and doubled the black into the opposite one instead, to Nick's good-natured chagrin.

'Flash bastard,' he muttered, slotting in another fifty-pence piece.

My streak continued and I took the next two games easily. During the first I looked up to see the two sisters in a huddle by the side of their table, and got the very clear impression that it was me they were talking about. She could, of course, be saying that the weird bloke down the end was staring at her, but 'I'm on Fire' was playing and I didn't believe she was. She had stared at me just as much as I had at her. Then, looking like someone in a video for the song, she raised her head slightly and our eyes met again. There was a faint smile curling on her lips. I was right. It was mutual.

Halfway through the second game they left the pool hall. Something immediately went out of the evening and my game lost a bit of its sparkle, but I was on enough of a roll to win. We were about to set up again when Nick noticed that it was nearly eleven and, doubtless keen to get back to Zoe, called it a night. I gave him a dose of my running joke about him having to get back before curfew, which he accepted with good grace while giving me one of his customarily alarming lifts home in his mad Mini.

While I waited for the water for a final cup of coffee to boil, I looked at my face in the bathroom mirror. It's not especially good-looking, but it's all right, apparently. I genuinely can't tell. I have greeny-brown eyes and a high forehead, prominent cheekbones and dark brown hair that insists on a slavish adherence to the laws of gravity. My lips are full, my nose is definite and my skin is generally pale. I hate my face, and have done for as long as I can remember.

The kettle in the kitchen pinged electronically to signify that it had boiled, but I ignored it for a moment, just to piss it off.

Around my right eye there are a number of scars. I don't know if you've ever noticed this, but by far the majority of people have a little scar somewhere near their eyes, the remnant of some childish fall. Most people can remember how they got them, and the ensuing frantic trip to the hospital, panicky parents and ice cream afterwards for being good. I can remember how I got mine too.

Sitting on the sofa with my coffee in the silent flat, I noticed that the answering machine was flashing. It was a message from Jo, my ex-flatmate, asking if I was doing anything tomorrow night. I called her back, knowing that she went to bed late, and arranged to play pool with her in the Archway Tavern. The girl might be there again and now that contact, however nebulous, had been made, I didn't want to miss a chance of seeing her again.

I took the remainder of my coffee to bed with me, and drank it with a cigarette, staring across the bedroom. It's far too large, the bedroom, given that nothing interesting ever happens there any more. There's a huge walk-in wardrobe down the end, crammed with my junk from the last two years, and a large dresser up against one wall. Stuck in the mirror are two photographs, one of my parents and one of Siobhan.

She left me, is what happened, if you want to know. Several times, indecisively, intermittently, and painfully. The reasons were complex and various, and not all her fault, but by any scale of reckoning she done me wrong. As I've said, I've thought about it too much now, and never expect to be able to untangle it. It isn't even the leaving that I hold against her. People fall in love, meet someone who strikes a deeper chord: that's the way life works, and I could have respected that. Siobhan didn't have the courage to do what she wanted to do, however, and so she played the percentage game with me as the comfortable option. She left, and as soon as she had gone, called me up to say she loved me. When she was with me I never had her, and when she was gone, she didn't let me go. I wanted her back, and couldn't break free, but when she came back each time it was unwillingly and incompletely, and that felt even worse. I couldn't have her, but I wasn't allowed to have anyone else. And then finally she left for good. So there you are.

I dreamed that night, of my mother. I was in our old house, looking out into the garden at night. My mother stood alone in the moonlight, her back to me, holding a long stick that looked a little like a pool cue. She turned back towards the house and when the wind moved her long brown hair from her face, I could see that she was crying. When she looked up at my window the light glinted on the tears round her eyes, making them look like shining scars.

Thursday at work was long and tedious, as Thursdays always are. The chief graphic designer on *Communiqué* is a bit too hip for his own good, and for the third week running I had to remind him with some vehemence that our first priority is getting all the words on the pages they're supposed to be on, not just making pretty pictures. I later overheard him describing me as a philistine to the chief sub-editor, so I accidentally spilt some coffee on some personal work of his he'd left lying around in the office. Just another morning in a small organization.

The afternoon was less fraught. I spent most of it at my desk, the neatness of which I know irritates the chief graphic designer immensely. By five o'clock I had nothing to do except stare at the photos I keep there – one of my parents and one of Siobhan – and so I went home early.

Jo was already there by the time I got to the Archway Tavern, and clearly somewhat relieved to see me. I've never felt directly threatened there, but I suppose for a lone non-Irish female it's probably different. Once we'd bought our drinks we set up camp round the table in the top corner. The twins weren't anywhere to be seen, which was both disappointing and somehow a bit of a relief.

Jo is actually bloody good at pool, and by nine we were fully absorbed, conversation chugging along in a pleasantly desultory fashion. We've known each other since college, and shared a platonic flat for eighteen months a couple of years ago. I think we're probably both the only person of the opposite sex we know who we can be just straightforward friends with, and that's nice.

Then at ten o'clock they came in. I was coming back from the bar with a couple more beers, and passed just in front of her, holding my shoulders back and trying to look like a potentially desirable human being. She didn't look directly at me – we were too near each other for that kind of risk at this stage – but there was a definite atmosphere as I passed. I arrived back at the table with the smell of her perfume wraith-like round my neck.

'Are you all right?' asked Jo, who didn't know anything about the twins. 'You look like you've been punched in the stomach.'

'I'm fine,' I said, and I felt it. Something was going on. The look yesterday had raised the game, and now, however tiny, something was going on. She was still seventeen and I still felt stupid, but it was exciting all the same.

I gave her time to get settled before I glanced over in their direction. By dint of an inspired potting streak Jo won the game and only as she was setting the balls up for the next did I look over.

As soon as I did, I knew something was wrong. She wasn't playing, but sitting to one side while her sister did. She wasn't staring dreamily into space as yesterday, but looking down at the floor, her expression hard. Distracted, I broke the pack badly and Jo settled down to pot some of the many available balls. The girl was still staring, and one leg was now jogging up and down in obvious anger. Maybe something had happened over in her world. Maybe it was nothing to do with me. But it didn't feel like it.

The answer came when I straightened from taking my next shot. My eyes were drawn over to their table and I saw that she was no longer staring at the floor, but over in our direction. She wasn't looking at me, however. She was staring at Jo, and her eyes were flashing, her jaw set in a tight smile. Immediately, I understood.

When Jo next passed me I took great care to stand back as far as possible from her, making it as clear as I could that we were not a couple. There were some lads in the twins' group this evening too: surely she could understand that being with a girl didn't necessarily mean that there was anything going on. As the game progressed Jo seemed almost to be conspiring against me. She was in a good mood, looking at me and laughing prettily, playfully jogging my cue and generally destroying the impression I was trying to create.

This reached a peak as I chalked up before breaking in the next game but one. I take good care of my cue. It used to belong to my father, and every inch of it, right down to the dent in the wood near the base, is very dear to me.

I'd only dared to glance across at her twice in the last fifteen minutes, and both times she was talking to someone, her back to me. Just as I was bending down to break I saw her slowly start turning towards me.

'This may help,' said Jo, and covered my eyes with her hands. Dumbfounded, I broke, and she took them away again. I couldn't believe that she had done that. We've known each other for six years and tonight of all nights she had to behave as if we were lovers. In the centre of my wildly staring gaze was the girl, and she was looking right at me. For a moment I stood still, transfixed. That's done it, I thought, that's fucked it up for good.

Then, amazingly, the girl's expression softened. Something in my face must have communicated my distress to her, and I could see that in that instant, she understood. She tilted her head on one side and looked for a moment longer, and then turned back to her sister.

They left as Jo and I finished the next game. Just before she reached the door, and without breaking her stride, she quite clearly turned and looked at me. On her face was a quizzical expression, a combination of raised eyebrow and crooked smile that I understood perfectly. I'd got away with it, but only just. Long experience with Siobhan had shown me that the longer any problem is left unsolved, the more likely it is to leave a scar. What I had to do was find some way of healing the rift.

A means of attempting that occurred to me on the way to work the next morning. What I would do was ring Nick and ask him, applying pressure if necessary, to play pool with me that evening. If she was there, and saw me playing with him again, she'd have proof that Jo didn't mean anything to me, was just another person I played pool with. We'd be free to recommence the progression that the meeting of our eyes on Wednesday night had started.

I didn't get round to calling Nick until the afternoon, because of a long and extremely acrimonious row with the chief graphic designer.

What happened was this. I walked into the office, feeling almost cheerful now that I'd thought of a way of making things up with the girl, to find that someone had been at my desk. Not only that: the person had taken the photo of Siobhan out of the frame and had torn it up. They had also taken my parents' photo out and cut the half with my mother in to pieces.

I stared at the fragments for a long time, unable to move, unable to think. It was only when I noticed that I had tears running down my face that I pulled myself up. I looked at the pieces strewn across the desk and realized that there could only be one possible culprit. The graphic designer must have found out that it was me who had spoiled his personal work, which he should on no account have been doing in office time, and this was his revenge. For slightly messing up some piece of rubbish he had taken the photos of the two people who mattered most to me in the world and cut them up with a scalpel.

I immediately confronted him, and was so worked up by then that I almost punched him in the face when he denied it. He denied even knowing it was me who had messed up his work. The argument spread into unrelated areas and within ten minutes we were standing shouting at each other. In the end he stormed out to lunch. Ignoring the covert glances of some of the other staff I sat heavily back at my desk, and tried to piece the photo of my mother back together again. I couldn't stop myself from crying, and soon I was left alone in the room. My mother died five years ago, and I still miss her every day. I loved her very much.

Nick professed himself able and willing to go out that evening, which was good. After the morning I'd had I didn't feel up to applying any pressure, and certainly didn't want to cite the real reason for my escalating interest in pool. During the day I had to try not to think too hard about the girl. In daylight the image of what I felt about her wavered, was dissolved by the vestiges of pride. I couldn't believe that I was getting myself into this state over some seventeen-year-old I'd still not spoken to. It wasn't reasonable, it wasn't normal. Only at night could I believe what I had seen in her eyes, know that a bond was forming between us, a special link.

I went home early, walked straight into the sitting room and dozed off on the sofa for a couple of hours. I hadn't been sleeping too well for the last couple of weeks, and coupled with the morning's furore it had just got too much for me.

As I struggled back towards wakefulness, aware that it had become dark outside and that I should shower and eat before Nick came, I felt the shards of a dream fade around me. I had once more been looking out of my window in the old house, the house we lived in before my mother went away. My mother was standing out in the garden again, and this time I ran downstairs and rushed outside, feeling the damp grass beneath my feet in the darkness. As I got closer she turned and I saw that again she was crying. My mother had some minor emotional problems, and seeing her crying is one of my earliest memories of her. But as I looked at her I felt my skin begin to crawl, because although it looked exactly like her, though every line, every bone was in the right place, it wasn't her. It looked as though someone of the right general shape and build had been given the world's most perfect plastic surgery until there was no surface difference, none at all. As I stood looking at her the wind whipped the hair across her face and a dog barked somewhere nearby. She was tall and very slim, my mother, and as she bent down towards me I had plenty of time to turn and run. But I didn't. I never did. I loved her. The hair cleared from her face, thrown backwards by another gust, and I saw that it wasn't my mother after all. It was her. It was the girl.

The last thing I saw as I woke up was that she wasn't crying any more. She was smiling, a hard, tight smile that I recognized from somewhere.

I stood up slowly and wandered clumsily across the room, rubbing my face with my hands. I knew I should remember that smile, but couldn't. I looked groggily over at the clock, and saw that I still had an hour before Nick was due to arrive. Shaking my head against the heavy residue of afternoon sleep I walked into the bedroom.

At first I couldn't tell what was different. After a moment I realized it was that I could see the whole of my face in the dresser mirror. And then I saw. The picture of Siobhan had been shredded, and my mother's half of the other picture was a slashed and tangled mess. The chief graphic designer passed through my mind for an instant, but I knew that it wasn't him who had done this.

On impulse I flung open the doors to the wardrobe and dropped to my knees, flinging things out behind me as I dug for the box I kept in the back. When I'd found it I sat back cross-legged and opened it on my lap, trembling.

Every photo in the box had been slashed. Every photo had either Siobhan or my mother in it, and every one had been reduced to small strips of meaningless colour. My graduation photo, with Siobhan on my arm back in the days when she loved me, was in pieces. The photo of me on my fifth birthday, sitting on my mother's lap with the bandages still round my right eye, was little more than confetti.

Spilling the petals of colour out onto the floor I lunged and stuck my hand under the bed. In a box within a box within a box I found my special photos. Nobody knew I kept them there, nobody. I opened the cigar box that should have held my favourite three photos of my mother and the best two of Siobhan, and inside was nothing but a tangle of photographic paper. They'd not been cut calmly, neatly, but mangled, ripped and gouged apart, slashed and shredded with utter hatred.

I got the message, as I sat there surrounded by ruin. I understood. There are no compromises, there is no middle ground. You are with someone, or you are without them. You either have them or you don't, and if you have them, you have them and them alone. There can be no one else, ever. This was a warning, a message, a sign of the way things would stand. This was no normal girl, and if I was to have her, it was to the exclusion of anyone else, past, present or future.

The phone rang. Without thinking, out of pure reaction to the jangling sound, I snatched the bedroom extension. It was Nick. He couldn't make it. He was doing something else. He'd forgotten. He was sorry. Monday?

I put the phone down, and stood up, grabbing my coat from the wardrobe. I had to turn up, to show that the message was received and understood. If I had to do it alone, so be it. I called a cab and waited outside for it, swinging my cue case impatiently. It was full dark by then, and a dog barked somewhere nearby.

It was crowded in the Archway Tavern. By the time I got there it was after nine, and on a Friday it's just swinging into its busiest period by then. All the tables were taken, the air was laden with smoke, and the twins were nowhere to be seen. I bought a beer and waited, sitting near one of the tables at the far end of the bar.

They came in half an hour later, surrounded by their friends. The blonde pool-playing girl was there, as were the two lads from the previous night. I fought down the urge to get straight up and go across. That wasn't the way to do it. There is a right way to do everything, and everything must be done in the right way. I hadn't eaten all day, and the beer was going straight to my head. It was very noisy and hot and smoky and there were people all around shouting happily at each other and I sat there with my cue case on my lap waiting for the right time, waiting for the sign.

Then suddenly a ray of quiet cut across the bar as the song on the juke box ended. After a moment of relative silence I heard a distinctive piano riff, and then smiled as a familiar guitar chord scythed through the smoke. It was 'Secret'. That was it.

That was the sign.

I stood up and walked down towards the other end of the bar. The twins were standing in a gaggle round a pool table there. I worked my way round the back of the group, feeling my heart swell. I would let her know that I understood. When I was behind her I tapped her on the shoulder. She turned and looked at me. For a second, I thought I read something in her eyes, and then all I saw was distaste.

'Hello,' I said.

'Who the fuck are you?'

The others in the group were staring at me. I smiled at them and then turned back to her.

'I got your message. I understand.'

'What message? What the fuck are you talking about?'

I saw the others' faces again. Some of them were looking embarrassed. The blonde pool player was giggling behind her hand. The twin sister was looking at the girl, eyebrows raised, shaking her head. I began to feel very bad.

'You know what I mean. The photos.'

She gave an angry and embarrassed laugh, and shook her head.

'I don't know what you're talking about. Now piss off.'

'Yeah. Piss off.' This was from one of the lads. Maybe he fancied her. He reached out and shoved my chest. I wasn't ready for it, and fell backwards, banging into a table. The group turned its back on me and laughed. The blonde girl kept giggling, giggling.

I staggered upright, feeling the chorus of 'Secret' reverberating through my bones. The barman looked at me sternly, but it was okay. I was going.

In the car park I smoked some cigarettes and waited for an hour. Just after ten the group came out, and the girl separated from the rest of them and headed down the Holloway Road. I followed her, pausing for a moment to pick something up from outside a house.

I understood. I had made a mistake. I had brought it into the open in front of her friends, in front of people who knew nothing about it, who didn't know that she was special, that she was capable of unusual things. When I saw which house she was going into I went round the back and carefully climbed up the drainpipe to the balcony.

I understand things, you see. I learn very quickly. When I was four I dropped a bottle of milk on the kitchen floor. When my mother saw what I had done she got out my father's cue and calmly screwed the two halves together. Then she swung the cue with all her strength and smashed me round the face with it. That's how I got one of the scars round my eye. I told you I could remember. When I was six, I said something wrong and she grabbed my hair and banged my head into the corner of the kitchen table six times, once for each year. I had to go into hospital that time, with concussion. I didn't tell anyone what had happened. It was our secret.

I never dropped the milk again, and I never said anything wrong. I learn.

A light went on inside as the girl went into the kitchen. She opened the fridge and there was milk inside. She drank some and then put the bottle back. I eased the latch on the balcony door open and stepped soundlessly into the flat. As she came out of the kitchen I could see her face, and she was smiling a tight, hard smile. I remembered it now. It was the smile my mother had when she picked up the piece of broken glass from the milk bottle to run it across my stomach. It was the smile she had when she pulled my head up from banging it on the table and pushed her fingernail into the new gash by my right eye. It was the smile she had the first and last time she met my first girlfriend.

The girl walked into the living room and sat on the sofa without turning the light on. She was waiting for me. She knew I was coming.

The only girlfriend I had before Siobhan was called Sally. She went to the same school as me, and we went to the films a couple of times. Then I brought her home to meet Mum and Dad. Dad was in the garden so we went into the kitchen first to meet Mum. She was sitting at the kitchen table. There was a milk bottle on the table. When she saw us she gave that tight hard smile and stood up. I introduced them to each other, but I don't think I did it very well. I was distracted. I thought I could see blood on the corner of the kitchen table.

'So this is Sally,' said Mother, leaning back against the table, arms folded.

'Yes. Hello,' said Sally, smiling sweetly.

Moving carefully, I edged closer to the living room. I could hear the girl humming, and the tune was 'I'm on Fire'. She had sent her twin off with the others so she could be here alone.

Mother smiled at Sally for a moment, and then gestured me to come and stand next to her.

'She's a bit fat, isn't she?' Mother said, putting her arm round my waist. 'He normally prefers slimmer girls, don't you?' She turned to me, smiling, and ran a finger along the biggest scar by my eye. 'Tall and slim with long brown hair.' Then she pulled my head towards hers. Sally backed out of the kitchen as my mother pushed her tongue into my mouth, sucking my lips and sliding her hand up under my shirt. She pushed herself up against me and laughed as Sally ran out of the house. I never spoke to Sally again. Then Mother bit my face and shoved me away from her. Off-balance, I fell and banged my face on the side of the fridge. That's how I got my final scar. I learnt. I understood. I couldn't have her, but I couldn't have anyone else either.

I walked into the living room. The girl pretended to be surprised to see me, even screamed a little, but I wasn't embarrassed any more. I knew how things worked, knew that this had to remain a secret between us. I pulled my cue out from behind me and belted her across the face with it. She went down onto the floor. She tried to speak but her nose was broken and blood was running into her mouth. I couldn't hear what she was saying, but it didn't matter, because I knew what the score was, and I was doing what I was supposed to. I didn't need instructions. I smashed the milk bottle I'd picked up on the Holloway Road across her forehead, and pushed the broken neck into her right eye. Now she had some scars, and I pushed my fingers deep into them, feeling the bone beneath, feeling what Mum had felt. I pushed my tongue into her mouth, sucking her lips, and slid my hand up her shirt. She struggled as I pushed the bottle into her stomach, and screamed as best she could as the soft skin there punctured and my hand fell in. I knew there wasn't that much time so I pulled my hand back out and linked it with the other one round her throat. I put my face as close to hers as I could as I squeezed, watching the blood from her scars trickle into her eyes and down her cheek.

As she gasped I looked up for a moment, looked at the room, the chairs, the carpet. This was our place now, somewhere only she and I had been. Blood and saliva ran out of her nose and mouth as she choked and I put my cheek right next to her mouth, waiting to see if I could tell.

And I could. I knew which was the last breath, I could feel it on my face, and I sucked it up into my body. I held her for a while, rocking her close, and we shared a happiness that I cannot describe, that is impossible to explain. She'd needed to be the only one, to have me completely, and she did. As we sat there we were the only two people in the world, and I thanked God she'd had the ingenuity and the magic to give me a message I could understand. This place would never stop being ours, and its power would never fade. I felt her slimness against me, and pushed my hands through her long brown hair, looking at the scars we shared.

DIET HELL

WHAT YOU MAKE IT

Jeans, is how it started.

About a year ago, I'm having problems buying a simple pair of blue jeans. For years I'd been a Gap man, then I discovered Calvin Klein, which frankly are a better cut. I'd been buying CKs for about three years when suddenly they stopped working for me. Didn't fit as well as they should.

I keep buying new pairs, hoping I'll find some that do, but I don't. Then one day I'm in a store, still searching for that elusive batch which have been cut the way they used to be, but they don't have my size. I'm looking for 30 waist, 30 leg, but all they have is 32 waist. So I think shit, I really need some new jeans, I'll try them on anyway. And guess what – they fit.

In other words, I'm now a 32 waist, is what the jeans are saying.

Now I don't mind this too much. Hell, I've been a 30 waist since I was twenty, and that's twelve years; figure sooner or later I'm going to go up a size. It's in the nature of things.

I go home with my new jeans, take the others back to the stores if I've still got the receipts, or throw them away if I haven't, and everything's cool again jean-wise.

Then nine months later, Calvin Klein start cutting the jeans weird again. Don't fit the way they should.

I muse on this for a while. Couple months, in fact.

Then one dread afternoon I go back to the store, stand in front of the 34 waist pile for a while. I grab a pair, put them back. This is a big step here, and I don't want to make it. But I pick 'em up again, buy 'em, take 'em home.

Guess what? Heart-in-elevator time. They fit.

Not perfectly: truth be told I'm probably more of a 33 and

a half than a 34. But the cut is back again, and I have to face facts. Basically, from here on in, if I want my jeans to fit I'm going to be walking up to that 34-inch pile.

Now this I'm not too happy about. Like I say, after ten years, you expect a change, especially if you like to eat and drink like I do. And fail to exercise, like I do. Exercise? Excuse me? Screw that. The thought of exercise makes me feel so tired I just flop right down on the couch and turn on the TV. So I can see there's going to be a trade-off. But another two inches in less than a year? This is not good. A 34 waist is a bad thing. It's in the Bible.

I try to find a mental workaround. Maybe, I think, this is just my body settling into its next phase. Maybe I'm going to be 34 for the next ten years. 34 at forty? That's not too shabby.

It nearly works. But there's a nagging voice in the back of my head. Maybe this is just the start of it, it says – and at this rate of progress, it's not going to be long before you're going to be moving along *another* pile.

That made me really stop and think a moment. I've *never* bought jeans – or any other type of trouser, for that matter – at a waist size with a 6 in it. Last time there was a 6 in the number was when I was a 26, and back then the sizes came in small, medium and large and my mother was doing the buying. I've never bought no 6-suffixed trouser, and I wasn't going to start now.

I turned the TV off, stood up, and got to it.

I started doing a little running. I went to the gym. I dropped my beer consumption back down to the level of a normal human being, and then cut it out altogether. I ate healthy food, and not so damned much of it.

Sorta.

The thing is, I did all this apart from a beer here and a beer there, and apart from skipping the run every now and then. Most days, in fact. I mean, running is dumb. Animals only do it when they're frightened, right? And why do you think that is? Because it's no fun at all. I didn't really join a gym either: they're real expensive and full of body Nazis. And shit – what's the point of being alive if you can't have a halfpounder with cheese when you feel like it, and a couple beers to wash it down? I mean, really? And do I have to spend the rest of my *life* dieting the whole time? Is this a reasonable way to live?

No. I don't think so.

It's my body's fault, I decide. It's reached a certain age, and it's tired of being trim. Probably even if I kept doing the good stuff it's just going to do its own thing.

So I come at the problem a different way. What I want, I realize, is the body I used to have back when I could eat what the hell I liked, and do no exercise, and my body would just happily metabolize all that shit away without me having to do anything about it. I don't want this diet and exercise crap: I just want the body I had before.

Then I get an idea. If I want that body, I just got to go back and get it.

So I build a time machine.

It wasn't so hard. Just muse on magnetism and tachyons a while and you'll be on the right lines. I cracked the basic principles on paper, then went down to Radio Shack and Toys R Us and Moss Bros, bought what I needed, and hacked the thing together in a couple evenings.

When I finished I got a copy of that day's paper, put it on the temporal diffusion plate. I set the dials, and pressed the button. The paper disappeared.

Then I remembered that six years ago, walking into that very room, I had found a paper with a date from the future on it. I was kind of drunk at the time, and don't remember what I did with it. Probably threw it away. It freaked me a little.

So I know the machine functions. Now I have to work out how to use it. I don't want to actually go back in time, you see: the early nineties weren't that special a period for me. Or the late eighties, come to that. Plus I've got an okay job these days and I'm halfway through a rerun of the last series of *Friends* and I want to see what happens.

So I realize that what I actually want, once I sit down and define my goals properly, is that my body's *nature* should go back in time say, five years, while both it and my mind stay right where they is. Be free, in fact, to travel forward in time the old-fashioned way, at a rate of one day every 24 hours.

So I check this idea out. I do an experiment first, because I'm a cautious man. I get one of the houseplants which is looking a little sorry for itself and like it could do with a new lease of life, and I send its nature back three months – to just after I bought it.

After I press the button the plant shimmers for a moment, and then suddenly it's looking bright and perky, like it used to.

I'm jubilant, obviously.

Then it occurs to me it was a crap experiment. Sure, the plant's body has gone back to an earlier state, while remaining rooted in the present – which has got to be enough to win me an award somewhere all by itself. But because it's a plant, and thus not much of a conversationalist, I've got no way of telling what happened to its mind. Did *it* stay in the present, or has the plant reverted to speaking plant baby talk and thinking the colour pink is cool?

I may be a tad chubby, but I'm definitely cautious. I needed another experiment. I drink beer for a while, which always makes me think better, and then it comes to me. I've got a dog, called Max. He's a great dog, but he's old. He doesn't hear as well as he used to, and his back legs are getting vague. If anyone could do with a body resurrection, he's got to be first in the queue. Ahead of me even, because my back legs work just fine.

So I stir the hound from where he's asleep in front of the fire, and I get his dog treats down from the shelf. Even at his advanced age this is news worth taking notice of, and he wakes right up and follows me around. I hide the box of treats under the cushion on the chair, making sure he sees me doing it, then I grab him, lift him over to my time machine, and put him down on the plate.

Set the dial for five years back. Press the button.

Shimmer.

Max is five years younger. He comes bounding off the plate, looking very pleased with himself. And then, and this is the cool part, he heads straight for the chair, sticks his nose under the cushion and turns it over. Finds the treats, chews them open.

I let him have half the box.

By this time it's late, and I've had maybe three six-packs of beer. I go to bed, knowing that tomorrow I'm going to have the body I always wanted. Well, maybe not always wanted, because I don't recall being that psyched with it at the time, but that's because I didn't realize what I had. It was good enough then, and that's good enough for me now.

I wake up early the next morning, because there's a weird yipping sound next to my ear. I open my eyes and see a puppy sitting on the blanket right in front of me, trying to lick my nose. At first my muddled brain wonders how the hell it got in the house, and then I recognize Max and leap out of bed like someone cattle-prodded my nuts. I run downstairs, the puppy Max still yapping away and trying to bite my heels in play, like he used to about ten years ago.

Downstairs on the table the plant has almost gone. But not quite. There's a seed lying there. I know shit about horticulture, so I couldn't swear to it, but it looked like the kind of seed which might have grown into the plant I'd owned the day before.

I played with Max for a while, but after a while his little eyes closed, and then he became a curly foetus. Got smaller still, and smaller, till I couldn't even see him any more. I guess the last thing was an egg and one lucky sperm, and then he was gone.

I was glad I'd decided to leave my trip overnight.

I went back to the drawing board, in theory and practice. I tweaked the machine a little and then tried again with next door's cat, but the little thing got younger even faster than Max had done. I tried blipping it *forward* in time at the last minute, see if that made a difference: but all that happened was the cat disappeared for an hour, then reappeared, having gotten even younger in the meantime. I futzed around a little more, then tried again, with the Great Dane from across the road. Same outcome. Except it took longer. And it bit me.

Once the body's nature had been sent back in time, it kept just slipping further back.

Now at this point the whole thing is fucked up and costing me a fortune in replacement pets, plus all the stress is making me drink more beer and eat like a hog, and the cut on those 34-inch waists seems to be going a little haywire.

Luckily, I'm standing in front of the mirror one night, thinking, '36. 36. Fucking 36 . . .' when I realize that's the answer.

I'm not just dealing with time here. There's a matter of *space*.

The 'one constraint' approach wasn't working. Max knew where the box of treats was until he was the size of my thumb, but that wasn't a lot of help to him. Or to me. You can't go walking into a good men's store and buy jeans when you look two years old and are getting smaller in front of the assistant's eyes. Trust me, no reputable department store will stand for that kind of thing.

But what if I locked down two constants? What if I kept the mind latched in place, and threw a physical limitation in too, like maintaining the length of my body? If I made it so my body couldn't get any shorter, then it had to stop going back in time when I reached my current exalted height of 5 feet 10 inches, say when I was in my late teens. My mind stays where it is, my body goes as far back in nature as possible while keeping the same length, but remains locked here in time.

Cool.

I hit the sums again, and by this time the math *is* kind of hairy. I'm way past tachyons and am getting upside charmed quarks and shit. I didn't want my face to get younger, or people might think something weird was going on. So I had to factor in getting my head to stay where it was in time, while getting the rest of my body to go back, but remaining the same length. This is math with big fucking wheels on, I'm telling you.

But I cracked it. I cracked that equation wide open. It's truly astounding what a man will do to avoid going jogging or giving up his Miller time.

By this time I've run out of neighbourhood pets, and anyway I'm getting desperate and wearing my 34s with the button and half the fly undone. So I sit myself on the plate, turn the dial. In the second I pressed the button I realized I was going to have to throw away all my new jeans and go out and buy 30 inchers, which was going to cost well over 200 bucks, but the thought just made me smile.

I felt weird for a second, and I guess I must have shimmered.

Then suddenly there's enough room in my pants for two people, and even my shirt feels loose. I got off the plate, went and looked in the mirror. It worked. I'm slim again. Took me two months of leisure time, and cost nearly four hundred bucks in parts and another eighty in replacement pets, but it worked.

Except in one niggling regard.

About a week afterwards, I noticed that my back was looking a little hairy. I figure what the hey, maybe some hormonal thing.

Then it started getting harder to hold things. My thumb seemed to be going a little weird, not as opposable as it used to be.

There were a couple of days when it looked like there was some kind of tail deal developing. That passed off, and the hair went away. My skin started getting a little scaly instead.

I'm still the same height.

But now I've got these, like, fins.

THE OWNER

When she realized she'd been staring at the flame from her lighter for more than five minutes, spinning the wheel time and time again in a mindless daze, Jane decided it was time to go to bed. She glanced at her clock on the filing cabinet – 12.35 a.m. – then let her head loll back, listening to the bones click in her neck and trying to summon up the energy to move. The flat's owner, a Mr Gillack, had wallpapered the ceiling and it was coming apart in a line down the middle. There was a crack in the plaster by the window, the baby sister of another running down the wall by the kitchen.

It cost £230 a week to live here. £1.36 an hour. Jesus Christ. Just having a *bath* was 60p.

While she waited for the computer to finish juggling 0's and 1's she stood with her mug at the window, looking down into the garden of the flat below. Thin moonlight glinted off a few pieces of iron furniture. One of the white chairs had been half-painted black in a desultory way, making it look like a frozen Dalmatian. The set looked like a tableau, the kind of thing the self-proclaimed avant garde at college would have celebrated as subconscious art. Unconscious shite, Jane had always felt.

Jane had been living in the building at 51, St Augustine's Road for two weeks, but still hadn't spoken to the young couple who owned the ground-floor flat. She hadn't spoken to anyone in the building, in fact. They never seemed to be in. Mail came and went from the downstairs hallway, and sometimes she heard voices and thumps at night from the flats above and opposite. That was all. It was like living in the *Marie Celeste*, but without the view.

As she walked across to the tiny kitchen to rinse her mug, the floorboards creaked massively. The boards were right at the top of the list of things which most irritated her about her new flat, along with the tiny kitchen full of hideous 1980s cutlery. Her mug was the only thing in there which was hers.

When she walked back out, the floorboards in the centre of the living room squealed extravagantly again. 'At least I don't live underneath,' she muttered, suddenly feeling a little better. It really was time to go to bed. If she kept staying up so late she was bound to get tired, and if she was tired she was bound to feel grumbly. There was no point doing that. Upwards and onwards.

In the hallway she clicked the catch down, then pushed it again as hard as she could, counting quickly to eight out loud. It was a source of more than a little irritation to her that she seemed to feel compelled to do this. She wasn't especially concerned about the prospect of intruders, and the house's main door was double-locked. So why this big thing over the lock?

She pushed down on the catch once more, and counted to eight again, twice, maintaining the pressure throughout. Then she twisted the knob hard, reassuring herself that the door was indeed secure. It was, not surprisingly, but she twisted it again, counting to eight three more times to make sure.

In the bedroom she undressed quickly and hopped beneath the duvet. She smoked her customary final cigarette propped up on one elbow, looking at her room. She hadn't got round to moving any of the furniture around in it, simply stowing her clothes and leaving it at that. It was the biggest room in the small flat, unhelpfully. She would have preferred an extra couple of feet on the living room. A large bedroom seemed too much like a taunt.

Catching yet another negative thought romping through her head, Jane stuck out a foot and tripped it up. Christ, she thought, what a wingebag. Shut up and go to sleep.

She rolled onto her side and snuggled up into the duvet. At least the pillows were good and thick.

A few minutes later she was on the edge of sleep when she heard a creaking sound. When it came again, louder this time, her eyes flicked wide open. She stared at the wall, listening. The creak had sounded as if it was coming from the hallway.

Then voices boomed from the hallway outside the door, and the light in the corridor flicked on, sending shadows through the pane of glass over her front door. The boards obviously stretched from her hallway into the corridor. The people returning to the flat opposite had set them off. That was all.

Jane closed her eyes and headed back towards sleep.

She felt much better when she got up the next morning, and determined to shape up. It was pointless dwelling on negative things. There was no problem in the world which could be solved by feeling depressed about it, and the world was a much drabber and more dangerous place if you allowed yourself to feel down.

This state of Genial Positiveness took a heavy knock when she discovered that there was no hot water. Again. Swearing vigorously, she turned the tap off and stalked into the kitchen to boil the kettle.

Before leaving the flat she stood on the creaking floorboards in the hallway for a moment, checking the lock. It seemed fine. Reassuringly sturdy.

A man in overalls was touching up the paint on the steps outside the house. She wondered briefly who'd hired him, and then dismissed the thought.

When she walked into reception at FreeDot Communications, Whitehead was standing in the middle of the main office area smugly surveying his empire. On seeing Jane he stared theatrically at his watch.

'Bright and early this morning,' he beamed, surprising her. She'd been expecting a dose of his running joke about part-timers sneaking in at the last moment. Then she realized it was only 9.50, and that she was ten minutes ahead of schedule.

'Keep forgetting I don't have to leave home so early.'

'How is the new flat? Compact and bijou?'

'Compact, mainly. Compact and expensive.'

Whitehead glided alongside Jane as she walked down the corridor, heading towards his own spacious lair at the far end. 'Ought to buy, you know,' he opined. 'Buying's the thing.'

'So everyone tells me,' said Jane. They did, and it was beginning to piss her off.

They paused briefly outside the door to Jane's room. 'I'll pop in a bit later,' said Whitehead. 'See how you're getting on.' Then he ducked into his own office, where his phone was bleating. He spent most of the day murmuring into it, reassuring people that the association he ran really did have a purpose. Up until recently Jane had been his right-hand person in that endeavour, and it wasn't something she missed.

Walking into her room, she took her filofax out and got straight to phoning Klass 1. It was only as she sat listening to the phone ringing that she noticed something had happened to the office. A desk had been placed along the window wall, and a computer sat squarely on its empty surface. Not only that, but one of her shelves had been unceremoniously cleared, its contents stuffed into crevices in the shelf above. Jane reached out and pulled one of her software manuals from where it had been wedged. The cover was crumpled and torn.

When Victor – the tall and elegant Indian half of the double act that was Klass 1 Accommodation – eventually answered, Jane was too distracted to be properly cross about the hot water. The letting agent expressed sympathy, tutted, and promised to get something done about the boiler that very day. Jane replaced the phone, then went back to frowning as she took in the room once more.

As she stood in the kitchen area, waiting for the kettle to boil and smoking her third cigarette of the day, she was joined by Egerton. Her heart sank, as always.

'Morning!' he sang, rosy-cheeked face beaming with idiot good humour. 'And how are you!'

Jane had tried long and hard to work out quite why Egerton

irritated her so much. Her provisional conclusion was that it was partly his continual chirping banter, partly the fact that he swanned about the place as if he owned it, partly that he had a ten-word job title which didn't actually define whatever it was he spent most of the day avoiding doing, and partly that his hair was so bloody curly. But mainly it was just that he was incredibly irritating.

Egerton yanked the lid off the kettle and peered into it, checking the amount of water inside. He looked like he was appearing in a pantomime for intellectually challenged children. Satisfied, he nodded curtly, slammed the lid back on, and went back to beaming at Jane.

'How was your weekend?' he shouted.

'Fine,' she replied, dismissing a conversational sally that had palled for her after the first fifty or so Monday mornings she'd spent at FreeDot. 'I couldn't help noticing that there appears to be another desk in my office.'

'That's right,' Egerton confirmed cheerily, nodding several times, as if she'd complimented him on something.

After a pause in which Jane realized that he really didn't understand the subtext of her observation, she continued. 'Why?'

'You're going to have company. Didn't Whitehead tell you?'

'No.'

Egerton waggled his eyebrows at her, still beaming, and then sailed off down the corridor just as Whitehead emerged from his office.

'I gather I'm going to be sharing my office,' she said.

'That's right.' Whitehead nodded. 'Bit of a reshuffle after the staff meeting on Friday. Decided to reorganize things a little, maximize resources. Getting a bit crowded in the main office, so . . .'

He trailed off smoothly, as if there was no more to be said. Making an effort to speak as conversationally as possible, Jane pressed him. 'But why my office? It's not the largest.'

'True, but you are only here three days a week now, and not really a member of staff any more, so . . .'

Jane nodded, to show she understood. She understood all right. After three years of doing half of Whitehead's job for him she was now just a freelancer, and bought labour sat where it was put and did what it was told. 'I see. So who . . .?'

'Camilla.'

'*Camilla?* But she's only been with us, with you, for three months.'

'I know, but she's coming on very well. And she's used a Macintosh before, so . . .'

'Isn't she mainly a secretary though?' Mainly an ambitious, flirtatious and smug little smartarse, was what she meant, but tried not to let it show.

Whitehead finished manufacturing his coffee and floated back in the direction of his office, where the phone was once more ringing. 'Won't do any harm to have someone else who knows how to run up a bit of design. Can't have all our eggs in one basket, can we?'

By the time she was standing on the Northern Line platform, waiting to go home, Jane had calmed down. The buzzing irritation that had built up in her during the day had burst the moment she left FreeDot, leaving her feeling empty and tired.

Sodding Camilla. Minutes after her conversation with Whitehead, the secretary/flavour of the month employee had slipped into Jane's office and settled herself at the new desk. She then spent the rest of the day alternating between typing fantastically loudly, and looking over Jane's shoulder as she finished the layout for the inside of FreeDot's new brochure. At one point she had asked Jane if there wasn't an easier way of doing the task she was currently engaged in. The politeness of Jane's reply, Jane felt, should have shut the girl up for the rest of the week. But it didn't.

As she sweltered on the tube, buffeted by meaty bodies and smothered by lank hair, Jane tried to rationalize her feelings about the girl. She was nineteen. She wanted to get on. There was nothing wrong with that. The fact that her star was in the ascendant at the same time as Jane's was taking a nosedive was not her fault. Jane closed her eyes and tried to tune out the people around her, tried to grope once more for Genial Positiveness.

When she opened them, the tube was stationary at Mornington Crescent. On impulse she got out.

Walking down the road she fought hard against the feeling that this probably wasn't a good idea. They were supposed to be friends, after all. And friends called on each other, didn't they? She stopped at the flower seller at the corner and bought a small bunch of irises.

At the entry phone she pushed down another surge of doubt, and pressed Andrew's bell. After a pause a disembodied voice said something, accompanied by the familiar whine of feedback.

'Hi,' she said brightly, her heart beating irritatingly hard, 'it's me.' There was a pause. 'Jane,' she added, less brightly.

'Oh, right, hi.'

'Are you going to let me in then?'

'Yeah . . . yeah, sorry.'

The lock buzzed and she pushed the door open.

His door was ajar when she reached the top of the stairs and she walked straight in. 'I picked up some flowers,' she said, smiling, 'Because I know you never bother . . .'

Andrew was standing awkwardly by the door, hands thrust deep into his pockets. Sitting on the sofa was a tall and deeply tanned girl, dressed in a racing green suit that went perfectly with her carelessly blonde hair.

Jane faltered, and came to a halt a couple of feet into the room. 'Well,' said Andrew heartily, 'Jane, Nikki, Nikki, Jane.'

'Hello,' the girl said, and before she dropped her head Jane noticed just how nauseatingly perfect her cheekbones were.

'Nikki was just passing,' Andrew volunteered with elaborate blandness. Jane nodded. She was looking at the table under the window. On it stood Andrew's large vase, filled with a huge bunch of uncut flowers, still in their paper. The same paper that was wrapped around hers.

'Well,' Nikki said into the silence. 'I must be going.'

When Andrew returned from seeing her to the door he went to some lengths to convince Jane that Nikki really had just dropped in. He needn't have bothered: Jane believed him. Her shock had simply been that of seeing her for the first time, seeing the girl who previously had only been the shadowy cause of thirty different kinds of hurt. Now that Nikki didn't have Andrew either it didn't seem to matter so much.

Yes it did, actually.

And he'd lied. Nikki *was* more attractive than her.

The conversation limped along for a while. At first she said her flat was great, then admitted how much she hated it, how tired she was of living between someone else's walls, surrounded by someone else's furniture. Of hiring her life. When Andrew asked her why she didn't buy somewhere she couldn't help reminding him that she'd wanted to. She'd wanted to buy somewhere with him.

Each time she said something like that he sat back with a patient expression which seemed to be saying he was doing his best in the face of difficult odds. And each time she brought herself to say something that wasn't small talk she felt a twist of resentment. He didn't deserve to hear about her feelings. He wasn't close enough to her any more.

In the end she stood up. 'This was a mistake,' she said firmly, and shook her head when he halfheartedly disagreed. 'I'm obviously not ready for friendship yet. I'll try again later.'

It wasn't until she was at the door that she noticed she was still clutching her bunch of irises. She thrust them at him.

'Here,' she said. 'To add to your collection.'

She spent the evening on the sofa pretending to read, but really just trying not to think. Whenever her mind drifted from the words in front of her, her head was suddenly full of pictures, fragments of imaginary scenes. Nikki, laughing, seen in profile against the white wall of Andrew's flat. Nikki, holding something playfully out of reach, and Andrew's hand and wrist as he stretched for it.

Each time Jane shook herself away from the images, her eyes searched around the room for something to hold them, something to bring her back into herself. But there was nothing there. Her books and her objects were like moss on a pavement, toys in an empty playground. Not meant, or meaningful. All they did was accentuate how much the place wasn't hers, how much it was the owner's. It was as if he'd seeped into the walls.

The phone rang, surprising her so much she cried out. She leapt across to it, heart thumping. It was for Mr Gillack. The owner. She gave the caller Klass 1's number and clunked the phone bad-temperedly back down.

It took her five tries at the lock before she was satisfied that evening. She pushed down the catch and counted ploddingly to eight, leaning down on every number. She did it again, and then once more, twisting the knob so hard her knuckles went white. She got as far as the bedroom door and then had to go back again. She undid the lock, showed herself it was open, and then pushed the catch down, watching the bolt slide through the crack between the door and the frame. Then she pushed it down hard for two more counts of eight. She knew it was no good asking herself why she did this. It was better to just get on with it.

When she opened the wardrobe to hang up her blouse something in the back made her start. Then she realized it was just Mr Gillack's most hideous possession, a large champagne bottle with a huge frond of pampas grass sticking out of it, which she'd chucked into the back of the wardrobe within ten minutes of moving in.

She moved one of her coats to hide it more thoroughly.

In the morning, she spent a good fifteen minutes under the shower, braising her skin, waking herself up.

She felt better. It was time to accept that Andrew was no longer part of her life. He wasn't even going out with the girl he'd been unfaithful to her with. It was over, history. Not even very interesting history, she decided: more like the history of welding. She was squeezing the soap so hard in her hand that on one particularly dramatic sweep up her arm it squirted out and ricocheted off the tiles on the wall to smack her in the chest. For a moment she felt like a hurt child, as if the world had unexpectedly slapped her, and then she burst out laughing.

By the time she was finishing her tea and simultaneously slipping on her shoes, she felt positive enough to even wonder if her lock ritual was something to do with the last year. She could remember the night Andrew had told her about Nikki, her feeling of complete and utter shock in the face of something so unexpected, so much at odds with the way she thought things had been. When you believed you knew your world and suddenly found out that you didn't know anything at all, maybe you came to doubt your own perception, even distrust your memory. Maybe you had to keep suspecting things just for your own peace of mind, then keep reassuring yourself again and again through endless rituals of self-protection.

Remembering for once that she lived closer to the centre now, Jane glanced towards the filing cabinet to check the time. The clock wasn't there. Puzzled, she slowly panned round the room until she found it. It was on the bookshelf. Shaking her head at her own absent-mindedness, she returned it to its proper place and left for work.

When she arrived at FreeDot Jane went straight to the kitchen to make her first cup of coffee. The Northern Line had pulled off one of its occasional bouts of suspicious efficiency and she was both early and feeling relaxed. Perhaps today she would be able to make an effort, get Camilla on her side.

Then she passed her office.

Her machine was on, and Camilla, a model of bright young ambition, was sitting at it, manual in hand.

Jaw clenched, Jane stood over Camilla for almost a minute before the girl noticed, so absorbed was she in invading someone else's territory. When she eventually registered her presence she smiled without a trace of guilt and moved, rather than retreated, back to her own desk.

Jane sat down, turned her back on her, and started work to a soundtrack of incessant typing.

The morning passed slowly in a low monotone of boredom. Halfway through, the phone rang, and Jane reached out without looking. When her hand felt the cradle the sound of typing had stopped, and the phone was no longer there.

'FreeDot,' sang Camilla. 'Certainly. May I say who's calling?' She held the call and said, unnecessarily loudly, 'It's for you Jane. A *personal* call.'

Jane took the phone. She found that it was Lucy on the line before she noticed that the din of typing had not recommenced. She turned to Camilla, who was covertly watching her, and the girl started to type immediately.

She wanted to talk to Lucy – an old friend and someone who might understand the way she was feeling – but not with Camilla in the background. It made her too conscious that this was office time. Instead she arranged to call her in the evening and settled back once more to her screen. The new FreeDot corporate brochure was still at least a day's work away from completion, and each time she looked at it she felt an increasing sense of dull frustration, bored beyond belief at the task of designing yet another leaflet saying the same things in the same way for the same organization. If she did anything unconventional it would be rejected by one of the innumerable committees, but if it looked the same as last time it would seem that anyone could do her job. She couldn't afford for it to look that way, especially now.

Egerton popped his head in during the afternoon. Grinning inanely, he asked Camilla if she'd like a cup of tea.

'Hmm, lovely,' she replied, turning and favouring him with a winning smile. Egerton disappeared. Then a beat later his head reappeared, less energetically this time.

'Jane?' he said.

*   *   *

She stopped at Sainsbury's on the way home, and struggled back up Agar Grove with a heavy bag in each hand, sure that her arms were actually lengthening. The bags were full of things she liked to eat, including a tray of fresh brownies. Standing at the checkout she'd been filled with a complex mixture of feelings: guilt at buying so much fattening food, and a sad defiance. She could afford to put on a few pounds – and after all, who was there to care? If no one else was going to spoil her, she'd do it herself.

Some phantom or shade which inhabited the house liked to sort the mail in the morning, and when she stood outside the door to her flat, fumbling for her keys, she saw that a pile of letters had been propped up against her door. It was all for the owner, apart from a Barclaycard bill.

There was a message on her answering machine. It was for Mr Gillack.

Jane had purposely not brought a copy of the brochure file home with her, feeling that she ought to get into the habit of only working the time she was paid for. But as she sat on the grubby sofa letting banal television wash in front of her, she wished she had some work to do, anything to inject some purpose into the wasteland of the flat.

Instead she ate three brownies, swearing each was to be the last, and tried moving the furniture in the bedroom around. No new arrangement seemed any better, and the pieces of heavy pine furniture seemed to feel a pull from their original positions, as if the owner's arrangement was the only one they would accept. In the end, hot and irritable, she put them back the way they had been.

Mid-evening, she called Lucy back but barely had time to tell her about the way things were going at work before she heard a doorbell down the line. Lucy's boyfriend Steve had turned up unexpectedly to take her out. As she hurriedly signed off Lucy sounded delighted and alive, and Jane wondered if Andrew had ever had the same effect on her.

Without thinking, she picked the phone up again and her finger was millimetres from the button which would speed dial his number before she stopped herself.

At eleven, she decided that there wasn't any point staying up any longer. She did quite well on the lock, only checking it three times. Then she went to bed.

Half an hour later she found herself suddenly awake, without knowing why. Then she heard a creak, and another, even louder. Turning very slowly in her bed, Jane held her breath. There was another creak from the hallway, this one quieter. It was followed by three more, each soft and at regular intervals, as if someone was walking in her hallway. Then they stopped.

This time there was no sound of the door of the flat opposite being opened, and Jane remained poised, lying tense as a board. In the end, she knew she wouldn't be able to sleep unless she checked it out, and quietly slid out of bed. Peering into the hallway she saw a light in the bathroom, a kind of blue glow. Keeping her feet at the edges of the corridor, where the boards creaked less, she crept towards it and pushed the door open tentatively.

Just a streetlight seeping through the blind. Sighing heavily, she went back to bed.

'What the *hell*?'

'Profanity, Jane?' Whitehead said, from the doorway.

Jane glared up from her screen. She was early again, and still had the office to herself. Camilla usually got in at ten on the dot. Somehow that was punctuality in her, not 'sloping in at the last moment' as it would have been for Jane.

'Someone's been messing around with the file.'

'"Messing around"?' asked Whitehead airily, coming closer, hands held behind his back.

Struggling to keep her voice steady, Jane gestured at the screen. 'There's new lines all over the place, and the rest of the copy's been typed in, it's . . . Christ – the *pictures* have all been shifted around too.'

'It's been finished, you mean.'

Jane turned to stare at him. 'Finished?'

'Yes,' said Whitehead, and then expanded with patronizing clarity, 'those things which remained to be done have been done.'

'You knew about this?'

'Well . . .'

'Camilla, yes?' Furious, Jane turned back to the screen.

'She stayed late last night, decided to have a go. I think she's done rather well, don't you?'

Jane took a deep breath, and decided to let herself be angry. 'Two points. Everyone here works on computers. They have *their* files on *their* computers. If I hung around late at night messing around with their work, I'd get the sack. Camilla does it, and she gets a brownie point.'

'She wasn't "messing around". She asked permission.'

'And you *gave* it?'

'Yes.' Whitehead looked calmly back down at her. 'And the second point?'

'These lines aren't aligned properly. I'm going to have to redo all of them. This text isn't locked to the baseline, so redo that – including repositioning all the pictures. Moving that logo has skewed the whole layout, which will have to be put back, and she's somehow mangled all the leading. Tidying all that up will take me three times as long as it took me to do it in the first place, and I can't even go back to the way I left it last night, because she's done it to the master copy. Yes,' Jane spat, feeling dangerously light-headed, 'she's done *really well.*'

'Jane.'

'Doing this isn't as easy as it looks, you know.'

'I know it isn't,' said Whitehead, abruptly and transparently switching into conciliatory mode. 'Look. She's got a bit to learn, and she shouldn't have altered the master. I'll tell her off for that, okay? She's learning.' He smiled meaninglessly at her and left.

'Yeah,' Jane said, to his back.

Later, as she stood waiting for the kettle to boil, Egerton wheeled up with her pay cheque for the month.

'Re your invoice of the 28th!' he warbled, and then, although he'd written the cheque himself, took a long unnecessary look at what it said before handing it over, as if he couldn't fathom what this piece of paper might be for.

As he strode off again, fingers clicking on the end of arms which swung like a demented toy soldier's, Jane noticed that Whitehead was standing talking to Camilla in the main office area.

As she watched, he made a comically cross face and mimed angry speech. Camilla laughed, her head thrown back, pretty in profile against the white wall.

When she left at five Jane was feeling marginally better, purely because her three days were up and she was almost done with FreeDot for the week.

'Have a nice weekend,' howled Egerton, from his position at the fax machine. He seemed to like standing there, watching the incoming tedium as if it was crucial news from some distant battlefront.

'I'm back in on Friday,' she said, managing a smile for him. 'Board presentation.'

'All set, are we?' said Whitehead, looming up as she put on her coat. 'All our lines in the right place?'

Jane looked at him, recognizing this kind of joke. For a moment it was as if she was still an employee there, still Whitehead's valued aide. 'I think so.'

'Good.' He winked. 'See you Friday.'

Jane smiled back and headed for the door.

'Wait for me!' called Camilla.

In the lift Jane kept silent, then realized it would be rude not to speak. She didn't care about hurting Camilla's feelings, but she didn't want to allow herself to be churlish. The most harm people can do to you, she thought, is making you behave in ways you can't respect.

'Bit early for you, isn't it?' she said, which seemed a good compromise between remaining silent and not giving an inch.

'Yes, I know. My boyfriend's got us tickets to see Les Mis.' The door opened and they walked across the foyer. 'Have you seen it?'

'No,' said Jane. Camilla smiled smugly, not realizing that wild horses couldn't have dragged Jane anywhere near Les bloody Mis. Outside, Jane was about to walk off when Camilla stopped. 'I'm sorry if I messed up your work,' she said, 'I'm a butterfingers really. Don't know what I'm doing.'

The insincerity with which she spoke was a clear taunt, and Jane thought, right: I don't have to put up with that.

'I think you know exactly what you're doing,' she replied, and walked away.

As she hurriedly squeezed the teabag in her mug Jane reached across for a brownie, humming. A programme Lucy had worked on was about to start, and she didn't want to miss the beginning. She was still feeling chipper at having called Camilla's bluff. Best of all, she didn't have to go to FreeDot the next day. Apart from the meeting on Friday, this week's time had been sold.

With the brownie an inch from her lips, she stopped. There was a bite missing. Surprised, she stared at it, trying to remember when she might have done that. Last night she'd eaten three, but finished them all. Not this morning, surely.

Still pondering, a small frown on her face, she settled onto the sofa. The adverts finished and a programme started, but it wasn't Lucy's. Confused, she looked up at the filing cabinet to check the time.

The clock wasn't there.

Still chewing slowly, Jane looked around the room, and found the clock. It was on the bookcase. She stared at it for a long time. She thought she remembered putting it back on the filing cabinet.

Suddenly she felt frightened, in a vague, formless way, as if some infinitely deep bedrock had shifted. On impulse she got up and sat at her desk. She pressed a button on the phone and waited for it to connect.

'Oh, hi . . .' she said, unsure of what to say, just needing some contact, something to tie her back down.

'. . . sorry but I'm not here at the moment. If you leave a message I'll –' A pause, as if Andrew had been distracted by something. '– I'll get back to you. It's going to beep any second.'

Jane pressed the pips down and dialled again. This time she heard it more clearly. Andrew had paused because someone was making him laugh. If you listened carefully you could hear him saying, 'Shh,' and the sound of female laughter.

In the hallway she reached out for the lock, preparing to go through the ritual again and seal herself safely in, but then stopped.

No, she thought, I'm not going to do that. I know what's done this to me, and I'm not going to let it. She reached out and simply pushed the catch down.

As she lay in bed, drowsily awakened once more, Jane heard creaking from the hallway again. She closed her eyes, determined to ignore it, but the creak came once more, much louder this time. Then there was a series of quieter creaks, as there had been the night before. Jane breathed deeply, vowing irritably not to get out into the cold to check it again.

Then there was another sound, and her eyes swivelled quickly. That creak hadn't come from the hallway. It sounded as if it came from the boards in the living room. Through the noise of rushing in her ears she heard it again, and this time there was no doubt. It was a board in the living room which had creaked.

Quietly, Jane slipped out of bed.

The hallway looked the same as it had the night before, dark with blue light seeping out from the bathroom doorway. Tonight there was something else, a slight flickering quality to the light. Feeling silly, but knowing she had to check for her own peace of mind, she padded silently down the hall towards the bathroom.

239

Just before she got there she realized that the flickering was reflected on the wall opposite the living room door, and she turned to glance in. Her television was on.

Her computer was also on, and there was a man sitting at her desk.

He wasn't looking at the computer but sitting side on, legs outstretched, watching the television with the sound turned down. He was drinking coffee out of one of the flat's mugs.

Feeling the tiny hairs on the back of her neck rise in swathes, Jane stared at him. She swallowed, too astounded to be more than very, very frightened.

'What do you think you're doing?'

The man turned slowly to face her. In his late thirties, he was of medium build and had short dark hair slicked back. There was something odd about his face.

'Watching television,' he said, and then turned back to the screen. Jane took a small step into the living room.

'Who the fuck are you?' she said, and was glad to hear that her voice carried anger as well as fear. The man turned his head back towards her, but kept his eyes on the screen.

'The owner,' he said.

'What?'

He flicked his eyes lazily towards her. They were calm, unre-markable. 'The owner,' he repeated.

'The hell you are. The owner ... Mr Gillack is in Belgium. On business. This is not your flat.' The man shrugged, and went back to watching the television. 'How did you get in?'

'Through the door,' he said. Jane was trying to remember if she'd put the catch down when suddenly she noticed something by the side of the desk. It was the champagne bottle with the pampas grass in it.

'What the hell is that doing there?'

'I put it there,' said the man, reaching for something on the desk. He picked it up and took a bite. 'Good brownies. Not home made, I assume.'

Jane was confused, and afraid, but the brownies gave her

something to hold onto. Whoever he was, those were her brownies, which she'd paid for, and he had no right to be eating them. 'Get out!' she shouted.

'I'm the owner,' the man said.

Jane took another step into the room. 'I don't give a toss. Those are my brownies. And neither you or anyone else has any right to come in here without my permission.'

The man looked at her mildly, sipping his coffee.

'Get out!' she screamed. 'Get out!'

After a pause he raised his eyebrows and slowly got up. Jane stepped backwards into the hall, and shrank into the bathroom as he passed. The man reached out and slid the catch up before opening the door. He took one step out and then turned, standing facing back in, hands behind his back. Jane leapt to the door and slammed it in his face. She jammed the catch back down and then feverishly lunged for the small bookcase in the hall, pulling it round to wedge it against the door, spilling books that were not hers all over the floor.

She slid down the wall, sobbing quietly, to land in a heap by the door, her leg poked painfully by a book. She snatched the book up and ripped it, pulling the covers off and mangling it, and then hurled it at the wall. She toppled slowly over to the floor to tuck herself up into a foetal position, hugging her legs and crying.

Next morning found her striding up the Pentonville Road at ten o'clock. It was light, it was daytime, and she was furious.

Alex, the second half of Klass 1 Accommodation, stood up with some trepidation when Jane swept into their office. He was much shorter than the pony-tailed Victor, and Greek rather than Indian, but just as courtly. 'Er,' he said. 'Oh, Jane, isn't it? St Augustine's Road?'

'Yes,' she said curtly.

'Is there a problem?'

'Yes. There is a problem.'

'Some coffee, I think,' said Victor, rising to assume command. Alex set about wielding the kettle.

'What exactly . . .?' Victor started to ask, but Jane cut him off.

'I want to know what the hell the owner was doing in my flat.'

Victor and Alex looked at each other, and then at Jane. 'I'm sorry?' they said, simultaneously.

'I woke up last night,' she said, 'to find Mr Gillack in my living room.'

'What was he doing?' asked Alex.

'Watching television,' Jane snapped.

Victor held out his hand to forestall further questions from Alex. 'Mr Gillack is in Belgium at the moment, on business. He isn't due to return until two weeks after your lease runs out.'

'He was in my living room! He has no right to come into the flat. Not without my permission, and certainly not in the middle of the night.'

'Absolutely not,' said Victor. 'You're sure this, uh, person, was Mr Gillack?'

'Yes. He said he was the owner. He said it several times. The only way he could have got in was with a key.'

'True. Well, this is very irregular. Alex, do we have a number for Mr Gillack?'

'I think so,' his colleague said, turning to hunt through a chaotic filebox.

'He's not in Belgium. He's here.'

'Jane,' said Victor calmly and seriously. 'The only means Alex and I have of contacting Mr Gillack is at his office in Belgium. So we must try that first.'

Alex triumphantly produced the right card, and Jane watched stonily as Victor dialled the number.

'Good morning,' he said after a while, enunciating clearly. 'Could I speak with Mr Gillack please?'

'Is he there?' asked Alex in the pause, and Victor shrugged.

'Is that Mr Gillack? Ah. This is Victor here, from Klass 1. Oh no, everything's fine.' Victor looked around for inspiration, and caught sight of a Post-it note. 'Just a message. American Express rang for you. Could you call them? No problem. Goodbye.' He put the phone down. 'That was Mr Gillack. He is in Belgium.'

Jane felt confused, but adamant. 'He was in my flat last night eating my brownies.' Victor held his hands up apologetically. 'Belgium isn't exactly Mars,' she added. 'He could have gone back this morning, or last night. You didn't ask him if he'd been there all the time, did you?'

'It would have been rather difficult.'

'Great. So what am I supposed to do?'

'Well, if it happens again . . .'

'What, if I wake up in the middle of the night to find a man in my flat again, you mean?'

'Yes, call the police. Make sure you lock up securely at night.'

'I do,' Jane shouted. If they only knew how bloody securely. Then she stopped short. Had she checked the lock last night? She couldn't remember. She remembered thinking about her ritual earlier on in the evening, but what had she done when she went to bed?

'Also,' concluded Victor, 'you have our number. Call us if there is the slightest cause for concern.'

'I should have spoken to him on the phone,' she said, her mind elsewhere. Maybe she hadn't checked it. But she had definitely pushed the catch down. Hadn't she? 'I would have recognized his voice.'

'The fact that he said he was the owner,' offered Alex, 'that could have been untrue.'

'No. He sat there as if he owned the place, and . . .' Suddenly she went cold, putting something together that she should have realized some time ago, should have known immediately. He'd been in her room. 'The bloody champagne bottle was back in the living room, and I put it in the cupboard.'

Victor and Alex looked at her like a pair of bemused cats. They had no idea what she was talking about.

'Why would anyone except the owner do that, hmm?'

'Jane . . .'

'I know, I know. He was in Belgium. Well, thank you anyway. And yes, you can rest assured that if it happens again you'll know all about it.'

The two men watched her sweep out, and then breathed a sigh of relief. 'Some more coffee, I think,' said Victor.

Jane was still fuming when she got to St Augustine's Road. She was glad to still be angry. If she stopped feeling angry she might have to think about the logistics of what had happened, and she didn't want to do that. She knew what she'd seen. She could remember it clearly. She didn't want to call her memory into question again.

The man in overalls was back, fiddling with a fusebox or something attached to the side of the building's stairs. In the house hallway was a pile of mail, sorted into flats. All the mail for Flat 8 was for Mr Gillack. Jane grabbed it furiously and spun it out into the street, slamming the door after it. She stomped upstairs and opened the door as viciously as she could. The light on the answering machine was on again and she slapped the button.

'Could Mr Gillack call –'

'Fuck off!' she shouted. A little frightened at herself she put her hands to her ears to blot out the sound of the message and walked jerkily out of the room. Suddenly a thought struck her, and she trotted back outside the house and leaned out over the banister.

'Do you do locks, by any chance?' she said.

An hour-and-a-half of loud banging later, the man stuck his head into Jane's living room, where she was supergluing the clock to the filing cabinet and humming.

'Miss, I've finished,' he said.

In the hallway she inspected the lock. It looked even more solid than the last one, and the catch went down with an irrevocable clunk. She flicked it up again, and then pushed it down.

'That's your set of keys, and the spares,' the man said, jangling them at her. He nodded approvingly at the door. 'Good lock that. British.'

'Have you got the old one?' Jane asked, flicking the catch up again. The man nodded out into the hallway. 'Do you mind if I keep it?'

Slightly surprised, he picked it up and gave it to her. 'It's your lock.'

'Nope,' she replied, pushing the catch down again, counting to eight silently in her head. 'This is my lock.'

The afternoon passed slowly. She stayed in, nothing to go out for, with the catch down and a chair wedged behind the door. The light changed outside the window and it got dark. She sat in front of her computer listening to the whirring sound it made, staring blankly at the FreeDot brochure on the screen. When she looked at the clock on the filing cabinet it said eight o'clock.

Then she looked again and it said nine. She got up and wandered into the kitchen, barely hearing the floorboards creak. When she reached into the cabinet above the sink she caught her hand on one of the other mugs, and hers fell out and smashed in the sink.

Instantly, her face crumpled and she found herself crying. The blurred mugs in the cabinet all belonged to the owner. The mug Andrew had given her, her mug, was in the sink. It was in the sink and it was broken. She didn't have another mug. None of the others were hers. Her mug was in the sink and it was broken.

She walked unsteadily back to her chair and picked up the phone. Pride lost a very brief battle and she pushed the programmed button. After three rings, it picked up.

'Hello?' she said, quietly.

'Yes?' said a voice. A woman's voice.

'Oh sorry,' Jane said, waking up a little and hoping she didn't sound too sniffly, 'I was trying for Andrew Royle.'

'Oh no, you've got the right number. He's just popped out to the off-licence. Who's calling?'

Head tight, feeling as if she was watching herself from several yards away, Jane said her name.

'Ah,' the voice replied, after a pause.

'Who's that?'

'Nikki.'

'Just passing again, were you?'

'Yes, as it happens.'

'And Andrew has popped round the offy.' It felt like a thing of cold logical beauty, being able to say that. She'd caught the woman out. Let her try to get out of that.

'Look Jane,' Nikki replied immediately, and at the tone of her voice Jane felt suddenly bad. 'He was going out with me more recently than you. Okay, not for very long, but more recently.'

Face creasing with misery, Jane realized her logic had been faulty, that her memory had tricked her again.

'You don't own him,' Nikki went on, with a calmness it hurt very much to hear. 'He's not yours any more.'

'What is?' said Jane quietly.

'What?'

'Nothing.' There was a long pause, in which Jane felt like a balloon that was dropping with eerie slowness towards the earth. She couldn't beat this woman, because things were different now. She wasn't in the right any more. Jane was just another girl, someone Andrew had once known, an entry in an address book that wouldn't be updated. If anyone was history, she was.

'Do you want to leave a message?' Nikki asked, eventually.

'Yeah,' said Jane, 'Tell him: "Jane says, fuck you."'

When she went to bed she checked every lock in the flat, screwing the window locks down as tightly as she could. It was unlikely that anyone would be able to scale three floors, but that wasn't the point. In the hallway she checked the chair was wedged firmly, but didn't bother to check the catch. It was too late now.

Listlessly unbuttoning her jeans, she opened the closet. The owner was inside.

Jane stumbled and fell as she tried to step backwards. The man from the night before was standing bolt upright amongst her clothes, hands folded together at waist height as if he'd been waiting there all day. He was wearing the same dark suit and a patient smile.

Jane scooted backwards, trying to get up and to rebutton her jeans at the same time. The man stepped out of the closet and beamed suddenly.

'Hello,' he said.

Jane's head banged into the bed frame and she clutched it and pulled herself up. She backed towards the wall, hands held weakly out in front of her.

'Please,' she said, 'please . . .'

'Please what?' the man said, cocking his head. 'Hm? Please what?' Back against the wall, Jane sidled towards the door. 'Please . . . and thank you?' He took a step towards her, blocking the way to the door. 'Please? Please?'

'Please, go away.' Jane shrank back as he took another step, staring at his blank, anonymous face. Her neck spasmed wildly and her mouth opened. Her face wanted to cry but she was too frightened. 'Please just go away.'

'Oh I don't think so,' the man said mildly. 'I don't have to go away. I'm the owner.'

Jane's teeth crashed together as her face responded to anger from somewhere inside her. She pushed herself from the wall and shouted: 'Get out! Get out! GET OUT!!'

'No,' he said, with a winning pout. He took another step towards her and before he could get any closer Jane lunged to the side and got round him. As she ran to the door he turned elegantly and made a swipe for her, tearing her blouse, but she made it past him and into the hallway.

She was halfway to the living room before realizing that was stupid, and instead swerved towards the door. She grabbed at the chair and yanked at it but it wouldn't budge. The wood from the chair seemed to have flowed into the wood of the door, jamming it shut.

As she tugged uselessly at it the owner watched her from the bedroom, smiling indulgently. Just as he started to move towards her she realized the chair was merely jammed under the handle. She yanked it aside and pulled at the door but it wouldn't budge. The owner stepped into the hallway and she grabbed the chair and flung it at him. She tugged frenziedly at the door again and then saw that the catch was down. She flicked it and swung it open just as a hand fell towards her shoulder.

She moaned as she stumbled out onto the tiny landing, and leaped straight for the stairs. Her heel caught and she fell most of the way down the flight, banging her face against the railing and tearing the nails out of one hand, but she got up as soon as she hit the bottom and careered out into the street.

She found a phone booth and rang a number. As soon as Klass 1's answering machine message started, she began to scream at it.

'He's in my flat! He's in my flat! He's in my flat!'

She kept screaming until even she couldn't hear the whisper of her voice.

Camilla reached out and took the brochure proofs from the printer. 'There,' she said. 'And it does look better than hers.'

Whitehead nodded and smiled. 'Good,' he said. 'Now all we need is Jane.'

Camilla looked at her watch. It was ten to four. 'She's cutting it a bit fine, isn't she?'

'She'll be here,' said Whitehead. 'Whatever her faults, she's reliable.'

Meanwhile, Jane was stepping out of the lift and opening the door to FreeDot. As she walked into reception, she shook her head. Her hearing appeared to be slightly deadened, and there was a buzzing sound. The office seemed very quiet, calm with quiet business. People came and went, passing paper. Egerton plucked a piece of paper from the fax machine and marched across the room to drop it heartily on someone's desk. People answered the phones though they weren't ringing, and looked as if they were talking into them. She took a step towards the corridor. Egerton plucked a piece of paper from the fax machine and marched across the room to drop it heartily on someone's desk. Jane blinked at him, watching him stop to answer a phone, his whole body declaring buoyant stupidity. Then he was at the fax machine again and she turned away.

Slowly she walked down the corridor. Behind her she thought she heard the ghost of a voice call her name, call it as a question.

When she got to her office Whitehead and Camilla turned to smile at her. There was a new plant on Camilla's desk and a poster for *Les Misérables* on the white wall. Suddenly, the buzzing stopped as their faces dropped.

'Jane, what's happened?' Whitehead asked, the lying fuck pretending to be concerned as he stared at the blood under her nose and her torn clothes, the bruise on her cheek and her ragged hair.

She ignored him, and swept her arm along the desk. 'Get OUT!' she screamed at Camilla. The plant sailed along the desk and flew straight out of the window.

As Whitehead lunged with a cry to watch it fall, Jane ripped the poster from the wall and began tearing it to pieces, arms flailing.

'Jane, please,' Camilla stuttered, cowering.

'Please WHAT?' Jane leaned over until her face was right up against hers, until she could see the mascara glistening on her lashes and smell the make-up, and screamed, 'Please *can I have everything*?'

She stuffed a section of the poster into her mouth and hummed while she chewed.

Whitehead stepped warily towards her. 'Er, Jane . . .'

'What?' she said, blowing the pieces out of her mouth at him.

'Perhaps you'd better go home.'

She fell towards the door, laughing weakly. 'Go home? Go HOME?'

Egerton was in the doorway, staring at her with childish surprise.

'Yes?' she shouted. 'What the fuck do you want?' He stumbled backwards, hands held up, and she turned to look once more at the room, at the shelves, at the machines, at the acres of white wall with so many things in front of it and none of them hers. Before she could cry she ran out into the corridor.

The door to Flat 8 was still ajar. She walked in and shut it behind her. The buzzing in her ears had returned.

The furniture was back where it had been when she moved in, the champagne bottle in position, his pictures back up on the walls. Her things had disappeared from the bathroom, and shaving foam and aftershave had materialized in their place. The fragments of her mug were gone from the kitchen sink. The bedroom seemed least altered because it had been least changed by her, but her clothes and the photo of Andrew were gone.

She walked back into the living room and looked out of the window. It was getting dark outside, and someone had taken the garden furniture and stacked it up so it stood like a sculpture.

When she turned, the owner was behind her, hands behind his back like a solicitous waiter.

'Yes?' he smiled.

'I'm going,' she said dully.

He looked disappointed with her, and spoke with a slow, mocking kindness. 'You can't go.'

'I am,' she replied, feeling about four years old.

'Where?' he asked. 'Where are you going to go?'

'I'll find somewhere.'

'You won't. There isn't anywhere.' He took a step towards her and suddenly her breath was hitching, uneven, because it hurt and she wanted to cry again. She backed away.

'Please . . .'

'What do you have, Jane?' he asked quietly, cocking his head like a robotic dog. 'Some have, some . . . haven't.' Still advancing, he threw his hands out expansively. 'You haven't. Everywhere's somebody's. There's nowhere to go.'

Then suddenly he shouted terrifyingly loudly, and Jane flinched as she had just before Andrew slapped her the night he left. 'WHERE'S THERE TO GO, JANE?'

She broke and tried to run for the door, but he intercepted her. She darted the other way along the wall, but he got there first. As she slid back and forth along the wall he tracked her and backed her into the corner.

'WHAT DO YOU HAVE, JANE?'

He slammed her against the wall and she dropped to the floor, her lungs suddenly empty. He grabbed at her and she rolled and tried to stand, but he slammed her over again and leaned down towards her, mouth hanging open as he reached to choke her. She fumbled out with her hand and found something and swung it round to smash it on his head.

The champagne bottle didn't break, but bounced out of her hand as he fell with a grunt on top of her. She squirmed away and stumbled towards the door but his hand whipped out and grabbed her ankle, tripping her so that she fell onto the sofa. She tried to pull free but his hand was too strong and snatched up her leg, tugging at her. Scrabbling out with her hand she found the bookcase. The old lock was on it and she grabbed it as his hand wrenched her thigh, turning her round to face him. Blood was seeping out of his matted hair and down his neck but he wasn't going to lie down.

'Mine,' he said.

She smashed the lock down into his face, feeling his nose momentarily resist and then spread like butter. For a second his head remained upright, and then he toppled over onto his front.

Jane staggered up, using the wall for leverage, watching him. His hands were flapping up and down, like a pair of damaged birds. She stared round the room and could see nothing that was hers, so she grabbed a picture off the wall and threw it at him. The owner's hands started flapping more wildly, beating against the carpet, and he began to make a humming sound that got louder and louder as his whole body began to vibrate.

He wasn't going to die. People like him never did.

She pulled out her lighter and held it next to the curtain. She spun the wheel.

'Own this,' she said.

The cheap curtains caught quickly, flames licking up towards the ceiling. Jane limped towards the door, coughing, stumbling round the owner whose whole body was whipping back and forth with an insectile violence.

She ran out into the hallway and as she wrenched the door open she heard his voice shouting from the depths of the fire.

'Where, Jane?'

Victor and Alex leaped straight out of the doors of the car, but Mr Gillack beat them to it. They'd been inclined to treat the whole thing as a joke, but to be on the safe side Mr Gillack had come back from Belgium. Suddenly, it didn't seem very funny any more.

'That's our commission down the pan,' muttered Alex, as they trotted after Mr Gillack towards the blaze.

A policeman brusquely stopped them from getting too close. His manner softened when he heard Mr Gillack was the owner, but he still wouldn't let them go any nearer. Mr Gillack just stood and stared, running his hands wildly through his long blond hair, watching his flat burn down.

Jane sat in the back of a police car, her legs outside. She felt cold, even though a blanket was wrapped around her. The inspector snapped his pad shut. 'We're going to have to ask you a few more questions later,' he said, 'but for now . . .'

He stopped then, and glanced at a constable who'd just returned from talking to the fireman. Out of sight of Jane, the constable mouthed the news. There was no one else in the flat.

'Ah,' said the inspector, very slowly nodding and turning

to look warily at the woman in the back of his car. 'But for now,' he concluded, 'I think we'd better get you down to the station.'

He gently lifted Jane's legs and swung them round into the car. Quietly shutting the door, he looked at the constable over the roof of the car and they both breathed out heavily.

Jane stared at nothing as they pulled away past the knots of bystanders. She still felt cold, but it was nice to have the blanket.

She looked out at the pavement. Standing there neatly, smiling and waving like a child as they passed, was the owner. He was on fire.

She turned back and looked down at the blanket for a while. The pattern was unfamiliar. It didn't look like one of hers.

FOREIGN BODIES

'Well?' I said.

'Well what?'

'You know very well. What happened last night?'

Steve laughed. I groaned loudly, enjoying every minute. 'You did it again, didn't you.'

'Yes.'

'She stayed round yours.'

'Yes.'

'You berk. You utter spanner.'

'It wasn't my fault.'

'Yeah. Try telling her that. Another scratched fixture, was it?'

'Nope. Reached the finishing post.'

'You idiot.'

'Twice.'

I sighed theatrically, and Steve laughed again, slightly embarrassed. He knew what I was going to say, not least because he agreed with me. 'You've been a *very silly boy*, haven't you?'

'I know, I know,' he said happily.

'What *happened*? We spoke, what, three hours before? I thought you'd told her it was just going to be a meal.'

'I did.'

'So what happened?'

'Well we were there, mid-evening, in this restaurant I wanted to try. That Bolivian place.'

'How was it?'

'Fucking terrible.'

'What, worse than that Korean?'

'No, not that bad, obviously. But still bad.'

'Anyway.'

'There we were, it was all going fine, and then suddenly she looked at me and said: "You know what I suggested last time?" and I said "Yes . . ."'

'What, about why don't the two of you just do it anyway?'

'Exactly. And so she said, "Well, how about it?"'

'And you said yes.'

'Well what *could* I say?'

The answer, of course, was nothing. I knew this, to my cost, but I continued giving him a hard time for a while, and then we signed off the phone and got on with our jobs. Steve didn't mind me giving him the third degree – it was the equivalent of doing a penance. Talking to me after an Ill-advised Sexual Encounter was the nearest thing he was going to get to saying ten Hail Marys.

There are men who will go out, see a woman they fancy, and chat her up. I know it happens because I've heard about it, seen it, marvelled at it. I've never done it myself. In all the time I've been meandering around the planet, I can honestly say I have *never* had the courage, confidence or whatever it is that it takes to be as proactive as that. But, on the other hand, if you're a reasonable-looking bloke, keeping half an eye open but never really trying very hard, there's a certain kind of situation you're going to find yourself in. While not especially charming, I can string coherent sentences together. While not handsome, I don't inspire outright terror when I hove into view. More importantly, I can listen. Boy, am I good at listening. And therein lies the problem, because there is a certain type of woman out there for whom I, and men like me, appear to be the answer. These women are intelligent and attractive, interesting and sophisticated. They are also, unfortunately, all as mad as snakes. In the two years I was a single variable, I spent time with four women of this type. They were either people I worked with or met through friends, and I didn't approach a single one of them. They started it. I'm not boasting or gloating here, completely the opposite. Think about it. In my circles women don't approach men. They don't need to. They spend enough time fending off members of the opposite sex without starting trouble for themselves. So what does that say about the women who do such a thing? It says they come with problems. It's different in some other countries, America for example, where perfectly sane women will sometimes make the running. In London it doesn't work like that. Or it doesn't for me, anyway. I was approached by four women, of widely differing ages, appearances and personalities, and I ended up spending time with them purely because I didn't realize that's what I was doing until it was too late.

And the simple fact was, each of these women was mad.

That sounds sexist. It's not. Not deliberately, anyway. There are a vast number of disastrous men out there, too. I'm probably one of them. I'm not characterizing the female sex as in any way unstable. If anything, I'm taking the blame back, because I can't understand how some women get the way they are unless it's through a long-term, recurrent, almost *concerted* campaign of subtle mistreatment by men.

My point is, I'm the guy they latch onto when someone else has brought them to that state. These other men sow the seeds through years of desertion, mixed messages and callous indifference, and then they trade up to a younger model and abandon these women to the world. The women regroup, do their jobs, live their lives and carry on, all the time keeping an eye out for someone who looks nice. Someone who looks like they're not going to hurt them, who looks as though they'll listen. In other words, looking for someone like me. The sad punchline of the story is that, despite appearances, I'm just as bad as everyone else, and I'm the last thing that they need. I'm just another of the guys they've met before, but with a slightly kinder smile and an even colder heart.

Or was, anyway. After two years of sexual hit-and-run accidents, each of which left me feeling more damaged and damaging than before, I simply gave up. I gave up right at the start of another one, finally having the experience and bloody-mindedness to spot it for what it could become. I backed out, pulled down the shutters, and resolved to sit tight for a while. If I wanted company I had my memories, and if I wanted sex I'd hotwire my imagination or buy a bloody video. Sounds pathetic, but it's not. There are advantages to virtual relationships. They don't leave you with someone you don't know to talk to in the morning, someone's calls you have to take when you've got nothing to say. They don't present you with someone's faith to destroy when you never promised them anything in the first place.

And then, out of the blue, I met Monica. I made the effort for once, and she reciprocated sanely and slowly, and suddenly everything was different.

Steve was still in the position I'd been in a year before, and although I'd never met her, this girl Tamsin fitted the mould perfectly. She was supposed to have temporarily split up from someone else, someone who was bigger than Steve, had a flasher job, but who happened to be out of the country. Steve had met her through the usual splatter of coincidence that in retrospect looks too dark and foreboding to be the result of pure chance. He had, to give him credit, pegged her as an 'unusual person' from the very first date.

At first fairly subtly, and then with surprising persistence, Tamsin had suggested a period of casual acquaintance, to include excursions into the sexual arena. This period would end with no strings, it was proposed, when her boyfriend returned from abroad. She would return to him, Steve could get back to his life, and everything would be neatly tidied away.

Though this was the sort of suggestion which is supposed to send male hormones ricocheting round their glands in a frenzy of joy, it had struck Steve as rather odd. In my capacity as a scarred foot soldier in similar campaigns, he chewed it over with me. My advice had been simple.

Don't even fucking *think* about it.

Why? Because.

Because it wouldn't work that way. Because the sex wouldn't

be as good as he hoped, and wouldn't make him any happier. And because when you've slept with someone once, there's no good reason for it not to happen again – and once it's happened twice you're in a relationship, never mind what it says in your contract.

I could picture, almost as though it was happening in front of me, what would take place the evening before Tamsin's boyfriend returned. She'd meet Steve for a drink, in some pub that meant something to both of them. The stage would be carefully set. Steve would be nervous, but relieved that the strange interlude was over. You don't get anything for free, and few things make you more nervous than an apparent gift from the Gods. Steve would buy a couple of drinks and sit down, ready to be hearty and make the usual promises of friendship, and then Tamsin would speak.

'Well,' she'd say, and pause, and smile brightly, 'what are we going to do?'

Steve would cough, and stare, and ask what she meant, and then it would all come out. She'd changed her mind. After all, there was something between them, wasn't there? Something *important*. She was going to tell her boyfriend she'd fallen in love with someone else. He'd be angry, of course, and she'd have to move out of his flat, and she'd have nowhere to stay . . . but between her and Steve, and the love that they shared, she was sure they'd be able to work it out.

When someone says something like that to you, you're not allowed to just run yelping out of the bar, although that's much the best thing you could do. There are rules of human engagement. And so Steve would swallow, try not to pass out, and settle down to having one of the worst evenings of his life. There would be tears, brave smiles, and a horrendous scene in a public place. Possibly screaming. I've seen it happen. After four hours he'd think he'd got away with it, and would limp sweating back to his flat.

Then the next day the calls would start, and the letters, and the visits. Steve would spend a month looking like a hunted animal, and would eventually emerge bewildered, frightened, and feeling absolutely terrible about something he'd never done.

And if he was anything like me, in four months he'd end up doing exactly the same thing again.

I knew Steve well enough to be able to plot all this with absolute confidence, and so I told him to stay well clear. He was my friend, so he listened, and thought about it, and realized I was speaking not with forked tongue.

And then, being a man, he'd gone ahead and done it anyway.

Two days later I was sitting at my desk again. I spend a lot of time sitting there. Working at it, rather less.

I was staring out of the window, and I was smoking. I am a keen, dedicated, probably almost *professional* smoker, and recognize a period of time I call 'a cigarette's-worth'. It's about five or six minutes, the length of time it takes to smoke a fag, but the actual duration isn't really the point.

Thus when I'm supposed to be working, I'll take a break to do a cigarette's-worth of reading, a cigarette's-worth of leafing pointlessly through magazines, or a cigarette's-worth of staring into space. This is different from the usual reading, leafing through magazines and staring into space which I do when I'm supposed to be working – though I'll almost certainly be smoking when I do those too – in that it's a conscious decision, a marked-off period of time during which I am deliberately, instead of merely effectively, not working.

I sighed and turned my intellect to the task of staring at the computer and randomly spiralling the cursor round the screen. This, I find, can keep me occupied for hours. Sometimes, as that afternoon, I dally with a variant of the technique, which involves clicking the mouse at intervals while I'm spiralling. This is both pointless and silly, as sometimes it accidentally moves some of my folders around on the computer desktop. But that's all right, because I can then do a cigarette's-worth of moving them all back so they're neat and tidy again.

When I finally started to resurface from my reverie, I noticed that I was whirling the cursor over the folder which holds my letters. I could tell that at a glance because I'd once spent most of an afternoon – on a client's time, naturally – making its icon look like a little letter coming out of an envelope. I work for a number of people in a variety of capacities, but I can't honestly say I represent value for money to any of them.

I double-clicked on the folder to open it, and stared vaguely at the sub-folders inside, each labelled with the name of the person to whom the contents had been sent. The names on some of them were enough to make me wince, without even exploring the terrible stuff inside. Like I said, I advised Steve on the basis of my own experience. Ginny's folder was there, as was Jackie's, Yvonne's and Mel's, amongst less frightening ones holding letters to various other ex's, friends and the tax office. There was also, I noticed, a folder which didn't appear to have a name. I was about to investigate when the phone rang.

It was Steve, and he'd done it again.

I should stress here that, despite appearances, Steve and I are not a couple of typical lads who can't wait to swop tales of sexual derring-do with each other. Over a long and arduous period we've earned our Politically Correct badges, and are in any event both fairly private people. I would never discuss Monica with him even if he asked, which he simply wouldn't. Reports on random sex are different, though – it's more like a sports news update. And don't try telling me that women don't do it too.

The last time we'd spoken Steve had sworn curiosity had now been satisfied, and that he wasn't going to end up in bed with Tamsin again. I'd been sceptical. If someone wants to do it again, how are you going to avoid it? Turning down a man is one thing: women have a right not to sleep with someone if they don't want to, and many men will respect that, intellectually if not in practice. It's the way of the world. Being denied sex is a key feature of being a male earthling, and it's only the grace with which you accept it that determines how you're perceived.

Turning down a woman is something completely different.

Turning down a woman, when she has taken that step and made that offer, comes across as such a wholesale rejection, such a spine-chillingly loud slap in the face, that it's almost impossible to do, however much you want to.

Steve had gone out to dinner with Tamsin, armed no doubt with the best of intentions, and it had happened again.

Sighing heavily, I got down to the task of telling Steve yet again that he was making a mistake. I see it as my role in life, discouraging other people from having fun. We knocked it back and forth for a while, and then there was a pause.

'There's something else,' he said, eventually.

'Oh yes?' I said. 'What? She doesn't believe you've got some-one else?' Steve had told Tamsin that he too was loosely attached to someone abroad, and that she was coming back soon. I'd liked the way he was thinking, but hadn't held out much hope that it would make a difference.

'No. She told me that she'd taken something. She took something last time as well, apparently.' I assumed that he was talking about drugs, and was about to wax indifferent when he continued. 'Last time it was photos.'

'What do you mean?'

'Last time she stayed round mine, when I was in the shower, she took some photos from the flat.'

'She did *what*?'

'She had prints done, large prints, and then gave the originals back to me this morning.'

'Photos of what?'

'Of me.'

I didn't say anything for a moment. I was reeling slightly. Though I enjoy being proved right as much as the next man, I didn't like the sound of this.

'Where were they? The photos? I mean, were they just lying around, in a drawer, or what?'

'They were in an album. It was on my desk.'

'Did you show them to her?'

'No.'

'She just opened it, without permission, and took the photos.'
'Yes.'
'That's not ideal, is it.'
'No.'
'And now she's taken something else?'
'Yes.'
'What?'
'I don't know. She wouldn't tell me.'

At the weekend Steve called me again. Monica and I were splatted in front of the television, stupefied with pizza. When the phone rang Monica advised me to ignore it, but I find that difficult to do if I haven't spoken to my parents that day, which I hadn't. So I answered it, and on finding it was Steve settled back to banter with half my mind, while trying to keep track of whatever it was we were watching. A documentary on Cane Toads, I suspect – comfort television. Monica had just walked out to make some coffee when Steve stopped abruptly, and said he wanted to ask me a favour. Something in the tone of his voice made me sit up and tune out the toads, despite the fact that they were cutely rolling onto their backs to have their stomachs rubbed, just like my cat used to do.

Steve wondered whether Monica and I could be talked into going out the following night. The fact that he was asking in those terms made it obvious what he was really saying. I asked, and he admitted that a double date was what he had in mind.

I breathed out heavily for comedy value, pretending that what he was asking was a bit of a tall order. Normally, he would have got the joke. He didn't. He rapidly said that he wouldn't have asked, except he didn't know what else to do. Tamsin had phoned him at least three times each day since they last saw each other. He was calling from his office rather than home, late on a Sunday afternoon, because pretending he had work to do was the only way he'd been able to avoid spending the day with her. Nothing else he'd been able to come up with, from the fact that he was tired to claiming that he needed to paint the ceiling, had been able to dissuade her. Because, after all, she could come and help paint the ceiling. And if he was tired, well, they didn't have to *do* anything, did they? She could just come round, bring some food, and they could curl up together . . .

When he got to that point, I stopped pretending and rapidly agreed, making it clear what I was doing and waggling my eyebrows at Monica for her approval. She rolled her eyes but then nodded with a smile. '*Men*', she was clearly thinking, and who can blame her? I made arrangements with Steve to meet him at a cinema in town the following evening.

When we'd finished I put the phone down and sipped my coffee. Monica nudged me a few minutes later to bring me out of my reverie, but it stayed on my mind. Steve was a calm, level-headed person. He'd known what he was getting into – I'd warned him often enough.

I could understand him being rattled. But he'd almost sounded afraid.

I had to spend the afternoon at a client's on Monday, which I didn't mind too much. It meant I could drink their coffee and waste their time, instead of merely my own. I hung around till half-six and then went round the corner to meet Monica in a pub.

We were both in high spirits when we left an hour later. Neither of us had bothered to eat any lunch, and after three drinks in quick succession peered rather owlishly at each other when we re-emerged into the fading light outside. Hand in hand we walked down the street towards Oxford Circus, and I sent up silent thanks To Whom It May Concern.

There'd been times when I thought I would never have this again, when I thought I would spend the remaining evenings of my life nodding in polite fury at the utterances of someone I didn't really know, never mind like, much less love. It wouldn't have been their fault, nor even mine really. It's simply the way things are when people come together out of hurt rather than happiness. When you try to use people as band-aids you merely reinfect the wound, and every moment you spend with them is like a speck of glass working itself deeper into your flesh. If it gets in far enough then the wound closes up, sealing the alien matter inside you. Women are used to having their lives and bodies invaded; men aren't, and so I think they struggle against it more. On the outside everything looks good enough, and you are the only person who can feel the fresh little cuts that tear every waking moment. The only way to get it out is to rip yourself apart, and so instead you sit and nod, and pretend that nothing matters.

The difference between that state and the one I felt with Monica was the biggest difference in the world, and as we careered slowly down the pavement towards Piccadilly I gripped her hand very, very tightly.

We were a few minutes early at the cinema, and while Monica went off to the toilet I sourced a large amount of soft drinks from the counter in the centre of the foyer. I considered buying a tray of tacos, cheese and jalopeños, and then patiently talked myself out of it. There are things that one likes that one simply should not have, and in my case thin slivers of green plutonium are among them. As I counted out my change I thought I saw some familiar colours pass on one side of me, but when I looked up Monica hadn't yet returned, and there was no sign of Steve.

I took the drinks, stood next to one of the free-standing ashtrays, and set about mainlining as much nicotine as I could before the show started. It's impossible to find a cinema you can smoke in these days, though I see that rustling, clearing one's throat repetitively and loudly explaining the plot to your neighbours are still very much allowed. Monica still wasn't back, but that didn't surprise me. I know what happens in women's toilets. They step through a portal to another dimension, where they assume their true form and gambol through dream-lit forests, tarrying awhile on their home planet to bask in the last moonglow of autumn, before returning to the cursed twilight of this dread prison world. At least, I assume it has to be something like that. I can't see any other conceivable explanation for how bloody long it takes. Yes, I know there are often queues, but that's because everyone takes so bloody long, isn't it?

I was halfway through my first cigarette when I spotted Steve on the other side of the room. He was wearing his leather jacket, hands thrust deep in pockets, and craning his neck as he looked round the foyer. People kept coming between us and so I had a minute to observe him, and to see that a woman of average build was standing fairly close to him. She had her back to me, but there was something familiar about her, and suddenly I knew what Tamsin had taken the last time she'd stayed at Steve's. She was wearing one of his sweaters, a sweater that Monica and I had given him at Christmas.

I faltered, stopped waving, and withdrew my hand, needing a moment to assimilate this.

Okay, so it wasn't any big deal. A jury of her peers would be unlikely to give her the death penalty. But it was wrong. It was wrong in some way that seemed to strike at me personally. When Monica and I had chosen the sweater we hadn't been going out with each other for very long, and she'd only met Steve on one rather stilted occasion. Steve and I never exchanged more than perfunctory gifts, and so I'd been surprised at her suggestion that we look for a sweater for him. He'd commented on his wardrobe when they met, apparently, bemoaning the fact that he never got round to buying anything presentable. I understood that Monica's desire was due partly to the fact that she was simply very nice, but also out of a wish to start forging a bond between her and my best friend, so we'd had a merry time trawling round a variety of men's clothes shops before finding one we both thought he would appreciate.

He'd liked it, and wore it often. And now this woman had taken it without his permission, and was wearing it as proof of a relationship which Steve didn't want to have. Okay, it was his fault for not being strong enough to keep away from her. But this was something else, something more than a misjudgement on her part, more than demanding too much too soon. It was invasive.

Steve eventually saw me, and I smiled and started towards them. At the same moment Monica emerged from the women's toilets, and we reached them at about the same time. Doubtless reading Steve's face, Tamsin turned to face us.

When I saw her my heart stopped, and I felt as if I had fallen suddenly into a dream of freezing water. The brief, liquid spell came and went in a moment, and I dragged my eyes off her to listen to what Steve was saying. I heard the words, but couldn't make any sense of them. My mind was elsewhere.

I'd met Tamsin before, and her name was not Tamsin.

When the film finished at half past ten, I wanted to go. I'd spent the last two hours taking covert looks to my left, where 'Tamsin' had been sitting, and while the initial spasm of complete panic had passed, I still felt extremely bad. I wanted to say goodnight and go home, but the look in Steve's eyes told me that my job wasn't yet finished.

So, after a pointless few moments of dithering, we went round the corner to a pub Steve and I occasionally drank in. Tamsin took Steve's hand and led him to a table. I asked everyone what they wanted to drink, avoiding Tamsin's eye, and went towards the bar. On an afterthought I diverted my course towards the Gents. What I wanted most of all was a chance to think without anyone being able to see my face.

Inside, I splashed cold water over my hands and rubbed them over my cheeks and forehead. Then I just leaned on the basin and stared at nothing at all.

I'd seen Tamsin before. More than that. I knew her.

Sometimes when you catch a half-glimpse of someone across the street you mistake them for someone else, most likely a person you're missing, or you've just loved and lost. This was not like that. This was not a chance similarity. This was the actual person herself. The problem was that I didn't know who the hell that person was.

When we'd stood in that little foursome in the foyer, Steve making the introductions in an endearingly embarrassed way, I'd felt my mind running at screaming pitch, trying to resolve the question of who she was. But I knew there was no solution, that however fast my mind ran the wheels were being held off the ground. I had no recollection of this person, except for knowing that I knew her.

My memory's fine, in case you're wondering. I may not always pay my Visa bill on the nail, but I don't forget names and faces. As far as I could remember – no, fuck that: it's for sure, and definite. I'd never met this person. But I knew her. I'd never known her name, but I knew it wasn't Tamsin.

Monica had noticed the sweater immediately, and preoccupied as I was, I'd felt the ambient temperature drop by about ten degrees. She knew about the photos, and about the second 'borrowing'.

'That's a nice sweater,' she'd said, with a smile that was bright enough to blind. The girl had nodded self-deprecatingly, and took a step closer to Steve, who was sending me signals I couldn't interpret.

'It looks just like one of Steve's,' I said, woodenly, staring at him. 'You know, the one Amanda gave you.'

Amanda was Steve's fictitious girlfriend, an imaginary medical student allegedly out of the country doing an elective in Canada. I know it sounds vile to have ploughed straight in like that, but I was all over the place. It was a wonder I could say anything at all, and not surprising that I fell immediately into my programmed role. I had a job to do, and I was going to do it, not least because now I'd seen Tamsin, or whatever her name was, she was sending shivers up my scalp. Something was very wrong, and the worst thing was that I didn't know what it was.

'It's the same sweater,' Tamsin said, smiling winningly. 'Steve lent it to me.' The look in Steve's eyes as she said this confirmed what I already knew. No, he hadn't. But she'd turned up this evening wearing it, and he could hardly have demanded she take it off. Why? Because she doubtless had nothing else with her, and nothing on underneath. But that wasn't the real reason. The real reason was that you simply can't do that kind of thing.

After all, she'd only borrowed a sweater. It wasn't a crime, was it? And she'd only done it so she could have something of his with her, so she could smell him while they were apart. That was sweet, loving, a sign of how much she was beginning to care: surely not a reason to be shouted at?

With each moment I spent in this woman's company I was feeling worse and worse. And the next thing that we did, after Steve had stocked up on soft drinks, was to go and sit together for nearly two hours. Tamsin ended up between me and Steve, and I had Monica on my other side. We sat, in the darkness, and the film spooled on, and I have not a clue what it was about. Sitting next to Tamsin felt about as comfortable as sitting next to a corpse, and all I had in my head was one thought.

Why did I think I knew her?

Eventually I left the pub toilet, and bought the drinks. When I returned to the table I was expecting to see Monica sitting with her arms folded, looking stern and ill at ease. Instead I was perturbed to see her chatting affably with Tamsin. Steve looked up, took his drink – and Tamsin's – and then carried on listening to what the girls were saying. He didn't try to catch my eye, and neither did Monica when I sat down. In fact, as far as I could tell, normality had broken out all around me. The undercurrents and strangeness had disappeared, except for in one place. My head.

We stayed in the pub until it shut. I probably said about thirty words while everybody else chatted away, having what appeared to be a good time. I tried to start a subsidiary conversation with Steve, but it petered out almost immediately, partly out of my frustration at his apparent refusal to receive the messages I was sending. He was sitting close to Tamsin, his arm behind her on the bench, and every now and then she'd let her hand fall on his knee. I felt like a jealous lover watching them together, but I simply couldn't understand what was going on. At one point her eyes fell on mine and I looked away quickly, almost as if they'd burnt me.

When we were standing outside, the foursome dividing into two pairs again, I threw one last rope in Steve's direction and asked if he wanted to share a cab. He said no, he was fine. Tamsin put her hand in his, looked at me, and they walked off up the road.

As soon as Monica and I were in a taxi I started talking fast, and didn't stop for several minutes.

What, I enquired, the *fuck* did Steve think he was doing? Why was he sitting in a pub next to a woman he didn't know – and who kept riffling through his possessions – and looking like he was enjoying himself? If he wanted this thing to stop before it got any further, why was he playing up to it?

'What was he *supposed* to do?' Monica demanded, when she could get a word in. 'Sit there looking miserable?'

'Yes,' I shouted, 'Yes, that's *exactly* what he should have done. Otherwise it'll be taken as a sign. Otherwise, what was this evening about?' Monica tried to interrupt, but I overrode her. 'As far as she's concerned, this evening will now have been about Steve introducing her to two of his best friends. It's just going to make things worse. Now, for the first time, she's going to have something solid to clobber him with when the time comes.' Without knowing I was going to do it, I savagely mimicked Tamsin's rather hard-edged voice. 'There *must* be something between us, Steve, because you went to all the trouble to introduce me to your friends.' I paused, and furiously lit a cigarette. 'He's digging his own fucking *grave*.'

'Put that out, would you, mate,' the taxi driver said firmly.

'Jesus fucking Christ,' I muttered, and ground the cigarette out in the ashtray.

Taking her time, speaking calmly and rationally, Monica told me I was overreacting. She pointed out that they'd seemed to enjoy each other's company, and suggested that maybe Steve was changing his mind. She inquired as to what it was exactly that I had against Tamsin, and went so far as to offer the opinion that imputing such cold-hearted deviousness to a woman qualified as misogynous.

At this I turned and stared at Monica, feeling the blood drain from my face. We teetered for a moment on the brink of a vicious argument, and then I calmly but firmly stood down. Like everyone else, I only know one side of the sex war story, but that doesn't stop me being right every now and then. I wasn't saying Tamsin was a mad *woman*. I was simply saying she was mad. Mad men would doubtless behave in ways that I would find equally abhorrent. I'd just never had the misfortune of getting emotionally entangled with one.

The whole discussion was nonsense anyway, because it was the furthest thing from my mind. I was focusing on it purely as a diversionary tactic, as a way of shouting down the other thoughts that were fighting for my attention. After an hour sitting in the pub looking at her, I still knew both that I'd never seen Tamsin before, and that I knew her very, very well.

'What about the whole sweater issue, then?' I said finally. 'What about that?'

Monica smiled and rolled her eyes. I remembered briefly that the last time I'd seen her do that was when Steve had asked me if we'd come out tonight, to dilute the presence of a woman he didn't want to be with. I didn't bother to mention it.

'Steve lent it to her. What more do you want?'

I sighed and stared out of the window, willing myself to calm down. Ultimately, it wasn't my problem.

'What's so strange, anyway?' Monica said suddenly. 'She's well-spoken, obviously intelligent, and she's certainly pretty.' She paused, and the cab seemed to go very quiet, with just the sound of wheels on wet pavements outside. '*You* looked at her often enough.'

I resisted the urge to whimper as the last sentence curled lazily in front of me, like a live electricity cable on wet grass. Then I clamped my mouth over Monica's and kissed the danger away. After a few moments the cab driver coughed aggressively enough to stop us and so we sat in companionable silence instead: Monica humming quietly to herself, me wishing fervently that I belonged to a species that reproduced by binary fission.

Next morning, I was at my desk at nine o'clock sharp. There

was no one there to see it, but it made me feel diligent and worthy, and there was, moreover, a reason for it. The portable handset of the phone was sitting in front of me, and for once I'd remembered to replace it on the charger unit before going to bed, so the batteries were good and full.

Steve got into work at nine-fifteen, and boy was he going to have a phone call waiting for him.

While I waited for the time to roll round I booted the computer into life and, sipping a cup of coffee, gazed upon the outside world with reasonable goodwill. In the cold light of morning the state I'd got myself into the night before seemed unnecessary, even ludicrous. I'd mistaken Tamsin for someone else, that was all, and if Steve was now intent on seeing her, then that was no one's business but his. I was feeling good, looking good, and juggling three oranges in one hand.

None of that is true, unfortunately.

I was staring out of the window, rather than gazing, and my jaw was rigid. I hadn't slept well. The morning light was not cold, merely bright, and it was failing to do what it was supposed to. It was failing to make me feel any better.

I wanted to call Steve, but I felt nervous about doing so. I wanted to believe that last night had just been some weird mental belch on my part, but I didn't. I'm not a complete idiot. If I feel something, really feel it, it's not suddenly going to go away. It's not a whim. It's real.

When we'd got home Monica had gone straight through to get ready for bed. As she wears not only make-up but contact lenses she generally starts about half an hour before me, so as only to have about another half hour's worth to do by the time I come through. I padded around in the kitchen making tea, and then wandered into the living room.

It didn't matter where I was. I was in the same place wherever I was standing, and I finally knew what was wrong.

Three years ago, before the mad women period, I had a girl-friend called Katy. She was the last real person I went out with before Monica. Katy was fun, warm and a very good friend, but she had some problems. We talked them back and forth over the years, tried different ways to work round them, and in the end she went to a psychiatrist. He started her off on hypnotherapy, and during the second session the bombshell landed.

There were things in her life, events, which she had completely blanked. I'm not saying what they were, because it's her life, but they're the kind of things you really don't want happening to you. These events had taken place, mainly when she was very young but a few when she was older, and then had simply disappeared from her mind as if they'd never happened.

Except they hadn't, of course. They were still there: she just didn't know about them.

It's not like forgetting. When you forget you can remember, given the right cues. When you blank something, it's like someone throwing a coin into a pool of opaque water when you aren't looking. However hard you stare at the surface, you're not going to know that the coin is there. You may experience ripples every now and then, and you may realize that *something* is buried inside you, but unless you're taken back in time to see the coin sink, the event simply never happened for you.

I was at home when Katy came back from the breakthrough session, and I can still remember the look of horrified astonishment in her eyes. The rug had been pulled out from beneath her in a way that normally only happens in dreams, and she didn't know what to trust any more. What else might she have forgotten? What else had happened that she hadn't been a party to? It was a bit like living a completely normal human life for thirty years and then overhearing someone say it was about time they whipped your motherboard out and upgraded the CPU.

'What?' you think, feeling very cold inside, 'what?'

As I stood in the living room waiting for the kettle to boil, that was how I felt, and as I sat at my desk the next morning, I felt exactly the same.

At that moment the phone rang, scaring me half to death. It was Steve, bizarrely. He thanked me and Monica for coming along the night before, and said he hoped we'd had a reasonable time. As he talked about the film I listened to him carefully, wondering if he was an impostor.

Finally, I said something. 'So. You had a good time last night, did you?'

'Yeah, great.'

'And afterwards?'

Steve laughed, and I nodded to myself and grabbed the mouse, nervously making the cursor move around. Careful not to prejudge the issue, I asked if he'd found out what Tamsin had taken.

'Oh yeah. It was just that sweater.'

'But you lent that to her, apparently.'

There was a brief pause, and then Steve laughed again. I couldn't tell whether he thought I was being weird, or if he was covering up some confusion of his own. 'Yeah, well I probably did. I was quite drunk that night. No big deal, anyway.'

'No. So. Has she taken something this time?'

'Yes, I expect so.'

'And you don't know what.'

'No.'

'She's a one, isn't she,' I said, and we laughed again.

I dropped the subject. I wanted very much to tell Steve how the sight of Tamsin had affected me, but I couldn't. Believe me, no one hates tension more than I do, the feeling that 'nobody knows but me'. If there had been any point in mentioning it to Steve, I would have done. I couldn't. It would have felt like I was prying, which was a big change from the last time we'd spoken about it.

I'd been on the brink of telling Monica the night before as we lay in bed, but again I hadn't. I could still picture that live electric cable in my head, and I wasn't going anywhere near it. No earthing would be enough for that conversation.

So Steve and I chewed the rag a little longer, arranging in our roundabout way to play pool at some unspecified venue on an undetermined date in the future. I was only listening with half an ear, watching the cursor whirl round the screen.

Then suddenly the cursor was over my letters folder, and I wasn't listening at all. I opened the folder, grunting distractedly in response to Steve's ongoing banter, and saw again the folder without a name. Yesterday it had merely made me curious. Today my reaction was far more extreme. I stared at it, mouse still.

The folder looked no different to the ones called 'Ginny' or 'Mel', except that it didn't have a name. Or it did, as I discovered through a little technical messing around, but it was a special one. It was simply a space.

When the call was over, I hesitated for a long moment, cursor hovering over the folder. Then I double-clicked. Inside was a list of files, eight in total. They didn't have names either.

It was just possible that the folder could have been renamed accidentally, that I'd carelessly deleted everything but a space character. It was inconceivable, however, that I would have done that to the eight files inside. I must have done it deliberately. Needless to say, I had no recollection of having done so.

I opened one of the files at random. The computer whirred into life, loading up my word-processing software. A few seconds later I knew what the file was. It was a letter of a type I've written several times, other examples of which currently resided in the 'Jackie' and 'Yvonne' folders, as well as in 'Ginny' and 'Mel'. A letter which said that while we'd had some fun, I didn't really feel that things could continue in the way they had. That I didn't feel that I was up to the rigours of a full-blown relationship, and didn't want to let them down. A letter that struggled valiantly not to say, 'Christ, I didn't ask for any of this. All I wanted was a friend. You were the one who pushed things into sex and commitment', a letter which tried to pull the blame onto me instead, in the hope of an easy getaway.

Reading the letter made me cringe way deep down in my soul. It was one of mine all right. I recognized the studious reasonableness, the calm hatred, the cultivated air of distant melancholy. Between the lines it said that I *was* to blame, in fact, that I should have had the sense not to get involved when

I knew I couldn't deal with it. That I was just another bloke, as shallow as the rest, who'd taken what was on offer against his better judgement, because he didn't have the character to turn it down. It was the letter of a confused child, denying responsibility for his actions by using all the tricks of an articulate adult.

The only problem was, I didn't know who it was to.

There were references in the letter to events, to times and places. None of them rang a bell. A few sentences didn't make any sense at all, unless they were in-jokes I'd shared with the person I'd been writing to. One read: 'I'm ready for the airlift to Bourbon Street'. It was meaningless, as far as I was concerned. It didn't make me smile sadly, as similar parts of the letters to Ginny or Jackie would have done. It was simply baffling.

I read the letter three times before sitting back with a cigarette, distractedly rubbing my temples. The letter made perfect sense. But then it would. I'd obviously written it.

But to whom, for fuck's sake? To whom, and when?

Without closing it, I opened another letter from the folder. This one was lighter in tone, but just as impenetrable. The fact that I sounded more relaxed probably meant it had been written earlier in the relationship than the other one. Probably, but not necessarily. With Yvonne, for example, there had been two waves, a second period of light-heartedness after we'd explicitly agreed that it was all just in fun, that we weren't playing for keepsies. Then, of course, the agreement had fallen apart, soon after she had put her apartment on the market.

'Why did you do that?' I'd asked, stupid old me. 'So I can come and live with you,' she'd said, smiling as if she'd finally given in to what I'd always wanted. Yvonne had been bright, funny and a successful businesswoman. She had also tried reasonably hard to slash my face with a breadknife.

I spent the next hour reading the rest of the letters, trying to get them into some sort of order. It should have been easy. They should have triggered an unwelcome series of memories which would have helped to put them in context. They didn't. They didn't trigger anything at all. They just read like a distillation of the letters from the other four folders, as if someone had fed them into a computer and the machine had spat out an averaging of them all.

In the end I just sat, staring out of the window. I couldn't see what was beyond the glass, and if the phone had rung I probably wouldn't even have heard it.

I was remembering Jackie, who'd once jumped so massively during a horror film that she'd sprayed an entire carton of popcorn over me and the surrounding rows. She had been really nice, in retrospect, simply a little uptight and justifiably wary of me. I was too fucked up by the time I met her to be able to tell the difference. I was remembering Mel, who kept insisting on taking me to little out-of-the-way upmarket cafés, each full of older versions of herself. Each venue was presented like a prize, and held some glorious memory for her that she would recount at stupefying length while I twisted with boredom in my seat. I was remembering Ginny, whom I'd liked, lying with her head upon my chest in bed one evening and telling me she'd slept with her ex-boyfriend that afternoon.

I was remembering Yvonne, who had a habit of pointing at me whenever she said something, head cocked to one side. At first I'd found this endearing; by the end it symbolized everything I hated most about her. When I thought of the others I could remember the line of their jaws, the curve of their hair, something personal about them and the way they looked. With Yvonne, only coldness and fear and that pointing finger.

I was remembering the fact that she'd rung me up two days after my cat had died, and asked me out to dinner. We'd stopped seeing each other three weeks previously, at my insistence, but we had a quiet and friendly meal. She was very supportive about my cat, because she'd known how much he meant to me.

During the meal she gave me a shirt that she'd bought. She'd seen it in a shop, she enthused, and simply had to buy it for me. The best manipulators are always those who've been manipulated to death themselves. Afterwards, she drove me home, and asked if she could stay. After all, she'd helped me –

279

surely I could do the same for her? I said no, and eventually left the car, clutching the little bag with my shirt in it. I felt awful, but what else could I have done? I couldn't just leave it there, and even she probably knew in her heart of hearts that she'd only bought it to make me feel I owed her.

I stood in my apartment and watched as she sat crying outside for half an hour, and then she left. She returned at three in the morning, and rang the doorbell until the house shook and I had to let her in. She then very loudly regressed to the age of five on my living room floor, and appeared to think I was her father. She grabbed a couple of knives from the kitchen, offered to cut herself up for me, and when I demurred, tried to cut me up instead.

It was, without exception, the worst night of my life.

It was only much later that I realized that she'd already sounded concerned when she'd rung up to ask me for dinner, as if she knew something would be wrong. Before she could have known I would be grieving for my pet, before she should have been aware that Ginger had died, apparently run over in the street by a car whose driver didn't stop.

I sat there and remembered all these things, watching them process in front of me like ghosts down a spiral staircase. Pieces of glass, still left inside, waiting to be recalled so they could shift and cut again.

But I couldn't remember a single thing about the folder of unnamed letters, or who I'd written them to. And all the time a name kept hammering in my head, a name I didn't even believe in.

Tamsin.

I worked for most of the afternoon on autopilot, bashing together some stuff for one of my major clients. It wouldn't matter that it was a bit below standard. They hardly noticed what I did so long as it was done on time.

Monica got back from work at about seven. It would make more sense for me to cook, given that I'm kicking around the house all day. But she's better at it and enjoys it, whereas I don't. It's one of the many things I'm completely talentless at. I don't know anything about cars' innards either.

She had the radio on in the kitchen while she was cooking, and when the phone rang shouted for me to get it. I picked it up and walked towards the window in the living room, away from the anaemic single-sex crooning that passes for popular music these days.

When I'd switched the phone on I said hello. There was no answer, and I was in the middle of shrugging and putting it back when a voice spoke.

'Hello David,' it said.

'Hi. Who's that?' I asked cheerily, assuming it was one of Monica's mates, all of whom are much better at remembering my name than I am at recalling theirs.

'It's Tamsin,' the voice said.

There was a very long pause, and I unconsciously moved a little further away from the kitchen door.

'Oh. Hello,' I said warily.

She laughed, a sound which had about as much humour in it as a door being shut at the end of a very long corridor. 'Yes, hello. Are we going to go on like this all night?'

I didn't know what else to say. In the end all I could come up with was an enquiry as to how she was.

'I'm fine,' she said, as if sharing a private joke. 'Excellent, thank you. How are you?'

'I'm, look . . .' At that moment Monica called to me, asking who it was. Without thinking, I said it was a client, and Tamsin's laugh carried to me from the phone. 'Look,' I repeated, feeling guilty and implicated, 'what can I do for you?'

'I don't know. What do you suggest?'

'Well . . .'

'I was just calling to say hello. After all, we know each other.'

'Yes,' I said, guardedly.

'I got the impression last night that maybe you don't approve of me.'

'What Steve does is up to him.'

'I'm not talking about that. You acted as if you didn't like me.'

'I . . . look, I hardly know you.'

'No?'

'No,' I said firmly. 'We only met last night.'

'That's right. Well, it was nice to talk to you, David.' At her second use of my name I felt something clench inside me. I'd noticed yesterday evening that she was a little familiar with it, and it's something I don't like. It's too personal, somehow. When someone uses my name like that, it feels like they're claiming squatter's rights on my soul.

'And you, Tamsin,' I said.

She laughed yet again, and the line went dead.

I felt like a bastard as Monica commiserated with me over clients who think they can call you up at all hours, but I wasn't going to tell her who it was. I was quiet over dinner, and ate little. For the rest of the evening Monica retreated to the sofa with a book, looking puzzled as I blanked my mind with work.

As soon as she'd gone to bed I called Steve. He sounded a little tired, but I ploughed on regardless. Tamsin could only have got our number from Steve's address book, and I'd come up with a pretext to get him to look for it. After a little preliminary chat I went for it.

He said he'd do it in the morning. I was about to press him, and then realized why he was sounding strange. There was someone with him, and she would have already returned his book.

I apologized for disturbing him, put the phone down and went to bed.

Nothing untoward happened the next day. That's the only way I can put it. I got up, did my work, spent the evening watching a film with Monica, went to bed. That was it.

Or nearly it. Each time the phone rang I expected it to be someone I didn't want to talk to, and after a while I just put the answering machine on and turned the volume down. I even considered taking half an hour mid-afternoon to go through the box file of letters and mementos I kept in the bedroom cupboard, looking for something, anything. But I didn't. I could remember what was there.

In the evening Steve called, and we arranged to play pool the following evening. I did some more work, and Monica finished her book, and then we went to bed. At some time in the night the phone must have rung, because when I got up the next morning the light on the answering machine was flashing.

Whoever it was didn't leave a message.

Steve got to the pub before me, and was at the bar making short work of a Budweiser when I turned up. We got another round and headed downstairs to the cold and deserted pool room. There was only one table, but as no one else seemed to know it was there, we rarely had much competition.

We didn't say much for a while, as was our wont. Eventually, Steve said I looked tired, and I agreed that I was. I went on to say that he was looking decidedly spruce for someone who was involved in as much nocturnal activity.

He smiled, and straightened up. He looked at me for a moment, paused, and then spoke. 'Well, you would know.'

'About what?'

Steve laughed, and appeared to make a decision of some kind. 'She told me,' he said. 'I don't mind.'

'About what?' I repeated.

'About you and her. You could have said, but it's not a problem.'

'Steve, what are you talking about?'

'About Tamsin,' he said, and for a moment he looked annoyed. It took me a moment to realize, because I'd never seen him look like that. Not at me, anyway.

I was completely confused. Okay, so he knew she'd called me. Surely it wasn't that big a deal.

'Steve, she just called me. To say hello, allegedly.'

'When?' he said. 'When was this?'

'Last night.'

'I didn't know about that.'

I stared at him. 'Well then what the fuck are you talking about? She called me. That's why I wanted you to look for your address book. She must have taken it last time she was at your place.'

Steve just looked at me.

'Steve, if there's anything else, you're going to have to spell it out for me, because I've no idea what you mean.'

Steve laughed angrily, and slammed his glass down on the table. I jumped, visibly. 'I'm talking,' he said, slowly and clearly, 'about the fact that you and Tamsin used to know each other. That you had an affair. That you fucked each other. Is that clear enough?'

For a brief, absurd moment, I was four years old again.

My parents had a vine in the back garden, back then, on which chilli peppers grew. Time and again I was told not to eat them, and so I didn't. I was relatively well-behaved in those days. Then one afternoon I touched one of the fascinatingly plump and glowing chillies, and a little while later was in agony, my lips burning as if I'd pressed them against an oven door. My parents, of course, assumed I'd eaten one of the peppers. I hadn't. All I'd done was accidentally rub one of my fingers against my lip, and that had been enough. As they applied ice to my lip and ice cream to my mind, my parents good-naturedly said they'd told me so, told me not to eat the peppers. When I protested that I hadn't eaten one they just smiled. The fact that they weren't shouting or angry made it worse. I hadn't eaten one. I hadn't eaten a pepper.

And so with Steve. I denied it. I said I'd never met her before, and it was true, but I felt like a liar. Steve didn't believe me. I tried to tell him about the way it had felt when I'd first seen her, when we'd all met in the cinema, but he took it the wrong way. As far as he was concerned, what she'd told him was the truth. He was the other side of the wall, and I couldn't reach him, no matter what I said. What's more, he now thought that I was trying to reactivate the affair behind his back.

I got angry, furious that he would rather believe someone he'd only met a couple of weeks ago. Again and again I said I didn't know her.

'Then how come,' he shouted eventually, 'how come she knows everything about you?' He slugged back the last mouthful of his beer, and then he stormed out of the pub.

I sat for a moment, shocked into immobility. Then I grabbed my coat and ran out.

I jogged down the road in the direction Steve would have taken, but there was no sign of him. I walked quickly back up to the pub, struck by the thought that he might be sitting fuming at one of the tables round the other side, but he wasn't. He'd gone.

I did a cigarette's-worth of standing against a nearby wall and smoking, in the hope that he'd reappear, but he didn't. I walked to the nearest phone box, and left a message on his machine saying that I had to talk to him. I didn't have to load fake sincerity into my voice: the real stuff was there in spades. I hoped he'd be able to tell that, even if these days he was choosing to believe Tamsin rather than me.

Then I walked home. There was a tube station nearby, but I couldn't face the thought of going underground and standing fretfully on the platform for ten minutes. I didn't think I could stand still for ten seconds, never mind longer. I turned in the direction of home, and walked stiff-legged up the road.

It was just turning dark by then, and the streets were deserted. I guess it was soap opera time, or dinner time, or some other period where everyone else just happened to be otherwise occupied. I felt utterly adrift, examined and found wanting. I couldn't explain why I'd felt the way I had on meeting Tamsin. I couldn't explain the letters either, but it wasn't as if they were to her. The letters I'd written to Yvonne were called 'Yvonne 1' to 'Yvonne 14'. I'm organized like that. The letters in the folder with no name had no names, so they couldn't be to Tamsin: otherwise they'd be called Tamsin 1-8. They were to someone with no name.

To no one at all.

It took less than half an hour to get home. I was striding quickly, wanting to be inside, anxious to be somewhere where I could be surrounded by things I recognized and understood. I found I was muttering and swearing to myself, on the verge of tears. I hadn't felt like that since the excruciating night nearly four years before when Katy and I had broken up. I was frightened to discover that side of me was still intact, that beneath the carefully cultivated exterior a lonely and hurt little boy was still jabbering and screaming to itself.

By the time I got to our street I was almost running. I scooted up the stairs to the flat, and was fumbling with the keys when the door opened and Monica was standing there, looking sane and wonderful and whole. She was surprised to see me, but as I started upon the drawn-out process of feeling my way towards an explanation, I realized that there was something a little strange about her. Not strange, exactly, but 'public'. She wasn't being quite herself. I asked her if she was okay, and she nodded vigorously.

'Oh yes,' she chirped, leading me up the couple of steps which led to the kitchen. Then: 'We've got a visitor.'

Steve had come to our flat. He'd thought better of his outburst, realized I was telling the truth, and had come to talk it out. It wouldn't be ideal with Monica around, but I felt so anxious that any resolution was welcome, even if it meant a tense hour or so with her. It felt as if the last few days were drawing to a point, a moment when, finally, the world was going to start making sense again.

That's what I thought as I strode across the kitchen towards the living room, feeling nervous but glad of something concrete to say and do. That's what I was expecting as I walked into the living room and looked across at the sofa, ready to be hearty and businesslike and to talk to Steve like we always used to.

I wasn't expecting to see Tamsin.

I stopped a yard or so into the room. I'd been so convinced it would be Steve that I'd almost been able to see him sitting tensely on the edge of the sofa, feeling a bit of an idiot. But it wasn't him. It was her.

This can't be happening, I thought. This is *Fatal Attraction* and it isn't happening to me.

'Hello David,' she said, looking up bright-eyed over the cup she was sipping from. She was holding it a little strangely, but I was too stunned to work out in what way.

'Tamsin was nearby and stopped in to say hello,' Monica said, unnecessarily. I stared at her while she was saying this, but there appeared to be no subtext to the announcement. 'Isn't Steve with you?'

'No,' I said. 'No. He went home.'

'Oh,' Monica said, puzzled. 'Why?'

As I struggled to come up with an answer, I glanced at Tamsin. She was smiling, a little cat smile that curled up at the corners into a mind whose strange angles I was still struggling to comprehend. 'Ask her', I wanted to say. Why don't you ask her what happened this evening, and why?

In the end I just shrugged, said that the pool hadn't been happening, and that Steve was tired and called it a day. I sat down on the sofa next to Monica, making it as clear as I could without recourse to speech that I felt there was one too many people in the flat. No one appeared to be listening on the body language wavelength.

'We were just talking about holidays,' Monica said, and for the first time ever I felt a twist of irritation for her. I can't do that kind of conversation, as she fully well knows, can't sit and swop sentences on subjects which are of no interest to me. What is the point? I don't give a shit what other people are going to do for their holidays. Why should I? It's just white noise, information which has no impact on me. Sitting and listening to it very rapidly drives me into a state of cold and furious boredom. I don't ask for in-depth discussions of weighty issues – I hate those too, as it happens – but I can't sit and listen to people reading out the ingredient list of their lives.

'Oh yes?' I said, hoping to kill the conversation stone dead.

'Tamsin's hoping to go to New Orleans,' Monica continued with, as far as I was concerned, a surreal level of enthusiasm.

'Why?' I said. I knew I was behaving badly.

'Oh, just everything,' Tamsin said, and Monica nodded at me, as if this explained something. 'French toast, the old town, jazz. I've always wanted to go. It sounds wonderful.'

'Holidays are always wonderful,' Monica chipped in, tellingly. 'They take you out of yourself, don't they?'

'That's it,' Tamsin agreed. 'That's exactly it. Sometimes when I'm sitting at my desk, doing something boring, I wish it could happen right there and then. I wish I could just be airlifted straight to Bourbon Street and sit on the pavement drinking cold beer and listening to Dixieland. Don't you feel like that sometimes, David?'

As I stared horrified into her eyes, a half-image passed through the back of my mind. A picture, combined with a fragment of sound, a wisp of scent, a beat of atmosphere. A glimpse of the side of someone's face, the sound of a tenth of a word being spoken. The noise of a pub, the smell of beer on a warm evening. Like a memory it was there, a half second of the past, and then it was gone, unrecoverable.

From that moment, I knew I couldn't try to explain away what was happening. It must have been me who was there, in that pub. That moment was part of me. Something had been forgotten, and I had to find out what it was. I must have been there, doing that, at that time, with someone.

'David doesn't dream about things like that,' Monica said suddenly, covering what must have been a very pregnant pause. 'He's happy.'

'Is he?' Tamsin asked. 'He doesn't sometimes want to call up his clients in the wee small hours and shout abuse?' I shivered, but Monica didn't notice. I hadn't said anything like that since we'd known each other. But I used to. I used to all the time. 'Or put razor blades in the parcels he carefully sends to them?'

'Stop talking about me as if I'm not here,' I said, mainly to convince myself that I was. 'No, I don't wish any of those things.

I'm happy now. I've got Monica, for a start.' I hadn't said this for political reasons, but it went down well with her, and she looped her arm around my back.

Tamsin looked at the two of us with a little smile that made me want to take a hot iron to her face. Somehow this woman was holding everything I had in her hand, and she was ready to clench her fist. I didn't know why, or what she was waiting for, or how much longer she'd hold off.

Suddenly I knew what I had to do, what I should have done half an hour before. Thinking fast, I groaned and went through a great show of irritation at my forgetfulness, tutting and virtually slapping my forehead in order to get the message across. Tamsin and Monica stared at me with bright smiles.

'What an idiot,' I said, shaking my head. 'Got to go.' I stood up, and reached for the car keys.

'Where?' Monica asked.

'To see Steve,' I said. 'Completely forgot something.'

'Can't you call him?'

'No,' I said. 'Got to get something from him.' It was weak, and I knew that Monica wasn't convinced, but by that time I was backing towards the door. Unless one of them was prepared to call my bluff, they couldn't stop me going. 'Won't be long.'

I turned on my heel and walked rapidly through the kitchen, willing them not to say anything, hoping against hope that Monica wouldn't come up with the bright idea of suggesting that I give Tamsin a lift somewhere. I heard her call out just before I got to the door, but I ignored it, shut the door quietly after me and ran downstairs.

I went through two red lights on the way to Steve's, using all the rat-runs I knew to get me there as quickly as possible. Tamsin was building a trap around me. I didn't know what kind, or why, but she was. The only way to stop the circle from closing was to jam something in the way: to ensure that Steve knew what was going on. I had to speak to him. I had to convince him that he was dealing with someone whose word could not be trusted. Not even on something as basic as her name. How I could do that without knowing what her real name was remained to be seen. But I had to do it.

When I pulled up outside Steve's flat I was relieved to see that his light was on. I'd spent the last five minutes of the drive convinced that he might have gone to mine, or even that something might have happened to him. There was no reason for the latter suspicion, none at all, but once it had entered my head there seemed no way of dislodging it. But he was obviously home, and would have heard the message I'd left on the answer machine. That was good. I strode up to the door and pressed the entry phone buzzer briefly. It was one of our running gags, seeing how short a buzz we could generate. Partly a joke, partly a subversive dig at all those in the world who leaned on buzzers until the building shook. It was a good buzz, short and probably barely audible. I knew he'd be impressed.

There was no answer. Puzzled, I pressed again, less briefly this time. After a pause a burst of feedback leapt out of the speaker.

'Steve,' I said. 'It's David.'

'Hello David,' said Tamsin. 'Why don't you come up?'

I stared at the speaker, feeling sick, then took a quick step backwards. As a blurred afterthought I moved so that I remained close to the front of the building, so that someone looking out of Steve's window wouldn't be able to see me. Heart pounding, I gazed unseeingly out across the road. There was no way.

No way she could have got here more quickly than me.

No way.

'What are you doing here?'

At the sound of his voice I refocused suddenly to see Steve walking down the pavement towards me. He was still wearing his coat, and looked cold. Moving quickly and silently, as if in a dream, I raised my hand to my lips and ran towards him. He stared at me as I grabbed his arm and pulled him towards the car.

'Dave . . .'

'Steve, get in the car,' I hissed. 'Just get in the fucking car. Please.'

He got in.

It took an hour, but in the end I did it.

I didn't say anything as I drove. I glanced across once to see him sitting looking affably out the front, and decided against breaking the silence. I hate talking about important things when I know I'm about to be interrupted by admin such as getting out of cars and buying drinks.

I drove to another pub that we sometimes went to and bought a couple of beers. When we were comfortably sat, when he'd been for a piss and I'd lit a cigarette, I began. I told Steve again that I'd never met Tamsin before. He started to shift in his seat, but I kept going. I told him that I'd just got home to find Tamsin in my flat, talking to my girlfriend, and that she'd made a reference to something that had spooked me. I told him that there was no way she could have beaten me to his flat. He nodded at that one: he's been driven by me, and knows the routes I take. I realized suddenly that he had only my word for the fact that she'd been there when he turned up, but he didn't question it.

He believed me, finally. At least, he believed that I'd never gone out with Tamsin. I firmly drummed into Steve the precise number of times I'd seen or spoken to Tamsin, and what the circumstances had been. He seemed willing to disregard any-thing Tamsin said which contradicted my version, and that was enough to be going on with. In my relief I was willing to back off the weirder stuff. It seemed the right thing to do. I think Steve was inclined to see it as slightly hysterical exaggeration on my part, done for comic effect. I wasn't prepared to sound any stranger than necessary, so I let it go. The sentences concerning it washed down through the conversation and disappeared, leaving us with something more explicable. A mad woman. We both knew about those.

In the end I drove him home, and felt a weight lift from my

shoulders as our familiar banter started up. As he got out of the car he laughed and shook his head.

'I should have known it was bollocks,' he said. 'In all the time I've known you I've not seen you even *look* at a blonde, never mind go out with one.'

I laughed, and waved, and drove away and because I was so relieved that I'd sorted things out with Steve it was only when I'd got about halfway home that I absorbed what he'd said. When I did I steered the car over to the side of the road and just sat for a while, engine idling, staring at the condensation on the window.

Tamsin's hair was brown. A rich, dark brown. Exactly the kind I liked.

When I got home I smoothed over my abrupt departure. Tamsin had stayed another five minutes after I'd left, apparently, and then gone to take the tube. I nodded distantly. It didn't make any difference. If she'd left a second after I had she still couldn't have beaten me. I tuned out while Monica free-associated on the subject of holidays, and worked on a way of asking a question so that it wouldn't cause trouble.

'Tamsin's hair,' I said eventually, with the air of someone who thought it looked terrible. 'Is it natural, do you think?'

'Oh yes,' Monica said seriously, giving the subject the full weight of her attention. 'You can't fake a blonde like that.' I nodded, dismissing the subject, but Monica held onto it. 'Do you like it?'

'Babe, you know I prefer brunettes,' I said, in a just passable Bogart voice, and Monica laughed. She knew.

So did Tamsin. Perhaps that's why I was seeing someone different. They saw blonde Tamsin. I saw someone with dark hair who didn't have a name. I thought it was more likely that I was the one seeing the truth.

She had power of some kind. That was clear. What was less apparent was what the hell she wanted.

The subject changed and we watched some television and went to bed and I lay all night staring at the ceiling.

The next morning it started in earnest.

I was sitting at my desk, as ever. I felt hollow, too blank to be tired. It was grey outside, and the leaves of the trees which lined the other side of the road were stirring constantly and silently behind the glass of my window. Monica had gone quietly to work at half past eight, and since then it felt as if I hadn't heard a sound.

Until the phone went, and I dropped my cigarette. The ring isn't that loud, but it was much closer than I was expecting. I realized that the phone was lying to one side of the desk. I'd forgotten to put it on the charger overnight. Again.

It rang twice more, and then I picked it up.

'Hello,' I said.

'Hello David,' said a voice, and in a way it was almost a relief.

'Tamsin,' I said.

'No,' she said. 'You know it's not. You know that's not my name.'

'Yes,' I said.

'So what is it?'

'I have no idea.'

'Bullshit. You know. You just don't fucking remember.' I was startled by the tone of her voice. For the first time it had lost its gloating pseudo-politeness and was on the verge of anger. It raised hairs on the back of my neck, and I didn't want to hear it get any worse. But I didn't know her name. I simply didn't know.

'What do you want from me?'

'What do I want?' she shouted, and I could feel myself shrinking with a familiar fear. 'What do I want? You're such a shit, David, such an utter, fucking shit. You fuck me up, throw me away, and you want to know what I want from you?'

'Tamsin, I . . .'

'*Don't call me that!*'

'I don't know what else to call you –'

I stopped not because I'd run out of things to say, or because I was interrupted, but because I heard the all too familiar tones the handset makes when the battery has run out.

The line went dead, and I was just trying to decide whether to run to get the other line in the bedroom, or just to be thankful that the conversation was finished, when I heard Tamsin's voice again, coming from the phone.

'Yes you do,' it said. 'Yes you do. And you'd better remember, because I need to know.'

'Can't you just leave me alone?' I stuttered, not knowing if she'd hear me. The battery indicator light had gone out. The phone should have been dead.

'Why should I? How can I? If you don't even have the decency to remember my fucking name?'

'Please,' I said, 'please, just go away.'

'I can't,' she said, abruptly no longer sounding angry.

Then there was no more sound. I looked at the handset. The battery indicator was still out. Our last couple of sentences couldn't have happened. I put the phone back on the desk. I didn't want it recharged.

Her name wasn't Tamsin. She'd admitted it now. I had to find out what it was, or remember it. Until that happened, it would go on, and from the tone of her last sentence I wondered if it was more than that. Maybe it wasn't just me who was being persecuted. Maybe I was involved. Perhaps she couldn't go until I remembered who she was.

Maybe she really didn't know.

I spent the rest of the morning ignoring my work, thinking until my brain hurt. I couldn't get anything to come. I couldn't think of anyone who I'd shared dreams of New Orleans with. I couldn't remember who the letters were to. In the end I called Steve, from the phone in the bedroom. The first minute or so of conversation was a little stilted, and I wondered how long it would be before our shouting match completely left both our minds. But it relaxed soon enough, and after a while I asked him.

'Steve, got a weird question for you.'

'The answer's no, Dave. I like and respect you, but I simply can't do that other thing. I'm just not attracted to you in that way.'

'Very funny. Since Katy, how many girls have I been out with?'

'Is this a rhetorical question?'

'No.'

There was a pause, and all of the light-heartedness went out of Steve's voice. 'Are you okay, David?'

'Not really. How many?'

'Well, there was Ginny, then that one I never met.'

'Jackie.'

'Yeah, her, that skinny one – Mel, was it? Oh, Christ, and that complete nutter. Yvonne. Whatever happened to her?'

That was something I'd often wondered. Exactly what had happened to Yvonne, why she had backed off in the end.

'She went away. Eventually.'

'Right. So, four.'

'That's what I thought.'

Back in the living room, I stood and looked out of the window at the drizzle. Outside on the pavement a cat ran past, as if fleeing from something. But they always look like that: probably it was only the rain.

It should have made me feel better to get confirmation from Steve that there couldn't have been anyone else. It didn't. Instead, it opened up a portion of my mind which hadn't really been paying attention. It melted suddenly, as if I was relaxing a muscle which I hadn't realized had been clenched for months, maybe years.

There had only been four. There was no one else.

Tamsin had to be one of them.

I turned and walked back into the bedroom. I opened the cupboard and sat down in front of it. Reaching beyond the hanging tails of coats and shirts I found my box file. For a moment I just let my hands rest on it, sensing that I could simply leave it there, that its contents could remain half-buried. But half-buried is not enough. You can put rubbish as deep in the bin as you like, and cover it with whatever you can find, but it will still be there. Even when the truck has come to take it away you'll know, know that somewhere the evidence remains. It may be hidden so that no one will ever find it, and it may be destroyed, but you'll still know it's there, or that it existed once.

Once a coin has been thrown in the water, it's always going to be lying at the bottom of some pool or other.

I pulled the box out and opened it on my lap. Unlike the files for my 'proper' ex-girlfriends, Katy and her predecessors, the contents were a jumble. Letters, cinema ticket stubs, wine corks and dried-out flowers mixed together so thoroughly that they could have related to just one person. I pulled out a couple of letters and glanced at the writing on them.

Letter from Ginny. Card from Mel. Unwisely, I glanced inside. There, in an untidy biro sprawl, was a message saying that she thought she loved me. Carefully phrased, so as not to go too far out on a limb, but there in black and white all the same. Cringing to the depth of my soul with shame, I put it back in the envelope. I hadn't loved Mel, or any of them. It wasn't that I had taken advantage. I simply hadn't felt anything at all.

Two consecutive postcards from Jackie. The first a tirade. The second a numb acceptance. A CD single of the theme song from a long-forgotten film which I went to see with Mel, a song which would have been 'our tune', if we'd stayed together long enough to have one. If I hadn't left, walked out dead into the night, leaving her tearless and bewildered.

Rain spattered against the window suddenly, and I looked up. I caught a glance of a photo of Monica and I which hung on Monica's side of the bed. Her face looked down at me, brown from the holiday she'd been on before we met. It was a pretty face, but it took me a moment to recognize it. Even longer to recognize myself.

I pulled another handful of letters from the box, mostly from Ginny. It was odd I couldn't find anything from Yvonne. I must have thrown them away. I was still leafing through cards and letters, feeling more and more horrified at myself, when my heart nearly stopped at the sound of the doorbell. Scattering the contents of the box I leapt awkwardly to my feet.

In the hall I paused. We don't have an intercom system, and so I had to go downstairs to answer. I didn't know whether I wanted to. After a pause the bell rang again, and I opened the door to the flat and walked slowly down.

No shape bulked through the glass of the front door, and when I opened it, there was nobody there. On the mat lay a small bundle wrapped in brown paper, and I picked it up and closed the door.

In the bedroom I took the paper off. Inside, damp from the rain, were seven letters. They all bore the same address, written in my handwriting, and none of them had a name.

Sitting suddenly down on the bed, as my legs went from under me, I took the letter out of the first one. It was neatly laser printed, and I recognized the typeface. I recognized the contents too. It was the first letter from the nameless folder. No name at the top, but my initial at the bottom, and a kiss.

Another clatter of rain hit the window, but I barely heard it. Fragments came at first, and then whole scenes, pushing through the cracks like eyeless animals wriggling from the earth. In slow motion, my vision blurred, I reached down and pushed my hand through the articles scattered around the file box on the floor, the remains of what should have been friendships, the debris of shattered people. The person I had thought was me watched as someone else searched for what he knew was there to be found.

A small bottle, and a key.

I found them.

The key fitted a door which I now remembered. The bottle held formaldehyde, and something else. The last joint of a finger, a finger which always used to point. Something which belonged to a woman whose face I could suddenly recall.

*   *   *

The rain was so furious that I had to lean forward and peer through the windscreen, and I skidded at one junction and nearly totalled a cyclist. On the passenger seat lay the letters, though I didn't need the address any more. The bottle was in my pocket.

The road was in a tangle of dead streets between Finsbury Park and Archway, an area I'd unconsciously avoided for two years. As I drew closer I noticed how many windows were still boarded up, the remnants of some developer's dream which had yet to come to fruition, waiting out the fallow years in a little patch of temporary ghost town. Most of the houses had already been abandoned when I'd last been there, when I'd last visited Tamsin Road.

The closer I got, the slower I drove. It wasn't reluctance. I knew I had to go. It was caution, because of the wetness of the roads, and because I didn't trust myself to drive with so much still flooding into my head. It was like suddenly discovering a new room in a house which has always seemed too small, except that I knew this room from before.

Turning into Tamsin Road was like finding a drawing you did as a child. It's a short street that curves, and on both sides the eyes and mouths of the buildings were boarded over and nailed shut. Dirty fragments of litter scuttled down the gutters, but not as much as you'd expect. No one was coming here to top the level up, and I suspected that if you caught one of the fleeing fragments of newspaper with your foot the date would be from some years ago. From 1993 itself, perhaps, the year I'd last been here.

I pulled up outside number 12 and killed the engine. After gathering up the letters I got out of the car, locked it and walked up towards the door. It was two years older and grubbier, paint peeling a little more than before, but I recognized it. For a brief moment I thought of the people I knew, of Steve and Monica, and realized that they were somewhere in the city now, doing their jobs and – who knows – maybe thinking of me. But I wasn't there anymore.

I was here again.

I felt in my pocket for the key and slipped it into the lock. She gave me the key herself, obtained by some means from the company she helped to run. I don't think they were the people who were planning to redevelop the area, but I can't remember. I hadn't blanked that fact, like all the others, but simply hadn't listened when I was told. I listened to her a lot at first, because she was funny, and clever. But after a while I didn't listen to her at all, like I didn't really listen to Mel or Jackie, or even to Ginny, whom I'd liked.

The lock turned with a little effort, and I let myself in. The hallway was dark, but I saw the letter lying on the mat and picked it up. It was the last one, covered in dust and beginning to discolour, with the address in my writing but no name at the top. I added it to the others and walked quietly to the staircase. After turning for no reason to look at the dirty yellow light which seeped through the boards across the door's thin and filthy window, I went upstairs.

The door was shut. I'd always closed it after me, as if that would make some difference, as if throwing something away and piling rubbish on top would really hide what was at the bottom of the pile. Realizing I was crying, I rubbed the back of my hands across my eyes and turned the handle of the door.

The room was exactly as I now remembered it, though deeper in dust. It was brighter than the rest of the house, more light coming through the windows, which had been papered rather than boarded over. The corkscrew we'd opened our wine with lay by the wall, and the mattress where we'd fucked was still beneath the window, now heavily stained with damp.

I walked to the middle of the room and looked down, and was not surprised to see that the ragged patch of carpet looked as though it had recently been disturbed. Slowly I sat down cross-legged next to it, and took the bottle out of my pocket.

We hadn't needed to come here. I had a flat, and so did she. We'd just done it occasionally to be different, to be sleazy in the way that middle-class yuppies sometimes think is exciting. We came on autumn afternoons, letting ourselves in separately, then shared a bottle of wine and had sex on the mattress and carpet and floorboards; her eyes flat with lust and hurt, mine with lack of feeling. Rubbed into the walls of the dead room I could almost smell the only two emotions I ever experienced in it: jittery, perfunctory desire, and bored, selfish remorse. The first time I'd said I didn't think our relationship was going anywhere was in this room, but of course we'd come back several times after that. It was as if I deliberately ended up sleeping with women after saying we shouldn't, as if I wanted to hurt them as much as possible. I didn't. I just followed the line of least resistance, lived out my programming like an abandoned automaton.

I smoked a cigarette, ground it out on the floorboards, and then reached out and pulled up the carpet. The boards looked loose, as indeed they were. Not knowing how she'd look, or caring, I pulled the middle one up, and then the two on either side.

She lay there, caved in and empty, body curved a little because she had been too tall to fit in the space. A last faint remnant of the smell I'd buried drifted up, but not much. Not as bad as it had been when I'd come here before, on the seven occasions I'd come and sat with her, watching the body decay, seeing the parts I'd kissed or sucked decomposing into sludge.

It wasn't just that she'd killed my cat. It was what she'd done to me before that, or helped me do to myself. Every time I tried to break loose from her she appeared in front of me, and diverted me to the side. She needed me to say I loved her, and manoeuvred me until I did, standing in the kitchen at her office and blurting it out in the hope that she'd stop crying. That was the only time I've ever lied in a sentence with that word in it, and it was the beginning of the end for me, the last time I could tell the difference between loving and not caring. That was when my feelings finally died, where I lost the battle to keep myself alive.

She was mad, but she was also a little girl who deserved and needed someone better than me. She killed my cat to try to keep me, and when I realized what she'd done, I killed her back. I rang her up at work and hinted that I wouldn't mind an afternoon behind papered windows, and she'd purred and said she'd be there as soon as she could. I knew she would. Being fucked in the afternoon by someone she knew didn't care about her was exactly the kind of self-inflicted wound she was incapable of rejecting.

I was standing behind the door when she walked in, and brought a brick down on her head as hard as I could. It took a couple more blows to finish the job, but I got there in the end. I cut off part of her pointing finger to prove to myself that I was free, put it in my pocket and then hid her body under the boards.

I wrote the first of the letters in my head as I stayed with her that afternoon, a letter that I needed to write. In these years since Katy I've had someone in my mind, someone I will be able to care about, someone I will come back to life for. Yvonne hadn't been that woman, and neither was Mel or Jackie or Ginny. That woman had no name, no address. She was the best of all of them, the opposite of their worst, all of that and more. She was me, I suppose, transposed and set apart, an idea to comfort me across cold evenings and grey years. Sometimes I'd thought I could almost picture her, almost smell her skin.

But she was everyone, and no one, and I never found her.

In my head I wrote a letter to that woman, pretending she really existed. Maybe, for a while, I even believed she did. I went home and typed it, and then posted it to Tamsin Road. I didn't know where else to send it.

A few weeks later I came back, picked up the letter in the hallway and read it out to what was under the floorboards. As a punishment, I suppose. To show her what I would have written if she had been the one, if she hadn't got a name.

I wrote seven more letters, but on the last occasion I didn't come to read. By then it didn't seem so important, because I'd given up. The letters had started to follow their own course, to replicate the only kind I was capable of writing. I could make up dreams like going to Bourbon Street, but I couldn't carry them through. Without the nameless woman to hold me, I couldn't keep them alive. Soon afterwards I must have blanked it altogether.

I didn't kill Mel or Ginny or Jackie, in case you're wondering. They didn't kill my cat. I'm not a violent man. I was just trying to find someone who was never really there.

After I'd looked at the remains for long enough, I opened the bottle and tipped the finger joint out onto the floorboards. I picked it up and placed it as close as I could to what was left of her right hand. Then I took a pen from my pocket, wrote her name at the top of each of the letters and on the envelopes, and placed those in there with her. The letters had never been to Yvonne, or to anyone who'd really existed. But they had confused what was left of her, and until she knew her name, she wouldn't be able to go.

I kissed the tip of my finger and touched it to where her lips used to be, remembering for a moment how much fun she'd been in the beginning, how often she'd made me laugh. Then I replaced the floorboards one by one and moved the carpet back over them. I ground the bottle to fragments under my foot, took a last look round, and then left. The key I dropped down a gutter as I got into the car.

I spent two hours driving, but have no idea where I went. Round and round the backstreets, not paying attention, just trying to find my way back to the present. When I'd come far enough I pulled over at a public phone box and called Steve.

Tamsin had already called him. Her boyfriend had returned, and she'd decided to stay with him. She felt it was for the best that they never saw each other again. Steve sounded both relieved and mildly put out by the news. I said I'd call him soon.

I went home, changed my clothes, and then sat at my desk watching the clouds. After a while Monica came home, and I stood up to give her a hug. I could see in her face when we parted that it hadn't been tight enough, but it was the best that I could do.

People always have names. Yvonne, or Monica, in the end it doesn't make much difference.

Not tight enough is the best that I can do.

SORTED

Alright. Here it is.

Friday night – lads' night out. Down 'Club Bastard'; owner's a big fan, what can I say. Beautiful. Everything on tap. Something to drink. Something to snort. Something to shag.

Sorted.

Roll up about ten; fucking photographers outside. No, love them, actually. You got to. Helped put us where we are, know what I mean? Stand outside, with the lads – in our top Armani coats. Flash Flash Flash.

Questions; what about that penalty, eh? What about the ref? Are we going to win the Cup?

Course we fucking are.

Inside, rows of shag; take your pick. Bottle blonde, extra tits, legs up to their arses. Lovely. Stand at the bar, lads together – like fucking kings. Free bubbly? Yeah, I should think so mate – just give us the fucking bottle.

Who've we got? Ted Stupid. Man in goal – safe. Top lad. Kevin Legg – out on the left. Goes like the clappers – excellent. Paul Tosser; solid at the back. Try to get past him – seven types of shit kicked out of your shins. Ha ha ha ha ha. No, seriously; great little player, great skills.

And me. Gavin Mate. Fucking midfield general, innit.

Do we dance? Do we fuck. No need mate. Stand there in a circle and the club fucking dances around us. Big laughs – Ted sticks his hand down some shag's top. Lobs her tit out – signs it. Excellent. Some cunt tries to muscle in – boyfriend. Paul elbows the twat in the face; end of problem. Great skills. Great little player.

Go behind the bar; help ourselves. Barman gets shirty; bunch

of arse. You don't understand: *we can do what we fucking like.*
Owner comes down – I pour him a drink. He's fucking loving
it. Flash flash, more pictures. Great on the back page. Nice little
advert. No fucking problem.

One o'clock, Kev's pissed as a twat – Paul's chewing face
with some top black shag. I'm caning it with Ted at a table in
the corner. Hundred notes of charlie up each nostril by then –
fucking flying. Then:

See this shag, other side of the room. Red mini, no top to speak
of. Gypsy skin, Bambi eyes. And an arse to fucking die for. Suzy
all over again: I'm thinking – right. That's me fucking sorted.

Go over, bit of chat. She's loving it. Put in half an hour's worth
– time to go. Give the nod to the lads; later – yeah, cheers.

Flash flash out the front so slip out the back; I'm Gavin Mate,
I am. Shag's wetting itself – ten seconds of fame, innit. Limo
pulls up, pile in. More charlie, obviously. Roll up the fifty, cut
the rocks. Show her how it's done. Excellent. Tweak a nipple,
just for a giggle. She's going to go off like a fucking rocket.

Back to the flat. Get more bubbly down her then think why
fucking bother. It's in the bag. Get on the pitch, black satin
sheets. She's wriggling like a pig in a tin. Another line, I dump
the Paul Smith and then it's game on.

Fuck her. Fuck her again. And then;

Hang on. Start again.

Gavin Mate. Midfield supremo. But not always, obviously.

Eighteen. Tipped up at the gate. You going to give me an
apprenticeship, or what? Guy takes the piss until I show him
what I've got.

Silky skills.

Team's going nowhere – the whole fucking point. They said
that one man can't make a team; proved what a bunch of twats
they are. Straight in the A's: slow start – playing with wankers,
aren't I. Couple of games, goals slotted in. Crowd loves it. Owner
goes 'Hang on – could have a winner here': stumps up for some
decent players. Kevin Legg. Ted Stupid. Suddenly we're a fucking

team. End of first season – promotion, thanks very much. Gavin Mate, hero of the hour. Course I fucking am.

Meanwhile, outside world; it's a performance, innit. Got the lads out on the prowl – flash flash, people talking. Bought top suits. And bearing – made old Eubanks look like a twat. Not difficult, of course. Joking – Chris and I are mates. Serious. He's the only loser I go round with. Ha ha ha ha ha.

Couple of seasons, build the rep and up the ladder. Receipts through the roof; owner's like a pig in shit. Going lovely. Manager knows I'm top lad. Royalty. Paul Tosser joins the back – World War Three on a stick. Night life. Shag on tap. Fun to be had; up the nose and up the arse. Money in buckets. Respect.

Dodgy moment; some slag from the *Sun* starts nosing into where Gavin Mate comes from. Can't have that; had a word. Slag never works again. Sorted. Manager's not going to let anyone piss off Gavin Mate – too fucking important. Gets the goals. Gets the press. Gets the sponsorship.

Meet the untouchables.

Now. This season. Premiership's in the bag. Just the Cup to play for. We going to win it?

Course we fucking are. I'm Gavin Mate, I am.

Leave the shag in the bedroom; go for some bubbly. Thirsty now. She's saying come back; begging for it. Course you got to oblige.

Give Ted a call first; getting his knob polished by a couple of teenies. Hear the girls laughing in the background – he's fucking sorted. They're sisters, innit.

Shame about mine. Suzy was good value. Shame she had to go.

Back in the bedroom, give one to the shag again. She falls asleep after. Finish the bubbly, go for some more. Sit in the kitchen a while. Know it's going to happen. Nothing I can do about it. Artist, I am. Artist of the pitch. Got to do what I fucking feel like.

Top plan: find a way of getting away with it. Stop being poncy Nigel Smith, lose the accent, fuck the past; find a way of being untouchable. Off the parents – car crash – shame Suzy had to go too. Probably her fault though, if you think about it; shouldn't have let me watch her. I'd give her one now, if she was alive. Slag. But she isn't. Probably give her one anyway.

Disappeared for a while – Middle East. No one's going to find the ones out there. Then back, become Gavin Mate, and a knock on the right door. Goals. Welcome to the untouchables.

Finish the bottle, raring to go. Pissed as a twat, good news; more blood and guts that way. Back in the bedroom, tape the shag's mouth up. Then break the bubbly bottle and have some fun. Manager'll sort it during the game tomorrow: get back here, be like it never happened.

Are we going to win? Course we are.

Nice one.

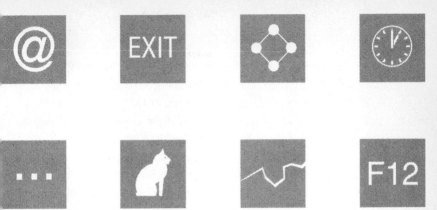

THE DARK LAND

WHAT YOU MAKE IT

It started with the bed.

After three years at college I'd come back home, returning to the bedroom I'd grown up in. It was going to be a while before I could afford to move out for good, and so in the intervening month I'd redecorated the room: covering the very 1970s orange with a more soothing shade, and badgering my mother into getting some new curtains that didn't look like they had been designed on drugs by someone who liked the colour brown a great deal. I'd also moved most of the furniture around, trying to breath new life into a space I'd known since I was ten. It hadn't worked. It still felt as if I should be doing French verbs or preparing conkers, musing on what girls might be like. I knew it was largely an excuse for not doing anything more constructive – like filling out the pile of job applications which sat on the desk – but that afternoon I decided to move the bed away from its traditional place by the wall and try it in another couple of positions. It was hard work. One of the legs was rather fragile and the bed had to be virtually lifted off the floor rather than dragged around – which is why I hadn't tried moving it before, I remembered. After half an hour I was hot and irritated and developing a stoop. I had also become convinced that the original position had been not only the optimal but in fact the *only* place the bed could go.

It was as I struggled to shove it back up against the wall that I began to feel a bit strange. Light-headed, nauseous. Out of breath, I assumed. When the bed was finally back in place I lay back on it for a moment, feeling rather ill – and I suppose I just fell asleep.

I woke up about half an hour later, half-remembering a dream in which I had been doing nothing more than lying on my bed and remembering that my parents had said that they were going to extend the wood panelling in the downstairs hallway. For a moment I was disorientated, confused by being in the same place in reality as I had been in the dream, and then I drifted off again.

Some time later I woke up again. I found it very difficult to fight my way up out of sleep, but eventually managed to haul myself sluggishly upright. After a while I lurched to my feet and across to the sink to get a glass of water. Drinking it made the inside of my mouth a little less dry, but no more appealing. I decided that a cup of tea would be a good idea, and headed out of the bedroom to go downstairs.

As I reached the top of the staircase I remembered the dream about the panelling, and wondered where a strange notion like that could have come from. I'd worked hard for my psychology paper at college, and was confident that Freud hadn't felt that wood panelling was even worth a mention. I trudged downstairs, still feeling odd, my thoughts dislocated and fragmented.

When I reached the halfway landing I ground to a halt, and stared around me, astonished. They *had* extended the panelling.

When you enter my parents' house you come into a two-storey hallway, with a staircase that climbs up three walls to the second floor. The panelling used to only go about eight feet up the wall of the front hall, but now it soared right up to the ceiling. And they'd done it in exactly the same wood as the original. There wasn't a join to be seen. How had they managed that? Come to that, *when* had they managed it? It hadn't been like that this morning, but both my parents were at work and would be for hours and ... well, it was just impossible. I reached out and touched the wood, bewildered at how even the grain matched, and that the new wood looked just as aged as the original, which had been there fifty years.

Then: Wait a minute, I thought. That isn't right. There hadn't used to be *any* panelling in the hall. Just simple white walls.

The stairs themselves had been panelled in wood, but the walls were just plain white plaster. How could I have forgotten that? What had made me think that the front hall had been panelled, and think it so unquestioningly? I remembered that I'd recently noticed, sensitized to these things by having repainted my room, that the white in the hall was a little grubby, especially round the light switches. So what was all this panelling doing here? Where had it come from? And why had I been so sure that at least some of it had always been there?

Something wasn't right. I walked into the kitchen, casting bewildered glances back into the hall. I absently-mindedly registered a soft clinking sound outside, and automatically headed to the back door – too puzzled about the panelling to realize that it was rather late in the day for a milk delivery.

Both the front and back doors of the house open onto the driveway, the back door from a little corridor full of muddy shoes and rusting tools which connects the kitchen to the garage. I threaded my way through the gardening implements and wrenched the stiff door open. It was late afternoon by then, but the light outside seemed very intense, the colours rich as they are before a storm.

I looked down and saw the milk bottle holder, with four bottles of milk in it. They weren't normal milk bottles, however, but large American-style quart containers somehow jammed into slots meant to take pints. Someone had taken the silver tops off.

A movement at the periphery of my vision caught my attention, and I glanced up towards the top of the driveway. There, about thirty yards away, were two children. One was fat and sitting on a bike, the other slim and standing by his side. I was seized with sudden irritation, and started quickly up the drive towards them, convinced that the clinking sound I'd heard was them stealing the tops off the milk.

I had covered scarcely five yards when someone who'd been at my school appeared from behind me, and walked quickly past me up the drive, staring straight ahead. I couldn't remember his name, had barely known him. He'd been two or three years older than me, and I'd completely forgotten that he'd existed, but as I stared after him I remembered he'd been one of the more amiable seniors. I could recall being proud of having some small kind of communication with one of the big boys, how it had made me feel a bit older myself, more a man of the world. And I remembered the way he used to greet my yelling his nickname, with a half-smile and a coolly raised eyebrow. All this came back with the instantaneous impact of memory, but something was wrong. The man didn't seem to register that I was there. I felt disturbed, not by the genuinely strange fact that he was in the driveway – or that he was wearing school athletic gear – but merely because he didn't smile and tilt his head back the way he used to. It was so bizarre that I wondered briefly if I was dreaming, but if you can ask yourself the question you always know the answer. I wasn't.

My attention was distracted by a reflection in the glass of the window in the back hallway. A man seemed to be standing behind me. He wore glasses, had a chubby face and basin-cut blond hair, and was carrying a bicycle. I whirled round to face where he should have been, but he wasn't there.

Then I remembered the kids at the top of the driveway, and turned to shout at them again, needing something to take my bewilderment out on. Almost immediately a tall slim man in a dark suit came walking down the drive; briskly, as if slightly late. Maybe it was a trick of the light in the gathering dusk, but I couldn't seem to fix on his face. My eyes just seemed to slide off it, as if it were slippery, or made of ice.

'Stop shouting at them,' he snapped. He strode past me, towards the back door. I stared at him open-mouthed. 'They're not doing anything wrong,' he said. 'Leave them alone.'

The kids took off, one on the bike, the other walking alongside, and I turned to the suited man. For some reason I felt anxious to placate him, and yet at the same time I was outraged at his invasion of our property.

'I'm sorry,' I said. 'It's just, well, I'm a bit confused. I thought

I saw someone I knew in the drive. Did you see him? Wavy brown hair, athletics kit?'

For some reason I thought the man would say that he had, and that that would make me feel better. All I got was a curt 'No' as he entered the back hallway.

Then another voice spoke. 'Well then. Shall we go into your old house?'

I realized that someone else was already standing in the back hall. The man with the blond hair and glasses. And he really was carrying a bicycle. He wasn't talking to me, but to the man in the suit.

'*What*?' I said, and hurried after them, catching a glimpse of the suited man's face. 'But it's *you* . . .' I stopped again, baffled, as I realized that the man in the suit was the same man who had been in athletics gear.

The two men marched straight into the kitchen. I followed them, impotently enraged. *Was* this his old house? Even so, wasn't it customary to ask the current occupants' permission if you wanted to visit? The suited man was peering round the kitchen, which looked very messy. He poked at some fried rice I'd left cooling in a pan on the stove. At least, I *seemed* to have left it there, though I wasn't sure when I would have done so. I don't just cook up rice in the afternoon for the pure hell of it. I still felt the urge to placate the man, however, and hoped he would eat some of the rice.

He merely grimaced with distaste and joined his colleague at the window, looking out onto the drive, hands on hips. 'Dear God,' he muttered. The other man grunted in agreement.

I noticed that I'd picked up the milk from outside the back door, and appeared to have spilt some of it on the floor. I tried to clean it up with a piece of kitchen roll which seemed very dirty and yellowed as if with age. I was trying to buy time. I felt very strongly that there must be some sense to the situation somewhere, some logic I was missing. Even if the man had lived here once he had no right to just march in here with his friend, but as I continued trying to swab up the milk before he noticed it – *why*? – I realized that there was something far more wrong than a mere breach of protocol at stake.

The suited man looked about thirty-five, much older than he should have been if he was indeed the guy I'd been to school with. Yet that would still leave him far too young to ever have lived here. Between our family and the previous occupants, I knew who'd lived in the house for the last forty years. So how could it be his old house? It didn't make sense. And was it actually him? The boy from my school? Apart from being too old, it looked like him, but was it actually *him*?

I did the best I could with the milk, and then straightened up, staggering slightly. My perception seemed to have become both heightened and jumbled, as if I was very drunk. Everything pulsed with an unusual intensity and exaggerated emotional charge, yet there also seemed to be gaps in what I was perceiving, as if I was receiving an edited version of what was going on. Things began to flick from one state to another – with the bits in between, the becoming, missing like a series of jump cuts. I felt hot and dizzy and the kitchen looked small and indescribably messy, the orange of the walls, the same colour my bedroom had once been painted, seeming to push in at me beneath a low and unsteady ceiling. I wondered if I was seeing the kitchen as *they* saw it, and then immediately wondered what I meant.

Meanwhile, they stood at the window, occasionally turning to stare balefully at me, radiating distaste and impatience. They were evidently waiting for something. But what? Noticing that I still had the piece of kitchen roll in my hand, I stepped over all the rubbish on the floor – *what the hell had been going on in this kitchen?* – to put it in the overflowing bin. I squeezed my temples with my fingers, struggling to stand upright against the weight of the air, and squared up to the men.

'L-look', I stuttered, leaning on the fridge for support, 'what exactly is going on?'

I immediately wished I'd kept quiet. The suited man slowly turned his head. It kept turning and turning, until it was looking directly at me – while his body remained facing the other way.

Like an owl, though he wasn't blinking. I could feel my stomach trying to crawl away and fought the need to gag. I sensed he'd done it deliberately, done it because he knew it would make me want to throw up, and I thought he might well be right.

'Why don't you just *shut up*?' he said. Then he twisted his head slowly back round until he was looking out onto the drive once more.

I decided not to ask any more questions.

Meanwhile, the mess in the kitchen seemed to be getting worse. Every time I looked there were more dirty pans and bits of rubbish and old food on the floor. My head felt thicker and heavier, as if everything was slipping away from me. I slumped against the fridge and clung to it, almost pulling it away from the wall. I began to cry too, my tears cutting channels in the thick grime on the fridge door. I dimly remembered that my parents had bought a brand new one only a few weeks before, but they must have changed it again. This one looked like something out of the 1950s. Very retro. Or original. To be honest it was hard to tell, because it was swimming back and forth and there was a lot of white in my eyes. Both the men were watching me now, as if mildly interested to see when I'd fall.

Suddenly, there was a terrible jangling impact in my head. I flapped hysterically at my ears, as if to stop someone hammering pencils into them. Then the pain happened again, and I recognized first that it was a sound rather than a blow, and then that it was the doorbell.

Someone was at the front door.

The two men glanced at each other, and the blond one nodded wearily. The suited man turned to me.

'Do you know what that is?' he asked.

'It's the front door' I said quickly, still trying to please him.

'So you'd better answer it, hadn't you?'

'Yes.'

'Answer the *door.*'

'Should I answer it?' I queried, stupidly. I couldn't seem to remember what words meant anymore.

'*Yes*,' he shouted, and picked up a mug – my mug, the mug I'd come downstairs, I remembered, to put tea in – and hurled it straight at me. It smashed into the fridge door by my face. I struggled to pull myself upright, head aching and ears ringing, aware of a soft crump as a fragment of the mug broke under my foot. The doorbell jangled again, the harshness of the noise making me realize how muted all other sounds had become. I fell towards the kitchen door, sliding across the front of the fridge, my feet tangling in the boxes and cartons that now covered the filthy floor. I could feel the orange of the walls seeping in through my ears and mouth, and kept missing whole seconds of time – as if I was blacking out and coming to like a stroboscope.

As I lurched across to the kitchen door and grabbed the handle to hold myself up, I heard the blond man say, 'He may not go through. If he does, we wait.'

It didn't mean anything to me. None of it did.

I made my way towards the front door, ploughing clumsily through drifts of rubbish in the hallway. The chime of the doorbell had pushed the air hard, and I could see it lapping towards me in waves. Ducking to avoid the sound, I slipped on the mat and almost fell into the living room. As I crouched there on my hands and knees I saw it was getting dark in there, really dark, and I could hear the plants talking. I couldn't catch the words, but they were definitely conversing, beneath the night sounds and a soft rustling which sounded a hundred yards away. The living room must have grown.

I picked myself up and turned to the front door. The bell clanged again, and this time the sound caught me full in the face, stinging bitterly. It should have been about four paces across the hall from the living room door to the front door, but I thought it was only going to take one and then it took twenty, past all the panelling and over the huge folds in the mat. It was not an easy journey.

Then I had my hand on the doorknob and then the door was open and I stepped out of the house.

'Oh hello, Michael,' said a voice. 'I thought someone must be in, because all the lights were on.'

'Wuh?' I said, blinking in the fading sunlight.

The woman in front of me smiled. 'I hope I didn't disturb you?'

'No, that's fine.' Suddenly I recognized her. It was Mrs Steinberg, the woman who brings us our cat food in bulk. 'Fine. Sorry.' I glanced covertly behind me into the hallway, which was solid and unpanelled and four paces wide and led to the living room, which was light and airy and the size it had always been.

'I've brought your delivery,' the woman said, and then frowned. 'Look, are you all right?'

'I'm fine,' I replied, turning to grin broadly at her. My mind felt like a runaway lift, soaring back upwards to reality. 'I just nodded off for a moment, in the kitchen. I still feel a bit, you know.'

Mrs Steinberg smiled. 'Of course. Give me a hand?'

I followed her to the top of the drive and heaved a box of cat food out of her van, watching the house. There was nothing to see. I thanked her and then carried the box back down the drive as she drove off. I walked back into the house and shut the front door behind me.

I felt absolutely fine.

I walked into the kitchen. As I'd expected, the men had disappeared. I looked slowly around a kitchen which looked exactly as it had since before I was too young to remember. Everything was normal. Of course.

I must have fallen asleep making tea, and then struggled over to the front door to open it while still half asleep. I could remember asking myself if I was having a dream, and deciding I wasn't – but that just showed how wrong you could be. It had been unusually vivid, and it was odd how I'd been suddenly awake and all right again as soon as I stepped out of the front door. But it had been a dream. Here I was in the kitchen again, and everything was normal. Clean and tidy, spick and span, with all the rubbish in the bin and the pans in the right places and the milk in the fridge and a smashed mug on the floor.

That was less good. It was my mug, and it lay smashed at the bottom of the fridge. How had that happened?

Maybe I'd fallen asleep holding it. Not terribly likely, but possible. Or perhaps I'd knocked it over on waking, and incorporated the sound into my dream. This was slightly more credible, but where exactly was I supposed to have fallen asleep? Just leaning against the counter – or actually stretched out on it, using the kettle as a pillow?

Then I noticed the fridge door. There was a little dent in it, with a couple of flecks of paint missing. At about head height. That wasn't good either.

I cleared up the mug and switched the kettle on. While it was boiling I wandered into the hall and the living room. Everything was fine, tidy, normal. Super. I went back into the kitchen. The same. Great. Apart from a little dent in the fridge door at about head height.

I made my cup of tea in a different, non-broken mug, and drank it looking out of the kitchen window at the drive. I felt unsettled and nervous, and unsure of what to do with either of those emotions. Even if it had been a dream, it was a very odd one, particularly the way it had fought so hard against melting away. Maybe I was much more tired than I realized. Or ill. Food poisoning could make your head go very strange, as I'd learned after a couple of college friends' attempts at cooking anything more complex than toast. But I felt fine. Physically, at least.

I carried the box of cat food into the pantry, unpacked it, and stacked the cans in the corner. Then I switched the kettle on again. Suddenly, my heart seemed to stop.

Before I had time to realize why, the cause repeated itself. A soft chinking noise outside the back door. I moved quickly to the window and looked out. There was no one in the drive. I craned my neck, trying to see around to the back door, but could only see the large pile of firewood that lay to one side of it.

Then I heard the noise again. I walked slowly into the back hallway and listened, slowly clenching my fists. I could hear nothing except the sound of blood pumping in my ears. I grabbed the knob and swung the door open.

Stillness outside. A rectangle of late afternoon light, a patch of driveway, and a dark hedge waving quietly. I stepped out into the drive, and stood and listened again.

After a moment I heard a very faint crunching noise. It sounded like pebbles softly rubbing against each other. Then I heard it again. I looked more closely at the drive, peering at the actual stones, and noticed that a small patch about ten yards in front of me appeared to be moving slightly. Wriggling, almost.

They stopped, and then the sound came again – and another patch stirred briefly, about a yard closer than the first. As if registering the weight of invisible feet.

I was so engrossed that I didn't notice the whistling straight away. When I did, I looked up. The blond man was back. He was standing at the top of the driveway, carrying a bicycle with the wheels slowly spinning in the dusk. He whistled the top line of a perfect harmony, the lower line just the sound of the wind. As I stared at him, backing slowly towards the house, the crunching noise got louder and louder.

Then the suited man was standing with his nose almost touching mine. 'Hello again,' he said.

The blond man started down the driveway. 'Greetings indeed,' he laughed. 'Come on, in we go.'

Abruptly, I realized that the very last thing I should do was let them back into the house.

I leapt back through the door into the hallway. The suited man, caught by surprise, started forward but I was quick and whipped the door shut in his face and locked it. That felt good, but then he started banging on the door very hard, grotesquely hard, and I saw that the kitchen was getting messy again, and the fridge was old, and I could barely see out of the window because it was so grimy. A slight flicker in my mind made me think that maybe I'd missed the smallest fraction of a second, and I realized that it really hadn't been a dream. I was back in the bad place. As I backed into the kitchen I tripped and fell, sprawling amongst cartons and bacon rind and dirt and what appeared to be puke on the floor. The banging on the back door got louder, and louder, and louder. He was going to break it, I knew. He was going to break the door down. I'd let them back and they had to come in through the back door. I'd come in through the wrong door . . .

Suddenly understanding what I must do, I scrambled to my feet and kicked my way through the rubbish. The fridge door swung open in my way. The inside was dark and dirty and there was something rotted inside, but I slammed it out of the way, biting hard on my lip to keep my head clear.

I had to get to the front door. I had to open it, step out, and then step back in again. The front door was the right door. And I had to do it soon, before the back door broke and let them in. I could already hear a splintering quality to the sound of the blows. And the back door was about two inches thick.

The hallway was worse than I expected. I skidded to a halt, at first unable to even *see* the front door. I thought that I must be looking in the wrong direction, but I wasn't, because I finally spotted it over to the left, where it was supposed to be. But the angles were all wrong, and to see it I had to look behind me and to the right, although when I saw it I could see that in reality it was still over to the left. And it looked so close – could it really be less than a yard away? – but when I held my hand out to it I groped into nothing, the fingers still in front of the door when they should have been past it.

I stared wildly around, disorientated and unsure even of which way to go. Suddenly, the banging behind me got markedly louder, probably as the blond man joined in, and this helped to marginally restore my sense of direction. I found the front door again, concentrated hard on its apparent position, and started to walk towards it. I immediately fell over, because the floor was much lower than I expected. It actually seemed be tilted in some way, although it looked flat and level, because although one of my legs reached it easily enough the other dangled in space. I pulled myself up onto my knees and found I was looking at a sort of sloped wall between the wall and the ceiling, a wall which bent back from the wall and yet out from the ceiling. The door was still over on the left, although to see it I now had to look straight ahead and up.

Then I noticed another sound beneath the eternal banging, and whirled to face the direction it was coming from. I found that I was looking through the living room door, and that it gave into sheer darkness, a darkness which was seeping out into the hallway like smoke, clinging to the angles in the air like the inside of a dark prism. I heard the noise again. It was a deep rumbling growl, far, far away in there, almost obscured by the night noises and the sound of vegetation moving in the wind. The sound didn't seem to be getting any closer, but I knew that was because the living room now extended out far beyond the house, into hundreds and hundreds of miles of dense jungle. As I listened carefully I could hear the gurgling of some dark river far off to the right, the sound of water mixing with the warm rustling of the breeze in the darkness. It sounded very peaceful and for a moment I was still, transfixed.

Then the sound of another splintering crack wrenched me away, and I turned my back on the living room and flailed towards where the front door must be. The hall table loomed above me and I thought I could walk upright beneath it – but tripped over it and fell again, headlong onto the cool floorboards. The mat had moved, no, was *moving*, sliding slowly up the stairs like a draught, and as I rolled over and looked at the ceiling I saw the floor coming towards me, the walls shortening in little jerks.

As I lay there panting, a clear cool waft of air stroked my cheek. At first I thought that it must have come from the living room, although it had been warm in there, but then I remembered that I was lying on the floor. The breeze had to be a draft coming under the front door. I must nearly be there.

I looked all around me but all I could see was panelling and floor and what was behind me. I closed my eyes and tried to grope for it, but it was even worse inside my head so I opened them again. Then I caught a glimpse of the door, far away, obscured from view round a corner but just visible once you knew where to look. On impulse I reached my hand out in not quite the opposite direction and felt it fall upon warm grainy wood.

The door. I'd found it.

I pulled myself along the floor towards it, and tried to stand up. I got no more than a few inches before I fell back down again. I tried once more, with the same result, feeling as if I was trying to do something entirely against nature. Again, and this time I reached a semi-crouching position, muscles straining. I started to slump almost immediately – but as I did so I threw myself forwards. I found myself curled up, my feet a couple of feet from the floor, lying on the door. Electing to not even *try* to come to terms with this, I groped by my side and found the doorknob. I tried to twist it but the sweat on my hand made them spin uselessly on the shiny metal. I wiped it on my shirt and tried again, and this time I got some purchase and heard the catch withdraw as the knob turned. Exultantly, I tugged at it, as with a tremendous crash the back door finally gave way.

The door wouldn't budge. Panicking, I tried again. Nothing. By peering down the crack I could see that no lock or bolt was impeding it, so why wouldn't it bloody move?

There were footsteps in the back hall.

Suddenly I realized that I was lying on the door, and trying to pull it towards me against my own weight.

The footsteps reached the kitchen.

I rolled over off the door onto the wall beside it and reached for the handle, but I'd slid too far. As the footsteps came closer I scrambled back across the slippery wall, grabbed and twisted the doorknob with all my strength. It opened just as they entered the hall and I rolled out through it, fell and landed awkwardly and painfully on something hard and bristly and for a few moments had no clear idea of where or who I was, and just lay there fighting for breath.

After some time I sat up slowly. I was sitting outside the house on the doormat, my back to the front door. At the top of the drive a young couple were staring at me curiously. I stood up and smiled, trying to suggest that I often sat on the doormat and that they ought to try it as it was actually a lot of fun – hoping that they hadn't seen me fall there from about two-thirds of the way up the door. They smiled back and carried on walking, mollified or maybe even hurrying off home to try it for themselves.

I turned hesitantly back towards the door and looked in.

It had worked. It was all okay again. The mat was on the floor, right angles looked like 90°, and the ceiling was back where it was supposed to be. I stepped back a pace and looked down the driveway at the back door. It had been utterly smashed, and now looked like little more than an extension of the firewood pile.

I stepped back into the house through the front door, the right door, and shut it behind me. I walked carefully and quietly into the living room, and then the kitchen. Everything was fine, everything was normal. It was just a nice normal house. If you came in through the right door.

The wrong door was in about a thousand pieces. I thought about that for some time, with another cup of tea and what felt like my first cigarette in months. I saw with frank disbelief that less than half an hour had elapsed since I'd first come downstairs. The back door. The *wrong* door. It was coming in through there that took me to wherever it was that the house became. Coming in through the *front* door brought me back to where I normally lived. So presumably I was safe, so long as I didn't leave the house and come back in through the back door. They couldn't get me. Presumably.

But I didn't like having that door in pieces. Being safe was only half of the issue. I wasn't going to feel *secure* until that portal was well and truly closed.

I walked into the back hall and looked nervously out through the wreckage onto the drive. Everything was fine. There was nothing I needed protecting from. But I still didn't like it. Did it have to be me who came through the door, or what if a falling leaf or maybe even just a soft breeze came inside? Would that be enough?

Could I take the risk?

As I stood there indecisively, I noticed once more the pile of firewood propped up against the outside wall of the back hall. I probably still wouldn't have put two and two together had not a very large proportion of the pile been thick old floorboards – a donation from a neighbour. I looked at the tool shelf on the inside wall and saw a hammer and a big box of good long nails. Then I looked at the wood again.

I could nail the damn thing shut.

I flicked my cigarette butt out onto the drive and rolled up my sleeves. The hammer was big and heavy, which was just as well because when I nailed the planks across the door frame I'd be hammering into solid brickwork. I was going to have to board right the way up, but that was all right as there were loads of planks, and if I reinforced it enough it should be well-nigh impregnable.

Feeling much better, I set to work. I may even have hummed. Kneeling just inside the door, I reached out and began pulling the floorboards in, taking care to select the thickest and least weathered. I judged that I'd need about fifteen to make the doorway really secure, although that was largely guesswork as I'd never tried to turn the back hall into a fortress before. Pulling them in was heavy work. I had to stretch out to reach them, and I began to get hot and tired, and anxious to begin the nailing. Outside it was getting darker as the evening began, and the air was very cool and still.

As the pile in the back hall increased in size it became more difficult, and I had to lean further and further out to reach the next plank. This made me nervous. I was still inside, and my feet were still on the ground in the back hall. I wasn't 'coming back in'. I was just leaning out and then, well, *sort of* coming back in but not really, because my feet never left the back hall. But it made me nervous, and I began to work quicker and quicker, perspiration running down my face as, clinging to the doorframe with my left hand, I stretched out to bring the last few boards in. Eleven, twelve. Just a couple more. Now the last one I could possibly reach: that would have to be enough. Hooking my left foot behind the frame and gripping it hard with my left hand, I stretched out towards the plank, waving fingers little more than an inch from the end. Just a little further . . . I let my hooking foot slide slightly, allowed my fingers to slip round half an inch, and tried to extend my back as far as it would go. My fingers just scraping the end, I tried a last yearning lunge.

And then suddenly a stray thought struck me. Here I was, pulled out as if on some invisible rack. Why hadn't I just gone out of the front door, picked up piles of wood, and brought them back into the house through the front door? It would have been easier, it would have been quicker, and it wouldn't have involved all this monkeying around at the wrong door. Not that it mattered now, because as it happened even if I didn't get this last plank I'd probably have plenty, but I wouldn't have been so hot and tired. It was also worrying that in my haste I'd been putting myself in needless danger. I'd better slow down, calm down, take a rest.

It was an unimportant, contemplative thought, but one that distracted me for a fraction of a second too long. As I finally got the tips of my fingers round the plank I realized with horror that the hand on the doorframe was slipping. Desperately I tried to scrabble back, but my hands were too sweaty and the doorframe itself was slippery now. I felt the tendons in my hand stretch as I tried to defy my centre of gravity and think my weight backwards, and then suddenly my forehead walloped onto the ground and I was lying flat on my face.

I was up in a second, and I swear to God that both feet never left the hall floor at once. I leapt back into the hallway, grabbing that last bloody piece of wood without even noticing it.

I crouched in the doorframe, panting hysterically. Everything looked normal outside. The driveway was quiet, the pebbles were still and there was none of the faint deadening of sound that I associated with the other place. I was furious with myself for having taken the risk, for not having thought to bring them in through the front door – and especially for falling, which had been painful quite apart from anything else. But I hadn't fallen out, not really. I hadn't come back in, as such. The drive was fine, the kitchen was fine. Everything was okay.

Soothed by the sounds of early evening traffic in the distance, my heart gradually slowed to only about twice its normal rate. I forced myself to take a break, and had a quiet cigarette, perched on the pile of planks. During the fall my right foot had caught the tool shelf, and there were nails all over the place, both inside and outside the door. But there were plenty left and the ones outside could stay there. I wasn't going to make the same damn fool mistake twice.

Gathering up the hammer and a fistful of nails, I laid a plank across the door and started work. Getting the nails through the wood and into the masonry was even harder than I'd expected, but within a couple of minutes it was in place, and felt reassuringly solid. I heaved another plank into position and set about securing it. This was actually going to work.

After half an hour I was into the swing of it and the wood now reached almost halfway up the doorframe. My arms were aching and my head ringing from the hammering, which was very loud in the confined space of the back hall. I had a break leaning on the completed section, staring blankly out onto the drive. I was jolted back from reverie by the realization that a piece of dust or something must have landed in my eye, distorting my vision. I blinked to remove it, but it didn't disappear. It didn't hurt, just made a small patch of the drive up near the road look a bit ruffled. I rubbed and shut both eyes individually, and discovered with mounting unease that the distortion was present in both.

I stood upright. Something was definitely going on at the top of the drive. The patch still looked crumpled, as if seen through a heat haze, and whichever way I turned my head the patch stayed in the same place. It was flickering very slightly now too, like a bad quality film print, although the flecks weren't white, they were dark. I rubbed my eyes hard again, but once I'd stopped seeing stars I saw that the effect was still there. I peered at it, trying to discern something that I could interpret. The flecks seemed to organize into broken and shifting vertical lines as I watched, as if something was hidden behind a curtain of rain, rain so coloured as to make up a picture of that patch of the drive. This impression gradually strengthened until it was like looking at one of those plastic strip doors, where you walk through the hanging strips. It was as if there was one of those at the top of the drive, a patch of driveway pictured on it in living three dimensions. With something moving just the other side.

Then suddenly the balance shifted, like one of those drawings made up of black and white dots where if you stare at it long enough you can see a Dalmatian. I dropped to my knees behind the partially completed barrier.

They were back.

Standing at the top of the drive, their images both underlying and superimposed on it as if woven together, were the two men. They were standing in a frozen and unnatural position, like a freeze-frame. Their faces looked pallid and washed out, the colours uneven and the image flickering and dancing in front of my eyes. And still they stood, not there, and yet in some sense there.

As I stared, transfixed, I noticed that the suited man's foot appeared to be moving. It was hard to focus on, and happening incomprehensibly slowly, but it was moving, gradually leaving the ground. Over the course of a minute it was raised and then lowered back onto the ground a couple of feet in front of its original position, leaving the man's body leaning slightly forward.

I realized what I was seeing. In extraordinary and flickering slow motion, somehow projected onto the drive like an old home movie, the suited man was beginning to walk towards the house.

The image wasn't flickering so much anymore, the colours were getting stronger, and I could no longer see the driveway through them. Somehow they were coming back through. I thought I'd got away with it, but I hadn't. I'd fallen out. Not very far by anyone's standards, but far enough. Far enough to have come back in through the wrong door. And now they were tearing their way back into the world, or hauling me back towards theirs. And very slowly they were getting closer.

Fighting to stay calm, I grabbed a plank, put it into position above the others and nailed it into place. Then another, and another, not pausing for breath or thought. Through the narrowing gap I could see them getting closer. They didn't look two-dimensional any longer, and they were moving more quickly too. As I leaned towards the kitchen for a plank I saw that there was a single dusty carton on the floor. It had started.

I smacked another plank into place and hammered it down. The men were real again, and they were also much nearer to the house, though still moving at a weirdly graceful tenth of normal speed. Hammering wildly, ignoring increasingly frequent whacks on the fingers, I cast occasional wild glances aside into the kitchen. The fridge was beginning to look strange, the stark 1990s geometry softening, regressing, and the rubbish was gathering. I never saw any of it arrive, but each time I looked there was another piece of cardboard, a few more scraps, one more layer of grime. It had only just started, and was still happening very slowly, maybe because I'd barely fallen out. But it was happening. The house was going over.

I kept on hammering. I knew that what I had to do at some point was run to the front door, go out and come back in again, come in through the right door. But that could wait, would *have* to wait. It was coming on very slowly this time, and I still felt completely clear-headed. What I had to do first was seal off the back door, and soon. The two men, always at the vanguard of the change, were well and truly here, and getting closer all the time. I had to make sure that the back door was secure against anything those two could do to it, for long enough for me to get to the front door and jump out. I had no idea what the front hall would be like by the time I got there, and if I left the back door unfinished and got lost trying to get to the front door, I'd be in real trouble.

I slammed planks into place as fast as I could. Outside they got steadily closer and closer, and inside another carton appeared in the kitchen. As I jammed the last horizontal board into place the suited man and the blond man were only a couple of yards away, now moving at full pace. I'd barely nailed it in before the first blow crashed into it, bending it and making me leap back with shock. I hurriedly picked up more wood and slapped planks over the barrier in vertical slats and crosses, nailing them in hard, reinforcing and making sure that the barrier was securely fastened to the wall on all sides, furiously hammering and building.

After a while I couldn't feel the ache in my back or see the blood on my hands: all I could hear was the beating of the hammer, and all I could see were the heads of the nails as I piled more and more wood onto the barrier. I had wood to spare – I hadn't even needed that last bloody plank – and by the time I finished it was four pieces thick in some places, with the reinforcing strips spread several feet either side of the frame. I used the last three pieces as bracing struts, forcing them horizontally across the hallway, one end of each lodged in niches in the barrier, the other jammed tight against the opposite wall.

Finally it was finished, and I stood back and looked at it. It looked pretty damn solid. 'Let's see you get through *that*,' I shouted, half sitting and half collapsing to the ground. After a moment I noticed how quiet it was. At some point they must have stopped banging against the door. I'd been making far too much noise to notice, and my head was still ringing. I put my ear against the barrier and listened. Silence.

I lit a cigarette and let tiredness and a blessed feeling of safeness wash over me. The sound of the match striking was slightly muted, but that could've been the ringing in my ears as much as anything, and the kitchen looked pretty grubby but no more than that. I felt fine. I wondered what the two outside were up to, and whether there was any chance that they might have given up and be waiting for the change to take its course – not realizing that I understood about the right door and the wrong door. For a few minutes I actually savoured the sensation of being balanced between two worlds, secure in the knowledge that in a moment I would just walk out that front door and the house would come back and none of it would matter at all.

Eventually I stood up, wincing in pain. I was really going to ache tomorrow. I stepped into the kitchen, narrowly avoiding a large black spider that scuttled out of one of the cartons. The floor was getting very messy now, strewn with scraps of dried-up meat covered with the corpses of dead maggots, interspersed with small piles of stuff I really didn't want to look too closely at. I threaded my way over to the door, past the now bizarrely misshapen fridge, and into the front hall.

The hallway was still clear of debris, and as far as I could see, utterly normal. As I crossed towards the front door, anxious now to get the whole thing over with – and wondering how I was going to explain the state of the back door to my parents – I noticed a faint tapping sound in the far distance. After a moment it stopped, and then restarted from a slightly different direction. Odd, but scarcely a primary concern. Right now my priority was getting out of that front door before the hall got any stranger. Feeling like an actor about to bound onto stage, I reached out to the doorknob, twisted it and pulled it towards me.

At first I couldn't take it in. I couldn't work out why instead of the driveway all I could see was brown. Brown flatness.

As I adjusted my focal length, pulling it in for something much closer than the drive I'd been expecting, I understood. The view looked rather familiar. I'd seen something like it very recently.

It was a barrier. An impregnable wooden barrier nailed across the door into the walls from the outside. Now I knew what they'd been doing as I finished nailing them out.

They'd been nailing me in.

I tried everything I could think of. My fists, my shoulder, a chair. The planks were there to stay.

I couldn't get out. I couldn't come back in through the right door, and for the moment they couldn't get in through the wrong door. A sort of stalemate. But a very poor sort for me, because they were much the stronger and getting more so all the time, and because the house was still going over and now I couldn't stop it.

I strode into the kitchen, rubbing my bruised shoulder and thinking furiously. There had to be something I could do, and I had to do it fast. The change was speeding up. Although the hall still looked normal the kitchen was now filthy, and the fifties fridge was fully back. In a retro kind of way it was quite attractive. But it was wrong.

In the background I could still hear the faint tapping noise. Maybe they were trying to get in through the roof.

I had to get out, had to find a way. I tried lateral thinking. You leave a house by a door. How else? No other way. You always leave by a door. But was there any other way you *could* leave, if you were in, say, a desperate emergency? The doors . . . The windows. What about the windows? If there was a right door and a wrong door, maybe there were right and wrong windows too, and perhaps the right ones looked out onto the real world. Maybe, just maybe, you could smash one and then climb out and then back in again. Perhaps that would work.

I had no idea whether it would or not. I wasn't kidding myself that I understood anything, and God alone knew where I might land if I chose the wrong window. Perhaps I'd go out the wrong one and then be chased round the house by the two maniacs outside, as I tried to find a right window to break back in through. That would be a barrel of laughs. That would be Fun City. But what choice did I have? I ran into the living room, heading for the big picture window. Through the square window today, children.

I don't know how I could have missed making the connection.

Possibly because the taps were so quiet. I stood in the living room, my mouth open. This time they were one jump ahead. They'd boarded up the fucking windows.

I ran back into the hall, through into the dining room, then upstairs to the bedrooms. Every single window was boarded up. I knew where they'd got the nails from, because I'd spilt more then enough when I fell, but how . . . Then I realized how they'd nailed them in without a hammer, why the tapping had been so quiet. With sudden unpleasant clarity I could imagine the suited man clubbing the nails in with his fists, smashing them in with his forehead and grinning while he did it.

Oh Jesus.

I walked downstairs again, slowly now. Every single window was boarded up, even the ones that were too small to climb through. As I stood once more in the kitchen, amidst the growing piles of shit, the pounding on the back door started. There was no way I could get out of the house, and I couldn't stop what was happening. This time it was going over all the way, and taking me with it. And meanwhile they were going to smash their way in to come along for the ride. To get me. I listened, watching the rubbish, as the pounding got louder and louder.

It's still getting louder, and I can tell from the sound that some of the planks are beginning to give way. The house stopped balancing long ago, and the change is coming on more quickly. The kitchen looks like a bomb site and there are an awful lot of spiders in there now. Eventually I left them to it and came through the hall into here, only making one or two wrong turnings. Into the living room. And that's where I am now, just sitting and waiting. There's nothing I can do about the change, nothing. I can't get out. I can't stop them getting in.

But there is one thing I can do. I'm going to stay here, in the living room. I can see small shadows now, gathering in corners and darting out from under the chairs, and it's quite dark down by the end wall. The wall itself seems less important now, less substantial, no longer a barrier. I think I can hear the sound of running water somewhere far away, and smell the faintest hint of the dark and lush vegetation.

I won't let them get me. I'll wait, in the gathering darkness, listening to the coming of the night sounds and feeling a soft breeze on my face as I sense the room opening out, as the walls shade away, as I sit here quietly in the dark warm air. And then I'll get up and start walking out into the dark land, into the jungle and amidst the trees that stand all around behind the darkness, smelling the greenness that surrounds me and hearing the gentle river off somewhere to the right. And I'll feel happy walking away into the night, and maybe far away I'll meet whatever makes the growling sounds I begin to hear in the distance, and we'll sit together by running water and be at peace in the darkness.

WHEN GOD LIVED IN KENTISH TOWN

WHAT YOU MAKE IT

'I've found God,' the man said.

I groaned inwardly, and tried to will him not to sit at the table. I knew I was unlikely to succeed, because he didn't have a lot of other options, but I gave it my best shot anyway. I was in the Shuang Dou, it was dark outside, and I had only just started on the mound of food which was arranged around me in a neat semi-circle. I didn't want company. I wanted to be left alone.

The Shuang Dou is not at the prestige end of the Chinese restaurant market. Basically it's a take-away, with an even smaller waiting area than is usual, into which they've shoe-horned a couple of small tables for patrons who can't wait until they get home before eating – or who don't have a home to go to in the first place. It looks like the interior decor was done by someone extremely lazy about twenty years ago, and I don't expect it would survive anything more than a desultory glance from a health and safety inspector. Even the menus, which are printed – like those of every other Chinese restaurant in the land – to fold neatly into three, are rather haphazardly creased just once, across the middle. On the other hand the food is cheap and good, and the kitchen area is right there behind the counter, so you can watch the proprietors cooking your dinner. It seems to be run by one small family, the youngest member of which spends the evening in a papoose on the woman's back; her older sister takes the customers' orders and gives back change with faultless accuracy and an eight-year-old's engaging seriousness. Their parents are always friendly, in a guarded way, and I go in there so often that the patriarch generally has my order cooking before I've finished giving it, wielding wok and MSG with cheering skill and professionalism.

I was somewhere comfortable, in other words, surrounded by foil containers of food, and I wanted to just sit there and eat. I didn't want a conversation with someone strange, especially if it was to be about God. The guy sat down on the end of the table and opened his own container, which held a large portion of something noodle-based, possibly the squid chow mein of which the owners are justifiably proud. He squirted an alarming amount of soy sauce over it from the pot on the table and started eating with the plastic fork provided. Another of the other things I like about the Shuang Dou is that they don't force you to eat with chopsticks. Sure, it can be fun, when you're in the mood, or when you're surrounded by white linen and paying £40 a head; but when you really just want to get the food down your neck it has to be said that a fork is a better tool for the job.

The man munched meditatively through a couple of mouthfuls of his chow mein and then looked up at me, still chewing.

'I have, you know,' he said affably. 'I've found him.'

'Hmm,' I said, quietly, taking care not to catch his eye. While I don't believe that madness is communicable through eye contact, I believe that mad conversations most certainly are.

'You think I'm bonkers, don't you?'

'Hmm,' I said again, with a slightly different inflection, trying to suggest that while I was in no way impugning his sanity, personality or intellect I'd really rather just eat my special fried rice in peace. Special fried rice is a big deal to me. I'm a bit of a bore on the subject, to be honest. If I had to give up every other dish in the world and subsist only on that, I could do it without a second thought. At the Shuang Dou they prepare it differently to most places, cooking the egg last and laying it on top of the rice like a very thin and tasty omelette. I just wanted to sit and eat it.

'Not surprised,' the man continued, and I began to sense, with a mixture of relief and dread, that my participation in the conversation was unlikely to be required. While this meant I wasn't going to have to get involved on an active level, it also meant that he was probably not going to stop talking. 'Not surprised at all. I'd think the same thing myself.'

I stealthily reached for the soy and dripped a healthy dose over my Singapore Noodles. Perhaps if I kept my head down he'd come to believe that while God was real I was imaginary, and talk to the table instead.

'At first I thought "Who'd have thought it, eh?" I mean – you'd hardly expect him to be living in Kentish Town, would you?'

At this I found myself looking up, unable to stop myself. The man smiled genially at me, jaws still working. Seeing him properly for the first time, I saw that he was somewhere in his mid-forties, dressed in a dark and elderly suit with a grey sweater underneath, a generic blue shirt and an old but neatly knotted tie. His hair was grey around the temples and his face was rather red, either through an afternoon spent out in the cold or a couple of decades propping up bars. The whites of his eyes were a little grey, but not ostensibly insane.

'I mean, sounds a little odd, doesn't it?' he said, tilting his head and waggling his bushy eyebrows in a way evidently meant to indicate the world outside the window.

'Hmm,' I said, indicating cautious agreement. Kentish Town, I should explain for the benefit of those unacquainted with it, is a smallish patch of North London just above Camden and below Highgate and Hampstead. Many, many years ago it had the distinction of being at the very edge of London proper, a last stop before the countryside – and at that time was of considerably more note than, say, Camden. The Assembly Rooms pub, just across the road from the tube station, used to be a staging post or something. Nowadays, Kentish Town is just part of the sprawl and a not very attractive part at that; it has little of the cohesion of surrounding areas, and is instead a rather vague lumping together of roads, rail tracks, pubs and people. It's an interstice, a space between other places which has been filled by accident rather than design – like the corner of a cupboard which gets stuffed with the things you can't find another place for. It has none of Camden's joie de trendiness, and is a long, long way from Hampstead or Belsize Park's easy wealth. It's just a bit of London, and I live there because it's cheap.

'But then I thought about it a bit,' the man continued, 'and it makes perfect sense. Very convenient for the centre of town – just a couple of stops on the Northern Line – cheaper than Camden, quite a good little minimart down past the Vulture's Perch pub. And the food here's not bad, of course,' he added, winking at the little girl behind the counter.

'You're saying God actually lives here, in Kentish Town?' I asked, in spite of myself.

'Oh yes,' the man said comfortably.

I looked back at him levelly, trying to work out whether this made him more – or less – mad. In some ways it was preferable to born-again religious mania; simpler and less grandiose, at least. On the other it was clearly not the pronouncement of someone who had all his chopsticks in one hand.

In the background one of the woks hissed suddenly as the owners strove to fulfil a telephone order.

'Whereabouts, exactly?' I asked.

The man looked at me for a moment, nodding, as if conceding that this was a reasonable question. 'Not sure,' he said. 'Never been able to follow him all the way home. But it must be around here somewhere. Convenient.'

'Why convenient?'

'Because this is where he has his shop,' he said. 'Just round the corner from here, in fact.'

'His shop,' I said, thinking I was beginning to understand. 'You mean, like, a church?'

'No, no,' the man said breezily. 'Electrical shop. Second-hand mainly, though there's some newish stuff in the window. None of it's exactly *state-of-the-art* though.' The italics were his, not mine. He uttered the phrase as if aware he was being rather conversationally daring, and hoping that I was as up with the times as he was, and could follow his meaning.

I nodded slowly, wishing I'd had the sense to keep my mouth

shut. Remembering that I had some Hot and Sour soup, I opened the polystyrene carton carefully and spooned up a mouthful. I have a tendency to eat all of my courses at the same time, which has driven more than one ex-girlfriend to distraction.

'You must have seen it,' the man said. 'Near that, oh, what d'you call it? That restaurant. Spanish. All those little plates of food. Quite good, in fact.'

'The tapas place,' I said, hollowly.

The man smiled happily. 'That's the one. Forget the name. Between there and the estate agent's, little way up from the Assembly Rooms pub. You know the one I mean?'

I nodded but didn't say anything, mainly because I wasn't sure I wanted to prolong this nonsense. Also because I was trying to picture the shop he was referring to. I couldn't, quite. I knew the Assembly Rooms well – just enough of a local to be enticing, just enough *not* a local that you could go in there without any real danger of being stabbed, it sat where four grey and busy roads intersected in a ragged non-crossroads. A couple of shops further up the road was the bedraggled and dusty tapas restaurant. I could remember peering through the window once and deciding that it would just be too much of a health risk; and, as my patronage of the Shuang Dou shows, I'm not overly fastidious in such matters. I could also remember the estate agent's, which stood out on that stretch of road because someone had spent a little money trying to make it look as if it wasn't situated in some particularly depressed area of an East European town. I knew there were a couple of shops in between the two, but I couldn't picture them.

'You look, next time you pass that way,' the man said, and I realized abruptly that he was standing, wiping his mouth with a paper serviette. 'You'll find I'm right.'

He nodded, winked at the people behind the counter and walked back out into the night, leaving me feeling obscurely irritated; as if by quitting the conversation before I had he'd somehow made *me* out to be the lunatic. As I watched him disappear down the cold and lamplit street, I spooned another mouthful of Hot and Sour into my mouth, failing to notice that it contained an entire red chilli.

By the time I'd finished coughing, and had thanked the lady owner for the plastic cup of water she brought me, the man had disappeared. When I'd finished my food I crossed the street and walked directly down Falkland Road to my apartment. It was sleeting, and getting late, and I wouldn't have bothered going round the long way to check what was between the estate agent's and the tapas bar even if I'd remembered.

Two days later I walked out of the tube station at about three o'clock in the afternoon, serene with boredom after a long meeting with one of my clients. I write corporate videos for a living – telling people how to sell hoovers, why they shouldn't refer to their co-workers as 'wankers', that sort of thing. If someone offers you a job writing a corporate video, just say no. Seriously. Just don't get involved.

It takes about five minutes to walk from the tube to where I live. Mostly that's a good thing. When you know that once you get indoors you have to sit at the computer and write a corporate video, it can seem less ideal. On days like that, you can find yourself wishing it was a four-day trek over mountainous terrain, involving sherpas, a few of those little horse things and maybe even an entire documentary team to shoot lots of footage of you getting frostbite and wishing you were back at home.

It was in this spirit that instead of heading diagonally across Leighton Road and up Leverton Street, I walked across the road and then past the Assembly Rooms up Fortess Road. It was only as I was passing the tapas bar, whose name I once again failed to notice, that I remembered the conversation I'd had in the Shuang Dou. Mildly excited at the prospect of anything which would delay my return home, I slowed my pace and looked at the stores between the restaurant and the sloping glass of the estate agent's up ahead.

When I saw the shop I felt a brief quiver of some strange emotion, probably just because I hadn't expected it to be there

346

at all. I found myself casting a quick glance up the road, as if concerned that someone should see me, and then wandered over to the window.

The shop looked like the standard type of electrical store to be found in areas of London which aren't aiming to challenge Tottenham Court Road's domination of the consumer goods market. Some of the products in the window were evidently second-hand, and – as the man had said – those which did look new were hardly cutting edge. Tape-radios with tinny three-inch speakers and shiny plastic buttons. Plastic Midi systems which looked like they'd fracture at low temperatures. Video recorders from the days when Betamax was still in with a shout. There were other things in the display, however. A pile of storage units, evidently for sale. A wide range of alarm clocks. A faded poster of ABBA.

Surely *that* couldn't be for sale?

I couldn't see beyond the display into the shop itself, and reached out for the door. Only when I'd unsuccessfully tugged on it did I notice a handwritten sign sellotaped to it on the inside.

'Back later,' it said. I smiled to myself, wondering if that's what Jesus had left on his door. Then I tugged at the door again, obscurely disappointed that I wasn't going to be able to go inside. Probably it was still just a desire not to go back home and get on with earning a living, but I suddenly wanted to see what was there.

Instead, I had to trudge round the corner and down Falkland Road to meet my doom, in the form of thirty pages of still-unwritten shite about customer care for Vauxhall dealers.

At five I sat back from the computer, mind whirling. When I'm writing corporate videos I tend to visualize the facts and opinions I'm supposed to be putting into them as recalcitrant, bad-tempered sheep, which are determined to run away from me and hide in the hills. After two hours I'd managed to worry most of them into a pen; but they were moving restlessly and irritably against each other, determined not to pull in the same direction. It was time to take a break, before I decided the hell with it and started shooting the little bastards instead.

I put on a coat and wandered down the road to the cigarette shop on the corner, stocking up on my chosen method of slow suicide. As I did so I wished, not for the first time, that cigarettes weren't bad for you, or at least that I didn't know they were. That knowledge made every single one I smoked a little internal battle – never mind the *external* battles which cropped up every now and then, when some health freak gave me a hard time for endangering their life. These people, I had noticed, were invariably rather fat, and thus were doing their own fine job of reducing their own life expectancy; but that doesn't seem to be the point any more. What *we* do is fine – it's what those other bastards are doing to us which we won't stand for. I remembered reading a short piece in a recent *Enquirer* entitled 'How to stop your co-workers from giving you their colds'. After a line like that I'd expected advice on how to prevent deranged typists from injecting me with viruses, or marketing executives from coming over and deliberately breathing in my face. But no, it had been things like: 'Have a window open', and 'Eat vitamin C'. In other words, advice on how to stop *yourself* from acquiring the communicable colds which – through no fault of their own – other people might have.

But we don't see it like that, any more. Life's a constant battle to stop other people doing things to us, taking as hard a line as possible. We don't move tables or leave the room when someone is smoking – we stop them from smoking, anywhere, ever. We don't avoid watching videos which have a bit of sex and violence in them – we get them banned. And presumably, at some stage, we don't not read books we disagree with. We get them burned.

I recognized these thoughts as those of someone who was bored out of his tiny mind, and decided not to go back to the flat just yet. Instead I headed round the corner, sending a little nugget of goodwill to the Shuang Dou on the opposite side of the road, and walked back down towards Leighton Road. Initially, I was just taking a long way home, and then I realized I'd be going past the shop again, and that now might qualify as later, and it might be open.

It was. As I approached the shop I saw that the sign had gone from the door. Very slightly elated, in a vague way, I pushed it open and walked in.

There was no one behind the counter, and so I was free to look around the shop. It wasn't quite what I was expecting. Usually such stores have an air of thrift, of objects being widely spaced on shelves. This one was exactly the opposite. The area inside, which wasn't much bigger than my 'cosy' living room, was piled floor to ceiling with a bewildering array of stuff. Some of it was electrical – more of the period pieces from the window – but the majority was completely uncategorizable. Old toys, piles of ancient magazines. A few posters on the walls – ABBA again, together with other seventies bands. Small, chrome-plated appliances of indiscernible function. Even a few items of clothing, tired and out of fashion. It was like a jumble sale organized with some clear but not quite explicable purpose in mind.

There was a noise behind the counter, and I turned to see that a man had appeared. He was tall, in his early fifties, and looked Nigerian. He was dressed in an old blue suit which was shiny in patches, and he wore a white shirt without a tie underneath his buttoned jacket. His face was lined and he looked nervous, as if I was intruding.

'Hello,' I said, feeling strangely at ease – probably because he looked so unlike the smarmy and over-confident people you usually find in electrical shops: you know the type, the ones who pronounce: 'Can I help you at all' as one howling monosyllable and try to sell you a triple-standard VCR even if you just came in for batteries.

The man nodded cautiously. 'Can I help you?' he said. His voice was deep but quiet, and the words were clearly enunciated. A genuine question.

'Just looking around,' I said, and he nodded again. I turned away and ran my eyes over the shelves, realizing I had a bit of a problem. I couldn't just turn and walk out now. It would seem dismissive, of this man and his shop. I didn't want to do that. He looked like he'd been dismissed often enough already. On the other hand, I found it hard to believe that there was a single object in the shop which I would want. I already had all the recording, videoing, listening and watching equipment I could possibly need, none of it more than six months old; and all of the other stuff looked like junk you'd want to throw away rather than acquire.

I couldn't leave without at least making an effort, so I stepped over to one of the shelves and looked more closely at the objects strewn along it. Small pottery figures you might expect to find on surfaces in the room of a twelve-year-old girl. A very old copy of the *National Geographic*. A plastic alarm clock, manufactured back when people thought plastic was cool. A couple of 45s, by bands I'd never heard of.

I was very aware of the man standing silently behind me, and when I noticed a shoe-box full of watches I reached into it. My hand fell upon an oddly-shaped digital watch, which seemed to have been fashioned out of man-made materials to resemble what people two decades ago had thought of as 'futuristic'. Half of its strap was missing, and no numerals were showing in the window; but on the other hand I could possibly have some fun taking it apart, maybe even getting it going and turning it into some cyberpunky inside-out timepiece.

I turned to him. 'How much is this?' I asked, feeling like a minor character in some very old film.

'Two pound,' he said.

'I'll take it.' I nodded, and walked over to the counter, feeling in my back pocket for some change. He smiled shyly and found a small paper bag to put it in.

When I left the shop I crossed the road and stood there, looking across at the window. I couldn't see into the store, and wondered if the man was still standing behind the counter. I opened the bag I held in my hand and looked at the watch.

Why on earth had I bought it? It was just going to sit in a pile somewhere in an already overcrowded flat; next time I moved I'd either have to work up the resolve to throw it away, or tote it with me for ever more. I was surprised to see that I'd been mistaken in the store – something *was* visible on the screen. It wasn't numerals, or at least not whole ones, but little segments of the LCD figures seemed to be slowly flashing. Not very good news, of course; instead of simply being out of battery, it probably meant the watch was completely broken.

But when I'd been in the store it hadn't been working at all.

An hour later the man left the store, and I dropped the chip I had in my hand and stood up. I'd been sitting in the fish shop on the opposite side of the road, drinking tea and having an early and unhealthy meal. The food was actually quite good – I'm a connoisseur of cheap take-aways in North London – but that wasn't why I had chosen to eat there.

To be honest, I didn't really *know* why I'd stayed around. I'd stared dumbly at the watch for a while, and then simply decided I was going to wait. I didn't want to hang out on the pavement where passing trucks could spray me with dirty water, so I ducked into Mario's instead.

Now the guy was on the move, and I knew I was going to follow him. I didn't have a reason, and I felt like an idiot. But I was going to do it anyway.

I waited in the entrance to the fish bar until the man had got far enough up the other side of the street, then left and hurried across the road. Nobody ran me over, though several people had a bloody good try. The man was walking slowly, and I didn't anticipate having a problem keeping up with him. Quite the opposite; the challenge was to make sure he didn't see me. As discussed, I write videos for living. Tailing people was a bit of a departure for me. I walked along, head down and hands huddled into my coat, hoping this was the right sort of approach – every now and then I raised my eyes to check he was still in front of me.

The man continued up Fortess Road as far as the corner store where I'd bought cigarettes earlier, and then turned into Falkland Road. I picked up the pace a little, and made it round the corner about twenty seconds after him. By then he'd only got about fifty yards up the road, and so I dropped back again. He was walking more quickly now, head up, and crossed the road to the northern side, heading for the junction with Leverton street. I decided to cross immediately, and by the time he was approaching the corner he was only about twenty yards ahead. It was winter dark by now, but I could still see the shiny patches on the elbows of his suit as he turned the corner. About ten seconds later I followed him round.

He wasn't there.

I stopped. He couldn't have gone into a house, because there was a good fifty yards of wall before the nearest doorway. Across the street and up a bit was another corner store, but there was no way he could have reached that in the time he'd been out of my sight. I knew this, but I hurried across the street anyway, and peered into the window. The only people inside were the proprietor and his son. I turned back away from the window and looked up the street, listening for the sound of footsteps.

I couldn't hear any.

I wandered the area for a little while, getting progressively colder. Then I walked slowly back down Leverton Street and headed back to my flat.

I felt let down, and a little betrayed.

I also felt like concentrating on worrying some sheep for a while.

By the next morning I felt differently, or I'd reached my boredom threshold again. Either way, I found myself, mid-morning, standing outside the shop again. I had the watch in my pocket, and it was still blinking. I'd tried changing the batteries, but that hadn't made any difference. Parts of the numerals were still flashing meaninglessly on and off. Feeling slightly breathless, I pushed the door and walked in.

This time the man was behind the counter as I entered, and it was me who felt nervous. I ground to a halt a couple of steps in. He stared at me. He was wearing the same suit, and still looked rather wary.

'Hello,' I said, eventually. He nodded. Struggling for something to add, I held the watch up. 'I bought this yesterday.'

He nodded again.

'It doesn't seem to work,' I said, knowing that was hardly the point.

The man shrugged apologetically. 'It wasn't sold as working,' he said, quietly. 'All I have is what you see.'

'Oh, I know,' I said. 'It's just, it started doing something when I left the shop, and I wondered . . .'

I didn't really know what I was wondering, and neither did the man. He just stared at me.

'I'm, er,' I said, holding out my hands, 'I'm not here to cause trouble or anything.'

'I know,' the man said.

'You look a little nervous,' I blurted, immediately regretting it.

The man stared down at the counter for a while, and then looked up. 'This isn't right,' he said. 'Nothing's right, and I don't understand it.' He said these words quietly, and with great sadness. 'This isn't the way things are supposed to be.'

'What do you mean?'

'I don't think I'm supposed to be here.'

This wasn't making a great deal of sense to me, but I felt that it was something that had to be discussed. Part of my mind was sitting back with its arms folded, wondering what the hell I thought I was doing. The rest felt quite strongly that whatever it was, it was right.

'Where are you supposed to be?' I asked.

'I don't know,' he said. 'But this doesn't feel right. Something else should have happened by now.'

'What kind of thing?'

'I don't know that either.' He shrugged. 'That's what makes it so difficult.'

There was a pause then, neither of us apparently sure of how to proceed.

'It was simpler, before,' he said suddenly, looking down at the counter. 'People knew what they were, what they wanted. This time, no one seems to know. And if you don't know, you can't believe. Even those who think they believe are just cheerleading for something that was never meant.'

'I don't understand.'

'Exactly,' he said, smiling faintly. 'Once, you would have done. When I was younger, people knew what they were. Now they are less sure. A man can't be a man, because he thinks that's a bad thing to be. He has forgotten what it's like. Women too. People have forgotten magic. Things are better now for them, but also worse. Everything is surface, nothing is inside. The insides are empty. Do you not think this is so?'

I didn't really know what he was saying, unless it was this: that for the last twenty years everyone had been hiding, unsure of themselves, dancing to someone else's tune. That women have become more free to have jobs, and less free to have lives. That men run scared from their maleness until it twists and curdles into bitterness and resentment and rape. That everything is a constant battle not to think, not to feel, not to believe in anything which can't be said at a dinner party without offending someone. Men fall over backwards to prove they're not rampaging beasts, until the animal which still lives in them dies from lack of exercise, leaving only a shallow stick figure. Women run after the respect of people who don't care about them, forced to sideline the new-born into nurseries and day schools, because it's companies which are supposed to be important now, not families. Men *should* behave themselves, I thought, and women *should* be allowed to have careers; but this wasn't the way it was supposed to be achieved. The human has been lost, and all we have become is code in someone else's machine. We believe in flavourings, and correctness, in feelgood factors and learning curves, getting cashback and hoarding chainstore loyalty points – and trust in Sunday supplement articles refuting things which were too boring to say in the first place. Everything else is too difficult.

'Yeah,' I said, eventually. 'That's pretty much the way it is.'

The man nodded, as if coming to a decision. 'I thought so. Do you want a refund?'

It took me a moment to realize he was talking about the watch.

'No,' I said. 'That's all right. I'll keep it anyway.'

'Good,' he said, turning away. 'I'm sure that somewhere inside it still keeps time.'

I'm looking for work at the moment. I'm not sure what kind. I stopped writing corporate videos a few months ago, halfway through another one about Customer Care: thirty different ways to make your clients think that you give a fuck about them, when both you and they know you don't. I only got to number fourteen. I decided that I'd helped write enough code, and that I wasn't going to do it any more. The sheep can worry themselves.

I still eat in the Shuang Dou a couple of nights a week, but I haven't seen the red-faced man again. It doesn't matter. I don't think he could tell me anything I don't already suspect. I've still got the watch too, and sometimes it seems almost as if the flashing figures are going to settle, become strong enough to read again. It hasn't happened yet, but I believe that, some day, it will.

I went back to the shop the day after the conversation, but the window was vacant. By pressing my face up against the glass I could see that everything had gone from the inside too. It was completely empty, dust already settling.

On the inside of the door was a sign, roughly hand-lettered but securely sellotaped, as if to withstand a long wait.

'Back later,' it said.

ALWAYS

Jennifer stood, watching the steady drizzle, underneath the awning in front of the station entrance. She waited for the cab to arrive with something that was not quite impatience: there was no real hurry, though she wanted to be with her father. It was just that the minutes were filled to bursting with an awful weight of unavoidable fact, and if she had to spend them anywhere, she would rather it were not under an awning, waiting for a cab.

The train journey down from Manchester had been worse, far worse. Then she had felt a desperate unhappiness, a wild hatred of the journey and its slowness. She'd wanted to jig herself back and forwards on her seat like a child, to push the train faster down the tracks. The black outside the window had seemed very black, and she'd seen every streak of rain across the window. She'd stared out of it for most of the journey, her face sometimes slack with misery, sometimes rigid with the effort of not crying, of keeping her body from twitching with horror. The harder she stared at the dark hedges in shadow fields, the further she tried to see, the closer the things she saw.

She saw her mother, standing at the door of the house, wrapped in a cardigan and smiling, happy to see her home. She saw the food parcels she'd prepared for Jennifer whenever she visited, bags of staple foods mixed with nuggets of gold, little things that only she knew Jennifer liked. She saw her decorating the Christmas tree by herself in happy absorption, saw her in her chair by the fire, regal and round, talking nonsense to the utterly contented cat spreadeagled across her lap.

She tried to see, tried to understand, the fact that her mother was dead.

After her father had phoned she'd moved quickly through the house, throwing things in a bag, locking up, driving with heavy care to the station. Then there had been things to do. Now there was nothing. Now was the beginning of a time when there was nothing to do, no way to escape, no means of undoing. In an instant the world had changed, had switched from a home to a cold hard country where there was nothing but rain and minutes that stretched like railway tracks into the darkness.

At Crewe a man got on and sat opposite. He had tried to talk to her: to comfort her or to take advantage of her distress, it didn't matter which. She stared at him for a moment, lit another cigarette and looked back out of the window. She judged all men by her father. If she could imagine them getting on with him, they were all right. If not, they didn't exist.

She tried to picture her father, alone in the house. How big it must feel, how hollow, how much like a foreign place, as the last of her mother's breaths dissipated in the air. Would he know which molecules had been inside her, cooling as they mixed? Knowing him, he might. When he'd called, the first thing, the *only* thing she could think was that she had to be near him, and as she waited out the minutes she tried to reach out with her mind, tried to picture him alone in a house where the woman he'd loved for thirty years had sat down to read a book by the fire and died of a brain haemorrhage while he made her a cup of tea.

For as long as she could remember there had been few family friends. Her parents had been a world on their own, and had no need for anyone else. So different, and yet the same person, moving forever in a slow comfortable symmetry. Her mother had been home, her father the magic that lit up the windows, her mother had been love, her father the spell that kept out the cold. She knew now why as the years went on her love for her parents had begun to stab her with something that was like cold terror: because some day she would be alone. Some day she would be taken in the night from the world she knew and abandoned in a place where there was no one to call out to.

And now, as she stood waiting for a cab in the town where she'd grown up, she numbly watched the drizzle as it fell on the distant shore of a far country on a planet the other side of the universe. The trees by the station road called out to her, pressing their twisted familiarity upon her, but her mind balked, refused to acknowledge them. This wasn't any world she knew.

In three weeks it would be Christmas, and her mother was dead.

The cab arrived, and the driver tried to talk to her. She answered his questions brightly.

At the top of the drive she stood for a long moment, her throat spasming. Everything was different. All the trees, all the pots of plants her mother had tended, all the stones on the drive had moved a millimetre. The tiles had shifted infinitesimally on the roof, the paint had faded a millionth of a shade. She had come home, but home wasn't there any more.

Then the front door opened spreading a patch of warmth onto the drive, and she fled into the arms of her father.

For a long time she hung there, cradled in his warmth. He was comfort, an end to suffering. It had been him who had talked her through her first boyfriend's abrupt departure, him who had held her hand after childish nightmares, him who had come to her when as a baby she had cried out in the night. Her mother had been everything for her in this world, but her father the one who stood between Jennifer and worlds outside, in the way of any hurt.

After a while she looked up, and saw the living room door. It was shut, and it was then that finally she broke down.

Sitting in the kitchen in worn-out misery, she clutched the cup of tea her father had made, too numb to flinch from the pain that stabbed from every corner of her mother's kitchen. On the side was a jar of mincemeat, and a bag of flour. They would not be used. She tried to deflect her gaze, to find something to focus on, but every single thing spoke of her mother: everything was something she wouldn't use again, something she'd liked, something that looked strange and forlorn without her mother holding it. All the objects looked random and meaningless without her mother to provide the context they made sense in, and she knew that if she could look at herself she would look the same. Her mother could never take her hand again, would never see her married or have children. And she would have been such a fantastic grandmother, the kind you only find in children's books.

On the kitchen table were some sheets of wrapping paper, and for a moment that made her smile wanly. It had always been her father that bought the wrapping paper, and in years of looking Jennifer had never been able to find paper that was anywhere near as beautiful. Marbled swirls of browns and golds, of greens and reds, muted bursts of life that had lain curled beneath the Christmas tree like an advert for the whole idea of colour. The paper on the table was as nice as ever, some a warm russet, the rest a pale sea of shifting blue.

Every year, on Christmas morning, as she sat at her customary end of the sofa to begin unwrapping her presents, Jennifer had felt a warm thrill of wonder. She could remember as a young girl looking at the perfect oblongs of her presents and knowing that she was seeing magic at work. For her father would wrap the presents, and there were never any joins. She would hold the presents up, look at them every way she could, and still not find any Sellotape, or edges of paper. However difficult the shape, it was as if the paper had formed itself round it like a second skin.

One evening every Christmas her father would disappear to do his wrapping: she had never seen him do it, and neither, she knew, had Mum. In more recent years Jennifer had found the joins, cleverly tucked and positioned so as almost to disappear, but that hadn't undone the magic. Indeed, in her heart of hearts she believed that her father had done it deliberately, let her see the joins because she was too old now for a world where there could be none.

She could remember once, when she'd been a very little girl, asking her mother how Daddy did it. Her mother had told her that Dad's wrapping was his art, that when the King of the Fairies needed his presents wrapped he sent for her father to do it, and he went far off to a magic land to wrap his presents, and while he was away, he did theirs too. Her mother had said it with a smile in her eyes, to show she was joking, but also with a small frown on her forehead, as if she wasn't sure if she was.

As Jennifer sat staring at the paper, her father came back in. He seemed composed but a little shocked, as if he'd seen the neighbours dancing naked in their garden. He took her hand and they sat for a while, two of them where three should be.

And for a long time they talked, and remembered her. Already time seemed short, and Jennifer tried to remember everything she could, to mention every little thing, to write them in her mind so that they would still be there in the morning. Her father helped her, mixing in his own memories, as she scrabbled and clutched, desperate to gather all the fallen leaves before the wind blew them away.

Looking up at the clock as she made another cup of tea she saw that it was four o'clock, that it would soon be tomorrow, the day after her mother had died, and suddenly she slumped over, crying with the kettle in her hand. Because the day after that would be the day after that day, the week after the week after, next year the anniversary. It would never end. From now on all time was after time: no undoing, no last moment to snatch. There would be so many days, and so many hours, and no matter how many times the phone rang, it would never be her mother.

Seeing her, her father stood up and came to her. As she laid her head on his shoulder he finished making the tea, and then he tilted her head up to him. He looked at her for a long time, and she knew that he, and nobody else, could see inside her and know what she felt.

'Come on,' he said.

She watched as he walked to the table and picked up some of the wrapping paper.

'I'm going to show you a secret.'

'Will it help?' Susan felt like a little child, watching the big man, her father.

'It might.'

They stood for a moment outside the living room door. He didn't hurry her, but let her ready herself. She knew that she had to see her mother, couldn't just let her fade away behind a closed door. Finally she nodded, and he opened the door.

The room she walked into seemed huge, cavernous. Once cosy, the heart of the house, now it stretched like a black plain far out into the rain, the corners cold and dark. The dying fire flickered against the shadows, and as she stepped towards it Jennifer felt the room grow around her, bare and empty as the last inaudible echoes of her mother's life died away.

'Oh Mum,' she said, 'oh Mum.'

Sitting in her chair by the fire she could almost have been asleep. She looked old, and tired, but comfortably warm, and it seemed that the chair where she sat was the centre of the world. Jennifer reached out and touched her hand. Kissed by the embers of the fire, it was still warm, could still have reached out and touched her. Her father shut the door, closing the three of them in together, and Jennifer sat down by the fire, looking up at her mother's face. What had been between the lines was gone, but the lines were still there, and she looked at every one.

She looked up to see that her father had spread three sheets of the pink wrapping paper on the big table. He came and crouched down beside her and they held Mum's hand together, and Jennifer's heart ached to imagine what his life would be like without her, without his Queen. Together they kissed her hand, and said goodbye as best they could, but you can't say goodbye when you're never going to see someone again. It isn't possible. That's not what goodbye means.

Her father stood, and with infinite tenderness picked his wife up in his arms. For a moment he cradled her, a groom on his wedding day holding his love at the beginning of their life together. Then slowly he bent, and to Jennifer's astonishment he laid her mother out on the wrapping paper.

'Dad . . .'

'Shh,' he said.

He picked up another couple of sheets of paper and laid them on top of her. His hands made a small folding movement where they joined, and suddenly there was only one long piece of wrapping paper. Jennifer's mouth dropped open like a child's.

'Dad, how . . .?'

'Shh.'

He took the end of the sheet lying under her mother, and folded it over the top. Slowly he worked his way around the table, folding upwards with little movements of his hands. Like two gentle birds they slowly wove round each other, folding and smoothing. Jennifer watched silently, cradling her tea, at last seeing her father do his wrapping, and as he moved round the table the two sheets of paper were knitted together as if it were the way they'd always been.

After about fifteen minutes he paused, and she stepped closer to look. Only her mother's face was visible, peeking out of the top. It could have looked absurd, but it was her mother, and it didn't. The rest of her body was enveloped in a pink paper shroud that seamlessly held her close. Her father bent and kissed his wife briefly on the lips, and she bent too, and kissed her mother's forehead. Then he made another folding movement, brought the last edge of paper over and smoothed, and suddenly there was no gap, no join, just a large irregular paper parcel perfectly wrapped.

Then her father moved and stood halfway down the table. He slid his arm under his wife's back, and gently brought it upwards. The paper creaked softly as he raised her body into a sitting position, and then further, until it was bent double. He made a few more smoothing motions and all Jennifer could do was stare, eyes wide. On the table was still a perfect parcel, but half as long. He slid his hand under again, and folded it in half again, then moved round, and folded it the other way, gentle and unhurried. For ten minutes he folded and smoothed, tucked and folded, and the parcel grew smaller and smaller, until it was two feet square, two feet by one, six inches by nine. Then his concentration deepened still further, and as he folded he seemed to take especial care with the way the paper moved, and out of the irregular shape emerged corners and edges. And still the parcel grew smaller and smaller.

When finally he straightened there was on the table a tiny oblong, not much bigger than a matchbox, a perfect pink parcel. Jennifer moved closer to watch as he pulled a length of russet ribbon from his pocket, and painted a line first one way round, then the other to meet at the top. As he tied the bow she looked closely at the parcel and knew she'd been right all along, that she'd seen the truth as a child. There were no joins, none at all.

When he had finished, her father held the little shape in his hands and looked at her, his face tired but composed. He reached out and touched her cheek, his fingers as warm as they'd always been, and in their touch was a blessing, a persistence of love. All the time she'd been on this planet they had been always there, her father and mother, someone to do the good things for, and to help the bad things go away.

'I can only give you one present this year,' he said, 'and it's something you've already got. This is only a reminder.'

He held up the parcel to her, and she took it. It felt warm and comforting, all her childhood, all her love in a small oblong box. She felt she knew what she should do, and brought the present in close to her, and pressed it against her heart. As she shed her final tears her father held her close and wished her Happy Christmas, and when she took her hand away, the present was gone from her hand, and beat inside her.

The journey back to Manchester passed in a haze of recollection, and when she was back in her flat she walked slowly around it, touching objects in the slanting haze of early morning light. She wished she could be with her father, but knew he was right to tell her to go back. As she sat in the hallway she listened to the beating of her heart, and as she looked at reminders of Mum she let herself feel glad. It would take time, but it was something she already had: she had her mother deep inside her, what she'd been, the love she'd given and felt. She was her mother's pride and joy, and while she still lived her mother lived too: her finest and favourite work, the living sum of her love and happiness. There would be no goodbyes, because she could never really lose her. She could never speak to her again in words, but she would always hear her voice. She would always be inside her, helping her face the world, helping her to be herself.

And Jennifer thought about her father, and knew her heart would soon be fuller still. She knew it would not be many days before another parcel was delivered to her door, and that it too would be perfectly wrapped, its paper a pale sea of shifting blue.

WHAT YOU MAKE IT

Finding a child was easy. It always was. You waited outside one of the convenience stores that lined the approach, or trawled a strip mall at the nearby intersections for half an hour. There were always kids hanging around at night, panhandling change for a burger or twenty minutes on a coin-op video game in one of the arcades. Or sometimes just hanging there, with nothing in particular in prospect. You have to have seen something of the world to know what's worth looking for. These kids, the just-hanging kids, had seen nothing – and were mainly willing to be shown pretty much whatever you had in mind.

The only question was which one to pick. Too old, either age, and it looked weird at the gate. Too young, and people tend to wonder where the kid's mother is at. And of course sometimes it depended, and you had to find one that looked just right for the night. Early teens was usually best, acquiescent, not too scuffed up.

It only took Ricky ten minutes to find one. She was sitting by herself on a bench outside the Subway franchise, looking at her feet or nothing in particular, alone in a yellow glow. Ricky cruised by the sandwich store twice in the twilight, noted that though there were two groups of kids nearby, one just a little along the sidewalk and another loitering outside Publix, the girl didn't seem to have a link to either. He parked the car up, let the motor tick down to silence, and watched her a little while. The nearest group of kids walked right by her, in and out of her pool of light, without a word being exchanged. She didn't even look up. She wasn't expecting friends.

Ricky grabbed his cigarettes off the dash, locked the car, and walked over to her.

She glanced at him as he approached, but not with much curiosity. Something told him that this wasn't indifference, but a genuine ignorance of the kind of situations the world could provide. This meant she was even more likely to be what he needed, and it was just good luck for her that it was Ricky's eye she'd caught, instead of some kind of fucking pervert.

'Waiting for someone?' he asked, stopping when he was a couple of yards away. She looked up, then away. Didn't even shake her head. He took the last few steps, sat down casually on the next bench along. 'Right. I know. Just a good place to sit.'

There was no response. Ricky took out a cigarette and lit it, unhurried. She looked maybe twelve years old, pretty face. Blue eyes, fair hair in a ponytail. White T-shirt, blue jeans. Both recently clean. He noticed her eyes follow his match as it skittered across the way and went out. Despite appearances, he had her attention.

'You hungry?'

She blinked, and her head turned a little way towards him. Something changed. It always did. It's a very elemental question. Even if you've just eaten enough to kill a man, you think about it. Am I hungry? Have I had enough? Will I be okay? And if you're really hungry, the question comes at you like you've just been goosed, like someone's just guessed your worst secret, how close you are to being cancelled out. Ricky knew how it worked. He'd been hungry. You answered the hungry question quietly, so the vultures wouldn't hear.

'Kinda,' she said, eventually.

He nodded, looking out across the parking lot for a while. Partly to check how many couples were hefting grocery bags to their breeder wagons; mainly just to let the conversation settle.

'I could buy you something,' he said then, casually. 'What's the matter? Your mom didn't feed you tonight?'

'Don't have a mom,' she said.

'What about your old man? Where's he at?'

The girl shrugged. Didn't matter whether she didn't know or just didn't want to know. Ricky knew she was his.

Ten minutes later, as he watched her wolf down her sandwich and fries, Ricky asked the big question.

'How'd you like to visit Wonder World tonight?'

It was well after eight by the time they got to the entrance. The queue was pretty short. Ricky knew it would be: they had a parade every night at eight-thirty, down 1st Street, and anyone with park-visiting in mind made sure they were already inside by then. Even the girl, whose name was Nicola, knew about the parade. Ricky told her that this week it was at nine-fifteen because it was a special parade. She looked at him dubiously, but seemed hopeful.

As he turned into one of the lanes and pulled up to the gate Ricky felt a familiar flicker of anxiety. This was the part where it could all go wrong. It hadn't yet, because the kids had always wanted what they thought they were getting, but it could. It could go wrong tonight. It could go wrong any time. He wound the window down.

The gateman's head immediately bobbed down to grin at him. 'Hi there! I'm Marty the Gateman! How you doing?'

Marty the Gateman was in his late fifties, and dressed in an exaggerated version of the uniform of a cop from the 1940s. His face was pink with good cheer or make-up. Or alcohol most likely, Ricky thought. The other gatemen in all the other lanes looked the same, and said exactly the same things.

Ricky grinned right back. 'I'm good. You?'

'Me? I'm great!' the man said, and then laughed uproariously. When he did this, he leaned back from the waist, placed a splayed hand on either side of his ribcage, and rubbed them up and down with each chortle, like a cartoon. Nicola giggled, twisted in her seat.

Ricky let one hand drop to where the gun rested down between the seat and the door, waited for the man to stop. Fucking loser. He imagined the guy going home after his shift, taking off his stupid fucking costume, whacking off in front of the television or a stack of porno. He had to do something like that. Rick knew *he* would have done, that's for sure. Couldn't be any other way.

Eventually the man stopped laughing, wiped his eyes. 'Shee! So! Two happy travellers for Wonder World! You just here for rides and fun and all the magic you can find?'

'No,' Nicola said, leaning over Ricky so she could smile up at him through the window. 'We're visiting Grandma too!'

Ricky relaxed. The girl was going to behave. Better still, she'd got into the part. They did, sometimes. Kids loved make-believe.

Marty winked. 'Lucky Grandma! She know you're coming?'

'It's a surprise,' Nicola said, confidingly. 'She lives in Homeland 3.'

'Okey dokey!' the gateman yelped joyously, pulling a deck of tickets out of one of the oversize pockets on his uniform. 'So, Mr Dad – how long you going to be spending with us?'

'An hour, maybe two.' Ricky smiled. 'Depends on how strong Grandma's feeling.'

'Why don't we say three? Can always get you a rebate when you come out.'

'Sure, Marty. That'd be great.'

'All-righty!' Tongue sticking out of the corner of his mouth, Marty the Gateman tapped some buttons on the control unit on the side of his booth. As he tapped, the buttons got a little larger, and started moving around, so he had to keep his hand darting back and forth to keep up. Two twinkling animatronic eyes appeared at the top of the control unit, and one of them winked at Nicola. Within a few seconds the buttons, which were brightly coloured in primary hues, were a few inches long and bending every which way. Still the man poked at them, huffing and puffing.

'Hey!' he said, and Nicola laughed, when a couple of the buttons got even longer and started poking him back. When this gag was done, the gateman held a ticket out towards the machine, a slit opened in the unit in the shape of a cheerful mouth, and the ticket was popped inside, chewed for a moment, and then spat out, authorized. The eye winked at Nicola again, and then suddenly the control unit returned to normal and Marty was waggling the ticket right under Ricky's nose.

Any other time or place, Marty would have lost his hand. But Ricky gave him the money, and the gate opened. The gateman waved at Nicola through the back window.

As the car started to pull forward, all of the faces in the gate structure – each a classic character from a Wonder World cartoon, every one hand-tweaked by liars into joyous perfection – swivelled their eyes towards the car and started to sing.

China Duck was there, Loopy Hound and Careful Cat, Bud and Slap the Happy Rats and Goren the fucking Gecko and countless others, every face already hot-wired into your mind no matter how hard you'd always ignored them.

'The magic is what you make it,' they sang, a sonic tower of saccharine harmonies, 'make it, make it . . . The magic is what you . . .'

Ricky wound the windows up.

Lit a cigarette and stepped on the gas.

The kid was quiet as they headed towards Homeland 3. She had plenty to look at, and she drank it in as though even in darkness it was the greatest thing she had ever seen. Maybe it was. Unlike her, Ricky had seen it all before.

Monorail tracks arced gracefully in all directions, linking park to park. Mostly quiet for the evening, but occasionally a streamlined shape would swoosh past the road or over their heads. Taking happy families out, or back, for the evening: out to ridiculous themed restaurants, or back to dumb-looking resort hotels where overexcited kids would make so much noise you'd want to throttle them, and parents would reconcile themselves to another night without screwing and send out for room service booze instead. Probably even that was delivered by a fucking chipmunk.

Actually, Ricky had never stayed in one of the hotels. Never even been in one: the security was too good. But he felt he knew exactly how it would be. A great big stupid con, like everything else in Wonder World. Set up fifty years ago, and now so vast and sprawling it put most cities in the shade. Rides and enclosures and parks and theatres and 'experiences' and crap, all based around a bunch of cartoons and some asshole's idea of the perfect world. There was a fake big game reservation. A bunch of fake lakes, where fish and dolphins and shit swam about, like anyone cared. A fake downtown strip the size of a whole town, where people who were too scared to walk to the corner store in their own stupid bergs could wander around and buy up all the shit they wanted. Some sort of stupid futuristic park, where it was supposed to be like what it would be in a hundred years: like we were all going to be shopping from home and wearing pastel nylon and using videophones – standing in tight little nuclear family groups and talking to Gramps on Mars.

Ricky knew what it was really going to be like in a hundred years, and it wasn't going to be cutesy characters walking around, posing for photographs and making the little kids laugh. It wasn't going to be restaurants where the family could go and get good food and great service for ten bucks a head; it wasn't going to be endless fucking stores full of T-shirts and candy in painted tins, and being able to leave your door unlocked at night and no litter anywhere. It was going to be guns, and stealing things. It was going to be dog eat dog, and he wasn't talking the kind of dog which had some fuckass pimply kid inside, earning chump change for blow. It was going to be taking what you wanted, and fucking up anyone who got in your way. It was getting that way already, and only fools pretended otherwise. That's what kids needed to learn, not crap about talking bunnies. Wonder World pained Ricky personally, which is one of the reasons why he did what he did for a living. He hated the bright colours, the cheer, the stupid, kiddie nonsense, the lies about how the world really was, the conspiracy to believe that there was magic somewhere in the world. He hated it all.

It was a crock of utter shit.

The kid stayed good as he drove, even though weird and

miraculous buildings kept appearing in the darkness, each promising fun and games. She didn't ask to stop at every one, like most of them did. She kept quiet until the car swung around in the front of the massive portal into the heart of Wonder World, the original Beautiful Realm park. The gate was like a massive googie castle, every ludicrous '50s drive-in and coffee shop-erama mashed joyously together into an eight-storey extravagance that would have taken the Jetsons' breath away. Whirling spotlights sent beams of light chopping merrily through the night, and characters capered around the entrance, beckoning people in. The girl had wound her window back down by then, and could hear in the distance the sound of drums and music, the singing and dancing inside.

'The parade,' she said.

He shrugged. 'Fuckers did it early. Or maybe it's just beginning.'

She was calm, reasonable. 'You said we'd see the parade.'

'We will. It goes on for, like, an hour. We'll just do this thing, and then we'll go catch the end. It's better that way. Most of the people have gone home, you get closer to all the characters.'

'Really?' She was looking at him closely, her mouth wanting to smile, but nervous of being let down. Just then one of the lights cut through into the car, showing her in every detail. Pretty little face, red lips that had never been kissed. Big eyes, wanting him to tell her good news, wanting to see nice things.

And tiny new breasts outlined in a T-shirt one size too small. She was perfect, all the more so because she wouldn't even understand what he was thinking.

Ricky decided this one was going to play the game a little longer than most of the others, that she going to learn the facts of life. The facts that had to do with taking whatever he wanted to put inside her. A training session. Save some guy time and effort later on, except Ricky knew there wasn't going to be a later. Usually he lay the kid over the back seat on the way out, put a blanket over them like they were just sleeping, winked at some guy at the gate and laughed with him about how the child had too much excitement for one day. Tonight he'd find a way of getting this one out alive. He'd work it out.

'Really,' he said. 'Trust me.'

She smiled.

Ten minutes later he was scanning street names as he cruised slowly down Homeland 3's main drag. Every now and then they'd pass a toon character, who'd stop and wave at Nicola. Ranging from three-foot dancing toadstools to six-foot ducks, they were freaking Ricky out. You didn't normally see characters roaming this late: they were only there to magic the place up through the day, during the most popular visiting hours. Ricky was having trouble sorting through the names of the streets, which were also the names of fucking characters. Loopy Drive IV, Careful Crescent VI – how the fuck were you supposed to keep track? Nicola wasn't helping, having decided to tell him her life story. She was thinking of shortening her name, and spelling it Nicci, because she thought it was classy and presumably didn't know how Gucci was actually pronounced. She liked cats, like Careful Cat, but dogs were sometimes cute too. She didn't know where Daddy was because she'd never known. She said she didn't have a mommy because real mommies didn't do what hers did, and so two days ago she'd run away from home and she wasn't going back this time.

Jesus, only two days, Ricky was thinking. Are you lucky you ran into me so quick. Going to save you six months of turning into your mommy, then a short lifetime waiting for the hammer to fall. You're a lucky girl, little Nicola. Lucky, lucky, lucky.

Part of him was also shaking, because of what he knew he was going to do later. He didn't normally do it. He just disposed of them. Take a drive down the 'glades, dump the body, no one's going to know or give a shit. He didn't like doing anything else, made him feel like a pervert though he wasn't – he was a professional. Every now and then was okay though, even if it was clouding his mind right now, making it hard to make the street names out. Some guys bought themselves new guns, went on a coke bender, hired a couple of whores. Everyone needs a treat. Incentive scheme. Keeps your wheels turning.

Ricky gripped the wheel tightly, tuned out the noise of the kid's nattering, got himself straight. Eventually he turned the car in what looked like the right direction. Found his way down the grid of streets, each lined with houses, some streets like the 1940s, some the 1950s or 1960s. Or like those times would have been if they hadn't been shit, anyhow. Like those decades were if you looked back at them now and forgot everything that was wrong with them. The streets were quiet, because mostly the people in the houses were too old to be out walking this late.

Homeland 3, along with the four other near-identical districts which spread in a fan around the Beautiful Realm, was one of the newest parts of Wonder World. Five years ago, the suits who ran the parks realized they had yet another goldmine on their hands: managed communities of old farts. Cutesy little neighbourhoods in the sun, where the oldsters could come waste their final years, safe from the world outside and bad afternoons where they could be walking home from the store they'd used all their lives and suddenly find three guys with knives standing on the corner. Not only safe, but coddled, living somewhere where their grandkids could be guaranteed to want to come see them. You want to go visit Granny in Roanoke? I don't think so. Wonder World? – that's a pretty easy sell. They built the houses, any size, any style, so everyone from trailer trash to leather-faced zillionaires had somewhere to hang their trusses: houses that looked like whatever you wanted from a space podule to a mud hut on the planet Zog. All this and stores and banks and shit, all built to look like what they sold. That's what made it so difficult to find your way around. Was like being in a toy store on acid.

It got so popular that even the smallest houses started getting expensive, and a year ago Ricky had an idea. You've got house after house of old people. With money. People who can't defend themselves too well. With things worth stealing. You get yourself into one of the Homelands – with a cute kid, who's going to question you? – and you help yourself to some stuff, using the kid's voice to get the door open. You're in and out before anyone knows there's a few old people gone to meet their maker sooner than intended: kid's the only living witness, and not for very long. All you got to do is make sure you never get recognized at the gate, and with millions of people going in and out every week, it's never going to happen.

And the kicker – Wonder World covered the burglaries up. Of course they did. Very bad for business, because they showed the magic retreat was a crock of shit. Plus, and here Ricky witnessed something which made perfect sense to him, something which placed the whole world in context as he understood it – the families often didn't make too much fuss. Why? Same reason that, after a couple months, Ricky had a new idea and moved on to a different line of business, made himself a professional.

Lot of times the families weren't exactly too sad to see the old folks go, because they wanted the old people's money. Which is why Ricky didn't bother to steal any more. Now Ricky took contracts instead, made it look natural. Much safer, more secret, more lucrative – for the time being. Sooner or later the suits would catch on and increase security somehow, and Ricky would move out, and start blackmailing the families instead. Even the kind of people who'd pay to have Gramps whacked had to be living in a Wonder World of their own, if they didn't realize it would come back to haunt them some day.

Ricky finally found Gecko Super Terrace III, drove a little way along it. Pulled over to the kerb, looked up at a house and checked the address. Grunted with satisfaction. He was in the right place.

Margaret Harris, eighty-four years old, was worth maybe three hundred and fifty thousand dollars, all told, including the Homeland house. Not such a hell of a lot, but her son and daughter-in-law could get the bigger boat a couple years earlier, and without working all those unsociable hours and missing cocktail hour. Upgrade the satellite, get a widescreen TV for the den. Maybe they'd throw their children a bone too. A games station. A bike. A last visit to Wonder World.

As John Harris, the son, had put it while slurping a large scotch to blur his conscience: they were just realizing an unwanted asset.

Margaret Harris had herself a kind of tiny Tudor mansion, dark beams and whitewash, exaggerated leans in the walls and gingerbread thatch. There was a light on in a downstairs room, behind a curtain. The grass in the front yard was all the same perfect fucking length. Maybe it was animatronic grass. Maybe it sang a happy wake-up call in the morning, a million blades in unison.

Nicola looked at the house too. 'Is this where she lives?'

'That's right. You remember what I want you to do?'

She looked away, didn't answer for a moment.

'I had a grandma,' she said, 'I saw her twice. She gave me a ring, but Mommy took it. She died when I was six. Mommy got so drunk she wet herself.'

Ricky nearly hit her then, but stopped himself just in time. It was like that with the ones like her. Part of wanting to fuck them was finding them just too fucking irritating to bear. He forced himself to speak calmly. 'This isn't your grandma, okay? Do you remember, Nicola? What I want you to do?'

'Of course,' the girl said. She opened the door and got out.

Swearing quietly, Ricky got out his side, slipped the gun into his pocket, then followed her up the path to the Harris house.

Nicola rang the doorbell a second time, and Ricky heard someone moving inside the house. He stepped back into shadow. Nicola stood in front of the door, waiting.

'Who is it?' The voice was old, cracked but not quavery. The kind of voice that says I'm pretty old but not ready to drop just yet.

'Hi Grandma!' Nicola piped, leaning forward to peer through the diamond of swirled glass in the door. She waved her hand. 'I've come to see you!'

'Theresa?' The oldster's voice was uncertain, but Ricky caught the sound of locks being tentatively drawn. This was the second key moment. This was the moment where the kid had to be good enough so that the old woman didn't press the Worry Button put beside the door of every Homeland house. The button that would alert Wonder World's version of security that something was sharp and spiky in the dream tonight.

The final slide bolt, and the door opened a crack. 'Theresa?'

Margaret Harris was small, maybe five feet tall. She was grandma-shaped and had white hair done up in a curly style. Her face was plump and lined and she was wearing one of those dresses that old people wear, flowers on a dark background. You opened a dictionary and looked up 'Grandma' and she was pretty much what you'd see.

'You're not Theresa,' she said.

'Oh no,' Nicola laughed. 'I'm Theresa's friend. Theresa said if we were passing by we should call in and say hello.'

Ricky stepped into the light, an apologetic smile on his face. 'Hi there, Mrs Harris. Hope this is okay – Theresa's telling Nicola here about you all the time. John said you probably wouldn't mind. Meant to call ahead, but you know how it is.'

'You're a friend of John's?'

'Work right across the hall from him at First Virtual.'

Mrs Harris hesitated a final moment, then smiled back, her face crinkling in a pattern which started from the eyes. 'Well I guess it's okay then. Come on in.'

The hallway looked like a painted background from an old Wonder World cartoon: higgledy stairs, everything neat, colours washed and clean. When the door was shut behind them, Ricky knew the job was done.

'You can't be too careful these days,' the old woman said, predictably, leading Nicola through to the kitchen to make some coffee. Right, thought Ricky, following at a distance, and you haven't been careful enough.

He hung outside for a moment, scoping the place, listening with half an ear to the sound of Nicola chatting with the old bag in the kitchen. Jeez, the kid could lie: what's happening at school, party she went to with Theresa last week, Theresa borrowing her shoes. Listening to her, you'd think she really *did* know the woman's granddaughter. Make-believe again, some life she wished she had.

Ricky debated disabling the Worry Button, finally decided it wasn't necessary. Difficult to do, anyhow – and just smashing it would leave a clue. This one was too easy to make it worth taking the risk.

The kitchen was small, cosy, tricked up to look like the kind of place where there would always be something in the oven, instead of ready-made shit in the microwave. Pots, pastry cutters, a rolling pin. Probably Wonder World sent someone into everyone's house every day, made sure the props looked just right. Grandma Harris turned as Ricky entered and handed a cup of coffee up to him. She smiled, twinkle-eyed, relaxed – the kid had put her at ease.

Ricky made a mental note that the cup and saucer would need wiping when he was done. Nicola had a glass of Dr Pepper – that would need washing too. He sipped the coffee – might as well – and deflected a couple of questions about working with the great John Harris. Pathetic, really, the way the old woman was eager for any news of her son, wanted telling how people liked him. Suddenly, he just wanted to lash out and shove his cup right down the old fart's throat. It would be a whole lot quicker, and put her out of misery she didn't even know she was in. But he knew how it had to look, and death by ingestion of china tea set wouldn't play.

Meantime, Nicola and Grandma sat at the table, yakking nineteen to the dozen. Nicola had a lot of Grandma-talking to do, even if she had to make do with someone else's. Ricky let his eyes glaze over, mulling what he was going to do to the kid later. He enjoyed doing that, getting the comparison, just like he liked looking at girls in the street and imagining them on the job, their hands or mouth busy, face wet with sweat. They'd never know, but they'd been his. Ricky rode that line, that fine line, between the life they lived and the life that could come and find them in the night.

'Isn't that right, Daddy?'

'Huh?' Ricky looked at the girl dully, having missed the question. 'What's that?'

'Nicola was just saying how you and John were planning a joint vacation for the families later in the year,' Mrs Harris said. 'That's wonderful news. Do you think you might be able to make it up here again? We'd have such fun.'

'Sure,' Ricky said, abruptly deciding this had gone on long enough and was getting out of hand. 'No question. Hey, Mrs Harris – meant to ask you something.'

'Of course.' Grandma was beside herself at the prospect of another visit later in the year. She'd have agreed to anything. 'What is it?'

'John told me about some pictures, old photos, you've got at the top of the stairs? Kind of an interest of mine. He said you might not mind me taking a peek at them.'

'I'd be delighted.' The old woman beamed. 'Come, let's go up.' Nicola jumped to her feet, but Ricky flashed a glare at her.

Grandma raised an eyebrow. 'Wouldn't you like to come too, dear?'

Nicola avoided Ricky's eye. 'Could I have another Dr Pepper first?'

'Help yourself, then follow us up. Now come on – Rick, isn't it? – let's go take a look.'

Ricky sent another 'Stay here' look at the kid, followed Grandma out. Made interested grunts every now and then as the old woman talked and led him across the hall to the stairs. A couple of objects caught Ricky's eye on the way, and he planned on picking them up later, before he left. Little bonus.

Up the stairs behind her. Feeling very little. No fear, no excitement. Just watching for the best moment. Mrs Harris walked up the stairs slowly, hitching one leg up after the other. Her voice might be strong but her body was saying goodbye. She wouldn't be losing much.

They got to the first landing, and Ricky saw that there were indeed a whole bunch of really fucking dull-looking black and whites in frames there on the wall. John Harris had the whole thing planned out, gave Ricky this way of getting her up to the scaffold. Ricky debated telling the old woman about that, letting her see what lay beyond her wonder world, that the son she'd raised had sat in his study one night drinking cheap scotch and working it all out. But by then Margaret Harris was standing right by him, and he knew the time was right and he wanted to get it over with. The real bonus was waiting for him in the kitchen. He didn't need any cheap thrills first.

This picture was her mother, that one her grandpapa. Gone-away people, stiff in fading monotone.

Ricky leaned towards her, apparently to get a closer look at a bunch of people grouped in front of a raggedy farm building – but actually to get the right angle.

For a moment then he was distracted, by a scent. It seemed to come from the old woman's clothes, and was a combination of things: of milk and cinnamon, rich coffee and apples cooking on the stove. Leaves barely on the trees in fall, and the smell of sun on grass in summer. These things weren't a part of his life, but for a moment he had them in his mind – like they were part of some story he'd read long ago, as a child, and just dismissed.

Then he pushed her down the stairs.

Palm flat against her shoulder, feeling the bones inside the old, thin flesh. He straightened his arm firmly, which was enough – and wouldn't leave a bruise which some forensic smartass might be able to talk up into evidence.

The old woman teetered, without making a sound, and then her centre of gravity was all wrong and she just tumbled over sideways, over the edge and down the stairs.

Thump, crash, thud, splat. Like a loose bag of sticks.

Ricky walked briskly down the stairs after her, reached the bottom bare seconds after she did. Held back from kicking her head, which would have been risky and was clearly unnecessary. Huge dent in the skull already, eyes turned upwards and out of sight. Arm twisted a strange way, one leg bent back on itself. The usual anti-climax.

Job done.

He stepped quickly over the body and to the kitchen, stopping Nicola already on her way out. She ran into him, crashed against his body. He grabbed her shoulders, warm through the thin T-shirt.

'What happened? I heard a crash.'

Usually he killed the kid at this point, before they got hysterical and made too much noise or ran out of the house. Ricky pushed Nicola gently back into the kitchen, felt his temperature rising. Needed her alive to do things with, but he couldn't do them here. 'Nothing. Just an accident. Mrs Harris fell down the stairs.'

'Grandma?'

'She's not your grandma, sweetie. You know that.'

'We've got to get help . . .'

Ricky smiled down at her. 'We will. That's exactly what we'll do. We'll get in the car, go find one of the security wagons. They'll help her out. She'll get fixed up and we'll catch the end of the parade.'

The girl was near tears. 'I want to stay here with her.'

He pretended to think about it, then shook his head. 'Can't do that. Security gets here while I'm away, find you with an old lady at the bottom of the stairs, what they going to think? They're going to think you pushed her.'

'They won't. She was my grandma. Why would I hurt her?'

Ricky glared at her, good humour fast disappearing. 'She wasn't your fucking grandma. Just some old woman.'

Nicola pushed hard against him, momentarily rocking him on his heels. 'She was *too*. She knew about me. She knew things. She said not to worry about my mom any more. She said she loved me.'

Ricky lashed out with his hand, shoved the kid hard. She flew back, ricocheted off the table and knocked the coffee pot flying. It struck the wall, spraying brown gunk everywhere, just as Nicola crashed to the floor. Ricky cursed himself. Not clever. Just going to make it more difficult to get her out of the house, plus it was going to look like signs of a struggle. He took a deep breath, stepped towards her. Maybe he was going to have to just kill her after all.

'Nicola? Are you okay, dear?'

Ricky froze, foot just hitting the floor. Turned slowly round.

Grandma stood in the doorway. One eye fluttered slowly, the one below the huge dent which pulled most of the side of her face out of kilter. The arm was still bent way out of place. Her body was completely fucked up, but somehow she'd managed to drag herself to the door, to her feet.

Nicola struggled into a sitting position against the wall behind Ricky. 'Grandma – are you all right?'

Of course she's not fucking all right, Ricky thought. No way.

Grandma leaned against the door frame, as if tired. 'I'm fine, dear. Just had a little fall, isn't that right Rick?' Her working eye fixed on him.

Ricky felt the hairs on the back of his neck rise like a thousand tiny erections. Then her other eye stopped flickering. Closed for a moment, reopened – and then he had two strong eyes looking at him. Tough old bitch.

Ricky reached for the table, grabbed the rolling pin lying there. This job was getting very fucked up, but he was going to finish it now.

'Close your eyes, dear,' Grandma said. She wasn't talking to him, but the kid. 'Would you do that, for Grandma? Just close your eyes for a while.'

'Close them tight?' Nicola asked, voice small.

'Yes, close them extra tight,' Grandma nodded, trying to smile. 'And I'll tell you when you can open them again.'

Ricky saw the girl shut her eyes and cover her ears. He shook his head, turned back to the old woman, rolling pin held with loose ease. He took a measured stride towards her, not hurrying. Ricky had been in bad situations all his life, had been beaten up and half-killed on a hundred occasions, starting with the times that happened in his own bedroom, a room that had no posters on the walls or books on shelves or little figures of cartoon animals. Ricky's old man hadn't believed in make-believe either; was proud of being cynical – 'That's what I am, boy, I'm nobody's fool' – and working the angles and telling God's honest truth however fucking dull it was. His lessons had been painful, but Ricky knew he'd been right.

Ricky wasn't afraid of an old woman, no matter how tough she might be, and he just grinned at her, looking forward to seeing what the pin was going to do to her face. She looked back at him, head tilted up, grey hair awry and skin papery, and then her head popped back out.

One minute her skull was caved in, the next it was back where it should be, like someone pumped exactly the right amount of air back into a punctured balloon. It made a sound like cellophane.

Ricky gawped, arm aloft.

Grandma swallowed, blinked, then did something with her fucked-up arm. Swung it around from behind her – and as it came it seemed to become more solid, find the right planes to rotate on again. She bent it experimentally, found it worked, and used it to pat her dry hair more or less back into place.

'You're a very bad boy, Ricky,' she said, softly, too quietly for Nicola to hear. 'And bad boys never see Santa Claus. Hear what I'm saying, motherfuck?'

Before Ricky could even process this sentence, Margaret Harris had hurled herself at him. He tried to turn, bring the pin down, but only managed to twist halfway round at the waist. She smacked into him sideways, and the two of them spun off the corner of the table to crash into the wall. Ricky felt his nose bend and melt, and realized there was going to be blood to clean up as well as everything else.

He tried to push the old woman away, but she looped a fist straight into his face. It cracked hard against his cheekbone, far too hard. The rolling pin went spinning across the floor.

Ricky kicked and scrambled, lashing out feet, hands and elbows in a flurry of compact violence. Each time he thought he was finally going to be able to dislodge her, she seemed to gain a notch in strength. They rolled back and forth under the table, smashing a chair to firewood, and out the other side. Ricky heard Nicola squeal, and a small part of his mind was able to hope their neighbours hadn't heard. Then he found himself with two gnarled hands tight around his throat, and almost wished they had, and were sending help. For him.

He finally managed to pull his knee up under the old bitch, and gradually forced his hands in between hers. When they were in position he steadied himself for a second, got his breath – and then threw everything he had, chopping his hands in opposite directions, and kicking out hard.

The old woman flew a yard and hit the stove like an egg.

Ricky was on his feet almost immediately, hands on his knees and coughing like a bastard. When he swallowed, something clicked alarmingly in his throat. Nicola was still squeaking, eyes shut, but he heard it as from a great distance. He could taste his blood, and see it spattered on the wall and floor – in amongst the coffee and a few lumps of grey hair that he managed to yank out of the robot.

A fucking animatronic. Had to be. He'd been set up. John Harris had changed his mind, or more likely been a plant from minute one and there'd never been a real Grandma Harris. Fuckers. Wonder World weren't working with the cops. They were settling things their own way.

And so would Ricky. The job was over, and it didn't matter how much mess he left. He was getting out, and then going to find Mr Harris. The fee had just gone up to include everything the bastard owned, including his wife. And his daughter.

Grandma Harris was slumped on the floor, back against the cooker. Her throat was arced up like a twisted branch, a perfect target, but jerked back into position as Ricky pulled out his gun. No matter. The face would do just as well.

He held the gun in a straight-arm grip, sighted down the barrel.

'Don't even fucking think about it,' the rolling pin said.

Ricky turned very slowly to look. 'Excuse me?'

It had grown legs, and was standing with little hands on where its hips would be. Two stern eyes glared out of the wooden cylinder of its body, and it looked like a strange wide crab.

Ricky stared at it. Knew suddenly that it wasn't a machine, but an actual rolling pin with eyes and arms. He fired at it. The pin flipped out of the way, then switched direction and flick-flacked towards him, like a crazy little wooden gymnast. Ricky backed hurriedly, fired another shot. It missed, and the rolling pin flicked itself into the air like a muscular missile. Ricky wrenched his head out of the way just in time, and the pin embedded itself in the wall.

'Careful,' said the wall, slowly opening its eyes.

Over at the stove, Grandma Harris was pulling herself upright. Ricky blinked at her. She smiled, a sweet old lady smile that wasn't for him. Ricky decided he didn't have to mop up this mess. He'd go straight to talk with John Harris. He fired a couple of rounds into the wall, just between its huge eyes. It made a grumpy sound, but didn't seem much inconvenienced. A huge mouth opened sleepily, as if yawning, as it was only just getting up to speed. The pin meanwhile pushed itself out with a dry popping sound, and turned its beady eyes on Ricky.

'Shit on this,' Ricky muttered, as it scuttled towards him. He swung a kick at the rolling pin, sent it howling across the room. Fired straight at Margaret Harris, but didn't wait to see if it hit.

He turned on his heel in the kitchen door, bounded across the hallway and yanked at the door. It wouldn't open, and when Ricky tried to pull his hand away, he saw the handle had turned into a brown wooden hand and was gripping his like he was a prime business opportunity and they were testing each other's strength. Ricky braced his foot against the wall and tugged, for the first time hearing the sound of the beams whispering above. He glanced up and saw some of them were wriggling in place, limbering up, getting ready for action. He didn't want to see their action.

The door handle wasn't letting go, and so he placed the muzzle of the gun against it and let it have one.

It took the tip of one of Ricky's fingers with it, but the fucker let go. Ricky reared back, kicked the door with all his strength. It splintered and he barrelled through it, tripped and fell full length on the lawn. Face to face with the grass for a moment, he saw that he'd been right, and there was a little face on every blade. He heard a noise like a million little voices tuning up and knew that its song wasn't likely to be one he wanted to hear.

He scrabbled to his feet and careened down the path towards the car, bloody hand scrabbling for the keys. Before he could get even halfway there two trash cans came running round from next door. They made it to the car before him, and started levering one side off up the ground. Meanwhile the rolling pin shot out of the house from behind him, narrowly missed his head, and went through the windscreen of the car like a torpedo. Barely had the spray of glass hit the ground before the pin emerged the other side, turned in mid-air and looped back to punch through a door panel. It kept going, faster and faster, looping and punching, until the car began to look like a battered atom being mugged by a psycho electron.

Ricky began to realize just how badly his hand hurt, and that the car wasn't going to be a viable transportation option. He diverted his course in mid-stride, just heading for the road, for a straight line to run. He cleared the sidewalk, barely keeping his balance, and leaned into the turn. Ricky could run. He'd had the practice, down many dark streets and darker nights, and always running away instead of to. The way was clear.

Then a vehicle appeared at the corner in front of him, and he understood what the grass had been singing. Not a song, but a siren.

Wonder World's designers hadn't stinted themselves on the cop wagon. It was black and half as big as a house, all superfins and intimidating wheel arches spiked with chrome. The windows in the sides were blacker still, and the doors in the back might just as well have had ABANDON HOPE ALL YE WHO ENTER HERE scrawled right across them.

Ricky skidded to a halt, whirled around. An identical vehicle had moved into position just the other side of the remains of his car. Behind it a bunch of mushrooms and toadstools were moving into position.

The doors of the first wagon opened, and a figure got out each side. Both seven foot tall, with very long tails and claws that glinted. Bud and Slap, though rats, had been friendly rats in all the countless cartoons they'd appeared in over the last thirty years. They were almost as popular as Loopy and Careful and China Duck, and even Ricky recognized them. Cute, well-meaning villains, they always ended up joining the right side in the end.

But this Bud and Slap weren't like that. These toons were just for Ricky. As he held his ground, knowing there was nowhere to run, they walked towards him with heavy tread. They were stuffed into parodies of uniforms, torn at the seams and stained with bad things. Bud had a lazy, damaged eye, and was holding a big wooden truncheon in an unreassuring way. Slap had a sore on his upper lip, and kept running a long blue tongue over it, to collect the juice. Both had huge guns stuffed down the front of their uniforms. At least that's what Ricky hoped they were. From five yards away he could smell the rats' odour, the gust of sweat and stickiness and decay, and for a moment catch an echo of all the screams and death rattles they'd heard.

'Hey there, Ricky,' said Slap, winking. His voice was low and oily, full of unpleasant good humour. 'Got some business with you. Lots of different kinds of business, actually. You can get in the wagon, or we can start it right here. What d'you say?'

Behind him Bud giggled, and started to undo his pants.

Nicola stood at the window with Grandma, and watched the parade in the road. It wasn't the real parade, like the one in the Beautiful Realm where they had fireworks and Careful Cat and Loopy, but they were going to see that tomorrow. This was a little parade, with just Bud and Slap, and Percival Pin and Terrance and Terry the Trash Cans: sometimes they put on little parades of their own, Grandma said, just because they enjoyed it.

They laughed as they watched the characters play. Nicola had thought the man she'd come with had been a bad man, but he couldn't have been as bad as all that. Bud and Slap the Happy Rats were each holding one of his hands, and they were dancing with him, leading him to the wagon. They looked like they liked him a lot. The man's mouth opened and shut very wide as he danced, and Nicola thought he was probably laughing. She would be, in his position. They all looked like they were having such fun.

Finally, the wagon doors were shut with the man inside, and Bud and Slap bowed up at Grandma's window before getting back into their police car. The trash cans went somersaulting back to next door's yard, and the rolling pin came hand-springing up the path, leaving a trail of little firework stars in its wake. Nicola clapped her hands and Grandma laughed, and put her arm around the little girl.

Now it was time for supper and pie, and tomorrow would be a new and different day. They turned away from the window, and went to start cooking, in a kitchen where the tables and chairs had already tidied everything up as if nothing bad had ever happened, or ever could.

Meanwhile, well outside Wonder World, over on a splintered porch outside a small house the other side of the beltway, Marty the Gateman sat in his chair enjoying his bedtime cigarette. His back ached a little, from standing up all day, but it didn't bother him too badly. It was a small price to pay for seeing all the faces as they went into the parks, and when they came out again. The kids went in bright-eyed and hopeful, the parents tired and watchful. You could see them thinking how much it was all going to cost, and wondering whether it would be worth it. Then when you saw them come out, hours or days later, you could see that they knew that it had been. For a little while the grown-ups realized their cynicism was an emotional short-cut which meant they missed everything worth seeing along the way, and the children had proof of what they already believed: the world was cool. The gateman's job was important, Marty knew. You said the first hello to the visitors, and you said goodbye. You welcomed them in and helped them acclimatize; and then you sent them on their way, letting them see in your eyes the truth of what they believed – they were leaving a little lighter inside.

Marty's house was small and looked like all the others nearby, and he lived in it alone. As he sat in the warmth of the evening, looking up at the stars, he didn't mind that very much. His wife now lived with someone who was better at earning money, and who came home after a day's work in a far worse mood. Marty missed her, but he'd survive. The house could have been fancier, but he'd painted it last summer and he liked his yard.

He had the last couple of puffs of his cigarette, and then stubbed it out carefully in the ashtray he kept by the chair. He yawned, sipped the last of his ice tea, and decided that was that. It was early yet, but a good time for sleep. It always is, when you're looking forward to the next day.

As he lay in his bed later, gently settling into the warm train which would take him into tomorrow, he dimly wondered what he'd do with the rest of his life. Work for as long as he could, he supposed, and then stop. Sit out on the porch, most likely, live out his days bathed in the memory of faces lit for a moment by magic. Smile at passers-by. Drink ice tea in the twilight.

That sounded okay by him.

THE TRUTH GAME

The past is a game in which you, blushing, reveal
Where you were first kissed, and by whom –
And like the others I sit and listen,
But unlike them I do not grin; because
All I can see are the bars in the window
Which prevent me from being him.

Copyright Details

More Tomorrow
First appeared in *Dark Terrors*, edited by Stephen Jones and David Sutton, published by Victor Gollancz. Copyright © 1995 Michael Marshall Smith.

Everybody Goes
Copyright © 1992 Michael Marshall Smith.

Hell Hath Enlarged Herself
First appeared in *Dark Terrors 2*, edited by Stephen Jones and David Sutton, published Victor Gollancz. Copyright © 1996 Michael Marshall Smith.

A Place To Stay
First appeared in *Dark Terrors 4*, edited by Stephen Jones and David Sutton, Victor Gollancz. Copyright © 1994 Michael Marshall Smith.

Later
First appeared in *The Mammoth Book of Zombies*, edited by Stephen Jones, published by Robinson. Copyright © 1992 Michael Marshall Smith.

The Man Who Drew Cats
First appeared in *Dark Voices 2*, edited by Stephen Jones and David Sutton, published by Pan. Copyright ©1988 Michael Marshall Smith.

The Fracture
First appeared in *Dark Voices 6*, edited by Stephen Jones and David Sutton, published by Pan. Copyright © 1992 Michael Marshall Smith.

Save As. . .
First appeared in *Interzone*. Copyright © 1996 Michael Marshall Smith.

More Bitter Than Death
First appeared in *Dark Voices 5*, edited by Stephen Jones and David Sutton, published by Pan. Copyright © 1991 Michael Marshall Smith.

Diet Hell
Copyright © 1998 Michael Marshall Smith.

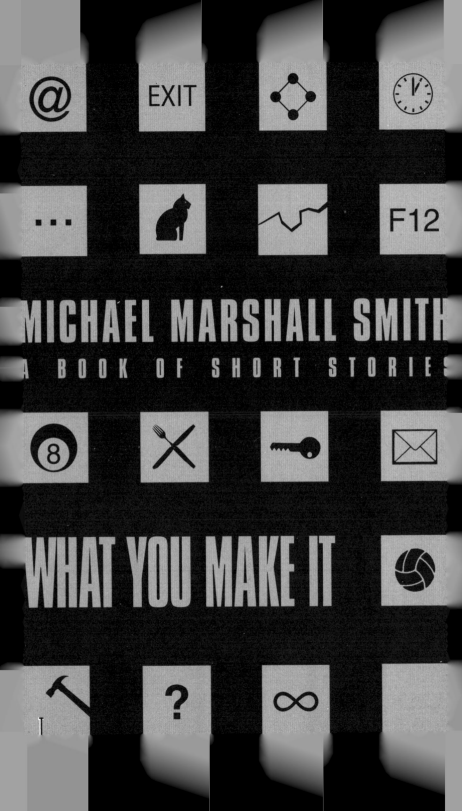